AN AIR FORCE COLONEL HAS BEEN MURDERED. AND IT'S ONLY THE BEGINNING.

"Jet-speed pace."
—*The Orlando Sentinel*

"Gripping twists and turns…will keep readers on edge."
—*Publishers Weekly*

continued . . .

THE COLONEL

PATRICK A. DAVIS

BERKLEY BOOKS, NEW YORK

THE COLONEL

A Berkley Book / published by arrangement with
the author

PRINTING HISTORY
G. P. Putnam's Sons hardcover edition / July 2001
Berkley mass-market edition / July 2002

Copyright © 2001 by Patrick A. Davis.
Cover art by Rob Wood / Wood Ronsaville Harlin, Inc.
Interior text design by Julie Rogers.

Visit our website at
www.penguinputnam.com

ISBN: 0-425-18560-5

BERKLEY®
Berkley Books are published by The Berkley Publishing Group,
a division of Penguin Putnam Inc.,
375 Hudson Street, New York, New York 10014.
BERKLEY and the "B" design
are trademarks belonging to Penguin Putnam Inc.

PRINTED IN THE UNITED STATES OF AMERICA

10 9 8 7 6 5 4 3 2 1

To Doug, Bonnie, and Barb,
for their faith and friendship

ACKNOWLEDGMENTS

My deepest appreciation to Katie and Bob Sessler, Linda and Nathan Green, Ann and Doug Anderson, Kathy and Bob Baker, Jo-Ann Power, Diana Barlow, Sue Veroneau, Colonel Dennis Hilley, Michael Roche, and the rest of my editing team, who patiently plowed through the early drafts and guided this book into something readable. I'd also like to thank Erika and Zane Harper, for keeping me straight on the FAA facts; Dr. Bill Burke, for his sage medical advice; Colonel (Dr.) Neal Barlow, the head guru of the Aeronautics Department at the Air Force Academy, for putting up with my endless questions on aircraft composites and structural designs; and Jean and Burt Fraleigh, for their encouragement over the years. My gratitude also to Chris Pepe and Lily Chin at Putnam and Tom Colgan at Berkley, for pushing me with my fingernails dragging to make this book better, and to my agent, Karen Solem at Writers House, for continuing to dream big.

Finally, I'd like to thank my wife, Helen Davis, and my parents, Betty and Bill Davis, whose love and support enabled me to realize my dream of becoming a writer.

THE COLONEL

THE DESK OF THE DIRECTOR OF EMERGENCY RESPONSE
ARLINGTON COUNTY POLICE DEPARTMENT
1425 NO. COURTHOUSE ROAD
ARLINGTON, VA 22201

To: Lieutenant Simon Santos   22 Mar 00
    Chief, Homicide Division
    Per your request: log #18836-042

Simon:

    Attached, find the transcript of the 911 call on the Wildman murder. Sergeant Railsbeck will run a voice analysis but she says don't get your hopes up for an ID. Says the caller sounds like a woman trying to disguise her voice. Voice inflections indicate the caller was extremely calm. Sergeant Railsbeck will call you ASAP if she turns up anything solid from the test.

    Good luck on getting this bastard, buddy. I mean it.

Paul

1 att. (1)

For Official Use Only

ARLINGTON POLICE DEPARTMENT

OFFICE OF EMERGENCY RESPONSE

Transcript #13642
Received: 21 Mar 00, 1612 hours.
Duration: 56 secs.
Dispatcher: Collins, Martha
Response Classification: Immediate

Transcript #13642, (1) of (2)

Dispatcher: Arlington 911. Is this an emergency?

Caller: (No response.)

Dispatcher: Hello. Is anyone on the line?

Caller: Yes.

Dispatcher: Are you calling to report an emergency?

Caller: Yes.

Dispatcher: What's the nature of the emergency?

Caller: I want to report a killing.

Dispatcher: A killing. Who's been killed?

Caller: Actually, there's more than one victim. The address is 235 North Seventh Street in Arlington. It's a private home.

Dispatcher: How many victims?

Caller: Three.

For Official Use Only

Dispatcher: And you're sure they're all dead?

Caller: Yes.

Dispatcher: You saw the bodies?

Caller: (long pause) Yes. They're not moving and there's a lot of blood.

Dispatcher: And your name?

Caller: I'd rather not say. I don't want to get involved.

Dispatcher: Wait. Don't hang up. If you have any information—

Caller: I don't.

Dispatcher: You must know the names of the victims—

Caller: (Hangs up.)

Dispatcher: Hello. Hello. Dammit. Billy, you get a trace on the call? No fooling. The same house? Give me the name of the owner. Got it. Colonel Margaret Wildman. Got two units rolling.

Dispatcher: (Hangs up.)

CHAPTER 1

WEDNESDAY

The thirty minutes or so before sunset is my favorite time of the day, and I'd just returned from work and was sitting in my battered rocker on the porch, sucking on a beer and scanning the paper. It was a warm spring evening and a few mosquitoes were buzzing around, but not enough to be annoying. Through an open second-floor window of my farmhouse, I could hear my daughter Emily singing along to the latest Backstreet Boys CD. Emily is almost eleven and she doesn't have much of a voice, but as a father you have to be encouraging with these kinds of things. And who knows, maybe her voice will change and someday she'll become the next Mariah Carey.

I winced as Emily butchered a high note. Then I flipped over to the sports section to check the basketball scores. Even though I lived in rural northern Virginia, about a seventy-minute drive southwest of D.C., I still got the *Washington Post* delivered. As usual, the Washington Wizards were stomped last night, this time by the Knicks. Never should have dealt Chris Webber, the only player they ever had that was worth a damn. I gloomily took a pull on the beer bottle, and glanced up when I heard the throaty purr of an airplane engine. I spotted the speck coming out of the setting sun and checked my watch. Right on time, I thought, tossing the paper aside to watch the landing.

A couple hundred yards from where I sat were two small wooden hangars and the grass runway my dad built thirty years ago when he decided to give up tobacco farming and become a crop duster. He did pretty well, too, at least enough to turn the place over to me and buy a condo in Florida when he retired. Dad's now got the golfing bug, so he and Mom stay there pretty much year-round except for the occasional holiday visit.

By now, I could see the plane clearly—an old single-engine Piper Pawnee that had been my dad's favorite. I squinted as the Pawnee banked toward the runway to set up for the approach. The windsock in the middle of the field stood straight out, indicating a strong crosswind. The pilot descended, holding down a wing to compensate for the drift. Moments later, the plane smoothly touched down first on one tire, then the other, which was exactly the way a crosswind landing is supposed to be made. Through the Plexiglas canopy, I saw the pilot wave as the plane taxied toward one of the hangars. I threw up a hand, feeling something approaching pride.

"Dinner. Ten minutes," a thickly accented voice behind me said. "Pork chops."

I glanced back to the stocky, graying woman with one of those square faces that always seem locked in a perpetual scowl. "Gracias, Mrs. Anuncio."

"Ten minutes," Mrs. Anuncio repeated, disappearing into the house.

I shook my head, holding back a smile. Mrs. Anuncio had worked for me for almost a month before I figured out that beneath that stern demeanor beat a heart of gold. She just had a military drill instructor's perspective when it came to running the household. She precisely scheduled each activity daily, whether it was the cleaning, laundry, or whatever. The way she looked at it, she was never late, so why should you be?

When my wife, Nicole, was diagnosed with cancer, I'd just retired as a lieutenant colonel with the Air Force after twenty years as an investigator in the Office of Special Investigations. It was a stressful time physically and emotionally, and I was running myself ragged trying to look after Emily and keep up with the house while shuttling Nicole to Walter Reed in D.C. for chemotherapy and radiation treatments. Out of the blue, Mrs. Anuncio appeared on my doorstep, announcing in very broken English that she'd been hired to provide "domestic assistance." My immediate reaction was that she either had a Mary Poppins complex or was trying to scam me, especially since she wouldn't tell me who was paying her. But she had a fistful of references and they all checked out. Against my better judgment, I accepted her help and it was the smartest thing I could have done. Almost overnight, my stress level diminished, and I could devote all my attention to Nicole.

Nicole fought the cancer for six months and when she passed away, Mrs. Anuncio stayed on without me having to ask. She's been with me well over a year now and I still haven't paid her a dime, which means my unknown benefactor is still footing the bill. She hasn't revealed who the person is, but I've got a pretty good idea. It has to be the same individual who anonymously flew out the high-priced New York oncologist to consult on Nicole's case and arranged for fresh flowers to be placed daily on her grave.

I put everything together when I saw him at Nicole's funeral, standing off in the distance. He left right after the ceremony, before I could talk to him. I sent him a thank-you note, but it was never acknowledged.

The plane lurched to a stop by the nearest hangar, the one with "Martin Collins Aviation" painted in gleaming white letters on the A-framed roof. Seeing my name up there still made me feel uncomfortable. I tried to talk my father out of painting my name over his, but he'd insisted, saying it was a rite of passage. As the plane's engine sputtered into silence, I unfolded myself from the rocker and strolled over.

The pilot popped open the canopy, then nimbly jumped to the ground and removed the flying helmet. Long straw-blond hair spilled out.

Gazing at Helen, I felt the familiar ache in my chest. She looked so damned much like my wife, Nicole. Same long, athletic build, flowing hair, and brilliant green eyes. Helen was Nicole's daughter from her first marriage. She'd grown up splitting her time between her father, a banker in Richmond, and us. Twenty-three now, and a business grad from the University of Maryland, she'd approached me last year with this crazy idea about taking a sabbatical from her stockbrokering job to give crop dusting a shot. I told her no way, pointing out the dangers. But she persisted, and I finally caved and taught her how to fly. She's been fully checked out for about three months and has been a big help. I'd pretty much been weaning myself out of the crop-dusting business, just doing a few jobs every now and then. Now Helen was taking care of those, which was fine with me. Frankly, I've never been crazy about flying. Maybe that's because I've always looked upon it as a job ever since I can remember.

Other kids grew up mowing lawns or pumping gas. I'd spent my formative years working as my pop's one-man ground crew, spending endless hours mixing vats of insecticide or fertilizer and washing down planes, and hating every minute of it. When I turned eighteen and started flying, I thought my attitude would change; it didn't. The thing that really got to me was the smell of the stuff we were dropping. It permeated your clothes and hair and never seemed to go away no matter how much you scrubbed. When I went off to college on an ROTC scholarship, I swore I would never set foot in a crop duster again. Before I was commissioned into the Air Force, I was offered a pilot slot, but turned it down. Everyone thought I was crazy, but I had no passion to fly. Zip. Still don't.

I swigged my beer as I sauntered up to the plane, trying not to be too obvious when I took a whiff. Nothing. I never understood why Helen never seemed to pick up the pesticide smell after a flight. "Dinner in ten minutes. You do Garber's place?"

Helen grinned, an exhilarated glow on her pretty face. "Yeah. Figure I'll get Mr. Ralston's tomorrow."

"I didn't know we were dusting Ralston's."

Helen gave me that slightly superior look of hers. "Are now. I also lined up Ben Miller for next week."

I was about to protest that she was taking on too much when I heard a shriek from the house. I turned to see Emily sprinting toward me, curly brown hair dancing crazily on her head. She was holding the portable phone.

"Daddy, come here! Daddy!"

"What is it?" I shouted, feeling a little alarmed as I hurried toward her.

She pulled up to me, panting, her freckled face flushed with excitement. "Tammy's got the flu. Her mom says she can't go. Can I buy her ticket, Daddy? Huh? Can I?"

I stared, confused. "What ticket—"

"To go to Arfkay. Millie is going. So is Jessie, and Laurie—"

"Slow down, honey." I took her hand, which was trembling. "What's arfkay?"

"She means RFK Stadium," Helen said. "The Backstreet Boys concert Friday night. Remember?"

I nodded slowly. I'd tried to buy a ticket a month ago, but things had been hectic at work. By the time I'd called TicketMaster, the concert was sold out. Emily had cried for two days and the guilt had eaten at me. It's the kind of thing my wife Nicole wouldn't have forgotten.

Emily's head bobbed. "That's what I said. RFK. Can I go? Huh? Please." She was squirming now.

Like I was going to say no. I smiled. "Sure, honey—"

An earsplitting squeal and Emily hugged me. "Thank you, Daddy."

"Give me the phone, hon. I'll call Tammy's mother, tell her I'll stop by tomorrow with a check."

She stepped back, dutifully handing it over. As I started

to punch in the number, she blurted, "Tammy's mom isn't going now either."

I stopped punching, wondering why I should care. "Okay..." I stared at her, waiting.

Emily looked down, kicking at the grass. She gave a couple of false starts like she was going to say something. Finally, she said, "Tammy's mom was going to drive. Millie's mom works nights. And Jessie's mom can't do it. I forget why..." She chewed her lower lip, giving me *the* look.

Behind me, Helen began to laugh. I shook my head, realizing I was being set up by my own daughter.

"You mean I have to drive you," I said.

"You're the only one, Daddy." Emily's voice was somber, like what she was saying was life or death.

Helen laughed louder.

As I stared into Emily's face, I knew I was beaten.

"Tammy's mom has a ticket, too," Emily added helpfully. "You can see the concert."

Me and fifty thousand screaming girls. The joys of fatherhood. "Fine. Okay. You can tell your friends I'll drive. Now wash up for dinner."

Emily's face went incandescent. "You're the best, Dad." She spun and skipped toward the house.

"Mom always said you were a pushover," Helen said. She sounded amused.

I turned and said dryly, "You'd have handled it differently, I suppose."

"Maybe. I might have tried asking someone else to take the girls."

I blinked. "You mean you wouldn't mind—"

"Unh-unh. Too late. Emily's expecting you to go now. Better take along some earplugs. By the way, don't fall over yourself telling me what a great landing I made." She winked and headed toward the house.

I smiled at her back. That's another thing Helen got from her mother. A confidence that couldn't be described as cocky, but came darned close. I felt the ache in my chest again. Christ, I missed Nicole.

As I headed for the house, I was about to call Tammy's mother when the phone rang. The caller ID read Warrentown Police.

I wasn't concerned. I'd been Warrentown's chief of police since my retirement from the military and routinely got calls at home. They never amounted to anything serious. A kid getting busted with a little pot, maybe a domestic violence situation or a fight at Jody's Bar. Usual small-town problems. And Warrentown was small: roughly four thousand people with three stoplights, three motels, four restaurants (eight if you count fast-food joints), nine churches, and a seven-man police department.

I recognized the slow drawl of Miles Brody, the night desk sergeant. Miles sounded puzzled, which wasn't unusual. He was a nice guy but not the brightest bulb in the room.

"Uh, Chief, did some woman Air Force captain just call you? A Captain Amanda Gardner."

"No. Why?"

"I got kind of a funny call from her a couple minutes ago. She said some general would be contacting you and wanted to know whether you were here or at home. She said you were being requested to help out on some kind of homicide investigation. You working on something with the Air Force?"

"Not that I know of. Did she say she was with the OSI?" The Office of Special Investigations was the primary criminal investigative arm of the Air Force.

"She didn't mention it. Anyway, I told her you were at home. Got her number if you want to talk to her."

"I won't need it, Miles. Call Burt and tell him I'll be busy for the next few days so he'll have to run the office."

"Huh? Chief, I thought you said—"

"What I said, Miles," I interrupted, "is I didn't know I was working on a case for the Air Force. But it seems I am."

A pause. "Okay, Chief."

I hung up with a grin. Poor Miles was still confused, but I wasn't even though I had no idea who Captain Amanda Gardner was. She'd obviously called at the request of her boss, General Gary Mercer, the head of the OSI. When I'd retired as a lieutenant colonel out of the Bolling Air Force Base office near D.C., General Mercer tried to talk me into taking one of the handful of civilian investigator billets. I was tempted for a couple of reasons. First, the job meant I could get my retirement pay plus a government salary. Second, I knew Mercer was desperate to keep experienced investigators since most of his people were bolting to better-paying jobs in the civilian world. The downside of his offer was that I'd continue putting in long hours and Nicole had her heart set on a husband who actually came home once in a while. After I turned Mercer down, he called again a month later, wanting to know if I'd be open to working as a consultant exclusively on homicides, which are something of a specialty of mine. It was too good a deal to pass up. I knew my workload would be light because killings among the military were relatively rare, and when I did work, I'd be getting roughly twice my military salary. I also liked the idea of working an occasional murder investigation as a change of pace from the small-town-cop routine.

Nicole's illness prevented me from handling a couple of cases, but I'd investigated three others: a domestic shooting involving an undersecretary of the Air Force, a drug-dealing sergeant's drive-by killing in D.C., and a general's son's suicide. In the first two, I actually didn't do much except assist the local civilian authority because the crimes had occurred off a military reservation. That was the rule. Location of a crime determined the primary investigative authority.

The phone rang again when I was almost to the house. I answered, expecting General Mercer's baritone, but was instead greeted by a familiar soft voice. In the background, I heard the jumbled sounds of conversation. Someone hollered out that the coroner had arrived.

"Hello, Martin."

To most of my friends, I'm Marty, but Lieutenant Simon Santos, chief homicide investigator of the Arlington County PD, always referred to me as Martin. "Hello, Simon."

"I'm wondering if you might have some time to help me on a case. It involves the murder of an Air Force colonel."

"I've cleared out my schedule. I take it you've spoken with General Mercer."

"A few minutes ago. I told him I'd notify you. Captain Amanda Gardner has already arrived. She'll be assisting you. Have you met her?"

"No."

"She's quite . . . young."

Simon's disapproving tone and the presence of Captain Gardner at the crime scene explained how things must have happened. Simon had notified the OSI that he was investigating an Air Force colonel's death and General Mercer had sent out Captain Gardner. Simon took one look at her and called Mercer back, demanding someone with more experience. Knowing Simon, he asked for me specifically, but then we'd known each other for a long time.

"I've sent Romero to pick you up, Martin," Simon went on. "He should be there in twenty minutes."

"That's not necessary. I can drive."

Simon let the comment pass, saying quietly, "This is a nasty one, Martin. The colonel's two young children were also killed."

I felt a chill. "I'll be ready."

After I hung up, I poured out the rest of my beer, and went up the steps into the house.

CHAPTER 2

Everyone was sitting down to dinner when I poked my head in the dining room. After I passed on the news that I had to go to work, Mrs. Anuncio gave a little sniff and said she'd put a plate in the oven. Emily made a sad face and Helen immediately challenged Emily to Nintendo, which brought out a dimpled grin. I smiled my thanks to Helen. I tried to spend an hour each evening with Emily, doing anything she wanted. Sometimes we'd play games, or go over a homework assignment, or just talk over her day at school. It's one of the suggested activities I picked up from a book on being a single parent, to keep me involved in Emily's life. Sounds hokey, but it seems to work for both of us.

I'd thrown on a pair of shorts and a T-shirt when I'd come home, so I went upstairs to change and clean up a little. Since I wouldn't be acting as the Warrentown Chief of Police, I put on a suit instead of my police uniform. As I dressed, I called Tammy's mom and arranged to pick up the tickets tomorrow. Forty-five bucks apiece and I tried not to choke on the phone.

Five minutes later, I dug out my OSI badge from the

dresser, then slipped my pistol into my waist holster and checked myself in the mirror. I'm not a big guy, a shade over six feet and around one-eighty. I still wore my blond hair in a flat-top, not because it was a holdover from my Air Force days, but because Nicole had always liked it that way. It was a little thing, but it reminded me of her. And that's all I had left. Little things. Like the pictures of Nicole I kept on the dresser. A psychologist buddy suggested I should put one photograph away each week as an exercise in letting go. I not-so-politely told him he was full of shit. I'd loved Nicole with all my heart and sticking her photographs in a drawer wasn't going to stop the way I felt.

Downstairs, I kissed Emily goodbye and as I went out the front door, I got a warm-and-fuzzy when I heard her chattering excitedly with Mrs. Anuncio and Helen about the concert. It was good to know she was finally coming out of the shell she'd withdrawn into after Nicole's death.

My watch said it had been fifteen minutes since Simon's call, so I sat in the rocker on the porch, creaking slowly, and gazed off in the fading light toward the gravel road that wound around the end of the runway. The road ended at State Highway 26 about a half-mile away, past the cattle guard. Staring at the intersection, my thoughts drifted to Lieutenant Simon Santos.

I'd first met Simon eight years earlier, when I was called out to assist his investigation into the beating death of a black sergeant found outside a redneck bar a couple of miles from the Pentagon. Back then, Simon was already something of a legend among local homicide investigators, and I was nervous about meeting him, unsure of what to expect. I'd heard him described as everything from eccentric and quirky to arrogant and ruthlessly efficient. On two points, everyone seemed to agree: Simon was a brilliant, unorthodox investigator with an uncanny ability to sniff out the truth, and he was rich as hell.

We solved the case in less than three hours. Simon followed a hunch, interviewed members of a local biker gang, pressured a witness and made the arrest. It was amazing, watching him work.

During my time with the OSI, he'd requested my help on four more murders involving military personnel. Since I've been retired, he's had General Mercer call me in on a couple others, the most notable being the one involving the Air Force undersecretary who'd been shot to death by his wife for diddling his female military aide. For some reason, Simon has taken a liking to me, but I'm not sure why. We're not really close friends, since we have little contact between cases. It bugs me that I've told him about my personal life, because he's never shared his.

What I've learned about him has come from reporters and colleagues, and the rumor mill that seems to work overtime around him. I knew Simon had once considered becoming a priest, spoke at least three languages, had a fortune estimated at many millions, lived in a mansion in Manassas, and was single. Now, that may sound like a lot, but it isn't: they're just isolated bits of information. Simon has never explained where his money came from, or what the hell a guy with his bucks was doing being a cop in the first place.

Anyway, when he needs me, he calls me up out of the blue, like tonight. He knows I won't refuse him except for something serious, like the situation with Nicole. There's a reason for my compliance, though. A large part of Simon's success is the way he obligates people so they'll do what he asks.

In my case, it's Mrs. Anuncio and the high-priced oncologist and the flowers for Nicole's grave. And, of course, sending the car, which makes it harder to say no.

I slapped at a mosquito. It was almost dark now and to the west I could just make out the clouds from the incoming cold front that the radio had mentioned. I was in the middle of a yawn when the headlights appeared at the intersection. As they came toward me, I rose from the chair and checked my watch.

Twenty minutes on the nose. But then Simon insisted on precision.

I waited in the middle of the driveway as a gleaming stretch limo rolled to a stop. A uniformed chauffeur the size of a small house emerged, smiling at me through a neatly trimmed goatee. He doffed his cap, which sat on a clean-shaven scalp. Romero had always reminded me of a white version of Mr. T, with a better vocabulary and without the jewelry.

"Good evening, Colonel Collins." Romero's voice was surprisingly high-pitched for a man his size, with a pronounced New York accent.

"Hi, Romero. And I'm a civilian now, so it's Marty."

Romero grinned and extended a small, gift-wrapped package. "A little something Simon got for your daughter, Marty. One of those portable CD players the kids like."

I smiled. "Thank you." I took the package into the house, and stuck it in the closet by the entryway because I didn't want Emily to stay up half the night listening to it. When I returned to the car, Romero was holding a rear door open.

As I crawled inside, I felt no surprise over the gift. In fact, I had half-expected it.

Like I said, Simon always managed to make people feel obligated.

Rolling down the driveway, I clicked on the overhead light and took in the interior of the limo. It was one of those custom models, equipped with a small bar and refrigerator down one side and a VCR and TV along the other. The only thing missing was a hot tub and a couple of groupies named Bambi and Ginger. I got comfortable on the rearmost seat and stared forward through the tinted partition at the back of Romero's domed head, which sat on a thickly muscled neck. His age was hard to estimate, but with the lines on his face, he had to be pushing sixty.

I'd never understood Romero's relationship to Simon, but whatever it was, it went way beyond just driving a car.

There was a familiarity between them that only comes after a lot of years together. I'd asked Simon about it once, but he did that annoying thing of his where he pretends he doesn't hear.

To be honest, sometimes Romero made me a little uneasy. Outwardly, he was personable and easygoing, but there was an aura of violence around him that didn't come from his size. You could see it in his eyes and the way he carried himself. A cop acquaintance once observed that Romero acted more like a bodyguard than a driver, and I agreed. In my first case with Simon, the biker we'd arrested for the killing pulled a knife when a cop tried to cuff him. Romero was there in a flash and the next thing everyone knew, the biker was screaming his head off, his arm broken at the elbow.

Don't get me wrong. I liked Romero. I just wasn't crazy enough to do anything to piss him off...ever.

We pulled onto the highway and headed east toward D.C. Traffic was light but would pick up when we approached the northern Virginia sprawl. Once the limo reached cruise speed, the partition whirred down and Romero asked, "Temperature okay, Marty?"

"Fine. Where are we going?"

"A house in Arlington."

"North or South?"

"North."

The response confirmed what I suspected. This time of night, the drive would take maybe forty-five minutes, which told me Simon must have sent Romero to pick me up before having even spoken to General Mercer. Hey, it's nice to feel wanted.

"How long has it been, Marty?" Romero asked. "A year?"

He was inquiring about the last time I worked with Simon. "A little longer." I paused. "Since before my wife became ill."

There was the awkward silence that always follows that statement. He said, "We were sorry to hear about her passing away." We, not I. Simon did that, too. And when they referred to each other, it was always by their first names. That's the familiarity I was talking about.

"Thanks." I listened to the hum of the tires on the road, then dug out my notebook. "You know any details of the murders?" I asked, knowing he would. Simon often used Romero as a sounding board. The first time I heard them discuss a case together, I was surprised. It didn't take me long to figure out that Romero was a lot smarter than he looked, and I'm not talking only common sense. His knowledge of police work went beyond what he could have picked up from working for Santos. Almost as if he'd once been a cop.

"Some," Romero said, looking at me in the rearview mirror. "Three victims. An Air Force colonel named Margaret Wildman and her two kids. Boy and girl."

"Husband?"

"Divorced. We've been trying to contact him, with no luck."

"Where did the colonel work?"

"The Pentagon."

I made a note, underlining the victim's name. It didn't ring any bells, but close to twenty-five thousand people worked in the building, essentially making it the size of a small city. "What office?"

"Haven't heard."

"You see the bodies?" Occasionally, Romero would accompany Simon into a crime scene, though he generally stayed away, knowing his presence pissed off some of the cops.

"Nope. Right after I dropped Simon off, he sent me to pick you up. Kinda glad I didn't go inside. I got a tough time when kids are . . ." He trailed off without finishing.

"How were they killed?" I asked quietly.

Romero took a deep breath. "Throats were slashed."

"Jesus," I murmured. An image flashed in my mind and I forced it away. "Who found the bodies?"

"A couple of cops who were responding to an anonymous 911 call."

I looked up from writing. Common sense told me a killer wouldn't have called the cops, so maybe we had a witness. I mentioned that point to Romero.

He shrugged. "Hell, who knows? People do screwy stuff all the time. Could be the killer had a reason for wanting the body to be discovered quick."

"To establish an alibi."

"Sure. Wouldn't be the first time. Besides, the 911 dispatcher managed to trace the call. Guess where it came from? Colonel Wildman's own house." Romero glanced back with a meaningful look.

I understood the implication. Assuming the killer had hung around to make the call, possibly to establish an alibi, this suggested an element of premeditation and planning. Odds were someone cool enough to phone the cops after slicing three people's throats wouldn't leave much evidence linking themselves to the crime. Still, it was possible someone else had called, someone who'd shown up and found the bodies. But if so, why didn't they hang around to—

"A little music, Marty?" Romero was again watching me in the mirror.

"Huh? Oh, sure."

Some light jazz, which was all Romero listened to, filtered back. He kept the volume low. I tossed out a few more questions, but he'd already passed on most of what he knew. The only other significant item was the children's ages. I'd asked because I wanted to know what to expect when I visited the crime scene. The girl was nine, her brother ten. So much like Emily.

The horror hit home then and I felt a little sick. Romero watched sympathetically as I cracked open the window. Just to get some air.

⇒ "That's it, the two-story brick job with all the lights on," Romero said, hanging up the car phone after a brief conversation.

He clicked off the radio, rolling out onto a tree-lined street in a quiet subdivision of older, red-brick homes in North Arlington, not far from the Balston Mall. The house Romero indicated was maybe a block away, on the right, and ablaze in light. I could see a county coroner's van and an EMT vehicle in the driveway. An assortment of plain and unmarked cop cars lined the curb out front, and roughly fifty yards beyond, a row of antennaed press vans. On the sidewalk across from the house, a crowd had gathered behind a wooden barricade manned by two uniformed officers. To the crowd's left, TV crews had set up, and a couple of talking heads were somberly staring into bright lights, giving their play-by-play.

"Good news travels fast," I murmured.

"Too damned fast," Romero grunted. "Simon and I arrived less than an hour after the body was found. A lot of the press were already here."

I understood. Romero was saying the media had been tipped off, probably by a cop. In the military we rarely had to deal with this problem, but in the civilian world it was a constant nuisance.

Romero slowed to a stop by a black-and-white near the driveway. "Hop out, Marty. That was Simon on the phone. He wants me to try and hunt down the ex-husband."

As I climbed out, someone from the crowd yelled, "Hey, buddy," and when I turned, flashbulbs went off. I blinked, rubbing my eyes. Laughter erupted and I resisted the urge to flip the bird as I crossed the lawn toward the front door. A couple uniforms were stringing yellow tape between the trees in the front yard. One looked over and squinted. "Help you, Mister?"

I was going for my badge when a female voice called out, "I'll handle this, Officer."

On the railed front porch, I saw a heavy man in a yellow plaid sports jacket and a tall woman in a dark green pantsuit. The man sucked hard on a cigarette, scowling in my direction. The woman quickly walked over. She was athletically built and strikingly pretty, in an outdoorsy sort of way. She wore her red hair almost boyishly short, and she looked young, mid-twenties. "Colonel Collins?" she asked tentatively.

"Yes. I go by Marty."

She relaxed into a smile. "Fine, Marty. I'm Captain Amanda Gardner, OSI." It didn't surprise me that she wore civilian attire. Military investigators rarely wore uniforms because of the rank problem. Enlisted men felt intimidated when questioned by someone they knew was an officer, and officers often proved difficult when being grilled by someone they outranked. Amanda stuck out her hand and we shook. Up close, she didn't appear to wear any makeup, and her grip was firmer than most men's.

I gazed at her for a moment. "I hope my involvement isn't a problem for you."

She grinned. "Heck, no, Marty. I've only worked a couple of homicides. I can use the help." She sounded like she meant it.

"Fine." I smiled back.

"You got gloves?" she asked, producing a pair of latex gloves from her jacket.

I nodded, reaching into my pocket. After we put on the gloves, we started for the house. To get a feel for her experience level, I casually asked her when she'd graduated from the OSI's Special Investigation School at Andrews.

"Almost two years ago. I spent another month at Quantico, attending the FBI's advanced forensics course. Before that, I coached the women's swim team at the Air Force Academy."

"You're an Academy grad, huh?"

She nodded. "Class of '92. Double majored in aero and computer science." She winked at me. "Have I mentioned I'm smart as hell?"

I shook my head, finding myself liking her, but then I tended to like most good-looking women. "So why does an aeronautical engineer join the OSI and not some military think tank?"

She made a face. "Christ, that engineering stuff is boring. I wanted a job that would hold my interest. I even did a stint working aircraft maintenance before deciding that was too dull."

We were approaching the stairs leading up to the porch, and I slowed to let her go ahead. "I understand you've never worked with Lieutenant Santos before?"

"Nope. Met him for the first time tonight. So are the stories about him true?"

"Depends on what you've heard," I said, following her up the steps.

"Well, for instance, that he has a closet full of suits all exactly identical."

"True. He likes to keep his life uncomplicated."

"He doesn't drive—"

"Rarely."

"He doesn't shake hands."

"Germs."

"Well, well, long time no see, Marty," the man on the porch said sarcastically. He stepped away from the railing, blocking our path to the door. "You here to babysit Santos again?" He made the statement sound like an accusation.

It took a sec before the fleshy face registered. Sergeant Brian McNamara must have put on thirty pounds in the past year, five of it in his three chins. "Hello, Mac."

MacNamara jabbed the cigarette at me. "Tell that son of a bitch what he's doing is bullshit. You got that?"

I sighed. McNamara was one of those tiresome people who always seemed embittered about something. To him, every slight, real or imagined, stemmed from a conspiracy and not his own ineptness. "Good to see you, too, Mac."

Another jab. "I'm not kidding, Marty. You tell that asshole what he did was way out of line. Tell him I'm gonna file a grievance."

I glanced to Amanda, who rolled her eyes.

"Nice jacket, Mac," I said.

McNamara blinked. "Huh?"

"Really, I like it." I smoothed out his lapel approvingly. "I just wouldn't have the balls to actually *wear* it."

McNamara turned bright red and began sputtering. Before he could say anything, I pushed past him through the open front door. Amanda followed, laughing softly.

"Fuck you, Marty," McNamara choked. "Fuck you and that—"

Amanda closed the door behind us.

➤ We were standing in a white-tiled foyer with a chandelier dangling above. Going clockwise from my left, I saw a curved staircase, an elegant dining room beyond, then a hallway and a formal sitting area. The furnishings were tasteful but modest, just what you'd expect on the salary of a colonel with a couple of kids. Amanda sidled up to me, still grinning. She really was quite attractive. "Nice move, Marty. You know that Neanderthal was actually hitting on me when you walked up."

"So when are you two going out?"

"Funny."

"Any idea why he's so pissed off?"

"He complained that this was supposed to be his case but Santos decided to take over."

"Mac *wanted* to work this case? That's a first."

"What do you mean?"

"He's got a rep for weaseling out of investigations. And the ones he does handle, he usually screws up because he's too damned lazy to put in the legwork. That's why Simon brought himself on board. No way he's going to let Mac anywhere near a high-vis case like this one." I faced her. "So where are the bodies?"

Amanda slowly exhaled, her pretty face turning serious. "The basement. It's pretty bad. Worst thing I've seen." She gazed at me for a moment. "You ever work a case with kids, Marty?" she asked softly.

"A few," I said. "But that doesn't make it any easier."

She nodded, then slowly led me down a carpeted hallway into the kitchen, stopping by an open door that led to a staircase. Amanda paused to look at a corkboard on the wall near the refrigerator, where a child's watercolor painting was tacked, marked with a big smiley face. She turned away, shaking her head sadly.

We went down the steps.

CHAPTER 3

I was struck by the quiet when we reached the bottom of the stairs, and wondered where everyone was. This portion of the basement was unfinished, just a dank square of concrete floors and walls, with a large sink and washer and dryer tucked in a corner. Fluorescent lights hummed from the open ceiling.

"In here," Amanda said, going to a doorway on the left. I trailed after her into a large game room of dark paneling and burnished oak flooring. A bar with a half-dozen stools stood at the far end, a dartboard hung on the adjoining wall. In the middle was a pool table, a crowd of maybe a dozen circled around it, backs to us, gazing down at something out of view. Moments later, everyone bent their heads respectfully and I understood the silence.

"I've heard he does this," Amanda murmured.

"Sometimes."

As we walked toward the group, our footsteps clicked loudly over the floor. People turned in annoyance. We took the hint and stopped.

Moments later, from somewhere behind the crowd, a voice began to pray.

When the prayer ended, the group began to disperse and Amanda and I drifted forward. I nodded to a couple of criminalists I knew. On the far side of the pool table, we saw a man slowly rise, gazing downward, rosary beads in his hands. We still couldn't make out what he was looking at. Then we came around the table.

My initial reaction was a mixture of shock and revulsion. In the military, I'd averaged only a couple of homicides a year and had never really gotten used to seeing the bodies of murder victims.

Colonel Margaret Wildman lay on her back, head tilted off to the side, a grisly red gash running across her throat. Her bruised and battered face indicated she'd been badly beaten before her throat was cut. One eye was blackened, her jaw was swollen and purple, and her lips were split and raw-looking. She still wore her Air Force uniform, and much of her blouse was stained with blood that had flowed down from her throat, pooling into a tacky puddle on the floor.

"Glad you could make it, Martin."

I nodded, gazing dully at Lieutenant Simon Santos as he slipped the rosary beads into his jacket. Simon was tall and dark, with a thin, gaunt face topped by longish black hair combed straight back. At thirty-four, he was considered young for a homicide lieutenant, which was the source of much of the department resentment. As usual he was dressed impeccably in a dark blue Brooks Brothers suit, white razor-pressed dress shirt, with a brightly colored bow tie and a red carnation clipped to the lapel. The only variation he ever made to his clothes was the bow tie, which he changed depending on the day of the week. Since this was Wednesday, he was wearing the yellow one with burnt orange polka dots. Even though it was ugly as hell, it jumped out at you, which was the idea. People never forgot meeting Simon.

"Someone sure did a job on her," I said to him.

Simon nodded. "Dr. Marbury said her jaw was fractured in at least two places and the socket below her left eye was crushed. She's also got a half-dozen broken teeth and two deep cranial contusions." Simon glanced behind the bar, where a balding man whom I took to be Dr. Marbury was squatting down, working on something on the floor. Two men in white coveralls stenciled with the word Coroner watched over his shoulders.

"The kids back there?" I said quietly.

Simon nodded again, shifting his gaze to Amanda. He gave her that piercing stare of his, the one he usually reserved for suspects. I immediately realized what he was up to because Simon had played the same game with me the first time we'd worked together. After a few seconds, he asked her, "Anything from the neighbors' interviews yet?"

Amanda calmly replied, "I checked about twenty minutes ago. No one reported seeing anything. I can check again if you—"

"No hurry. I need you to do a few things first." He paused expectantly.

Amanda looked back coolly, saying nothing. Good girl, I thought.

Simon said, "You might want to write this down...."

A tight smile. "It isn't necessary, Lieutenant."

Simon shrugged, and spoke very quickly. "I want you to phone in a request for a listing of Colonel Wildman's phone records, including her cellular, and her credit-card expenditures. Go back at least a year, but I'm particularly interested in the ones over the past month. I'll also need the name of Colonel Wildman's babysitter; she must have employed one. I think I saw an address book in the study upstairs. You might try that or maybe a neighbor will know. While you're in the study, you might look through the file cabinet for anything of interest. And please find Erika and ask her to come down. Tell her to bring her case." Erika was Erika Harper, a forensics specialist Simon usually brought into any cases he worked.

It occurred to me Amanda probably didn't know Erika, and I waited for her to mention it.

"Anything else?" Amanda asked.

Simon shook his head. He watched Amanda leave, a tiny smile creeping across his face.

"You know," I said, "if she wasn't damn good at her job, General Mercer wouldn't have assigned her to the case."

"Perhaps."

"You're wasting your time if you think you can intimidate her."

Simon ignored me, but the smile told me Amanda had passed his little test. I switched subjects and asked, "Why do you want to talk to the babysitter?"

No response, because Simon was again focused in the direction of the bar. "Martin, how old would you say a child would be when they no longer carry around a teddy bear?"

The question caught me off guard and it took me a few seconds to respond. "Emily outgrew hers around six. Some kids might hang on to them a bit longer."

"I thought as much," he murmured. He suddenly smiled at me and squeezed my shoulder, a significant gesture because he wasn't into touching. "It really is good to see you, Martin."

"You, too," I said. I didn't thank him for Emily's gift, because I knew it would make him uncomfortable.

"I almost didn't call you for this one. I thought you might need more time."

"It's better if I stay busy," I said, pulling out my notepad. "Romero mentioned the murder was called in anonymously."

"Yes. The dispatcher said the voice was heavily muffled, but sounded like a woman. The lab's going to analyze the tape, see if we can get something."

"The killer's definitely a man," I said. "I don't see a woman doing this."

"No?" Simon shrugged.

"What time was the call?"

"Four-twelve. Cops showed up four minutes later."

I made a notation. Like Amanda, Simon never wrote anything down, somehow managing to keep track of everything in his head. Me, I'm not that smart. "Estimated time of death?"

"Between three-thirty and four-thirty P.M."

"Remember," Marbury called out from behind the bar, "that's for the woman only. Her core temp's almost two degrees higher than the children's, which means they were probably killed before she was. Judging by the lividity and the extent of the rigor, I say as early as three this afternoon. When I do the autopsy, I can narrow down the times a little."

"Damn," I murmured, chilled by implication.

"Yes," Simon said, eyeing me. "Colonel Wildman watched her children die."

Marbury rose stiffly, handed a thermometer to one of the attendants, then hitched up his pants and walked over. I forced myself to look past him at the two small bodies crumpled in a pool of blood, their hands already covered by plastic bags to preserve trace evidence. The girl was heaped like a rag doll on top of her brother, her head back, mouth duct-taped, a bloody line across her small throat. Her eyes were locked open, staring up into nothingness. I thought of the terror she must have felt. On the floor near the girl's outstretched hand, I noticed something furry and shifted over for a better view.

A teddy bear, ripped apart, the stuffing visible. I now partially understood Simon's earlier question. The bear was the size of one that Emily had, and I felt something close to hate.

"Want to hear what I got so far?" Marbury asked. He wore a rumpled suit and had a pink face with no chin. He blinked at me. "Who are you, anyway?"

"A consultant with the OSI," Simon said.

Marbury shrugged, unimpressed. "Here's the scoop. The kids were killed first, within a couple of minutes of each other. The boy first, then his sister. Over there." He pointed to the wall next to us, roughly three feet from Colonel Wildman's body, where dark splatters were visible, blood collected on the floor below. "You can tell by the stains on the paneling and the blood trail."

"Close to their mother," I said softly.

No one spoke for a moment.

Marbury cleared his throat. "No indications of sexual assault on either child. Both died from a single slash to the throat, severing the carotid artery. Whoever did it has probably done this kind of thing before."

"How do you know?" I asked.

"No hesitation marks," Marbury said. "Not many people can slit someone's throat cleanly, especially a kid's. A lot of times you'll find tiny pricks or cuts, where the killer starts and stops before finally getting up the nerve to go through with it. By then, they're so worked up, they often use too much force, almost severing the head completely. In this case, the cuts were just deep enough to get the job done. The guy was also practiced enough to keep the arterial blood directed at the wall away from him. Held them by the hair while the blood pumped out before tossing them behind the bar. Bastard might as well have been gutting a fish."

Christ. I had to swallow to speak. "So the killer could be a professional."

"Oh, yeah," Marbury said with feeling. "The guy was definitely a pro. The only other possibility is some homicidal sexual fruitcake, but those guys are usually loners. In this case, I'm inclined to rule out the sex angle for a couple of reasons. First, I haven't found any semen stains, and second, I'm pretty damn sure there had to be at least two people involved to pull off this thing."

Simon nodded his agreement, and so did I. Sexual killing wasn't exactly a team sport.

"One to control the children," Simon expanded. "And one to handle Colonel Wildman."

The activity in the room was picking up. A photographer was standing by the bar, taking pictures of the children while one of the criminalists I'd seen earlier dusted the ends of the pool table. I noticed Erika Harper appear with her black "doctor" bag, the one filled with evidence-collecting equipment. She stopped a few feet away, waiting.

Tossing her a glance, Marbury continued, "Colonel Wildman's neck wound suggests she was probably killed by a second person. It's deeper, with two distinct hesitation marks."

"So one person killed her and the other the children," I said, making a note.

Marbury nodded, frowning. "The one thing I don't understand is why they beat the hell out of Wildman, unless maybe they just wanted her to suffer before she died." He shrugged, glancing at Simon. "But hey, figuring that out is your job, right?"

Simon nodded. "That everything you have?"

"So far. Now, I haven't examined Colonel Wildman to confirm definitively whether or not she was sexually assaulted, but she's clothed so I'd say that's not much of a possibility. You want a rush job on the autopsies, I suppose?"

"Please," Simon said.

"Tomorrow morning okay?"

"Tonight would be better."

"Aw, Christ, gimme a break, Simon. With the budget cutbacks, my people have been working double shifts—"

"Will this help?" Simon handed him an envelope.

Marbury opened the flap, peering inside. He sprouted a big smile. "You son of a bitch. Okay. Tonight it is. Hell, it's not like I need sleep." He slipped the envelope into his jacket and almost cheerfully returned to his men at the bar.

"*Aïda* tickets for tomorrow night's performance at the Kennedy Center," Simon explained to me. "His wife is an opera fan."

It had to be something like that. Depending on the season, Simon also walked around with tickets to Orioles, Redskins, and Wizards games. He didn't look at it as a bribe, because he didn't use money. Not that Simon was above doling out cash. Rumor had it there was a small army of informants on his payroll. It's a good thing, being rich.

Erika Harper gave a little cough. "You asked for me, Lieutenant?" Erika had one of those breathy Marilyn Monroe voices. The only problem was she was in her late fifties, square and graying. She'd been working forensics for thirty years and change.

"Yes, Erika. Over here." Simon drew her by an elbow toward Wildman's corpse and spoke softly into her ear. They crouched, and Simon pointed to Wildman's right hand. After a few moments, Simon said, "Call me if the fibers match." He rose and joined me. "I think we're finished here. There are a few interesting items upstairs I want you to see. Particularly in the study."

"Sure." As we made our way toward the door, I was about to ask Simon about the fibers when he said, "Your thoughts, Martin?"

"Any idea how the killers entered the house?"

"The back door was jimmied. We also found fresh tire marks in the alley behind the homes. From there, the intruders could easily have gained entrance without the neighbors seeing."

"Anything missing from the house?"

"Not that we've determined. Colonel Wildman's purse contains almost two hundred in cash, and we found her jewelry case seemingly untouched."

"Which means we can probably rule out robbery. Besides, thieves wouldn't kill like this or rob a home in the middle of the day with the occupants inside. If Dr. Marbury's right that the killings weren't sexually motivated—"

"They weren't."

"Agreed. So all we can determine now is the killings were well planned, apparently by people who specifically targeted Colonel Wildman for an unknown reason. Marbury raises a good point. Why work over Wildman if they were going to kill her anyway?"

"The killers obviously had a reason."

"Sure. One possibility is they had some kind of personal vendetta and were trying to inflict pain to punish her. A second is that they were trying to extract information from her." I paused, my brow furrowing. "But frankly that doesn't make a helluva lot of sense. They had her kids. By threatening them, the killers could have gotten anything they wanted from her."

We'd reached the stairs but had to wait for a guy with a video camera to come down. Simon turned to me with a smile. "Good, Martin. You're correct that the killers wanted something from her. But it was more than just information."

"It was, huh? Like what?"

Simon shrugged. "I'm not certain. Whatever it was, it had to be something quite small."

"How can you know that?"

"Hmm. Oh, because of the teddy bear." Then he nodded to the video guy and went up the stairs.

CHAPTER 4

"Okay," I said when we reached the kitchen. "Explain about the bear." We were standing next to the island with the stove and I had him by the arm. Through the window over the sink, I spotted three cops with flashlights slowly traipsing across the fenced backyard. The tree limbs were swaying back and forth as the wind picked up.

"You saw it?" Simon said, facing me.

"Sure," I said, letting go. "It's all torn up."

"Actually," Simon said, "it was cut."

"You think the killers were looking for something hidden in it?"

Simon nodded. "I'd noticed dark brown fibers under Colonel Wildman's fingernails. If Erika proves they came from the bear, we will know Colonel Wildman handled it recently."

"Maybe they're carpet fibers."

"There isn't any dark brown carpeting in the house, Martin." He gave me a long look. "Besides, the presence of the bear in the basement confirms its significance."

This explained Simon's interest in tracking down the children's babysitter. Normally kids nine and ten wouldn't be carrying a stuffed bear around, but he had to be sure.

"Even if you're right," I said, "that still doesn't help much. The killers obviously took whatever was inside the bear."

"Ah, but at least we have an idea what the object was."

"We do?"

"Upstairs, Martin," Simon said. "It's one of the things I wanted to show you."

As we went out into the hallway, I said, "By the way, where did Wildman work in the Pentagon?"

"Amanda said she was an aircraft maintenance specialist who worked in the Air Force Flying Safety office."

Not what I wanted to hear. I'd been thinking Wildman might have been killed for something related to her job, but that seemed unlikely. If she'd been an intelligence officer or a nuclear specialist, that would be one thing. But a military flying safety office wasn't exactly a hotbed of classified information.

Once we got to the second floor, Simon drew me to the first door on the left and we peered into a pale-pink bedroom with a white canopied bed, tiny blue birds stenciled on the headboard. "Notice anything of interest in the daughter's room, Martin?"

My eyes flowed clockwise around the room. Next to the bed was a pale-blue bureau and a child's-height wall mirror, then a miniature card table in the corner, a watercolor set open on it. I lingered on a wooden easel with a partially completed picture of a kitten. Continuing, I saw toys and games neatly stacked on a shelf by a small hutch with computer. I glanced down at the floor by the closet, pointing to an open suitcase, brimming with folded clothes.

I said, "Looks like the daughter was going on a trip."

"The boy, too." We crossed the hall into a bedroom that had posters of sports figures covering almost every inch of the wall. Michael Jordan and Shaquille O'Neal held the positions of honor above the bed. Another partially packed suitcase sat on the floor.

"The curious point," Simon said, "is Colonel Wildman wasn't going anywhere."

"She was just sending the children away?"

"Yes. We found plane tickets in her purse, purchased this morning. They were scheduled out on a nine-thirty A.M. American Airlines flight to Boston tomorrow."

"Any idea why they were going there?"

"Probably to visit Colonel Wildman's parents, who live there. We actually found three tickets. The children were going to be accompanied by their father, Wildman's ex-husband."

"Name?"

"Robert Baker. I've tried to phone him but couldn't get an answer. I sent Romero to wait at his home with instructions to notify us when Baker arrives. Apparently the man is something of a local sports celebrity. A baseball player."

I did a slow blink. "He's *Bobby Baker*, the pitcher?"

Simon nodded. "I understand he was quite good."

That was an understatement, but Simon didn't follow sports. The tickets he carried around were used exclusively for barter. Before Cal Ripken had appeared on the scene, Bobby Baker had been the Baltimore Orioles' biggest star. A flame-throwing southpaw, he'd won twenty-plus games in each of his first three seasons, then only a handful over the next two. Baker's problem was that he lived the way he pitched, fast and hard. A big-time party animal, Baker broke his left elbow in a bar fight and never regained his form. By the time he was twenty-seven, he was out of the big leagues. After that, his life pretty much spiraled downhill. He was an alcoholic who reportedly put away a bottle of vodka a day, and understandably had trouble getting jobs, much less holding them. For a while, you could occasionally catch him on local TV, hawking one product or another. Then came a well-publicized bust for drug possession, which ended his career as pitchman. Recently, there'd been a feel-good article in the paper about how Baker had finally kicked the booze and settled down. I hoped it was true because, like a lot of die-hard fans, I'd always pulled for the guy.

"You might have Romero troll the sports bars in town," I

said, only half-joking. I gave Simon a long look. "You know, tomorrow's a school day. Parents usually have to have a good reason to take their kids out of school."

A nod. "It's pretty evident Colonel Wildman knew she was in danger and was trying to protect the children. This seems to confirm it." He reached into his left jacket pocket, the one that didn't house his supply of tickets, and handed me a Baggie containing a single photograph. "We found similar pictures in an envelope on Colonel Wildman's dresser."

I pressed the plastic against the picture to see better. The photo showed four children standing in line, about to board a school bus.

"Colonel Wildman's children are the last two."

I'd recognized the daughter but not the boy. Unlike his blond-haired sister, his hair was dark brown. There was little resemblance between them. "So Wildman has a picture of her children..."

"It's taken with a telephoto lens. As were the other nine in the envelope. It's unlikely that Wildman would have taken what amounts to surveillance photos of her own children."

"Baker might," I said. "Maybe what we're dealing with is a domestic situation. Baker and Wildman could have been engaged in some kind of custody battle and he came here to have it out with Wildman. Things escalated and Baker lost it, beat Wildman and then killed the kids." I paused, then shook my head. "But I'm not sure I buy that scenario."

"Because of Baker's name on the plane ticket?"

"Sure. No way Wildman would have her ex-hubby escort her children if she'd considered him the threat." I gave the photo a last look and passed it back. "Too bad she didn't put the kids on an airplane sooner. You'd think if Colonel Wildman knew she or her kids were in danger, she'd have contacted the cops, the FBI or— What's wrong?"

Simon was frozen, staring at the photo. He snorted angrily. "The daughter. I missed it earlier. Her hair is quite a bit shorter in this picture."

"Is it?" I peeked over his shoulder and still couldn't be certain. I hadn't really noticed her hair in the basement. I said, "If you're right, then the photos must have been taken some time ago."

"Which means," he said, pocketing the picture, "they *weren't* what frightened Colonel Wildman. It had to be something else."

"The pictures could have been used to threaten her earlier," I pointed out.

But Simon was already moving down the hallway, his face knitted in thought.

CHAPTER 5

Colonel Margaret Wildman's study was a light and airy room with beige carpeting and pale-green walls. Large colorful flowerpots in the corners added a feminine touch, contrasting with the military mementos and photographs that seemed to be everywhere. Framed against a large window at the back sat a white-oak desk topped by a computer and a scanner, metal file cabinets on one side, a stand with a printer and fax machine on the other.

Simon and I entered to find Amanda hunkered over the desk, intently scrutinizing the contents of a bulky manila folder. Simon gave a little cough before she finally acknowledged us, saying, "I'm going through Colonel Wildman's credit card bills." I threw her a smile, but she kept her eyes on Simon, her face blank, showing no signs of the annoyance she probably felt toward him.

She went on, "The last charges in her files were almost two weeks ago. I spoke with the credit card and phone companies. They'll fax out her most current statements as well as a twelve-month summary sometime tomorrow. Also, I checked with Detective Reardon again. Nothing earth-shattering on the interviews." She held up an address book. "And no luck on coming up with a sitter in this."

"It can wait," Simon said. "Have you uncovered anything of interest in her records yet?"

"Couple items. There's a bank statement..." She reached for a second, even bulkier folder.

As Simon joined her, I hung back, looking over the pictures. One of the larger ones showed Colonel Wildman in a canoe with her children, who looked maybe four and five at the time. Wildman had been an attractive, sharp-featured woman, with short dark hair, a slender figure, and a dynamite smile. I tried not to think of the way she looked now. A few of the photographs included a tall, dark-haired man standing next to her and the girls. Bobby Baker had put on weight since his playing days, but I still easily recognized him. The fact that I was gazing at his image here in Wildman's office reinforced the realization I'd come to earlier—he hadn't been the one who sent her the school-bus photos.

I drifted over to the adjacent wall, where the pictures had a military theme. Most were of Wildman in green military fatigues, sometimes alone or with a group, standing in front of a variety of military transports, probably the ones she'd worked on as a maintenance officer. I studied them, hoping something would strike me as unusual. Maybe a photo of her standing by a missile silo or in front of some intelligence agency...anything that would indicate she had access to information that someone would kill her for.

But there was nothing in the background except airplanes.

"What were you going to show me in here?" I asked Simon.

He was standing over Amanda, watching her sort through banking envelopes. He looked over, gesturing to the computer. "It's completely dead."

"Okay..."

"The hardware is operable, but the memory is completely wiped out."

"Deleted?"

Simon shook his head. "We think erased. Perhaps by a

magnet. We'll send it to the lab to see if anything is recoverable."

"And you're convinced the killers zapped it?"

"I don't think there's any doubt, Martin. The two computers in the children's rooms are also inoperable."

I began to feel a buzz of excitement. "So Colonel Wildman was killed for something she knew, something she must have kept on a computer."

"A distinct possibility."

"I can tell you the lab will be wasting their time if a magnet was used," Amanda said. "Now if the killers employed a software encryption program to scramble the data, I might be able to recover some of it. You want, I can give it a shot later."

Simon seemed confused by her comment, so I jumped in, relating her background as an engineering and computer whiz. As I spoke, I noticed that Amanda didn't try to downplay her credentials.

"So you want me to take a look later?" she asked.

"Please," Simon said.

"Of course," I said to him, "there's the possibility Colonel Wildman would have copied what she had to a floppy—" I stopped. Simon was smiling knowingly.

"Shit," I said, catching on. "The bear? That's it, isn't it. You think there was a floppy disk hidden in the bear?"

He nodded. So did Amanda, indicating she was following the conversation. I wouldn't have thought Simon had mentioned the significance of the disk to her, so that meant she'd figured things out herself.

"So why hide it in the bear?" I asked.

Simon shrugged. "It's an unlikely hiding place."

"Actually," Amanda said, "the selection makes sense. Wildman was going to send her children away to keep them safe. Why not send the disk with them, especially if she thought her house might be searched?"

Simon practically beamed at her. And Simon rarely beamed. "Excellent, Amanda. I'm sure that's precisely what Colonel Wildman intended."

Amanda fielded the compliment with a look of bland indifference. But when she glanced my way, I caught a faint smile.

"Maybe so," I said. "But it seems Colonel Wildman would have made additional copies of the disk, given it to people she trusted."

"Who says she didn't?" Amanda said.

I looked around the office. Neat. No appearance of being searched. "Have you checked? Maybe she kept another copy in here?"

"Not in the desk or the file cabinet," Amanda said. "I looked."

"We'll conduct a thorough search," Simon said. "But if she had copies here, they're probably gone."

I nodded, thinking of the bodies in the basement. To save her children, Wildman would have given the killers everything.

"What about Colonel Wildman's office at the Pentagon?" I said. "We'll need to secure it."

"Already taken care of," Amanda said. "I notified the DoD cops to post a guard on her office until we can check it out." The Department of Defense, like many of the government agencies, had its own small police force.

"How about the systems administrator?" Each office had a system administrator who handled computer security. Without Wildman's password, we would need the SA to reinitialize her computer so we could access the system.

"Sergeant Rider at the ops desk is handling it. The SA will meet us at Wildman's office around nine." She checked her watch. "Gives us about forty-five minutes."

I had to hand it to her. She didn't miss much. I said, "You know if Colonel Wildman worked in anything besides maintenance before her Pentagon assignment?"

"Not as far as I know. I've put a request in to AFPC for her personnel records. Probably get them sometime tomorrow." AFPC was the Air Force Personnel Center out of San Antonio. Noticing my frown, she added, "It doesn't make sense to me either, Marty. I mean who the hell kills a maintenance officer?"

The million-dollar question. I didn't bother to reply.

Amanda waved a sheet of paper. "Anyway, guys, here's the first thing I turned up...."

Simon looked down while I scooted around the desk to see. A March bank statement. Colonel Wildman's account showed a balance of a little over five thousand dollars. Amanda indicated an entry about halfway down, a check written for seven hundred and thirty-three dollars.

Simon said, "So..."

"Maybe nothing, but I noticed the same charge on four earlier statements." She pointed out two other entries. "It's not her house payment or her car lease. I got curious and pulled her canceled checks from a file." Amanda's hand snaked to some checks paper-clipped together and held them up to Simon.

"Capitol Rentals," Simon read.

She flipped the check over, revealing the cancellation stamp of a local Sovran bank. "Funny, huh? I mean why would she be renting a second place around here—"

"I already know," Simon said.

Amanda's eyes widened, and so did mine.

"It's a rental house for Bobby Baker," Simon said.

"Huh? She's *paying* for his place?" Amanda said. "I thought Baker made millions playing ball—"

"He did," I said. "But he was in the majors before the really big money. And what he made he blew years ago."

A long pause as we considered the implication of the payments. The bottom line was if Margaret Wildman was shelling out for a place for her ex-husband to live, then it followed that she still *cared* for him. And if she did, maybe she confided in him whatever information she had. Simon, of course, had probably realized this, which explained why he was so hot to find Baker.

Simon stifled a yawn. "You said you had something else, Amanda?"

She kicked back in the chair, nodding toward the clamshell closet doors, which were shut. "In there. On the floor."

Since I was closest, I went over and pushed the doors open. It smelled faintly of mothballs. Winter clothing and long dresses hung from the rack, heavy blankets and linens stacked neatly on a shelf above. On the floor next to some ladies' shoes was a flat cardboard box, the name of an electronics manufacturer stamped on the side. The top said "Computer scanner." I touched the box lightly with my shoe. Empty. I glanced around for something else of interest.

"The box, Marty," Amanda prompted.

"What about it?"

"There's a receipt taped to the far side."

I turned the box around. The receipt indicated that the scanner had been purchased for almost a hundred and fifty dollars. I was still confused. I started to ask Amanda what she was getting at when I noticed the date. I plucked the receipt free and spun around. "Yesterday. Wildman purchased it yesterday. Hell, she must have used it to scan whatever information she had so she could transfer it to a disk."

Now this Simon didn't know. He snatched the receipt from me and hissed in approval. "Well done, Amanda," he murmured.

"I know."

"I mean it."

"I'm truly thrilled." She sounded both amused and sarcastic.

He gave her a funny look as if uncertain how to take that. Tucking the receipt into his jacket, he said, "The question now is whether Colonel Wildman had a chance to give someone a disk before she was killed. Because if she did—"

He broke off, looking to the door. From the hallway, we heard the sound of rapidly approaching footsteps. Moments later, a uniformed cop with a Marine haircut stuck his head inside. His forehead glistened and he was out of breath like he'd been running.

"Lieutenant, Detective Reardon found a witness," the cop said.

CHAPTER 6

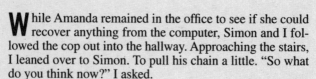

While Amanda remained in the office to see if she could recover anything from the computer, Simon and I followed the cop out into the hallway. Approaching the stairs, I leaned over to Simon. To pull his chain a little. "So what do you think now?" I asked.

"Hmm. About what?"

"Amanda."

A pause. "She'll do, Martin."

I grinned.

As we stepped out the front door, we saw that the crowd had almost doubled, particularly in the press section. The moment the media spotted Simon, questions erupted and cameras flashed. We followed the cop across the lawn toward the sidewalk. Across the street, reporters continued their verbal barrage as they scurried along to keep up. A couple of uniforms strolled beside the jostling stream, keeping them back.

"Lieutenant Santos, over here. Just a few questions..."

"Was Colonel Wildman raped? Is this a sex crime?"

"Can you confirm the children's throats were cut?"

"How badly was Colonel Wildman beaten before she was killed?"

"Christ," I muttered. "How the hell can they know all this so fast?"

"McNamara," Simon said automatically.

I glanced over, startled. "What?"

He pointed down the road where McNamara was pacing near a gleaming black Corvette, puffing away furiously on a cigarette, a cell phone jammed to his ear. McNamara stopped in mid-stride, staring at the phone. He shook his head, firing the cigarette angrily at the ground. Moments later he climbed into the car and the engine roared to life.

"Our angry friend has a nice car for a policeman, wouldn't you say?" Simon said.

I nodded.

"He also lives in a half-million-dollar home in Chesapeake. And his kids attend private school." Simon grimaced as McNamara peeled away, tires squealing and smoking.

"I thought he handled security consulting on the side," I said. Everyone knew McNamara had been moonlighting for years.

"He does, and has become quite successful, which puzzles me. The man is incompetent." Simon flashed a grim smile. "Anyway, we've suspected for a while that McNamara's been leaking information to the press, but we can't prove it." He shrugged. "Not that it really matters. He's not alone. There are half a dozen others who sell information."

"I thought the press didn't pay for information."

"Officially, no. But the growth of pseudo–media outlets like the TV gossip shows and scandal magazines has caused a bending of the rules. To compete, a number of the more traditional press organizations have quietly begun paying sources for their stories."

"Is that why he was so pissed off about you taking over the case? You were screwing him out of information he could sell?"

"Probably."

We walked along, ignoring the clamor from the press. The wind was turning the night air chilly, and I regretted not bringing my overcoat. I said, "McNamara seems to hate you."

"I know. I've heard he's been investigating me."

"Oh? Looking for what?"

"Who knows?" Simon looked suddenly uneasy. "Still, he could pose a problem."

"What kind of problem?"

But Simon wouldn't say anything further.

The cop turned into a driveway three houses down, and opened the front door without knocking. He led us into an alcove of Spanish tile and stained glass. To our right was a cozy parlor, three people seated inside. A white-haired couple in their sixties watched us nervously from a floral sofa. In an armchair across from them sat a large man with red hair, wearing a blue sports coat, a badge clipped to the pocket.

Detective Michael Reardon stood as we came in, acknowledging me with a slight nod. We'd met once, a few years back. He introduced the couple as Mr. and Mrs. Frawley, and explained that they had seen a car parked in front of the Wildman home around three that afternoon.

"That's right," Mr. Frawley said. "I saw it when I was taking the garbage out." He was a small, wiry man with a squeaky voice. His wife was even shorter, but about twice as wide. She kept dabbing her eyes, which were red.

"Any particular reason you noticed the car, Mr. Frawley?" Simon asked.

"Margaret doesn't get many visitors," Frawley said. "Besides, it was a late-model Sable. Tan. I noticed it because my son recently bought one, except his is silver."

By now I had my notebook out again and was scribbling away.

"Any chance you saw the license plate?" Simon asked.

"Noticed it. Didn't pay attention to the number."

"Any idea of the state?"

"No state."

I looked up from my writing. Simon was frowning.

"The plate was white," Frawley said.

I almost dropped my pen. Simon also looked stunned, but when he spoke, he sounded calm. "You're absolutely certain?" he asked.

"White," Frawley said again. "A government plate."

"You didn't see who was driving the car?"

"No. I just saw it parked there."

"Any idea how long it was there?"

A head shake. "But it was gone when I looked maybe an hour later."

"At four?"

"Actually a little before. I had a doctor's appointment at four-thirty. I left the house around ten 'til."

"You're absolutely certain the car was gone from Colonel Wildman's by then?"

"Sure. Drove right by. No car."

"Did you see anyone else visit Colonel Wildman to-day?"

"No. I think there might have been a second car parked across the street earlier. Wouldn't swear to it, though." Simon's eyes went to his wife, who meekly shook her head. "You might try Maggie Porter," Frawley added. "She's kind of the neighborhood busybody, runs the local crime watch. She's kind of a fanatic about it. Even set up a video surveillance system at her house. Understandable, though. A couple years ago, some guy followed her home and robbed her. She lives across from Wildman."

Simon turned to Reardon. "Not home," Reardon said.

Simon looked to me to see if I had any questions. I stepped forward, asking if Bobby Baker, Wildman's ex, had visited in the past few days. More head shakes from the Frawleys. Mr. Frawley squinted at me. "You don't think Bobby's somehow involved?"

"Do you?"

"Not a chance in hell," he shot back. "Bobby loved those kids. Came over at least a couple times a week. Took them to the movies, flew kites over at the park, anything they wanted. Played catch with his son in the backyard. He's a good man. All that crap about his drinking, I never saw it." Mrs. Frawley bobbed along in agreement.

"Mrs. Frawley," I said gently. "Do you know if either of the Wildman children still carried a teddy bear?"

She seemed flustered to actually be asked a question. Then her eyes filled with tears. "I...I don't think so. I don't remember seeing them with one."

"Do you happen to know who the children's sitter was?"

She wiped at her eyes, nodding. Before she could reply, Reardon said, "She already gave me the sitter's name. Marcy Rogers. A high school kid. I had dispatch run down the number and address."

I jotted the info down as he read it off, then thanked the Frawleys. Mrs. Frawley began saying things like, "They were such a nice family. The children...so sweet..." She finally broke down with a racking sob, and her husband gently placed his arm around her. After a few moments, Simon handed Mr. Frawley a card, telling him to call us if he thought of anything.

"Sure," Mr. Frawley said. "I wish I could have been more help. It seems that whoever was in the car isn't the bastard you're looking for. Not if it was someone from the government."

"No. Probably not. Good night." He flicked his head at Reardon, who followed us to the door. "How long until you finish the interviews?" Simon asked him.

"Mills is working the homes across the street and we still have to hit the neighbors out back. Couple more hours at least, then we'll have to come back tomorrow to get the ones who aren't home."

"Make the neighbor Maggie Porter a priority."

Reardon nodded.

"You have Mr. Frawley's statement about the car on tape?"

"Not yet."

"Get that first."

Mrs. Frawley was still crying as we left.

More reporters as Simon and I walked back. We didn't even look in their direction, which enhanced their frustration and made them even more vocal.

"I don't like this," I said.

"No . . ."

"If the killers were professionals somehow tied to the government—"

"The license plate doesn't prove anything, Martin. It could have been stolen."

"True."

"The car, too."

"I know, but—"

"Besides," he said, "the vehicle was parked in her driveway."

I nodded. Simon was probably right. Someone involved in the killing wouldn't park in the open like that. The only other explanation was that the car belonged to a Pentagon coworker who'd happened by. If so, unless they left right after Frawley saw them, maybe they noticed something—

"Remember, Martin," Simon said. "The key to this case is the way Colonel Wildman was killed."

I had a pretty good idea what he was getting at. Before I could follow up, shouts erupted to our right. A number of reporters began running toward the Wildman house. Ahead, we saw the two coroner's assistants rolling a gurney with a small body bag down the driveway. Cameras began going off as the men slid the gurney into the back of the ambulance. Across the street, TV cameras recorded the scene. Film at eleven.

"The beating," I said to Simon, resuming our conversation. He nodded.

"The excessive brutality of it," I said. "It suggests anger, hate—"

"And don't forget the children."

"The children?"

"Why they were killed. To me that's even more troubling."

"But they had to be killed. They were witnesses—"

"You're missing my point. The killers were obviously well-organized. They could have targeted Wildman when her children weren't home." He gave me a long look. "But they didn't."

I shook my head. Simon was implying that the killers had a specific reason for also wanting the children dead. I told him this sounded, well, a little nuts.

"Perhaps," he said stiffly. "But I am certain of one thing. Wildman was killed by someone she knew. Someone with an intense hatred who—"

He abruptly fell silent.

I frowned until I noticed he was looking at an altercation by the press barricade. A woman was waving her arms wildly at two burly officers blocking her way. She was really making a scene, screaming and cursing. She was a leggy, big-haired blond in a black, form-hugging sweater and matching slacks which seemed almost painted on. Her figure was spectacular. At first I couldn't quite make out her face. And then she turned toward a streetlight. I caught her profile and then—

I stared. I couldn't take my eyes off her. Even with her mouth twisted in anger, she was one of the most beautiful women I'd ever seen.

Simon and I kept walking as we watched the confrontation. The blond suddenly tried to squeeze by the cops, and one grabbed her by the arm. The woman snarled, slapping his hand away.

"That's assault!" she screamed. "Don't you fucking touch me!"

The cop recoiled, stunned.

"Assault!" someone from the crowd yelled. More voices joined in. "Assault. Assault."

We could see people laughing as they chanted. The woman flashed an arrogant smile. She looked taut and sleek, like a big cat. As the cop started to reach for her again, the woman glanced toward Simon and me. She began waving frantically, calling out something. We were still maybe thirty yards away and couldn't quite decipher her words over the chanting crowd.

As we came closer I finally heard her clearly. I immediately looked to Simon in surprise.

She was calling out to him by name. His first name. Pleading to talk to him. She sounded desperate. I expected him to go over, find out what she wanted.

But he kept his eyes focused straight ahead. People were staring at us. I said, "Simon..."

"I hear her, Martin."

And he quickened his pace to the house.

CHAPTER 7

We crossed Colonel Wildman's lawn toward the front door. Simon was really moving, and I had to hustle to keep up. The woman was still calling out to him. Reporters had gathered around her, flashbulbs popping all over the place. The whole thing seemed a little crazy. I asked, "Who the hell is she?"

But Simon was looking at the cops who were focused on him, their faces uncertain. He gave them an exaggerated head shake. The cops grinned and reached for the woman.

"God*dammit*, Simon!" she exploded. "This is important! You son of a bitch, Simon—"

We ducked under the yellow tape and went up the steps past a gaggle of uniformed officers on the porch. Most wore amused smirks. Before going inside the house, I looked back. The two cops were forcing the squirming woman outside the barricade as she kept up her verbal assault on Simon.

We finally stepped into the foyer. It was quiet. I said dryly, "Nice girl. Friend of yours?"

Simon gave me a dark look.

"C'mon. You obviously know her."

He hesitated. "Her name is Janet Spence."

"Huh? You gotta be kidding." *Now* I knew why he didn't want to talk to her. Janet Spence was a well-known syndicated gossip columnist who worked for the *Washington Post*. I asked, "So what's she doing covering a murder?"

"Who knows?" He stepped aside as the two coroner's assistants returned, heading toward the kitchen.

"Be outa your hair in ten minutes, Lieutenant," one of them said.

"Fine," Simon said.

I said, "Janet Spence seemed to really want to talk to you. Said it was important."

"She lies, Martin."

"Lies how?"

Simon ignored me, punching a number into his cell phone. I sighed. Turning toward the stairs, I told him Amanda and I were going to the Pentagon to check out Wildman's office.

"Wait, Martin."

So I did. From the conversation, I realized he was talking to the children's sitter. He hadn't bothered to ask me for her number. Simon, of course, remembered it.

After telling the sitter he'd be by in ten minutes, he ordered a car from one of the uniforms outside. To me, he said, "The car Frawley saw could have been driven by a military acquaintance of Wildman."

"I know. And that person may or may not know something about the murders. But it's unlikely they could have been the person who made the 911 call."

"That's assuming Frawley is correct on the time he said the car had left."

"He is."

Simon nodded thoughtfully. "Who in the government is responsible for allocating official vehicles?"

"Forget it, Simon. The General Services Agency bulk-purchases thousands of cars a year for various federal agencies. Without a plate, it's impossible to tie a vehicle to an organization, much less a person."

"Even with the make and color?"

"Doesn't matter. Got to be hundreds throughout the federal system. No way to narrow down the list to something manageable anytime soon."

Simon pursed his lips unhappily. I suggested questioning Colonel Wildman's co-workers to find out if any drove government-issued Sables. He was giving a look of disapproval before I finished.

"If you can be discreet, I'll allow it," he said. "But I don't want it to get out that we know about the car."

"Relax. I'll play it cool. Anyway, there won't be many candidates. You've got to have clout to be assigned a government vehicle."

He squinted. "Meaning a general officer?"

"At least a colonel or the civilian equivalent."

A female cop poked through the front door to tell Simon a car was waiting. As he left, I made my way to the stairs. After a couple of steps, I frowned, looking around.

Someone was calling my name.

"Hey, Marty! Marty!"

Down the hall, I spotted a familiar figure striding toward me, a cardboard evidence box tucked under an arm. Zane Carlson was one the criminalists I'd seen earlier. Zane was in his early fifties, small and wiry. He still wore what had to be the world's worst toupee, happily oblivious to the fact that it sat on his scalp like furry black roadkill.

Zane pulled up to me, grinning. "Been a while, Marty. Must be what? Two years." The grin faded into a sympathetic line. "Heard about your wife. Jeez, that must have been rough."

I nodded, hoping my silence would tell him I didn't want to go there.

But Zane went on somberly, "You know, I lost my wife almost five years ago. Goddamn drunk driver ran a red light."

"I didn't know that," I said.

"Yeah..." Zane looked off into space, remembering. "First year was hell. After that, it got easier. But the pain never really goes away. Sometimes, even now..." He swallowed, coming back to me. "Hang in there, Marty. You ever need to talk, I'm in the book."

"I appreciate it, Zane."

"That Simon who just left?"

"Yeah. Should be back in thirty minutes or so."

"You see him, tell him I got something from Wildman's car he might be interested in." He tapped the box, which had a cover.

I had to ask. "What's inside?"

Zane balanced the box on a bony hand and removed the cover. When I looked inside, my body began to tingle. A soft leather case, like a briefcase, only smaller. Colonel Wildman's initials were stitched on the side. As I reached for the handle, I kept my voice casual.

"I'll see that Simon gets this," I said.

Amanda was typing on the computer keyboard when I entered the study. She noticed me, and shook her head gloomily. "Nothing. If they scrambled the drive with software, I'd have found something. That means they used a goddamn magnet. Bastards knew what they were doing."

"Try this," I said.

And I held up the case containing the laptop computer.

CHAPTER 8

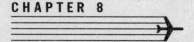

I stood over Amanda as she powered up the laptop. The screen flared to life and the hard drive chirped. "So far, so good," Amanda murmured.

"The computer will work. The killers obviously weren't aware of it or they wouldn't have left it behind."

The whirring stopped and the Windows desktop screen appeared. Amanda clicked on the documents folder. The screen filled with icons of files, most with military titles. She opened one that said Correspondence: a list of names, most with military rank attached. "Christ," she said, scrolling down, "must be over a hundred letters here. This will take a while." She closed the window and opened another document called Reports. More files.

"Give me twenty minutes," she said. "I'll check out the military reports first, see if there's anything—"

"No time. We've got to get to the Pentagon."

Her brow furrowed. "What's the rush? We still have a few minutes."

I told her about Mr. Frawley and the car he saw.

Amanda slowly ran a tongue over her lips, looking gradually stunned. "Jesus . . ."

I nodded.

"That means someone from the government—"

"More than likely it was someone from Wildman's office."

She started to push away from the desk, then stopped. "We got time to check out that disk you found? Only take a sec."

I hesitated, then reached into a zippered side pocket of the computer case and removed a floppy I'd discovered earlier. On the side, in neat print, it said "Disk 2," and below, "Press Clippings."

Amanda studied the disk. "Number two? No others in the case?"

"No."

With a shrug, she inserted the disk into the A-drive. A soft whir and three dates appeared on the screen. "Huh? That's all?" She sounded disappointed.

She clicked on the first date: December 17, 1997. A news article appeared. The headline read "Royal Saudi Airliner Crashes." We scanned the story, which had an Associated Press byline. The plane had disappeared from radar over the Mediterranean on a flight from Zurich to Riyadh. No survivors were expected.

We read the second file, dated November 3, 1998. Another article about a plane crash. This time a Colombian airliner had gone down over a remote part of the Andes.

Amanda sat back, looking a little puzzled. I said, "Colonel Wildman was a safety officer. It was probably her job to track airplane accidents."

"Civilian ones?"

Point taken. As far as I knew, the Air Force was only concerned with military crashes. I shrugged.

A click and the last article appeared: This plane crash had occurred less than two months earlier, on February 7, 1999. A Chinese airliner flying from Beijing to Pyongyang, North Korea, had gone down over the Yellow Sea.

"I don't remember reading about this one," Amanda said.

I didn't either. And I could only vaguely recall the first two crashes. "It probably didn't get much play in the U.S. papers. Foreign accidents usually don't. Scroll up to the beginning of the article."

She did, asking, "You looking for anything in particular?"

"I'm not sure— There." The cursor hovered over the second sentence, the one where the type of airliner was mentioned.

"A Global 626," I read.

"Wasn't that the same aircraft that crashed in Colombia?"

I nodded. "And the one in Saudi."

She sighed, shaking her head. "Can't think there'd be a connection."

She was referring to the murders. "No. We'd better go. We'll take the laptop with us. Maybe there's something in the files we can use. Grab your purse."

"I don't carry a purse," she said automatically.

Silly me. As she shut down the computer, I had her pass me the disk. I stared at it, dimly recalling a conversation with a pilot friend. It was a couple years back. He'd called to say he was being transferred to a new aircraft. He also mentioned something else.

I went over to the photos on the wall. I found what I was looking for in a picture along the top row. A shot of then Lieutenant Colonel Wildman standing in front of a line of aircraft. Most were C-141s, the Air Force's primary cargo jet. But the second aircraft from the right was larger than the rest, sleeker. I hadn't paid much attention before because I hadn't been interested in the planes.

"Say," Amanda said, coming up behind, "isn't that a picture of—"

"Yes," I said. "It's called a C-26. The military version of the Global 626."

"I didn't know the Air Force flew the G-626."

I faced her, sliding a hand in my jacket. "They're fairly new. The Air Force only purchased a handful."

"Guess that explains Wildman's interest in..." She frowned. "Hold on. Those the aircraft that were bought for some secret mission?"

"*Top* Secret," I corrected, punching a number into my cell phone.

Master Sergeant Rider at the OSI duty desk said it would take maybe an hour to run a query of the jet through the Air Force database. Because it was tied to a Top Secret program, our access would be limited. I told him to find out what he could and notify me ASAP.

When I hung up, Amanda was staring at me. "You think there's anything here, Marty?" Her tone indicated that she did.

I shrugged. "I suppose it's possible."

"*Possible?* Hell, this has to be it. This is the classified connection to Wildman we were looking for."

"What about her children?"

"Huh?"

I smiled. "Forget it. It was something Simon said. C'mon. Maybe we'll get lucky in Wildman's office."

CHAPTER 9

Five minutes later, I was camped in the passenger seat of Amanda's cherry-red Camaro, watching her nimbly weave between the southbound traffic on the George Washington Memorial Parkway. As she drove, her head bobbed to the pulsing beat of a rap song on the radio. I took it as long as I could before reaching for the volume button.

"You mind?" I asked.

"Not your style, huh? Sure, turn it off. What are you into, anyway? Big band music? A little Glen Miller maybe?"

"I'm not quite that old," I said dryly, punching the power button. She stole a couple of glances my way like she wanted to say something. "Shoot, Amanda."

"Just curious why the Air Force would classify a passenger aircraft."

I shrugged, and told her the jets were supposedly employed in counterterrorism missions. Insertion flights for units like the Navy SEALs or Army Delta Force. That sort of thing.

She frowned. "So you think maybe some terrorist group had her killed?"

I thought, then shook my head. "Why would a terrorist group target a maintenance officer? Revenge against a SEAL team member, maybe. Wouldn't be the first time."

"Colonel Wildman had knowledge of the plane's classified avionics and equipment. . . ."

"True, but—"

"Plus, a terrorist group explains why the killers were so organized. Hell, they not only knew how to wipe out a hard drive, they even brought the equipment to do the job."

"Assuming there was information on her computer, why would the killers zap it instead of taking it with them?"

"It's bulky. Cumbersome. Anyway, they wouldn't need it. Not if they already had the info on a disk. And they obviously fried Wildman's hard drive to prevent us from connecting the plane to the murders."

"Uh-huh," I said. "And why would terrorists want information on the plane?"

"Who knows? Sabotage, maybe."

"So the pictures of her kids we found. I suppose you think those were taken to force Wildman into cooperating.

"Why the hell not?" she snapped. "It fits."

I started to argue, but pulled back because Amanda was clearly annoyed. Besides, her scenario did seem to fit the facts as we knew them. But I couldn't swallow her initial premise, that terrorists would go after a maintenance officer.

For the next few minutes, Amanda hunkered over the wheel, giving me the silent treatment. She darted into the left lane to pass a van, then cut back over. A mile later, she finally looked my way. "Aw, hell, maybe you're right, Marty. The more I think about it, the more it all sounds a little . . ."

"Far-fetched?"

She nodded. "Christ, I thought maybe I had something."

"Still might. Stranger things have happened."

"Yeah, well . . ." Amanda stared out the window. "I suppose it could still be the husband. Or maybe someone from her office. Someone who might have felt threatened and . . ."

I settled back, half-listening as she droned through a list of possibilities. Amanda's impatience for answers reminded me of myself during my early investigations. Back then, I'd attack a case by happily bouncing from one lead to another, never sure where I was going but determined to do *something*. Experience had taught me that I could be more efficient by slowing the pace, thinking things through. That's how Simon operated and, though I didn't like to admit it, I'd honed much of my style after his. Not that Simon's circumspect approach didn't frustrate me on occasion. I've seen him spend days seemingly doing nothing, but the next thing I knew, he'd solved the case.

We were approaching the exit for Highway U.S. 1, except we were still in the left lane. I started to mention it when Amanda suddenly punched the gas and knifed over, cutting inches in front of a Mercedes. As we roared up the ramp, the driver behind rode his horn in annoyance.

"It'd be nice to reach the Pentagon alive," I said.

"Relax, Marty," she said, eyeing the rearview mirror. "I know what I'm— *Jesus*!"

"What?"

"Some red BMW. Practically ran another car off the road to make the exit."

I gazed back skeptically.

"Hey," she said, noticing. "There's a difference. I knew I had it made."

"Uh-huh. Tell me, how long have you had this little insecurity problem?"

She laughed at that. "Yeah, yeah. I know I come on a little strong. Blame my upbringing. I was the only girl with four brothers. Besides, it's hard to be humble when you know you're good."

"So you don't even try?"

"What's the point?"

I smiled at her frankness. "You impressed Simon tonight."

"Yippee. What's with him, anyway?"

"What do you mean?"

"Testing me. That's what he was doing. I want to know why."

I chose my words carefully. "Simon insists...demands competence. He's...uncomfortable working with someone new until he knows whether he can trust them. Most of the people on his team have been with him for—"

"Yeah, yeah. I get the picture. Simon gets his jollies playing mind games with people to see how they react. Nice guy. I had upperclassmen at the Academy do the same thing. We called them assholes."

"Simon is a nice guy," I shot back. "You'll realize that the longer you know him."

She blinked at me. "Hey, sorry. Didn't realize you two were so tight."

"We're not. It's just..." I didn't bother to finish.

After a few moments, Amanda said softly, "No harm, no foul?"

I hesitated. "Sure."

"You got any idea what we're looking for in Wildman's office?"

I shook my head. "But we'll know when we find it."

She glanced at me.

"Something worth killing for." In the distance, I picked out the Pentagon, glowing like a modern fortress against the skyline. We'd be there in minutes. I reminded myself to call my daughter Emily before she went to bed. After Nicole's death, nights had been particularly difficult for her. For the first few months, I'd sit up with her, waiting until she fell asleep—

"Uh, Marty..."

When I looked over, Amanda was again focused on the rearview mirror.

"I think that red BMW is following us," she said.

I turned to see the car camped on our tail. Through the glare of its headlights, I could make out the silhouette of the driver and no one else.

Moments later, the high beams began clicking on and off.

"I think he wants us to stop," Amanda said.

"You're mistaken," I said.

"Huh?"

"It's not a he."

CHAPTER 10

W e worked our way across traffic toward the shoulder, the BMW following. I kept trying to make out the driver. I could see the outline of thick cascading hair, but no facial features. We rolled to a stop under a streetlight, not far from the Pentagon's south entrance. The BMW coasted in behind. Its headlights went out, replaced by the pulsing of emergency flashers. The driver's door opened and a woman emerged—

My eyes widened in astonishment.

"Jeez, nice outfit," Amanda said. "You think she can breathe in that thing?"

The woman was walking toward my door. Her sweater hugged her every curve, running seamlessly down from the swell of her full breasts to the flare of her shapely hips.

"You know her, Marty?" Amanda asked.

"She's Janet Spence. The *Post* columnist. She's an acquaintance of Simon's."

"What's with the getup? She doing research on hookers?"

"Be nice, Amanda," I said, rolling down my window.

Janet Spence reached my door and bent down, flashing a

dazzling smile. Up close, her beautiful face looked perfectly made up, like a painting. "Thank God I caught you, Colonel Collins—"

"Marty. I'm not in the military anymore."

She blinked. "Oh? One of the policemen said—"

"Doesn't matter. What's this all about, Ms. Spence?"

"Hey, Simon must have told you about me." She looked pleased.

I nodded.

She leaned closer, the swell of her breasts inches from my face. I tried not to stare. She smiled at Amanda, who gazed back bleakly. "Look, Marty, it's important that I speak with Simon. I know he's upset with me, but I can't do anything about that. Convince him to call me, huh?" She handed me a card, her face softening. "Please. It really is very important."

"I can't promise anything."

She stared at me, gave my hand a squeeze, then slowly straightened. In a sad voice she said, "Tell him it's not what he thinks. Tell him Margie Wildman was my friend."

My eyebrows went up but before I could say anything, Janet Spence turned and walked back to her car.

As I slipped the card into my pocket, Amanda said dryly, "You believe Betty Big Boobs really knows Colonel Wildman?"

I shrugged. "She sounded sincere."

"Get real, Marty. She's just looking for a story and you know it."

"Amanda, she's a gossip columnist."

"Yeah, well . . ." She shrugged, checking the driver's-side mirror. "You'll come to your senses in a minute."

"What's that supposed to mean?"

"When the blood flow returns to your head." Then she flashed a sardonic grin, gunned the engine and peeled out into traffic.

 At precisely 8:44 P.M. we rolled into the parking area near the Pentagon's River entrance, the one on the east side usually reserved for the military's heavy hitters. In spite of the hour, the lot was still a quarter full, which was par for the course. On any given night, hundreds of staff officers could be found burning the midnight oil, trying to get some short-notice report or briefing ready for the constellations in the morning. I was familiar with the drill because I'd done a couple years in the building working OSI budget issues. One thing I'd never understood was why generals always seemed to wait until the last minute before asking for something. Management by crisis, which made me wonder how they ever planned a war.

We parked toward the front, and as we emerged from the car, Amanda put an AFOSI Official Business placard on the dashboard so it could be read through the windshield. As we made our way up the sidewalk leading to massive wooden double doors, we could feel a change in the weather. The night was quiet and had gone from chilly to downright cold.

"You know your way around in here?" I asked Amanda.

"Pretty much. I still occasionally get lost with all the construction going on. You know they got the whole area between corridors three and four closed up now?"

I nodded. She was talking about the billion-dollar renovation project that would be going on for the next ten years. I said, "When the Pentagon was built in 1943, it was supposed to be a breakthrough in efficiency. It was designed so that a person could go between any two points in the building in under seven minutes."

Amanda frowned. "What'd the guy do, sprint?" She scooted ahead and held open the door. "Age before beauty."

"Thanks," I grunted. We showed our OSI IDs to a tired-looking female guard at the security check point who had us push back our jackets to reveal our pistols before handing us no-escort-required visitors' badges and waving us around the metal detector.

Only a handful of people walked through the antiseptic

green corridors, which was a marked contrast from the daytime, when bands of tense-faced officers always seemed to scurry around. In the Pentagon hierarchy, anyone below the rank of colonel was considered an action officer, the official term for the worker bees who did the bidding of the generals.

The Pentagon was built along the number five: five sides, five stories, and five concentric rings that expanded outward. These rings were labeled A to E and interlocked with ten numbered corridors. Unlike Amanda, I thought the hub-and-spoke design was damned efficient, but you had to know what you were doing. For instance, if you wanted to get from one side of the building to the other, you generally should use the A or inner ring, not simply because it was the shortest distance to travel, but because portions of the other rings were often blocked off for additional office space. A major benefit to the design was that an office number gave you its precise location. Colonel Wildman's office was 5D161, which told me it was on the fifth floor, D-ring, between corridors one and two.

Our heels clicked on the linoleum up to the fifth floor, where we worked our way around the A-ring to corridor two, and took it to the D-ring. The Air Force Flight Safety Analysis office was located halfway down the hall on the right. We pushed into a cluttered room with pale green walls and partitioned cubicles. A short hallway on the left led to the private offices at the back—the ones usually occupied by the colonels. There didn't seem to be anyone around, but we could hear music playing. Moments later, a frizzy-haired female Air Force major poked out from a nearby cubicle. She had a file in her hand and her name tag read Sullivan—the name Amanda had given me for the systems administrator. Larger offices filled the SA's job with a contract civilian; smaller ones, to save bucks, assigned it to the most junior military member. In the Pentagon, this usually meant a major since captains were rare and lieutenants were practically nonexistent.

We went over and introduced ourselves. Afterward, Major Sullivan shook her head sadly, tossing the folder onto her desk in the cubicle. "When Sergeant Rider called me, I...I couldn't believe it. Colonel Wildman and her children... and then Officer Johnson told me how...how they died."

Johnson was probably the DoD cop who was guarding Wildman's office in the back. I expressed my condolences to Sullivan, then shifted to my interviewer's voice, asking if she knew Colonel Wildman well.

Sullivan swallowed hard, nodding. "Yes. I worked with her in AWACs maintenance at Tinker. She's the one that brought me here. She said working at the staff would be good for my career." Sullivan gestured vaguely. "This... this is going to devastate everyone. Margaret...Colonel Wildman was well liked." Her eyes misted. "It's such a shock. I...I just spoke with her yesterday."

Amanda and I nodded sympathetically. After Sullivan dabbed her eyes with a tissue, I asked, "Was that the last time you saw her?"

A head shake. "I didn't actually see her. She's been out on leave for the past week. I called her at home to check the status of a report she'd been working."

Taking leave to remain at home was a little odd, though not unheard of. Amanda mentioned this to Sullivan.

"All she told me was she had some work to catch up on," Sullivan said.

"What kind of work?" Amanda asked. "Something for the office?"

"I wouldn't think so," Sullivan said. "She wouldn't burn leave for that."

"Would anyone in the office know what she was working on?" Amanda asked.

Sullivan thought. "Probably not. I was closer to her than anyone else here. You might try Alma."

"Alma?"

"Alma Carter. One of the secretaries in the front office. Alma and Colonel Wildman often went to the POAC to jog together." The POAC was the Pentagon's athletic club in the north end of the building.

Amanda dug out a notepad, proving she had one. "You have Alma's number?"

"Sure." Sullivan stepped over to her desk and slipped an office roster from under the Plexiglas. She passed it to Amanda, telling her to keep it.

"Major," I said, "do you know of any reason why someone might want to harm Colonel Wildman?"

Sullivan looked shocked. "Of course not."

"Please," I said. "It could be anything. A project she was working on? Or maybe she'd met someone? A romance—" Sullivan shook her head emphatically at that. "Or perhaps she had a disagreement with someone— Who?" She'd started like I'd struck a nerve.

"It's probably not pertinent," she said. "I'm . . . I'm not sure I should even bring it up."

"Let us decide," Amanda said.

Sullivan was still reluctant, saying she didn't want to engage in gossip. I went through my spiel, promising that everything she said would be kept confidential. Then I reminded her that this was a murder investigation.

"All right," Sullivan said finally. "I wasn't actually there, but everyone in the office has been talking about it. Last week Colonel Wildman got into an argument with Major General Holland. Supposedly over the status of some report. It got pretty ugly and—"

"Holland?" Amanda said. "*Marcus* Holland?"

A nod. "He's the chief of Air Force Safety and— Did I say something?" Sullivan was struck by Amanda's reaction. So was I.

Amanda had gone completely still, staring grimly into space. I gave her a few seconds. When she didn't move, I lightly touched her arm. She flinched, coming back.

"So you know the general?" Sullivan said, stating the obvious.

Amanda nodded, tight-lipped. I gave her a questioning look, which she ignored.

I cleared my throat, returning to Sullivan. "About the argument, Major . . ."

"It took place in the general's office. I understand Colonel Wildman did most of the yelling, which surprised me. I've never, ever known her to lose her temper before. The confrontation lasted only a couple of minutes, then Colonel Wildman stormed out."

"This report," I said. "Any idea what it was about?"

A head shake. "I tried to ask Colonel Wildman but..." Sullivan shrugged. "She made it clear she didn't want to talk about it. She was like that. Very private. You might ask Alma. Her desk is outside the general's office and she overheard the argument."

I made a notation on my pad and switched gears, asking Sullivan if there was any reason why Colonel Wildman might have been interested in civilian airline crashes. Her answer verified what we'd figured: the office dealt exclusively with safety issues concerning military aircraft.

Sullivan explained, "We study the final accident reports to see if some of the maintenance procedures need to be changed, then rewrite the regulations accordingly." She gave me another sad smile. "I said we, but Colonel Wildman handled most of the workload. She was the only one with any hands-on experience."

Amanda said, "By experience, you mean..."

"As a maintenance analyst on aircraft accidents. It was her specialty. That's why she was so good at her job here. She knew which safety changes were important, how best to implement them. That sort of thing."

Amanda threw me a glance. As an accident investigator, Colonel Wildman probably had a professional interest whenever any plane went down, civilian or military. I took the disk from my jacket. "That probably explains this. We found it in Colonel Wildman's—"

I didn't get to finish, because Sullivan suddenly stepped forward, intently staring at the disk. "Is that— It is. That's mine."

"Oh?" I said.

She nodded. "I'm creating a database of civilian aircraft

accidents so we can identify safety trends that might benefit military flight operations."

Amanda said, "So you gave the disk to Colonel Wildman—"

"No, no," Sullivan said. "That's why I was surprised. I
thought it was still in my desk." She pointed to a lower
drawer.

Amanda frowned. "Did Colonel Wildman often take
material without your knowledge?"

"She usually left a note, but not always." She shrugged.

"Any idea why she might have taken the disk?" I said.

Sullivan's brow knitted. "Nothing comes to mind. She'd
have no official reason, since the Air Force doesn't fly the
G-626."

Amanda looked at me, perplexed. "Just a minute," I said
to Sullivan. "I thought the Air Force bought some G-626s a
few years ago."

"Oh, they did," she said. "But it turned out the planes
weren't suitable for the demands of the mission. The Air
Force ended up replacing them with Boeing 767s."

Amanda sighed, jotting in her notepad. "So much for the
terrorists," she muttered.

"What was that?" Sullivan said.

"Nothing," I said. I gave her what I hoped was a disarm-
ing smile. "We'd like to take a look at Colonel Wildman's
computer now."

CHAPTER 11

Instead of leading us to the private offices, Sullivan went over to a steel file cabinet a few feet away and began spinning the combination lock. It took me a moment to catch on.

"You keep a list of everyone's passwords?" I asked.

"Yeah. It's not exactly legal, but we've been burned a couple times." She glanced back at me. "You know how it is."

I did. In the Pentagon, everyone reacted to the whims of the brass. When I'd worked in the building, I once spent an entire weekend researching a question I *thought* the Air Force Chief of Staff was going to ask. He never did, but it's that kind of paranoia that leads office managers to keep personal-password listings. No one wanted to tell a general that the information he wanted had to wait until the action officer returned from either leave or a TDY.

The lock clicked and Sullivan slid open a drawer. As she rummaged inside, Amanda asked, "Did you know Colonel Wildman's ex-husband, Bobby Baker?"

Sullivan turned, holding a file. "Yeah. They were still married when I was stationed with her at Tinker. Not that

Bobby was around much. He's pretty much a free spirit."

"Colonel Wildman ever mention being afraid of him?"

Sullivan's eyes widened in disbelief. "You serious? Afraid of *Bobby*?" She started laughing.

Amanda watched her for a moment. She carefully marked in her notepad again before eyeing me.

"Scratch theory number two," she said.

Pinocchio.

That was Colonel Wildman's password. I thought it sadly fitting for a mother with two young children. As Amanda and I started for the private offices in the back, I asked Sullivan for the name of the DoD cop again.

"Officer Johnson, but he's not back there."

"Oh?" I said.

Sullivan said apologetically, "I was going to mention it earlier. I sent him to Colonel Wildman's new office. She was reassigned recently."

"When was this?" I asked.

"Ten days ago." She lowered her voice. "The day after the fight with General Holland."

"Fired?" Amanda said.

"Technically, she's still assigned to our department. But yeah, she was pretty much fired."

"Bastard," Amanda spat.

I flashed her a look of warning.

She disregarded it, saying, "Hey, I'm just telling the truth, Marty. This guy Holland's an asshole."

"That's enough, Amanda."

"Ask the major here. She'll tell you—"

"*Enough*, Amanda."

She glowered at me but fell silent.

I shook my head. The Pentagon grapevine was notorious. That last thing I needed was to get hauled onto the carpet because one of my investigators was bad-mouthing a two-star general.

"She is right, you know," Sullivan said quietly. "The

general can be . . . vindictive. That's why I really didn't believe that Colonel Wildman was returning to the office."

"Did someone say she was?" I asked.

"Colonel Burke, General Holland's deputy. He announced this morning that Colonel Wildman was being reinstated. But that doesn't make sense. I mean, why would General Holland fire her and a week and a half later bring her back?"

"Maybe she wasn't actually fired?" I said.

"Then why have her clean out her office?" Sullivan said.

She was right. It didn't make sense. But then nothing in the case did yet.

"So where is Colonel Wildman's new office?" I asked.

After Sullivan told us, I went to the door before realizing Amanda wasn't with me. When I glanced back, she and Sullivan were conversing softly. Sullivan was looking a little stunned. She nodded hesitantly and Amanda gave her hand a squeeze before coming over to me. I held open the door for her. "What was that all about?"

"Just wanted her opinion."

I followed her into the hallway. "On what?"

"On whether she thought General Holland might have anything to do with Wildman's murder."

I was incredulous. "Dammit. You can't ask her that. Holland's not a suspect. You have no right to accuse—"

My cell phone rang.

I glared at Amanda as I answered it. It was Master Sergeant Rider reporting on the computer query. Rider rarely sounded puzzled, but he did so now.

"I think I found a discrepancy, sir," he said.

I slowly tucked my phone away.

"Well?" Amanda said.

I hesitated. "Not quite sure. Sergeant Rider says the G-626 PAA numbers don't match."

Amanda's blank look told me she didn't speak Pentagonese.

I explained that PAA stood for primary aircraft authorized, which was the way planes in the Air Force inventory were tracked. I added, "Sergeant Rider confirmed that two jets were initially purchased in 1998. The odd thing is, only one aircraft was returned to the manufacturer."

"Maybe Sullivan was wrong and the Air Force kept a G-626."

"It's not listed in the inventory database."

We were both quiet.

Amanda gave me a long look. "Planes don't just disappear, Marty."

"No."

That wasn't quite true, of course. We both knew there was one way planes could disappear.

We went back inside the office to ask Major Sullivan.

"Sure," Major Sullivan said. "One of the G-626s crashed during an operational test flight. That's why the Air Force judged the aircraft unsuitable." She was sitting at her desk, with Amanda and me hovering over her.

"I don't remember reading about it," I said.

Sullivan gave a little shrug. "That's not surprising. The Air Force tried to downplay the accident. Supposedly because there was a lot of highly classified equipment on board."

Amanda immediately looked to me. I nodded, confirming I'd caught the implication. Downplay was a fancy word for cover-up. I followed up with the obvious question: Did Colonel Wildman work the accident investigation?

"If she did, she never mentioned it," Sullivan said.

I said, "I presume you keep a record of old investigation reports?"

"Sure. We've got an archive down the hall. Goes back twenty years. Any records before then are stored at the Safety Center in Albuquerque."

"We're just interested in the ones Colonel Wildman worked. Can you pull them?"

"Not a problem. Might take me twenty minutes or so. I need to run a computer search to identify—"

"That'll be fine. Call when you're ready." I gave her my cell phone number, then glanced to Amanda to see if she had anything. She didn't.

As we turned to go, Sullivan said, "Maybe I could help. Anything in particular you're looking for?"

She was fishing, curious about our interest in the accidents. I told her the truth anyway.

"I wish we knew," I said, before we finally left.

CHAPTER 12

The door clicked closed onto a deserted hallway. Since Wildman's office was on the other side of the building, we began working our way toward the A-ring. Amanda said, "If Colonel Wildman worked the G-626 crash, that might explain her interest in the disk."

"How does that lead to a motive for murder?"

Her mouth hovered open, then slowly closed. She wasn't taking the bait this time. Still, I knew the new theory she was considering. And if anything, I considered it more implausible than the last.

We turned a corner. We could hear the distant sound of jackhammers from the construction. My earlier annoyance with Amanda had faded, but I still wanted to know. She kept glancing over, so I decided to wait. I could tell she was trying to reach a decision.

Two steps later, she abruptly stopped, facing me. "Maybe I should just remove myself from the case."

"That bad?"

She nodded.

"If you just had some run-in with General Holland . . ."

"I wish. It's a little more serious than that, Marty. You

see—" Amanda squinted, gazing past me at the sound of clicking heels. I turned to see an attractive blond woman in a dark blue suit walking rapidly toward us. Her angular face was tense. I tossed her an automatic smile which caught her by surprise. She managed a faint one of her own as she went by. Amanda stared after her until she rounded a corner.

"Small world," she said.

"You know her?"

A nod. "She's General Holland's wife, Lucille. At Langley everyone called her The Queen."

"The queen?"

"Because she's such a bitch."

I sighed. "I suppose you hate their kids, too?"

Amanda gave me a dark look as we resumed walking. She asked, "Does the name Captain Marcia Brinkman ring any bells?"

Actually, the name *did* seem familiar.

"Captain Brinkman," Amanda said, "committed suicide about three years ago. At Langley. She was found in her apartment off-base—"

"I remember now," I said, the details jogging my memory. I told Amanda I'd read the final report when it crossed my desk.

"Marcia was a friend of mine, Marty. She's the reason I have to recuse myself from the case."

She'd lost me. "I thought you were pulling out because of General Holland?"

Amanda inhaled deeply, her expression turning serious. Softly, she said, "I am, Marty. You see, as far as I'm concerned, General Holland killed Marcia."

My head snapped around. "Jesus. Don't you listen? You can't go around accusing general officers of—"

She stuck a hand in my face. But instead of anger, Amanda's voice quivered with emotion.

"Just let me explain, Marty."

 Amanda and I circled the A-ring as she recounted the story. She spoke slowly, with long pauses.

The process was obviously difficult for her. In the end, I still had to disagree with her judgment. General Marcus Holland might be an arrogant, self-serving son of a bitch. But he certainly wasn't a killer, at least not in the legal sense.

Amanda had first met Holland four years earlier, when she worked maintenance at Langley Air Force Base in Virginia. She'd requested the assignment because her Academy roommate, Captain Marcia Brinkman, was stationed there as a supply officer. Shortly after Amanda's arrival, Marcia was selected to become the Wing Commander's executive officer. Marcia had been thrilled: an exec job was a plum assignment for a junior officer. It put them close to the seat of power, helped them get connected to a sponsor who could push their careers.

In Marcia's case, her soon-to-be sponsor was one of the Air Force's anointed—the ex–Stealth fighter pilot and Gulf War hero who was the youngest brigadier general in the Air Force.

Marcus Holland.

Within weeks, Amanda became concerned over Marcia's growing infatuation with her boss. Marcia spoke of Holland constantly, followed him around everywhere, even popped into the office on the weekends, hoping he'd be there. The tragic thing was that this obsessive behavior wasn't anything new for Marcia. As Amanda tells it, her friend lived in a world of romantic fantasies, always looking for a Prince Charming who would never come. At the Academy, she'd gotten involved with one guy after another. In the end, the men always left, leaving Marcia empty and hurt. Amanda took some solace in the fact that Holland was married; she knew a man in his position couldn't allow himself to become involved in an affair.

She was wrong.

Amanda found out when Marcia called to tell her she'd slept with Holland and was in love. She was sure Holland felt the same way. He was talking about leaving his wife, getting married.

Amanda reacted angrily, telling Marcia she was being reckless. Didn't Marcia understand Holland was using her and would never leave his wife? They argued and Amanda said things, things she later regretted. But the damage was done. From then on, Marcia wouldn't return Amanda's calls, wouldn't answer the door when Amanda dropped by.

The estrangement lasted four months, until Amanda returned to her apartment and found a tearful Marcia waiting outside. Marcia explained that she'd been suddenly transferred back to supply, no explanation given. In her heart, she knew Holland must have arranged the move. She was determined not to allow him to walk away. She couldn't. There was this problem.

She was pregnant.

Marcia's smile at that statement had given Amanda a chill. At that moment, she remembered being afraid for her friend, worried what she'd do when she was again rejected by Holland.

Amanda had her answer two weeks later.

According to the police report, that was the day Marcia had returned early from work, finished off a bottle of wine, then climbed into a warm bubble bath and slit her wrists.

CHAPTER 13

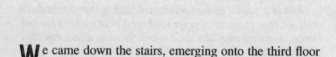

We came down the stairs, emerging onto the third floor of the A-ring. Colonel Wildman's office was up ahead, past the next corridor.

"I . . . I had to identify the body," Amanda said.

We went a few steps. I said gently, "The report was pretty clear, labeling it a suicide."

"I know. . . ." She abruptly pivoted, speaking rapidly. "Marcia may have killed herself, but Holland drove her to it. Marcia went to see him, tell him about the baby. The son of a bitch told her it couldn't be his. Said if she persisted with the accusation, he'd destroy her. He threatened to hire people to dig into her background, prove she was a slut. He called her nothing but a tramp and—"

She was getting herself worked up, almost shouting now. People passing by were staring. One young Navy commander had stopped to listen.

"Keep it down, Amanda," I said sharply. I fired off a menacing look at the commander. He did a double take and scurried off.

Amanda's nostrils flared. "*Fuck* keep it down, Marty. Holland's a scumbag—"

"Hey! I'm on your side, remember?"

She stared, surprised. Slowly the anger faded from her face. "Christ, I'm sorry, Marty. It's just that whenever I think about Marcia—"

"Try not to. It's easier that way."

Her expression softened. "I heard about your wife."

I nodded.

"I'm sorry."

"So am I. You okay now?"

She nodded.

We resumed walking. I said, "I don't remember reading in the report anything about your friend being pregnant."

"You read the autopsy . . ."

I shook my head.

"It was there. Not that she was pregnant when she died but that she'd recently had a miscarriage. I think that was a big part of it. What pushed her over the edge. She . . . she really wanted the baby." She paused. "And the harassment from Holland's wife sure didn't help."

"She knew?"

"Marcia was convinced that's why Holland dumped her. Because his wife found out. Probably not about the baby, but about their affair. The day they broke up, Marcia began getting threatening phone calls from some woman. Sick stuff about cutting her face. Throwing acid on her. Then someone tore up Marcia's apartment and killed her cat." Amanda glanced over. "Had to have been Holland's wife, Lucille."

I didn't comment. But I couldn't picture a general's wife running amok in a jealous rage. As we rounded the bend, I said, "You still want off the case?"

"It's probably best, considering."

"I don't have a problem with you staying on if we reach an understanding."

"Such as . . ." She sounded wary.

"I make all decisions regarding General Holland. I rule him out, he's out. And no more shooting your mouth off. That's critical. Agreed?"

She hesitated, then nodded.

"Welcome back." I smiled at her, but she wasn't looking at me anymore. Instead, she was focused ahead on the biggest cop I'd ever seen, standing outside an office door. I put him easily at six-six and three hundred pounds. He reminded me of the big guy in the James Bond movies, the one with the metal teeth.

"What'd Major Sullivan say his name was?" Amanda asked. "Johnson?"

"Yeah."

"He seems pretty uptight."

I'd noticed this, too. Officer Johnson was pacing nervously, looking down the hallway, away from us. His dark uniform had a large sweat stain in the middle of the back, which I thought odd. It wasn't that warm.

"Wonder what that's about," Amanda said.

Officer Johnson was in his early twenties, with a voice that sounded like he gargled with gravel. He broke into a relieved smile when he saw our IDs. "Christ, am I glad to see you two. Hell, I was thinking I might even lose my job, maybe already had."

"Lose your job?" I said. "Why?"

He waved a meaty hand to the office door. "Things were screwed up from the beginning. I was running late because I'd picked up the wrong key. There was a mix-up about the offices—"

"We know about that," Amanda said.

"Anyway," Johnson went on, "I had to swing by security again, get the right key. When I walk up the second time, I see a guy in an Air Force uniform going in. I hustle over, try the door, but it's locked. So I knock, identify myself, and tell the guy to open up. Nothing. Then I see a light go out under the door, you know, like he's trying to pretend he's not in there. I tell him I saw him go in. Still nothing. I finally use the key and find this officer sitting at the desk. He's got the computer on so I can still make out his face.

The guy freaks. Starts swearing like crazy, telling me to get the hell out. I try to explain why I'm there and why he's got to leave, but that just pisses him off more. He keeps right on hollering and I, well, I lose it and start shouting back. At first, I didn't see his rank, 'cause, you know, it was pretty dark and all. If I had..." Johnson wiped sweat from his brow. "But hell, I *didn't* know who he was and that's the truth. I figure he's just some asshole officer—" He stopped, looking down at us. "No offense—"

"None taken," I said.

"So," Johnson said, "I'm standing there, going at it with him when I flip on the light. *Now* I see his rank. Man, I can tell you I started to sweat. The guy had a young face, so I thought maybe he was a major or a lieutenant colonel. Around here, those guys are a dime a dozen—"

By now I knew. I cut in. "His rank?"

"A goddamn general. A two-star. The youngest one I've ever seen."

Beside me, Amanda sucked air through her teeth. I said, "And the general's name..."

"Holland. Major General Marcus Holland."

"My, my, imagine that," Amanda said dryly. She was looking right at me as she spoke.

"What happened next?" I asked Johnson.

A shrug. "Hell, I wasn't sure what to do. I mean I knew I was in the right, but the guy was a *general*. So I tell him he has to step outside while I call my supervisor. The general likes that idea. He comes right out into the hall, demanding to talk to Lieutenant French. I don't mind 'cause I know Frenchie's been around a long time and doesn't take crap from anyone. I get Frenchie on the radio, tell him what's up, then pass the radio to the general." Johnson grinned. "Man, I could tell Frenchie was saying all the wrong things to him 'cause he got even madder. After the call, he tried to go back inside the office, but backed off when I threatened to cuff him. That's when he took my name and badge number and said he was going to have my ass canned." Johnson looked to me for reassurance.

I told him I'd contact my boss, General Mercer, to make sure any potential complaint wouldn't go anywhere. Not that I thought that Holland was foolish enough to make one. If he did, he'd have to explain what he was doing in Wildman's office, and that's probably the last thing he wanted.

As Johnson passed me the office key, Amanda asked him if Holland had taken anything out of the office with him.

"He wasn't carrying anything, but it's not like I searched him," Johnson said. He hesitated as if wanting to add something.

Amanda studied him. "Go on, Officer Johnson."

Johnson ran a hand over his hair. "It's probably nothing. It was just sitting under his hat when—"

"His *hat*?" I said.

"Yeah. The general left his hat on the desk. One of those wheel-caps. I went back in to get it for him. When I picked it up—"

"A computer disk?" Amanda interrupted.

"No. Nothing like that. That's why I don't think this is any big deal. It was just a picture."

Amanda frowned.

"What kind of picture?" I asked.

"A woman and a couple of kids. Family photo. In a small gold frame. I figured it was Colonel Wildman's and the general had accidentally tossed his hat on it in the dark."

Amanda grudgingly nodded her agreement. So did I. From her description of Holland, he didn't exactly strike me as the sentimental type who'd want a picture of Wildman and her children.

"Anyway," Johnson said. "I left the picture on the desk."

"Fine," I said, turning to unlock the office door. The office number matched the one Sullivan had given us. I paused when I realized there was no plastic nameplate with Wildman's name and title.

At that moment, I knew Major Sullivan's suspicions

were correct. General Holland never had any intention of reinstating Wildman.

I unlocked the door and pushed it open with my foot. The room was dark. As Amanda and I pulled on latex gloves, I told Johnson he'd better remain for the rest of the evening. He made a face and went to get a chair.

"Worried General Holland might come back?" Amanda asked.

I didn't answer her. She knew I was.

I stepped inside the office. It smelled like a musty old sock. I felt for the light switch, clicked it on.

"Huh?" said Amanda. "You gotta be kidding. This is *it*?"

CHAPTER 14

Amanda's surprise at Colonel Wildman's office was understandable. She'd expected something suitable for an Air Force colonel. Instead we were in a cramped, windowless box, not more than ten feet by eight. Even with the door open, I felt slightly claustrophobic. The sparse furnishings consisted of two desks placed side by side, a battered metal filing cabinet topped by a coffeemaker, and nothing else. No chairs for visitors or even a bookshelf... not that there was room. The desk to our left was empty, suggesting it wasn't being used. The one on the right had a computer, a small printer, a phone and the small, gold-framed photograph Johnson had described.

"Jesus," Amanda said, "I'd go nuts if I worked in here." She went over to the first desk and opened a drawer. "Empty." She rapidly began going through the others.

"This office," I said, "is supposed to be unpleasant. Colonel Wildman wasn't simply fired; she was essentially banished here in an attempt to force her to retire. The same thing happened to my boss when I worked here. He had a drinking problem that got out of control. One morning he learned he'd been reassigned to one of these cracker-boxes.

He stuck it out for a couple of weeks before resigning from the service. He couldn't take coming in just to sit. And that's all you do in here. Sit, with nothing to do."

Amanda had finished with the desk and was checking out the file cabinet. Without looking back, she said, "So Holland sent Wildman here to end her career, huh?"

"Yes."

"If so, why would he bring her back?"

"Probably wouldn't." I went over to the second desk. The computer screen was dark but the power light was on. I tapped a key, and was curious when only a blank page appeared on the monitor. I opted to let Amanda check it out. I picked up the photo of Colonel Wildman and her children. They were posing next to a big Mickey Mouse.

"Everything's clean," Amanda said, joining me. "You're right. Colonel Wildman didn't do much work in here." She looked over my shoulder at the photograph. "Disney World," she murmured.

"Yeah . . ." Nicole and I had taken Emily there two summers ago.

"It makes me angry, Marty," she said quietly.

"It should."

She glanced at me. "The family will want the picture."

I nodded, slowly slipping it into my jacket. In twenty years, I'd worked four homicides involving children. Each small face still haunted my memory. Now there would be two more: a blond-haired girl and a dark-haired boy.

I felt a sudden rush of emotion. Fighting it off, I pointed Amanda to the computer. "You're the expert. I want you to tell me what General Holland was looking for."

Amanda studied the screen, tapping a finger on her teeth. "Interesting," she murmured.

"Why? It's just a blank page."

"This is a word-processing program. See the file name."

I did now. In the lower margin was a single word: Resignation.

"Now," Amanda said, "either Holland was about to type something, or..." She shifted the mouse to the header line and clicked the undo tab. "Bingo."

A standard military Subject-To letter addressed to General Marcus Holland. The body contained a single sentence: *This is to inform you that I intend to resign my military commission on 29 March.* And below: Colonel Wildman's signature block.

"Looks like Wildman decided to resign from the Air Force after all," Amanda said.

"Notice the date."

"March seventh." She glanced up. "Couple days after the confrontation with Holland. Explains how he knew about the letter."

"Why would he care?"

"What do you mean?"

"Holland obviously deleted the letter. Why would he care if anyone knew Colonel Wildman wanted to resign? It seems that's what he wanted. And if she was resigning, why the hell would he have bothered to reinstate her?"

She slowly pursed her lips, then nodded. "It also doesn't make sense that Holland would raise a stink with Officer Johnson over the letter."

"No."

"So there must be something else."

I nodded.

A tiny smile crawled across her lips. "This mean you consider Holland a suspect?"

I thought. "No. And neither should you."

"C'mon, Marty. He was here poking around within hours of the murder—"

"So what? He was her boss. He probably had a logical reason to be here."

"What about the argument?"

"What about it? Bosses argue with their subordinates all the time."

Amanda rolled her eyes. "Even you've got to admit it looks pretty bad."

"Fine," I said curtly. "If you won't at least attempt to remain objective, maybe you should withdraw from the case." I stepped aside, clearing her path to the door.

She looked stunned. Then her face tightened with anger. I'd only been trying to make a point. Now I was worried I'd overdone it and she might actually leave.

But with a final glare, she returned to the computer.

For the next few minutes, I watched over Amanda's shoulder as she sorted through the various files. There weren't many, which made sense; Pentagon computers were assigned to offices, not people. Wildman had only used this one for a few days at most.

Of the handful of files we did find, nothing jumped out. Three were partially completed military safety reports and the rest were personal letters. I noticed that there wasn't anything on the G-626 or any other civilian aircraft.

Amanda pushed back from the desk, shaking her head. "*Nada*. If there was something here, Holland must have deleted it."

"He wouldn't have had much time. You sure you looked in everything?"

"Except her e-mail." She sat forward, picking up the mouse.

My back was stiff from crouching. I stretched and went through Wildman's desk drawers. I found the prerequisite Pentagon phone directory, a stapler, a couple of pens, an opened packet of gum, some printing paper and a packet of manila folders.

There were no computer disks or files of any kind. Of course, if there had been a disk, Holland could simply have put it in his pocket when he—

"Marty..."

Amanda was staring at the screen.

"What is it?" I asked.

"Maybe a motive."

She shifted over so I could read.

Margaret,

WHERE ARE YOU??? I've been trying to reach you all afternoon. The situation is critical. I received a call from Fred Hilley, an engineer from my research lab. Fred said a team from Mr. Caldwell's office arrived to confiscate all the wing box data. It's only a matter of time until they discover the missing documents.

I know we are doing the right thing, but frankly, I'm having second thoughts. My wife wants me to take the next plane home and I'm tempted.

Call me the moment you get this. I'll be in my hotel until 6 p.m. If I don't hear from you, I'll return around 11. I don't think we can afford to wait any longer. We should turn the files over to the authorities immediately.

By the way, I left a couple messages on your answering machine. If I sound frightened, I am.

Douglas

"My God," I murmured.

"Yeah," Amanda said. "Explains Wildman's interest in the disk we found. And the documents mentioned here had to be what she was scanning into her computer."

I was still reeling, trying to understand. "The wing box is obviously something from an aircraft, but..." I trailed off. My expertise was light aircraft, not airliners.

"Actually," Amanda said, "it's the portion of the aircraft that secures the wings to the fuselage. Most are metal, usually titanium, but the wing boxes of newer aircraft are made from a composite material that is lighter and even stronger." She looked up at me. "At the Academy I took a couple of courses in aircraft structure and design."

Even though I knew the answer, I had to ask. "What happens if a wing box is defective?"

"Depends. Minor cracking would be hard to detect without a major inspection. There would probably be some

pressurization problems, but that's about it. A sudden cata-
strophic failure in flight could cause the wings to separate
from the plane."

"Shit." I rubbed my face hard. "Could a modern airliner
actually be manufactured with such a huge defect?"

"It's certainly possible. You know anything about composites? No? Composites are synthetic materials like Tho-
ratine or Moritium, which are mixed together with carbon
fibers and cured in sheets. Sort of like concrete. The sheets
are layered one on top of another, similar to plywood, until
the desired strength is reached. If the process is done cor-
rectly, the final product is incredibly strong and light. But
if something is messed up along the way—say the curing
time is too short or the temperature is wrong, or maybe the
mixture is somehow contaminated—you've got a big problem. It's not like metal; once a composite is finished, defects are almost impossible to detect."

"Why?"

"Because of the nature of the composite material. Say
one or more layers in the middle are defective, but the rest
are fine. Detecting those problems is extremely difficult
because all you can really check is the integrity of the material close to the surface. When I was at school, the
biggest problem engineers were facing was the air bubbles
between the layers. McDonnell Douglas lost a couple of
prototype fighters because of wing failures until they figured out the bubble problem. That was eight, nine years
ago. I'm sure that issue has been pretty much worked out
by now."

"The G-626 first appeared around what—ten or eleven
years ago," I said.

She nodded.

I closed my eyes, trying to think. "If a passenger aircraft
had such a serious flaw, wouldn't the FAA order them
grounded until repairs could be made?"

"Could be they don't know about the problem."

My eyes popped open.

"Yeah," Amanda said. "I agree that's pretty damned unlikely. The airlines are the most scrutinized industry in the country. If the plane's defective, the FAA would know. That means they must have cut a deal."

"A deal?"

"Replacing a wing box is a difficult process, Marty. It essentially involves rebuilding the plane's primary structural support. You're talking months per aircraft. Maybe the FAA is allowing the planes to fly until the repairs are made. And if Colonel Wildman knew this, maybe she was going to make it public..." She didn't finish. She just stared at me, waiting for my response.

I took my time. I looked at the monitor, then back to her. Finally, I said, "We need to be careful. The e-mail is completely unsubstantiated. Until we can prove—"

"For chrissakes, Marty. It makes *sense*. The facts all fit."

"I'm aware of that. My concern is this guy Douglas' credibility—"

"His last name is McInnes. And we know he works for Global Aviation.

"Oh?"

Amanda scrolled the screen up and sat back. There was the e-mail address: dmcinnes@globalaviation.org.

Amanda said quietly, "And notice when McInnes sent the e-mail. Explains why Colonel Wildman never answered his calls."

I nodded. The line showed today's date at 4:32 P.M. By then, Colonel Wildman and her children were either dead or dying.

"Well?" Amanda said.

I had no argument and she knew it. I told her we might have a motive.

"There," Amanda said, suppressing a smile, "was that really so hard?"

 "Wonder who this guy Caldwell is?" Amanda asked five minutes later. She was still sitting at

Wildman's desk and I was parked on the edge. We were both rereading copies of the e-mail she'd just printed, along with Wildman's resignation letter.

I folded my pages and stuck them in my jacket. Outside, I could see Johnson camped near the door in a chair, reading a biker magazine. "Obviously some bigwig with Global."

Amanda slid back her chair. "How many G-626s you think are flying now?"

"It's one of the most popular airplanes in the world. Hundreds. Maybe thousands."

"So if they were all grounded long-term, that would cost what, about a zillion bucks?"

I nodded.

"Helluva motive. So what now?"

"We need to figure if any of this ties in to General Holland. We should talk to the secretary, Alma Carter. Find out what she overheard."

"I noticed on the roster she lives on Columbia Pike. We could swing by when we're done here."

I checked the time. Nine-twenty. "Give her a call."

Amanda took out her cell phone. As I turned away, I heard a sudden intake of breath. When I glanced back, Amanda had an expression somewhere between fear and shock. She was gripping the phone so hard I thought she might break it.

"Amanda, what's the—"

"Jesus! The answering machine!"

"What answering machine?"

She spoke fast, stumbling over the words. "Wildman's goddamn answering machine, Marty. In the e-mail. McInnes. He called Colonel Wildman, left her messages."

"So what if . . ."

"I personally *checked* the machine. There weren't any messages. None. And we know Colonel Wildman couldn't have erased them. She was dead. Don't you see? That means . . ."

But I wasn't listening anymore. I was already going for my phone. I fumbled it, swore. When I finally punched the speed dial, I heard Amanda verbalize what we both now knew.

"The killers know about McInnes," she said.

•

CHAPTER 15

All right, Martin," Simon said from Wildman's home, where I'd called him. "We'll put an APB out on McInnes. Check with the hotels and car-rental agencies. Now, is there anything you haven't told me?"

"No." I'd filled him in on everything: Wildman's computer disk containing the aircraft-accident files, her confrontation with General Holland, her subsequent firing, Holland's presence in her office, the e-mail, Amanda and my suspicions. All of it.

Simon became silent, digesting the information. I knew better than to interrupt. Thirty seconds passed. A minute. Abruptly he asked, "Do you believe Colonel Wildman was killed because she was investigating this airplane, Martin?"

I hesitated. "It's the only explanation that seems to fit the facts."

"Colonel Wildman was a military investigator. Why would she be interested in civilian aircraft?"

I explained my theory.

"When will you know for certain?" he asked.

"In a few minutes, after we look at the military aircraft accident files."

"And if she *hasn't* conducted a G-626 investigation..."

"I don't know."

"I don't like this, Martin. You're suggesting a major conspiracy..."

"Yes."

"...orchestrated by a major corporation with a possible military tie-in."

"I know."

"Again that point bothers me. Why would the military be concerned about a civilian airliner they no longer fly?"

I was getting annoyed. Simon knew I didn't have the answers. "How should I know? Maybe the military isn't involved. It's possible General Holland is acting on his own because of some connection to Global Aviation. Or maybe he's just following orders. Maybe there's someone higher up—" I stopped. I knew I sounded like I was grasping at straws. "Look, if you think I'm way off-base—"

"No, no. It's certainly plausible." He let out an audible sigh. "Building a case will be difficult. We'll need technical information on the airplane."

I told him I had an FAA acquaintance who might be able to help.

"We'll also need to check out General Holland's background, Martin. Can you request his personnel file?"

"Yes." I'd been planning to do that.

Simon's call-waiting clicked. "Excuse me, Martin. That's Romero."

I killed time by drumming my fingers on the desk. Meanwhile, Amanda had sufficiently recovered from her shock and was busy making calls on her cell phone.

Simon came back, telling me Romero had gotten a lead on Bobby Baker from Baker's girlfriend. He passed on the name of a hotel in Crystal City, just five minutes away, where Baker was employed. He suggested I meet him there around ten.

"Baker know about the deaths yet?" I asked.

"His girlfriend said someone saw a newscast and told him."

"Any reason why he hasn't contacted us?" In most of the murder cases I'd worked, the victims' relatives usually swarmed around the cops, seeking details and demanding justice.

"Apparently, he's quite distraught."

"What does Baker do?" I asked.

"I understand he's some kind of a celebrity greeter. Oh, and it seems we were right about the teddy bear containing a disk. The babysitter confirmed that the children hadn't carried the bear around for years." Then he was gone.

I frowned, putting my phone away. A hotel with a celebrity greeter? That was a first.

Amanda finished her call moments later. She still looked upset. I gave her a quick rehash of my conversation, ending by mentioning that Simon had located Baker. "What about Alma Carter?" I asked.

"She's got three small children and two of them have the flu. Said it would probably be better if she came here to talk. She'll meet us in Major Sullivan's office in thirty minutes. I can talk to her while you go see Baker."

"Fine."

"I also called Sergeant Rider," she said. "He's sending a team out in the morning to print the office. And I checked in with Major Sullivan. She'll be ready for us in five minutes or so."

I nodded and told her to shut down the computer. Then I called information for the number of a Robert Sessler in Woodbridge, Virginia. Rob was the FAA acquaintance I'd mentioned to Simon. He and I have known each other since our days in ROTC at Virginia Tech. Even with our long history together, we're not particularly close; Rob had always been wrapped a little too tight for me. While the rest of us partied, Rob was the guy pulling extra time at the detachment, making points burying his nose up the colonel's behind. When he eventually became the ranking cadet, we expected the power to go to his head. It didn't. Rob remained surprisingly low-key when he ran the unit, earning our grudging respect. Upon graduation, we gave him a

commode lid made from beer cans inscribed with the
words Most Likely to Succeed. The Silver Crapper award.
You had to be there to understand, but it was a big deal.

And Rob had succeeded, but not in the military. After
his Air Force flying career was cut short by a devastating
leg injury from a skiing accident, he joined the FAA and in
ten short years had risen to head the flight certification office. It's considered a primo job because Rob essentially
determined the airworthiness of all commercial aircraft. If
anyone knew the problems of the G-626, it would be Rob.
Now the question was whether I could convince him to talk
to me.

Rob's teenage son Jack answered the phone and told me
his folks were at a fundraising dinner. That was Rob, always working the angles. I left a message for him to call.
"Tell him it's important, Jack," I said.

As I hung up, Amanda tapped my arm. She pointed to
Johnson, who was slowly uncoiling from his chair, nervously looking down the hallway.

Amanda shook her head in disgust. "Christ, don't tell
me that son of a bitch is—"

Then Johnson abruptly faced us, his anxious expression
confirming her suspicion. Moments later, we heard the
clicking of heels.

"Remember," I told Amanda, "let me handle this."

A grim smile. "You know me, Marty."

That was the problem. I thought I did.

We went out into the hall to talk to Major General Marcus Holland.

CHAPTER 16

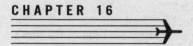

Watching Holland approach, I could understand the infatuation of Amanda's friend, Captain Marcia Brinkman. General Holland was handsome, head-turning handsome. Not that I was into guys' looks, but the man I saw could easily have been a movie star. He had the whole package: dark, wavy hair, chiseled features, muscular build. The only thing he lacked was height; he was maybe five-nine and reminded me a little of Tom Cruise.

But in a military uniform, what really stopped you in your tracks was the contrast between his youth and his rank. I had to agree with Officer Johnson. General Marcus Holland was the youngest-looking two-star I'd ever seen.

Holland continued toward us in measured strides, his face locked in a glare. About ten feet away, he slowed, his eyes settling on Amanda. For an instant, his face flickered in recognition. He seemed on the verge of saying something, but didn't.

I stepped forward and said pleasantly, "Good evening, General."

He scowled at me. "Who the hell are you?"

I told him, holding up my badge, which he ignored. I debated introducing Amanda but decided to pass. Holland already knew her. Besides, I didn't want to give her an opportunity to tell him to go screw himself.

"I've spoken with Captain Ritter, Collins," Holland said stiffly. "He's approved me retrieving some papers from Colonel Wildman's office."

"Who is Captain Ritter, sir?" I asked.

Behind me, Johnson said, "He's the head of the Pentagon police."

"Exactly," Holland said. "Now if you'll excuse me—"

"Sorry, sir," I said, bracing myself for a confrontation. "I can't allow it."

"Oh?" He appraised me coolly for a few moments. "I take it you haven't spoken to General Mercer recently?"

General Mercer was the OSI chief who'd assigned me to the case. I shook my head.

"I suggest you call him, Collins. He'll inform you that I'm authorized to enter the office."

My first reaction was that Holland was full of shit. In the ten years I'd worked for General Mercer, I'd never known him to be intimidated by rank. A gruff, outspoken man, Mercer had a history of knocking heads with senior officers who'd tried to poke their noses into investigations. That's one of the reasons he'd pushed hard to have civilian consultants like me placed on the OSI payroll. He wanted investigators who could operate with autonomy from the brass. I knew there was no way Mercer would have okayed Holland's interference.

Still, Holland's confidence worried me. I had just started reaching for my phone when it started ringing. In the background I heard what sounded like a ball game. Then a familiar voice: "We've got a goddamn problem, Marty."

I knew then.

"Excuse me, sir," I told Holland.

I stepped away to talk to Brigadier General Gary Mercer.

The frustration in General Mercer's voice confirmed my suspicions even before he spelled everything out.

"Look, Marty," he said, "I don't know what the hell is going on, but I just got a call from the chief. He told me General Holland is trying to locate some classified file Colonel Wildman had in her possession. The chief says we're supposed to cooperate on finding the thing." By "chief" Mercer was referring to General Neal Barlow, the Air Force Chief of Staff.

I felt a wave of anger. I kept my voice low, trying to keep Holland from overhearing. "Sir, I'm here with General Holland now, outside Colonel Wildman's office. I have to tell you this is bullshit, sir. I think Colonel Wildman was murdered for something she was working on. Something related to her job. The missing file could be critical to proving motive."

"The Chief assured me the file has nothing to do with—"

"Sir," I interrupted, "we know the killers were searching for information she had in her possession. It could be the file."

A pause. "This is straight, Marty?"

"Yes, sir."

"Any idea what's in the file?"

"We think something related to aircraft accidents."

"Huh?"

"That's just a theory, sir. But Wildman *was* an aircraft accident investigator."

General Mercer was silent. I could hear him breathing.

"Can you prove any of this?" he asked.

I hesitated. "Not yet, sir. We've got a few leads we're working."

Another pause. Longer. "Sorry. I got no choice but to cooperate with Holland. I can't buck the chief."

"I understand . . ."

"But that doesn't mean we can't *fuck* with them a little."

"Sir?"

"The chief ordered me to turn over the file to Holland *if* we find it. He didn't say we couldn't look at it, and he sure as hell didn't say we couldn't make a copy if we think it's crucial to the investigation."

I couldn't believe what I was hearing. While Mercer would confront his superiors, he was far too military to knowingly disobey a direct order. Of course, part of the reason could be that Mercer was retiring in a few months and knew the chief really couldn't do much to him.

Holland, Johnson, and Amanda were watching me. "I appreciate this, sir."

"We're cops, Marty," Mercer said, with surprising feeling. He added quietly, "Besides, I owe her. Wildman."

"Sir?"

I heard General Mercer take a drink, cough. "Colonel Wildman called me a couple of weeks ago. She had this crazy story that she was being followed. Even said her phone might be tapped. I sent Captain Sulley to interview her, see if there was anything there. He reported that she was vague as hell about the details. Couldn't or wouldn't tell him why someone would harass her or who it might be. What she wanted was for us to provide her with some protection. Just hang out and watch her. Hell, with what she gave us, there really wasn't much we could do. I told Colonel Wildman that since she lived off-base, the OSI really didn't have any jurisdiction. I suggested she contact the local police. She gave me an earful over that. She said she'd already spoken to them and they weren't doing anything. I had Sulley give the Arlington cops a call. They told him they'd checked out her story, and concluded that there wasn't really anything there. That it was just a domestic issue with her ex-husband and she was blowing things out of proportion."

The domestic comment surprised me. I made a mental note to have Simon look into it.

General Mercer was silent for a few moments. "You know, if she'd played it straight with me . . . maybe I could have done something. But the way it was . . ."

As he drifted off, I could almost feel his guilt through the phone. I didn't say anything. I just waited.

Finally, he said, "You do whatever you have to on this. You run this thing any way you want. Just try and finish it fast. Anyone gives you problems, call me. And one more thing..."

"Yes, sir."

"Watch yourself, Marty. I'm not sure what the hell this is really about. But when the chief personally gets involved, it's big. He usually plays everything by the book. He'd never have called me just because a goddamn two-star whined a little. So it had to be somebody with juice who pushed him."

"Yes, sir." I felt a chill at the implication.

"I'll nose around a little, see if I can find out who's really pulling the strings on this."

"Thank you, sir." I expected him to hang up.

"And do me a favor, Marty. Tell Holland I said to go fuck himself. One of the reasons I disregarded Colonel Wildman's story was because I personally checked with that son of a bitch and he told me she had psychological problems. If I were you, I'd make him sweat a little, see what he knows."

And he hung up with a bang.

CHAPTER 17

Well?" General Holland said when I walked back.

"You can go in, General," I said politely.

Amanda and Johnson both looked stunned while Holland flashed an arrogant grin.

I told Holland he'd have to wear gloves and asked Amanda to give him a pair. Her face darkened, but she passed him a pair with comment. He snapped them on, watching her with amusement.

"Asshole," she mouthed, as he went inside the office. Johnson grinned.

I told Johnson to get some yellow crime-scene tape, and said he could leave after he taped up the door. Originally, I'd wanted him to hang around to prevent Holland from gaining entry again, but that concern was moot now.

As Johnson hustled off, Amanda confronted me, hands on her hips. "What the hell is going on, Marty?"

I explained, keeping my eyes on Holland as he searched Wildman's desk.

Afterward, Amanda said, "Colonel Wildman actually *told* General Mercer someone was following her."

"Yes."

"Why didn't she tell him who it was?"

Good question. I shook my head, shifting my gaze to her. "Might want to rethink your decision to remain on the case."

She looked startled. "Huh? What the hell did I do now?"

"Nothing. It's Holland. He's obviously well-connected. He could hurt you. So maybe it would be better, smarter for you to—"

"Not a chance. I'm in."

"Sure?"

"I'm sure."

It was the answer I expected. But I had to ask.

As we watched Holland, I could see Amanda was getting increasingly pissed off. I was, too. His actions were outrageous. General or no general, he was blatantly interfering with a homicide investigation.

An idea occurred to me. But I would need something to pressure Holland. A glance at my watch told me I had twenty minutes until I had to leave. Enough.

"Amanda, I need a favor . . ." I quickly explained, telling her to hurry.

As she jogged off, I realized I was being completely unprofessional. Not that I gave a damn. Besides, General Mercer did say to sweat him a little.

I went inside the office.

 Holland was staring at Wildman's computer. He glanced up when I entered. "It's off."

I nodded.

"Did Officer Johnson shut it down?"

"No. We did."

"So you looked through her computer?"

I nodded.

"That means you already searched the office."

"Thoroughly."

His jaw tightened. "Why the hell didn't you tell me?"

"You never asked, General."

"You a smart-ass, Collins?"

I shrugged.

"So," he demanded, "did you find anything?"

"Depends."

His face turned hard. "Don't fuck with me, Collins. I asked if you found anything."

"You mean the file?"

"Of course, I mean—"

"Tell you what, sir. You describe what's in the file and I'll tell you if we found it."

That did it. His lip curled into a snarl. Then: "By God, you insubordinate son of a bitch, I'm going to have your ass!"

"Can't, General. I'm a civilian." I gave him a little smile.

He looked stunned. I could almost see the gears turn in his head as he tried to figure out his next move.

I calmly gazed back.

Holland stepped around the desk to me. "You have no idea what you're dealing with, Collins. I want the file. *Now.*"

I made like I was thinking things over. "I'll make you a deal, General. You answer a few questions, I'll tell you about the file. We both get something."

"I don't make deals," he snapped.

I turned to go.

"Wait."

I looked back.

"Damn you, Collins, I need that file."

I was silent. Waiting.

Holland gave a sigh of annoyance. "All right. Fine. But make it quick."

"Let's start with that," I said, nodding to the computer. "Why were you interested in what was on it?"

"No mystery. I thought maybe she'd copied the file into it."

From my jacket, I produced the two folded pages along with my notepad. I held one out to Holland.

He glanced at it, then shrugged. "She was resigning."

"I want to know why you tried to delete this letter from her computer."

He started to reply, then stepped back, thinking it over. He said, "Colonel Wildman called me to say she'd changed her mind, that she wouldn't be resigning. She wanted me to tear up the letter, and I did. When I saw it on the computer, I just deleted it. I can't really explain why, other than the fact that I knew it wasn't pertinent any longer."

A bullshit answer, but I knew it was all I was going to get. I returned both pages to my jacket, since I wasn't about to tip our hand about the e-mail.

"Who is Douglas McInnes?" I asked casually, flipping open my notepad.

"Who?" He sounded surprised. Almost.

"You've never heard of him?"

"No. Who is he?"

I changed the subject. "I understand you and Colonel Wildman had an argument recently."

Holland stiffened. "Who told you that? Was it Colonel Jessup? Major Brannigan?"

"Tell me about it, sir," I said.

"*That* was a matter between Colonel Wildman and myself. A private matter. That's all I have to say."

"But you fired her because of the argument?"

"She was insubordinate. I couldn't allow that."

"I understand you were going to reinstate her."

He blinked. "Why yes. She apologized and said it wouldn't happen again."

"When was this?"

"A couple days ago. Monday. She called me."

I jotted this down. "Where?"

"My office."

"What time?"

"Around three P.M."

He was rattling off answers without hesitation. If he wasn't telling the truth, he was one hell of a liar.

I cleared my throat and brought up the argument again.

"I told you I won't discuss it."

I didn't say anything. I played the staring game.

"Now look here, Collins—"

"General," I interrupted, "you're not being very smart about this. People overheard your confrontation. One way or another, I'm going to find out what it was about. Either you tell me or I hear it from them." I shrugged.

Holland's jaw tightened. I expected him to tell me to go to hell.

Instead, he said, "There was nothing to it. We had a disagreement over the findings of a recent accident investigation. She disagreed with the investigation team's report, which found the pilots responsible. I didn't share her view, and we argued."

His story matched Sullivan's comment that they argued over a report. "What was the mishap aircraft?"

"A C-130 out of Little Rock."

This time he'd hesitated fractionally before answering. That was enough. I sensed he knew I knew he'd just lied. But for some reason, he obviously felt I couldn't prove it, or didn't care if I could.

"Sir, you mind telling me where you were today between two-thirty and four P.M.?"

Holland looked incredulous. "Christ, you're really something, Collins. You saying *I'm* a suspect now? This is unbelievable."

"Sir," I said patiently, "we've got to clear everyone she worked with. If you would just please answer the—"

"My office," he snapped. "I was working in my office all afternoon. Now, if you're finished with this nonsense I'd like the—"

Someone coughed sharply behind me. "Uh, Marty."

Amanda was standing in the doorway, her face a sheen of perspiration. She must have run the whole way. I said, "Excuse me, General."

"Dammit, I'm in a hurry."

"It'll just take a moment, sir." I started to leave.

"Collins . . ."

Christ. I glanced back.

"...one question." Holland pointed to Wildman's desk. "There was a photograph here earlier. It's missing."

I tapped my jacket. "I have it."

He took a deep breath, nodding slowly. "Just thought you should know."

"Thank you, sir."

I joined Amanda in the hall, mildly puzzled. Up to now, Holland had displayed no remorse over Wildman's death. But just then I thought I noticed something in his face that surprised me.

A look of regret.

I shook my head, listening to Amanda. "Impossible. Major Sullivan must have made a mistake."

"No mistake, Marty. Sullivan checked all the accidents Colonel Wildman worked. No G-626. Now, what we did learn—"

"Dammit, that can't be. The only way this case makes sense is if Wildman was involved in the investigation. If not, why would she be interested in—"

I stopped. Amanda grinned broadly, removing a paper from her jacket.

"Relax, Marty," she said. "She found something even better."

"Oh?"

"She downloaded the names of the accident team members who worked the G-626 crash. Take a guess who headed it." She handed me the page.

I knew before I looked. My eyes went to the top line where the Board President was listed.

General Marcus Holland.

I asked, "Where's the accident file?"

"That's a problem. That's why Sullivan downloaded the team off the computer. It seems the file is missing."

"*What?*"

Amanda nodded. "Sullivan searched the cabinet twice. No file."

"Wildman," I said slowly, thinking as I spoke. "She must have taken it. That's got to be the file Holland was looking for."

"Probably. And if Holland okayed some kind of official cover-up, that would explain why he's so anxious to find it." Her eyes flickered past me. "Speak of the devil. Our boy is getting impatient."

I turned and saw General Holland, motioning to me from the doorway. Farther down the hall, Johnson approached, carrying a roll of yellow tape.

I sighed, handing Amanda the page of names. "Better wait here. This isn't going to be pretty."

"Like that's going to happen," she said, following.

CHAPTER 18

Enough," Holland said, leading me into the office. "You've jerked my chain long enough, Collins. I want the file."

"Sorry, General. I don't have it."

He spun around to me. "What the hell are you trying to pull?"

"Nothing. We didn't find a file in here." I glanced back to Amanda by the door, Johnson towering behind her. Amanda nodded in confirmation.

Holland's handsome face turned red. His hands balled into fists. "You *son of a bitch*! I'm going to have your job! Your fucking job!" He began gesturing wildly. "I told you not to screw with—"

What the hell. I eased forward. He accidentally tapped my shoulder.

"You saw that?" I called out.

"He struck you," Amanda said.

Holland blinked, startled. "What the hell do you mean I—"

"I saw it, too," Johnson said.

"Two witnesses, General," I said. "I can arrest you for assaulting a police officer in the performance of his duties."

"You moved into me!"

I shrugged. "Johnson, let me have your cuffs."

Johnson stepped forward, fighting a smile.

"You wouldn't fucking dare," Holland spat.

"General," I said quietly, "I just saw the bodies of a woman and her two children who were butchered. Yeah, I'd dare."

He puffed up in his uniform, but I could see uncertainty in his eyes. "You have no idea what you're doing, Collins. Your actions are reckless and—"

He was off-balance now. I took a shot. "Who is Douglas McInnes?" I asked again.

"Dammit, man, what does Douglas—"

He stopped.

He knew he'd made a mistake. He stared at me and calmly adjusted his tie. Without another word, he pushed past Johnson out the door.

As he disappeared down the hallway, I heard Amanda say into my ear, *"Now, Marty?"*

When I turned, her face told me what she wanted.

I thought it over. I wanted to be absolutely certain. I recalled the interview and my impressions before making a decision.

"Consider him a suspect," I said finally.

Officer Johnson and Amanda secured the office with tape while I placed a quick call to basically cover my ass. The ball game was still on.

"Goddamn Wizards are getting blown out by sixteen," General Mercer said.

I cleared my throat. "Sir, you might be getting a complaint . . ."

Mercer was actually laughing when I hung up.

But then, I'd been careful not to mention my suspicions about Holland . . . yet.

Amanda and I thanked Johnson for his help and headed down the hall. I would take her car to meet Simon while she went upstairs to interview Holland's secretary. At the stairwell, she brought up a point I hadn't considered: Did General Holland ask me whether the file had been found at Wildman's house? He hadn't, which only meant one thing.

He must have known the file wasn't there.

"And you notice he called McInnes by his first name," she said. "Almost like he knew him."

I'd noticed. "Confirm Holland's alibi with Alma Carter. If he was working at his office during the murders, she would probably know."

Amanda nodded.

"And find out whether he drives a Sable. Be discreet. Simon doesn't want the word to get out that we know about the car."

"Okay."

"There should also be a computer in Wildman's old office—"

"It's gone, Marty," Amanda said. "Sullivan told me it was removed last week. I can try and find out where it was taken, but . . ." Her shrug implied it was a waste of time.

"Sullivan might know who requested its removal."

"I'll ask. That it?"

"Unless you have anything."

"Thought I'd get Sullivan to dig out the office bios on Holland and Wildman."

"Fine."

She stood there for a moment, looking at me. "You know, Marty, I was thinking they already killed a colonel. And depending how high up this thing goes . . ."

I gave her arm a squeeze. "We'll be okay. It would raise

too many eyebrows if something happened to us."

But as I went down the steps, it occurred to me that Colonel Wildman had once probably thought the very same thing.

I checked my watch and took out my phone. Even though it wasn't rational, I felt a sudden need to call my daughter.

"Emily's on a roll, Marty," my stepdaughter Helen said. "She says she'll come over when she's finished playing. Might be a few minutes. She's going for a record."

As she spoke, I heard the familiar sounds of a Donkey Kong video game, punctuated by an occasional squeal of delight from Emily. "She'll be too excited to sleep," I said, disapprovingly.

"Chill, Dad," Helen said. "She's having fun. It's been a while since she's been able to just be a kid, enjoy herself."

I felt a trace of annoyance even though I knew Helen was right. "She get all her homework done?"

"Every bit."

"Make sure she brushes her teeth. Sometimes she forgets—"

"I will."

"I picked up the latest Harry Potter book for her. It's in my briefcase in my study."

"I'll see she gets it." Helen sighed. "Look, why don't I bring her to the phone now?"

I was tempted until I heard the sound of a loud explosion followed by Emily's high-pitched giggle. "Just tell her I'll see her in the morning. You lock all the doors yet?"

"Not yet. Why?"

"Do it now. And make sure you check all the windows."

"Christ, Marty. What's with you? You always been such a worrier?"

"Humor me. I'll feel better."

"Fine. Okay. But next time you need to work late, don't. You can't handle it."

"Thanks a lot."

She laughed. "Hey, don't take it personally. Actually, it's kinda cool. And if you want my vote, you're an okay dad."

She was teasing me. "Say good night, Helen."

"Nighty-night, Marty."

Helen was right. I was overreacting. Nevertheless, I made a second call to Roscoe at the station and told him to send a patrol car by my house every couple of hours. Just to be sure.

When I reached the exit, the same female security guard was sitting at the desk, thumbing through a tattered *People* magazine. I tossed her a smile as I went by. She yawned and flipped a page.

I'll admit I was disappointed that Emily would rather play a video game than come to the phone. I understood I was reading too much into it. Funny thing was, before Nicole's death, I wouldn't have given something like this a second thought. Of course I hadn't been much of a father back then. Like a lot of men, I had this arcane notion that my job was to provide the financial base while the woman handled the kids. It was a sexist attitude, but that was the way I'd been raised. My father's idea of being nurturing was for me to get him a beer. It took Nicole's illness to show me I was wrong, to show me how much Emily needed me.

Now the most important thing in my life was to make up for lost time, to be a good father to my daughter. I suppose that's why the thought that I couldn't compete with a silly video game—

I sighed, pushing through the wooden door into the chilly night. *Let it go, Marty.*

Going down the sidewalk, I noticed a stretch limo off to the left, sitting by the curb, the engine running. For a second, I thought maybe it was Simon, but the limo was larger than his. I glanced over a few times, wondering if I'd catch a glimpse of some bigwig politico or heavyweight DoD official.

Climbing into Amanda's red Camaro that still smelled

new, I cranked the engine and adjusted the seat. As I backed out, I spotted a figure emerging from the building, walking quickly. I came down hard on the brakes.

Holland.

I frowned, realizing he was angling toward the limo. He walked straight toward the rear door and bent down as if conversing with someone. He began gesturing. If anything, he looked more agitated than earlier.

Temper, temper, I thought, pulling around to get a better view.

Three minutes later, I was hunched forward, the defroster going full blast, peering through the window at General Holland still by the limo some thirty yards ahead. A nearby van partially shielded my car, not that I was worried that Holland would notice me. He was too busy mixing it up with the limo's occupant.

Finally Holland spun away and strode quickly toward the building. After maybe five paces, he stopped short and glanced back. A man had emerged from the back of the limo. Since the guy's back was to me, all I could tell was that he had dark hair and wore a gray suit. They seemed to speak for a few seconds, then Holland abruptly threw out a hand in obvious disgust and continued up the walkway. The man took a few steps toward Holland before giving up.

As he returned to the limo, I saw the guy's face. Mid-forties, pointed jaw, neatly trimmed mustache, wide-set eyes. If he was a senior DoD official, he wasn't anybody I knew. He climbed into the backseat and the limo rolled away.

I waited until it disappeared around the corner before calling Simon. When he answered, the muffled sounds of traffic meant he was en route to see Bobby Baker. He told me he was about ten minutes from the hotel.

Holding my notepad under the map light, I passed on the license number I'd copied, explaining why I wanted it. I also gave him a rundown of my interview with Holland and the conversation with General Mercer, ending with

Mercer's comment that the Arlington cops had looked into a harassment charge Wildman had made two years earlier.

"I'll check it out," Simon said. He paused, adding, "The timing of Wildman's complaint is suggestive, Martin. The surveillance photographs of her children could be two years old. And General Mercer's comment about government interest is particularly worrisome. Did he give any indication as to the source?"

"No. But it's got to be high up the chain to get the Air Force Chief of Staff involved." I tucked my notepad away and began cruising around the parking lot toward the exit.

"Meaning who?" Simon asked. "The Secretary of Defense? The White House?"

"At that level."

He got quiet. "All right, Martin. I'll run the plate. When you arrive at the hotel, wait for me in the lobby. I'll need to escort you to see Bobby Baker."

"Why?"

But Simon had hung up on me again. He did that a lot. He wasn't being rude so much as oblivious. He just assumed when he was finished talking, you were too. After six years, the hangups didn't bug me . . . much.

I kicked back in the seat for the five-minute drive to Crystal City. Traffic was light, and in the quiet, my thoughts shifted to Bobby Baker. If there was a top-ten list for promising ballplayers who'd squandered their talent, his name would be close to the top. In his prime, he was unbelievable, the most dominating pitcher in the game. Everyone had him tagged as the Orioles' savior, the guy who would finally take them to the World Series. And maybe he would have, except for the personal demons that got in the way. Before the scuffle in the bar, there were rumors he was hitting the booze hard, and had even been accused of taking a few belts before a game. But his arm always saved him. Even half in the bag, he was unhittable. Then came the injury and his slide to nowhere. Now, just when Baker finally manages to pull his life together, fate slams him with the death of his kids.

Life, I thought, *can really suck.*

Ahead, I spotted the bright-red neon of the Crystal City Marriott. As I slid into the turn lane, I was curious about why Simon insisted on escorting me to see Baker. It made no sense, but a lot of stuff Simon said didn't.

I put on my blinker and pulled into the hotel.

CHAPTER 19

The Marriott Hotel was one of an endless line of concrete-and-glass high-rises that defined Crystal City. I cruised past the valet-parking stand and made a swing around the crowded lot before I saw Simon's limo pull in. I honked, parked in an open space I'd remembered out back, then hustled around to the entrance.

Simon and Romero were waiting for me on the steps under the front awning, the limo against the concrete island in the middle of the circular drive. A bunch of cabs were parked farther down, the drivers clustered together, talking and smoking. Simon was chatting with one of the uniformed parking attendants, a skinny black guy with shoulder-length dreadlocks. The attendant kept calling him Simon like they were old friends. Simon handed the guy a bill. It must have been big, because the attendant's face broke into a wide grin, revealing more gold than teeth.

"Hello, Marty," Romero said as I walked up.

"Hi, Romero."

When Simon turned to me, I nodded to the attendant. "One of your informants?"

"Calvin's assisted me in the past. He confirmed that

Bobby Baker is still here." Simon pointed to an area set off by parking cones. "Baker's car is the black Cadillac."

"Nice wheels for a guy whose wife pays his rent," Romero grunted, disgusted. "Even springs for valet parking."

I nodded, sharing his sentiment. But maybe when someone's accustomed to having money, it's hard not to live like they still had it.

Simon told Romero to check the dealership marked on the car. To me, he said, "Calvin mentioned that the car is new, Martin. Baker's only had it two days."

I understood. In a murder case, whenever someone close to the victim seems to come into money, you have to wonder if there's a connection. Whether Baker financed the car or plopped down a wad of cash would tell us if we should dig further. In Baker's case, since he was something of a local celebrity, the dealer might simply have cut him a deal, maybe tied to a promotion.

"By the way, I ran that limo's license— Over here, Martin." Simon drew me by an elbow off to the side, so we'd be out of the way of a group coming out of the hotel. He kept his voice low. "You were right to be curious."

"Okay . . ."

"It's registered to a leasing company. Beltway Luxury Cars. I called the manager and he looked up the account."

"And?"

"A corporate account. Global Aviation."

I eased out a breath, saying nothing.

Simon appraised me for moment. "You act as if you expected this."

"I thought we'd eventually find a connection to Global, but not this soon."

"Did you see anyone else in the limo? An older man, in his seventies?"

"No. Windows were tinted dark. Why?"

"The manager said the vehicle was delivered on a short-term lease only yesterday to a Global executive." He paused. "Mr. Charles Caldwell."

Now I got excited. "Caldwell's the name of the guy McInnes mentioned in the e-mail. It was Caldwell's people who searched McInnes' research files."

Simon nodded. Of course, he knew this because I'd read him the e-mail. "I take it you've never heard of Charles Caldwell, Martin?"

"Should I have? "

"Caldwell," he said, "is the company's CEO."

"Jesus. Then maybe it's Caldwell who's behind the murders. He'd have the clout to arrange—"

I broke off when I saw Simon's head suddenly swivel to the left. His eyes widened in surprise. "Let's go inside, Martin."

"Huh?

"*Now*, Martin. Hurry." Then Simon took off rapidly toward the entrance, motioning to Romero by the Caddy. Romero broke into a jog. I trailed after Simon, confused. He went up the steps fast, glancing anxiously over his shoulder. I followed his eyes. I saw the group from the hotel getting into a cab, and a car pulling up to the front—

I stared.

The car was a BMW convertible. Red.

It rolled to a stop at the curb. I saw the long blond hair.

I hustled up the steps. By now Simon was already ducking through one of the glass doors. Romero came up behind me, breathing hard. We almost bowled over an elderly couple who had just exited.

Behind us Janet Spence called out. "Hey, Simon! Wait up! Simon! Romero—"

I tossed out an apology to the couple, yanked open a door, and went inside, Romero on my heels. When I glanced back, I saw Janet through the glass, clambering awkwardly up the stairs, a large handbag dancing crazily over her shoulder. She still wore the same skintight sweater, her breasts bouncing provocatively with every step. Calvin, the attendant, was watching her with a leering grin. He must have said something, because Janet suddenly turned and tossed him her car keys.

"Martin! Romero!"

The lobby was a sea of conventioneers wearing colored name-tags. I finally spotted Simon on the other side of the reservation desk, standing under a large corporate banner, waving both arms. He motioned emphatically toward the elevators on the other side of a bubbling water fountain. Romero and I headed over, weaving our way through the crowd. A couple of times I looked back. No Janet. I began to think we might get lucky and lose her.

When we got to the elevators, Simon was nowhere in sight. "This way, Marty," Romero said without breaking stride. I followed him around the back of the elevators and down a spiral staircase to the mezzanine, where the shops were located. He took me down a hallway and pushed through a door into another stairwell. We went down one more floor and emerged into a gray concrete corridor with exposed pipes along the ceiling. A door across from us said MAINTENANCE, and the sound of machinery hummed from within.

"You sure you know where you're going?" I asked.

But Romero was hurrying down the corridor. He hung a right into another long hallway. I caught up to him. At the far end we saw a figure standing by a door, waving to us.

It was Simon.

"She follow you?" Simon asked, as we came up. "I don't think so," Romero said. He glanced to me, and I shrugged. I still didn't get what the big rush was about to avoid her. I knew it couldn't be just because she was a reporter.

"So when are we going to see Baker?" I asked Simon.

Simon didn't reply. He began punching a code into a keypad by the door, which was unmarked.

"Baker's in *here*?" I asked, surprised.

A nod. At a click, Simon pushed in the door and stepped aside. Classical music wafted out.

"After you, Martin."

I entered a brightly lit foyer of plush carpeting and mahogany walls. A woman smiled pleasantly at me as she stepped out from behind an ornate reception desk. I did a double take at what she was wearing.

"May I help you, sir?" she asked.

I could only stare.

CHAPTER 20

Her name tag said MARLA.

She wore a shimmering black bikini, a black choker, stiletto heels, and nothing else. She was in her early twenties, blue-eyed, with flowing brown hair and the kind of figure that made guys walk into walls.

"Are you a member?" she asked.

I rejoined the living by shaking my head.

Her face brightened. "Is that— Simon! Jeez, it's been ages."

Simon came forward, smiling. "Quite a while, Marla. How is school?"

"Graduate next year. You believe it? And now I'm thinking about going for a master's. Hey, I'm getting married to Brice Williams." She held out her hand, showing an engagement ring with a diamond the size of a small marble.

Simon congratulated her and they chatted briefly about her upcoming wedding.

"So," Marla asked him, "you here for business or pleasure?"

"A police matter. Is Mr. Peters in?"

"Uh-huh. In his office." Marla's face was turning somber.

"I understand the ballplayer Bobby Baker works here," Simon said.

"You didn't know? Mr. Peters hired him...oh...must be going on two years now."

"That long?" Simon said, surprised.

"Bobby didn't work full-time until maybe six months ago. Could be you just missed him. The clients like him. You must be here about his wife and kids, huh?"

A nod. "Baker has been told, then?"

"Mr. Peters caught the story on the news and took Bobby up to one of the suites to tell him. The Jefferson room. Linda was pretty upset with Mr. Peters, thought he should have let her break the news."

"Linda?"

"She's a new girl—"

"Baker's girlfriend," Romero interrupted. "Linda Green. She's the one I spoke to."

"Is Baker still in the Jefferson room?" Simon asked.

"Far as I know," Marla said. "As you can imagine, he's taking it awfully hard. Those kids were his life. He talked about them all the time." She gazed at Simon, her voice softening. "He's really crushed, Simon. Maybe it'd be better, you know, if you give him some time. Maybe talk to him tomorrow."

I frowned. For her to make this suggestion was completely out of place. Simon also seemed puzzled by it.

He patted her hand reassuringly. "We won't disturb him long. Do me a favor and tell Peters we're on our way." When he drew his hand back, I saw he'd slipped her some money.

As we started to leave, Marla said, "Uh, Simon, could I talk to you for a minute?" Her eyes flickered uneasily to Romero and me.

"Of course," Simon said. To Romero and me, he said, "I'll meet you in the lobby."

Romero and I walked up to a massive wooden door affixed with a brass plaque that read THE PENTAGON CLUB. The door buzzed and as we went in, I looked back to see

Simon and Marla, talking softly. Marla's pretty face was knotted in worry. I wondered what she was telling him that she didn't want me and Romero to hear.

I watched until the door closed.

The lobby was actually a long corridor maybe ten yards wide, with more deep plush carpeting and shiny mahogany walls. Ornate gold-framed paintings lined both sides, presidents on the right and generals on the left. An enormous chandelier dangled from a twelve-foot-high ceiling, bathing the room in a soft light. Everything I saw projected a feeling of wealth and power. Farther down from us stood knots of serious-faced men talking quietly, most with drinks. A waitress in a black bikini shuttled between them, taking orders.

"Quite a place," I said.

"Yeah." Romero deposited himself heavily on a throne-like armchair in a sitting area by the door.

I joined him on a matching sofa, saying, "The name of the club implies a military connection. I wouldn't think military members could afford a membership."

"Not unless they've got fifty grand burning a hole in their pocket."

"That much?"

Romero nodded, crossing his legs. "And that's just the initiation fee. Dues run a couple grand a month. The club was built by defense contractors back in the fifties as a place to wine and dine the Pentagon brass. Most members are big-time defense lobbyists, so their companies pick up the tab."

Which explained the cloak-and-dagger gyrations. In the wake of the Tailhook scandal, the last thing a high-ranking military officer or DoD official needed was to be seen frequenting a place with semi-nude girls.

"I'm kind of surprised the Marriott okayed a place like this in one of their hotels," I said.

"That's because the original club was located here. Marriott wanted the land bad enough to allow a new club to be built discreetly in the hotel."

"Why'd Simon become a member?" I knew Simon had no military connection.

"A lot of politicians and D.C. power brokers come here. He figured it was a good place to make contacts. You know, just in case he ever needed anything. He's also a member of the Georgetown Club. It's kinda like this except it's used mainly by Capitol Hill types. I actually like this place more. Food's better."

I now understood how Simon had risen so rapidly up the cop pecking order. Funny thing was, until this moment, I'd thought he was apolitical.

The door buzzed and Simon appeared. I gave him a questioning look.

"Let's go, gentlemen," he said, striding by.

At the far end of the lobby, we passed a glassed-in room filled with books. A handful of men were sitting inside in overstuffed leather chairs, smoking cigars. In the short walk, we'd stopped three times so Simon could say hello to people he knew. This was a side of him I hadn't seen, the charming, affable Simon. The corridor turned right and we came to a softly lit dining room, figures dimly visible at the tables, bikinied waitresses hovering nearby. Ahead, I saw another open room with a sweeping wooden staircase that resembled something out of *Gone With the Wind*. Simon leaned over and said something to Romero, who went to the stairs.

"Baker," Simon said, as we made another right down a hallway.

I'd figured as much. Romero would make sure Baker didn't bug out on us before we could talk to him. Three men approached us, walking unsteadily. Two were in their sixties, the third maybe forty. The younger guy was talking loudly, slurring his words. His companions burst out laughing. I caught the punch line, a joke about the President's dick size. It wasn't that funny unless you were a Republican.

As they passed, I recognized one of the older men: Senator Clive Dugan, the Chairman of the Armed Services Committee. I mentioned him to Simon.

"You sound surprised," he said.

"I am. Considering the girls, I think it'd be a little risky politically. If some women's group found out, made a big splash—"

Simon laughed. "Senator Dugan isn't worried. He knows no one here will say anything. That's the purpose of the club. To ensure privacy for the political elite like Dugan, so he can meet with constituents without eyebrows being raised."

I shook my head, still thinking it was a risk. At the end of the hallway, we made a left past another glassed-in room with barber chairs.

"What you don't understand, Martin," Simon went on, "is clubs like this one are a way of life in D.C. There are similar exclusive venues throughout the city, all built by a variety of interest groups for the express purpose of catering to government officials. It's the way business in this town is done." We came to a set of double doors blocking the hallway. A brass plate on one said CLUB ADMINISTRATION.

As we went through, I said, "You mean the political lobbying business."

He nodded. "I take it you don't approve?"

I waved a hand around. "Bringing someone like Senator Dugan here, pampering him just so you can get your legislation passed. It's wrong. You're essentially buying their vote."

"That may be," Simon said. "But lobbyists do serve a purpose. They present a viewpoint to an elected official. The other side does the same. The official then weighs both alternatives and makes an informed decision."

I gave him a look of annoyance. "You really believe that?"

He smiled. "Of course not. But I've learned to accept that the process won't change until Congress enacts new laws, and probably not even then. The system is far too entrenched, and frankly, in spite of the rhetoric, the public really doesn't care. If they did, they wouldn't keep reelecting the same officials." He shrugged. "Besides, as political practices go, it's only slightly corrupting. Here we are."

We stopped at a door that said, Club Manager, Mr. Archibald Peters. From within, we could hear voices. As Simon reached for the knob, someone shouted: "Goddammit, William, just call Linda to get that son of a bitch out of here! Now!"

Moments later, the door flew open, revealing a flustered young man in a three-piece suit. He blinked at Simon.

"Good evening, William," Simon said cordially.

William swallowed. "Good evening, sir."

We moved aside. William tore down the hall.

"Hello, Simon," a man's voice said.

He didn't sound happy.

Peters looked like a guy who would be named Archibald, even though I couldn't recall knowing anyone by that name. Peters was fiftyish, short and bald, his grip bony but firm. He wore a tuxedo and smelled of flowers. From the platinum Rolex on his wrist and the porcelain figurines in his office, it was clear Peters was a man who appreciated nice things. I'd half-expected him to sound like an English butler, but his raspy voice suggested New York or New Jersey.

After the introductions, Peters camped behind his antique desk, which was bare except for a laptop computer in the corner. He gazed bleakly at Simon. "Marla says you want to talk to Baker?"

Simon nodded.

Peters sighed, rubbing his dome. "Your timing couldn't be worse. She mentioned his little problem to you?"

"Yes."

"I didn't know anything about it, Simon. I'd never have hired him if I did. You know that. Hell, I was just doing him a favor."

"It's not your fault, Archie," Simon said.

"I don't know how long it's been going on, and I don't give a damn. All I want now is to avoid a scene."

"Relax, I'm just going to talk to him."

Peters squinted suspiciously. "That's all?"

"That's all."

Peters looked relieved. "Thanks, Simon. The club can't afford a scandal. I appreciate this."

"Not a problem. But I'll need a favor in return."

"Name it."

"The membership list."

Peters' eyes widened. "Hell, you know I can't do that. The list is confidential. If it ever became public—"

"It won't."

Peters slowly eased back in his chair. He tugged on his cheek, looking at the wall. Finally, he came back to Simon. "I don't suppose I have a choice."

"None."

"Want to tell me why you want the list?"

Simon shook his head.

"You guarantee this thing with Baker—"

"Don't give it a second thought, Archie."

"All right." Peters drew his laptop over. "It's on the computer. I'll have to print out a copy. We've got almost a thousand members, so it'll take a few minutes." He started clicking the mouse, saying, "You know I liked Baker. Frankly, I couldn't help but feel sorry for him. Who wouldn't, after what he's gone through? And now with the murders . . ." Peters sat back as a laser printer in the corner began humming. "But Baker's only got himself to blame. I'd fire his ass if this wasn't his last day."

"What?" Simon asked.

Peters glanced up. "Marla didn't tell you? Baker gave me notice last week. He said he wouldn't be working after tonight. Caught me by surprise because only a couple of months back, I gave him a big raise. Forty percent. But hell, he seemed worth it. He's a hit around here. Japanese members went nuts over the guy. Big baseball fans. Now he ups and decides to leave. Go figure."

"He give you a reason?"

"He's got another job offer. Didn't say from who. Must be pretty big bucks, though, to match what I was paying him." Peters' phone rang, and he swiveled to pick up.

Up to now, I'd thought Baker's "little problem" was that he'd fallen off the wagon and it was affecting his job. If Baker was drunk, that would explain why Marla had wanted us to wait. But after listening to Peters, I knew it had to be something more serious than just booze.

I leaned over to confirm my suspicions with Simon. Before I could, Peters shot forward in his chair with a look of incredulity.

"Who?" he demanded. "Aw, for the love of . . . I can't believe this. Yeah, yeah. I can hear her. Fine. I'll tell him." He banged down the phone hard. "When it rains it fucking pours."

"What wrong?" Simon asked.

Peters eyed Simon. "Marla says there's some woman banging on the outside door. Asking for you."

For an instant, Simon looked angrier than I'd ever seen him. I thought for once he might actually swear.

Instead he spun and walked out.

As I started to follow, Peters said, "Collins, there's one thing I forgot to mention . . ."

I turned.

". . . about Baker. When you see him, go easy. He's a little . . . unstable."

"We can handle him."

Peters nodded, settling back in his chair like he wanted to talk some more. "This problem with Baker, I honestly didn't know about it until a few minutes ago. Marla thinks it's been going on for a couple weeks. Hell, I thought he was just a little stressed out. It's a real shame about that guy. He had it all, and . . ."

I didn't hear the rest, because I was walking out the door.

CHAPTER 21

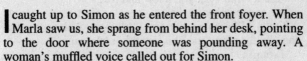

I caught up to Simon as he entered the front foyer. When Marla saw us, she sprang from behind her desk, pointing to the door where someone was pounding away. A woman's muffled voice called out for Simon.

"She sounds crazy," Marla said to Simon. "She's also demanding to see Bobby Baker."

Simon went to the door. He still looked angry, but not homicidal anymore. "Silence," he called out sharply.

The banging stopped.

He opened the door, and I followed him out.

I'd expected to find Janet Spence angry, maybe a little crazed. Instead she was relaxed and smiling. She winked at Simon. "What the hell took you so long? My hand was getting tired."

Simon glowered back. "What are you doing here?"

"I want to talk to you about the Wildman murders."

"Out of the question."

"You tell him?" she asked me.

I'd forgotten. "Sorry." To Simon, I said, "Janet says she knew Colonel Wildman."

Simon rolled his eyes.

"Dammit, Simon, I do," Janet said. "How do you think I knew about this place? Margie Wildman told me Bobby worked here. She and Bobby were both friends of mine."

Simon seemed on the verge of dismissing her, but changed his mind. He studied her as if trying to determine whether she was telling the truth.

"I'm not kidding," Janet said, her voice softening. "This is important. We need to talk. I have some information you might be able to use."

"What kind of information?" Simon asked warily.

"It's kind of complicated. Maybe there's somewhere we could go . . ."

"I won't give you a story."

"I know."

"I won't make any deals."

"Fine. Whatever."

"You tell me what you know and that's it."

She nodded obediently.

Simon still seemed reluctant. "All right. Wait for me upstairs by the elevators. This shouldn't take long."

"Promise?"

Simon nodded.

Janet gave him an odd smile. "I'll be waiting." She turned and went down the hallway.

As Simon punched the code into the lock, I asked, "You think she really knows something about the case?"

Simon looked at me as if I were crazy, then yanked open the door and went inside.

I took that as a no.

⟹ On the club's second-floor landing, we took a left down a red-carpeted hallway, passing heavy wooden doors with more gold scripted names of presidents and generals. Simon said these were private conference rooms. A couple of waitresses hurried by, wheeling silver carts laden with food. From the rooms, we could hear voices punctuated by an occasional laugh. The Jefferson

Room was next to MacArthur's, about halfway down.

Romero was waiting outside the door, leaning against the wall. He pushed upright as we approached. "He hasn't left."

On our way up, I'd told Simon about Peters' concerns that Baker might be a little unstable. Simon shrugged. He rapped hard once on the door and went in, Romero and me trailing. I'd barely stepped inside when all hell broke loose.

I heard Romero suddenly shout to me. Before I could react, he turned and shoved me, hard. My legs buckled and I fell awkwardly to the carpet. An instant later, something shattered against the wall inches from where I'd been standing and wetness sprayed my face.

"Dammit," I snarled, "what the hell is—"

A man swore viciously from inside the room. Then I heard Simon shouting for Romero. In the chaos, I caught movement, saw Romero rush forward. I pushed up to see, but Simon was crouching before me, blocking my view. We heard the sounds of a struggle. More swearing. Someone grunted loudly in pain.

Then Romero, calmly: "Move and I'll break your arm."

"Fuck you!" Another grunt of pain. "Dammit, okay, *okay*!"

"You can get up, gentlemen," Romero said.

As we did, I squeegeed the moisture from my face.

Beer.

The room could have passed for one of those luxury skyboxes at a ballpark, complete with plush carpeting, leather furniture, wet bar, large-screen TV, even a briefing table with phones and Internet connections. Everything a well-heeled lobbyist needed for a little friendly political arm-twisting.

I focused on the big man in a tweed blazer slumped on the couch, rubbing his left hand. On the coffee table before him were strewn at least a half-dozen empty beer bottles. Shattered remnants of another bottle lay on the carpeting by the door. I'd been lucky. From the way the bottle exploded, it was clear Bobby Baker still had a hell of an arm.

Up close, Baker didn't look like a guy who'd spent a lifetime abusing booze and whatever else. Instead of a face marked like a road map, his was tanned and smooth, and his thick brown hair showed no signs of graying. He was maybe fifty pounds heavier than his playing days, but his six-five frame could handle it.

What particularly caught my interest were his eyes: puffy and red like he'd been crying. But when I looked into them, I didn't see the grief I expected. Instead, they appeared glazed and the pupils unfocused.

I felt disgust, my earlier suspicions confirmed.

"Mr. Baker," Simon said harshly, standing over him. "That was extremely reckless. You could have caused a serious injury. Were you cut, Martin?"

"No." And I gave Romero a smile of thanks.

Baker gazed back sullenly. He looked accusingly to Romero and held up his hand. "You fucking hurt me, asshole."

Romero shrugged.

"Who the fuck are you guys?" Baker demanded.

Simon and I produced our badges and held them to his face.

Baker stared at them in disbelief. "*Cops!* Jesus Christ, why didn't you say so? Man oh man, I thought—" He caught himself with a nervous smile. "Goddamn cops, huh? Have a seat, fellas. Sorry about the scare I gave you." He was speaking fast, his movements edgy.

"You thought what?" Simon asked mildly.

Baker hesitated. "Nothing. I just...I don't know what I thought. I'm kind of all balled up. The shock...I just can't believe it. My family...that they're..." His eyes misted. He dug into his trousers pocket, produced a dirty hanky. He wiped his eyes and blew his nose.

Simon said, "This will be difficult, but we need to ask a few questions."

"I'm not sure I—"

"This isn't a request."

A nod. Baker's right foot began tapping. I didn't think he was aware of it.

Simon joined Baker on the couch. Romero and I settled on recliners across from them. Simon seemed interested in a corner of the glass-topped coffee table. Baker noticeably tensed, watching him. Simon slowly shifted his gaze to Baker. "I understand you kept in close contact with your ex-wife."

Baker nodded. "Because of the . . . kids. I usually went over there a couple days a week." He took a ragged breath. "Damn, this is hard. Anyone want a beer? Couple more in the fridge." He started to rise.

"No beer, Bobby," Simon said firmly. "Sit down, please."

Baker shrugged, easing back down. The foot began tapping again.

"When was the last time you saw your family?" Simon asked.

"Two days ago. I went over to take the kids to a movie. A Disney flick." He blinked, becoming dewy-eyed again.

At that moment, I was convinced Bobby Baker couldn't have had anything to do with the deaths. His pain was too real. In spite of my disgust, I felt sympathetic. Nicole's death had almost killed me. I couldn't imagine what it must be like to also lose two children, and so brutally.

Simon waited until Baker gathered himself. "Do you know any reason why someone might want to kill your ex-wife and children?"

Baker shook his head.

"Nothing at all?" Simon asked. "Perhaps a project she might have been working on recently . . ."

Another shake.

". . . something involving an airplane accident?"

The head shaking stopped. So did the foot tapping. Baker slowly looked up, his face puzzled. "A plane crash? No. Doesn't ring a bell."

I frowned at something in Baker's voice. A casualness

that sounded forced. "You've never heard her talk about the Global 626?"

Baker gave me a blank look. "What's a Global 626?"

The response caught me off guard. "It's one of the most popular airliners in the world," I said dryly. I glanced to Simon to see how he wanted to play it. He settled back, content to let me continue.

"Don't fly much anymore," Baker said, shrugging. "Not since I quit playing ball."

His hyper behavior made it difficult to pick up the normal cues that told you when someone was lying. I said, "So Colonel Wildman never discussed her work with you?"

"No. We just did stuff with the kids." He swallowed. "Family stuff."

"She didn't give you a computer disk recently? Maybe asked you to hold it?"

A pause that went on a beat too long. "Computer disk? Unh-unh. Course, I don't know nothing about the computers." He rubbed his face. "Look, fellas, how about we try this tomorrow. I'm not sure I can really handle much more now."

Before I could respond, Simon said, "Of course. You're under a terrible strain. Can we reach you at home tomorrow?"

"Sure."

I stared at Simon in disbelief. Why the hell was he suddenly agreeing to leave? It was clear that Baker wasn't playing straight with us. I wanted to argue, but Simon shut me up with a hard look.

As Romero and I stood, Simon slid close to Baker and began speaking to him in consoling tones. He went on for maybe a minute, saying he understood Baker's pain over his loss. Baker nodded along, but said little. As Simon rose to leave, he accidentally knocked over an empty beer bottle. He knelt down to pick it up, turning his back to Baker. The movement seemed awkward.

Then I noticed Simon's hand pass over the bottle and

feel under the sofa. He stood, replaced the bottle on the table, then patted Baker on the back.

As Simon went past me to the door, I noticed his right hand was cupped, like something was in it. He slid the hand inside his jacket before turning to Baker. "By the way, Bobby, Mr. Peters mentioned you have a new job."

"Yeah. A P.R. firm in D.C. Larson and Pinard. Start next week."

"That's quite a prestigious firm."

"I guess . . ." Baker stared at his hands.

As Simon and Romero left, I hung back because I had one final question. I asked Baker if Colonel Wildman had given him a reason why she was sending the children away.

Baker shook his head. "She really never said."

"And you never asked?"

"Never thought much about it. Just figured she wanted them to have a little vacation. See their grandparents."

Baker sounded and acted completely sincere. I knew he was full of shit. I told him goodnight and went to the door. As I drew it closed, I saw Baker bury his head in his hands and begin to cry. I shook my head in frustration. It was obvious Bobby Baker had loved his children deeply.

So why the hell was he lying to us?

CHAPTER 22

Simon and Romero waited for me at the end of the hall-way. Simon was talking into his cell phone. He ended the call as I walked up.

"You look troubled, Martin," Simon said.

"I am. I can't figure Baker out. He damn sure knows more than he's telling."

"I agree," Simon said. Romero nodded along.

"Look," I said, "I know Baker's hurting and all, but it seems to me we should go back in there, push him— Why the hell not?"

Simon was shaking his head, eyes on Romero. "We've discussed that option, but it's clear to us Baker isn't in any condition to be questioned. Tomorrow would be better, when he's more lucid and his paranoia has subsided. Right now he's compelled to lie, protect himself."

"Because he's higher than a kite," I said.

Simon nodded, reaching into his jacket. He removed what looked like a drinking straw, except this one was made of metal.

"The sofa," I said.

"Yes. In the commotion after we entered, I noticed him

stuff something under the sofa. He also tried to wipe the tabletop clean, but I still detected powder residue on it."

"Cocaine," I said, stating the obvious. "Man, the guy's a piece of work. His kids were murdered and he's sucking down nose candy."

Simon shrugged. "We all have our own ways of dealing with grief, Martin." He paused a moment, adding, "We'll question him tomorrow. I've arranged for a surveillance team to tail him when he leaves, keep him out of trouble until then."

I still disagreed. If it was up to me, I'd jack Baker up now and force him to tell what he knows. Part of me wondered if Simon's decision was driven by his promise to Peters that we wouldn't make a scene.

Romero cleared his throat. "We'd better get going, Simon."

Simon nodded vaguely, but just stood there, adjusting his tie. After a few seconds, he slowly took out a piece of gum, unwrapped it, and popped it in his mouth. Then he glanced down at his shoes and wiped the tops off on the back of his trousers. He checked them and wiped again. I became curious, watching all this. For some reason, Simon was reluctant to leave.

"You will have to talk to her eventually, you know," Romero said.

My eyebrows inched up. Simon was stalling because he didn't want to see Janet Spence?

Romero shot him a look of exasperation and went down the stairs. Simon shook his head, sighed deeply, then followed.

Sidling up to him, I said, "So the reason Baker chucked the bottle at us was to create a diversion to hide his drug paraphernalia?"

"Apparently."

"If that's true, then why did he act relieved when he found out we were cops?"

Simon shrugged.

We'd reached the lobby floor. Because it was getting late, the clusters of people had thinned. I spotted Romero's bulk heading toward the exit.

Simon stared after him. "Romero doesn't understand. He thinks I'm too harsh in my judgment of Janet."

This time I didn't bother wasting my time asking him why.

We turned down the hallway toward the administrative offices. I remembered we had to retrieve the membership printout from Peters.

I said, "Maybe Baker had another reason for lying to us besides drugs. Could be he's more involved in the murders than we think."

"It's certainly possible. Detective Reardon is checking if Colonel Wildman had any insurance policies benefiting Baker. We'll also look into his bank account, see if he's been the recipient of any windfalls."

"His pay raise probably explains the car."

"Probably." He glanced over. "Frankly, do we even care if Baker gained financially by his ex-wife's death?"

"What do you mean?"

"Assuming Wildman's murder is tied to the G-626, how could Baker be involved?"

He had me. I shook my head.

"Besides, Martin, it's quite apparent Baker wouldn't hurt his children. His anguish was real."

"But he's hiding *something*."

"True."

I sighed. The more we learned, the muddier everything became. Thirty minutes ago, General Holland was my prime suspect. Now Baker was right up there. Of course, it was possible they were both somehow—

"Simon!"

Peters was coming through the double doors, waving a folder.

We went over to get the membership list.

Simon waited until Peters headed back to his office before opening the folder. Inside was a sheaf of pages with roughly twenty names per. Simon immediately began flipping through the stack.

"Who are you looking for?" I asked.

Simon abruptly stopped, then began scanning again. I peeked over his shoulder.

Names beginning with C. I knew now. My eyes went down the page, but it wasn't there.

"No Caldwell," I said.

"No."

"Try Holland," I said.

He did. It wasn't there. He closed the folder and jammed it under his arm.

"Worth a shot," I said. "If either Caldwell or Holland had been members, we could have connected Baker to them. So maybe Baker's in the clear after all."

"Perhaps."

We retraced our steps toward the lobby. Simon said, "You know, Larson and Pinard is the largest P.R. firm in the city. Most of their clients are high-ranking senators and congressmen."

"Okay..."

"I'm curious how Baker obtained a job there, considering his questionable history. A firm of their stature normally employs people with impeccable credentials."

I shrugged. "People cut celebrities a lot of slack."

"I suppose..." Simon drifted off. As we went by the staircase, I noticed an anxious-faced young woman coming toward us. Her demeanor and the fact that she was dressed casually in a bulky pullover sweater and jeans clued me in to her identity.

She slowed, staring at us. Suddenly she angled our way.

"Simon..."

"I see her, Martin. Perhaps now we'll find out why Bobby Baker is so frightened."

Baker frightened?

Simon stepped toward the woman with a smile.

 "Lieutenant Santos?" the woman said tentatively, looking at Simon.

"Yes. You must be Linda."

She nodded, and confirmed that she was Linda Green, Baker's girlfriend. "Marla described the bow tie. That's how...well, anyway, I wanted to thank you. Marla said you aren't going to arrest Bobby."

"No."

Linda Green shook her head sadly. "Bobby's been doing so well. It's been a year since he had a drink. Almost two since he's done drugs. I don't understand it...why he started again. He...he promised me." She gazed past us, looking lost. "I've tried so *hard*. I thought if he was happy...if I could keep him happy...he wouldn't feel the need to..." She fell silent, staring.

We didn't say anything. We just waited.

Abruptly Linda looked at us, her face apologetic. "I'm sorry. It's just that...that I care about him so much."

"I understand," Simon said. "Do you mind telling me when he started using again?"

"I'm not really sure. Maybe a week. I've known for a week. You can always tell."

"Did you ask him why he started?"

A hesitant nod. Her voice became bitter. "He told me he wanted to, that it wasn't a *big deal*. He could *handle* it. But...I think maybe it was the stress. Lately, Bobby's been tense. Short-tempered. Saying things he doesn't mean. And that's not Bobby. He's usually easygoing. Kind." She gave a weary sigh, pushing hair from her eyes. "Of course, I asked him why he was so uptight. He said I was imagining things, that there was nothing wrong." She became quiet, distant again. "I was...I was thinking maybe I should take him away someplace, you know, where he could stay clean. But now, with what's happened with his kids..." She swallowed. "Poor Bobby. He never catches a break. Never."

"We'll need to talk to him tomorrow," Simon said.

She nodded.

"Take him home tonight and keep him there. I want him to be sober when we talk. No booze and no drugs. If he does either, I will arrest him."

Another nod.

He gave her his card. "Any problems, call me." I stepped forward and asked Linda for her address and number, and jotted them down.

"Thank you," she said to Simon. She hesitated. "I liked Margaret. She was nice to me. And those two kids..." Her lower lip quivered. "I hope you find who did it."

"We will," Simon said.

As she walked off, I said, "Nice girl. Better than Baker deserves."

Simon nodded thoughtfully. "Oh, Linda, one last question..."

She turned.

"...Bobby. Who is he afraid of?"

She looked startled.

"He is frightened, isn't he?" Simon went on.

"I...think so. He...he's nervous whenever he leaves the house. He also bought a couple of guns recently."

"When?"

"A few weeks ago. Keeps one in the house and one in the car."

"Has he given you any indication of who he could be afraid of?"

A head shake.

I'll be damned, I thought, finally catching on.

Gently, Simon said, "Try and find out why he's afraid. Get us a name. Can you do that?"

She nodded, big-eyed.

"Tell Bobby I can protect him. Convince him to talk to me."

"I'll...I'll try." She attempted a smile, then slowly walked away.

"Hell," I said to Simon. "No wonder Baker went nuts. He thought we were sent to hurt him."

He nodded. "He knows almost everyone that's a member. Seeing three strangers suddenly barge in, he panicked." He smiled wryly. "Having Romero with us didn't help matters."

We started back down the hall. I was thinking hard. "That means whoever he is afraid of is a member of the club."

Another nod. "If that's true, it suggests two key points. That Baker didn't actually commit the murders but is somehow involved."

The first part I understood, but the second— "Just because he won't talk to us?"

"What other reason could he have for not cooperating?"

I considered this. "Baker could still be in the clear. Suppose someone threatened him and that's the reason he's not talking?"

Simon's voice became quiet. "You're a father. If your children were murdered, would you stay silent?"

I shook my head.

"Then," Simon said, "there must be another reason."

"Over there," I said to Simon, pointing.

We were moving through a sea of conventioneers clustered around the elevators. Through the bodies, I'd spotted Janet and Romero standing by a large sculpture that resembled a giant cast-iron Rubik's cube. Romero noticed us and waved.

As they came over, men turned to watch Janet, which was natural. In spite of his expressed antipathy, Simon also had difficulty keeping his eyes off of her. I found his reaction curious, since I've never known Simon to display the slightest interest in women. In fact, one of the rumors going around was that he had to be gay. Maybe even had a thing going with Romero. Crazy, I know, but people talk.

"You guys ready?" Janet asked, walking toward us.

Simon nodded, and their gazes lingered on each other.

Watching them, a possibility occurred to me. Just maybe . . .

Simon said to her, "We can talk in the car. Remember, this doesn't change anything between us." Then he pivoted, heading for the exit.

For an instant, I saw a flicker of disappointment in Janet's eyes. Romero put a big arm around her shoulder and whispered something in her ear.

I was certain now.

By the time we got outside, Simon was again talking with the parking attendant, Calvin. Simon handed him money, pointing across to Baker's car. Calvin winked, pocketing the cash. I slowly shook my head, realizing what he was up to. But like Simon always told me, he wasn't technically breaking a law.

➤ It was almost a quarter after ten when Romero flipped on the blinker and rolled the limo into the late-evening traffic on Jefferson Davis Highway. Janet and I were camped on the backseat, Simon off to the side. Streetlights flickered off our faces as we picked up speed. Janet gazed out the window while Simon stared at the floor. They seemed to be avoiding eye contact.

I turned to her. "It's your nickel, Janet..."

She nodded. When she spoke, her voice was quiet but with an edge. "I want to make one thing clear first. I don't care about any goddamn story. All I want is to find who killed Margaret and her children. That's it. Period." Even though she was looking at me, we all knew she was really talking to Simon.

He remained silent but finally looked up at her.

Janet took a deep breath. "Here it is. I think the government might be responsible for the murders."

I stared at her. So did Simon. Romeo watched her in the rearview mirror. None of us said anything.

She blinked at us. "Did you hear what I said?"

"We heard," Simon said quietly. "We just don't believe you."

Janet's jaw tightened. "Fine. I know it sounds crazy. Maybe you'll believe me if you hear it from Margie herself."

Simon frowned, confused.

I said, "How can Colonel Wildman—"

And then I saw Janet remove something from her handbag. At first I thought it was a small radio. But as we passed under a streetlight I realized I was mistaken. It was a tiny microcassette recorder, the kind used for dictation.

"Son of a bitch," Romero murmured.

CHAPTER 23

We stopped at a red light near Old Town Alexandria. Even though it was a weekday evening, traffic was heavy. Janet inserted a cassette into the recorder, saying, "We went out to dinner about a month ago when I recorded this. That was the first time Margaret told me about the accident investigation she'd worked. I actually started recording our conversation a little late— There."

A click. The tape began to hiss.

By now I was digging my notepad out. I clicked on the overhead light.

The hissing ended, replaced by background noises: muffled voices, clinking glasses...restaurant noises. Then a tapping, like fingers drumming a table. The drumming stopped. An unfamiliar woman's voice came on abruptly: "All right, but I want you to promise that no one will know about this until I'm ready. These people are dangerous. I'm taking a risk by telling you."

Janet's voice: "Jesus. Aren't you being a little melodramatic?"

"Promise me."

"Okay, okay. Nothing gets out until you give the word."

"Maybe this isn't such a good idea. Forget I ever brought—"

"Dammit, Margie. I won't tell a soul. I want to help."

An audible sigh. "This is difficult. I...I haven't known who to trust. I have to be sure that..." She drifted into silence, as if trying to decide.

The light turned green. Cars began honking, making it difficult to hear. Simon told Romero to find someplace quiet and pull over.

On the tape, Margaret Wildman finally came back. In a quiet, weary voice, she began describing a fatal plane accident she was assigned to investigate two years earlier....

Romero pulled the limo into the Potomac Yard Mall and I started to write.

Ten minutes later, Janet clicked off the tape player.

Afterward, we sat almost in a daze. No one seemed to want to talk. Simon had his eyes closed and I knew he was trying to make sense of what we'd just heard. I was doing the same by looking over my notes. Romero was slumped against the driver's seat, watching us in the rearview mirror.

Our reaction was understandable. We'd just heard a dead woman calmly lay out the motive for her own murder.

According to Wildman, everything began two years earlier when she'd been assigned to an investigation team looking into the crash of a C-26, the military version of the Global 626. A few weeks into the investigation, her team was abruptly replaced, no explanation given. Months later, when the military released the final accident report, Wildman knew the reason cited for the crash was blatantly false. She confronted the team leader, demanding an explanation, but was rebuffed. She soon realized that a major cover-up was under way. She became obsessed with uncovering the real cause of the crash. From her earlier investigation, she'd developed the theory that the plane was inherently dangerous. The problem was that she had no proof.

When she tried to build a case, the walls went up. No one would talk to her, provide information. Most hid behind the plane's Top Secret security classification, claiming Wildman lacked "the need to know." Her superiors ordered her to drop her investigation, going so far as to threaten her with official reprimands and eventually a court-martial. Still she persisted, until the threats escalated to a level she could no longer ignore. In the end, Wildman made the only decision she could and reluctantly scrapped her investigation.

Over the years the guilt ate at her. With every subsequent G-626 crash, she felt increasingly traumatized, but saw no way out.

Until the night before the dinner with Janet.

Wildman explained that an opportunity had come up, one she hoped would allow her to finally come forward. But she had to act fast. She had less than a month to gather evidence for her case. She would need help.

She explained that this was why she'd contacted Janet. Janet's access to *Washington Post* archives would be invaluable. She again warned Janet of the risks.

At that point Wildman began to detail the threats she'd experienced two years earlier: the harassing phone calls, the strange cars following her, and the two men who were waiting in her living room when she came home. Wildman said they never raised their voices, just calmly handed her a packet and told her this was her final warning. Inside the packet, Wildman found pictures of her children, accompanied by an itinerary of their daily activities. When they went to school, when they came home, when they went out to play; it was all there. The implication terrified her.

As Wildman recounted her story, we heard her fear. A mother's fear. Even now her decision to renew the investigation was difficult. She spoke of sending the children away, to protect them. So they couldn't be hurt or—

That's the moment Janet had suddenly stopped the tape. As if she couldn't bear to listen.

Almost a minute later, Janet still seemed a little rattled. She was squeezing her hands together, taking slow, measured breaths. Finally she looked at Simon and broke the quiet. "What do you think?"

Simon was still leaning back, eyes closed. I asked, "Is there more on the tape?"

"A little. But Margie doesn't gives any specifics about the crash. She pretty much goes on about ... about how terrified she was when she saw those pictures. That's why she wanted me to take my time before I made the decision to get involved. She wanted to make sure I knew what I was getting myself into."

I said, "You obviously told her yes."

Janet nodded. "But not until two days later. To be honest, she had me spooked. Once I saw the photos, I ... I almost said no. But in the end, I just couldn't."

A surprisingly frank admission. I was deciding I'd misjudged her, that she had more substance than I'd first thought. "Colonel Wildman must have mentioned some details on what she thought was wrong with the airplane."

"A little. A lot of the stuff was extremely technical, so I didn't understand much. What Margie wanted was for me to use my paper's resources to check out Global Aviation. She requested pretty much everything: company history, organizational diagram, production figures, financial reports, component subcontractors, you name it. It took me a couple weeks. I turned everything over to her on Monday. That was ... that was the last time I saw her." She blinked rapidly, gazing out the window. Simon's eyes cracked open, watching her.

I said, "So you met her at her house and ..."

"Not the house," Janet said, returning to me. "Margie was too uptight for that. She thought her home was being watched. She also became paranoid about me calling her there. You know, in case someone bugged her phone. We met for lunch at the Pentagon cafeteria, the one in the lower concourse—"

"I know it."

"I gave her the disks then."

"Only disks? No paper copies?"

"No. She wanted disks because they were easier to up-load into her computer."

"You mentioned that she thought she was being watched," Romero said, shifting to face her. "Did she say by whom?"

"Yeah. That's what really shook her. It was the same two men who had given her the photos of her kids. She noticed a car following her one morning as she drove to work. When she parked at the Pentagon, the car cruised by her. She said she freaked when she recognized the two men inside. What really got to her was that she knew they had wanted her to see them."

"They never actually spoke with her?" Romero asked. "Confronted or harassed her in any way?

"Not that I know of."

"When did this occur exactly?"

"The day we met for lunch. Monday. That's what made her finally decide to send the kids to her parents'."

"She describe these men to you?" Romero said.

A nod. "She said one guy was white, kinda heavy. The other guy was smaller, dark. Maybe Hispanic."

Simon suddenly sat forward, surprising Janet. "You're certain about the description?"

She hesitated. "Uh . . . pretty sure. That's what she—"

"What else did Colonel Wildman say about them?"

"What do you mean?"

"Did she provide additional details when she described these men?"

Her brow furrowed. "I don't recall . . ."

"Think. Maybe their ages or— Yes?"

"There is one thing. She said the white guy was quite a bit heavier than she'd remembered when he came to the house."

Simon hissed like she'd said something important. "Nothing else?" he pressed. "A description of the car, per-haps?"

A head shake.

Abruptly, Simon sat back, signaling he was finished. I frowned, immediately looking at Romero. He shook his head. Like Janet and me, he was also confused by Simon's reaction.

Returning to Janet, I asked, "What did Colonel Wildman think was wrong with the airplane? The wing box?"

"You *know* about that?"

I nodded. "So she did confirm that was the aircraft's problem?"

"Yes. She said there was a manufacturing flaw. That it was failing somehow, cracking. She said most were designed out of some kind of super-hard metal called . . ." Her face went blank.

"Titanium," I said.

"That's it. Anyway, she said the G-626 wing box was made out of a composite material which was cracking, causing the wings to fall off."

"My God," Romero murmured.

Silence again as the horror sank in.

I automatically closed my eyes, visualizing the three plane crashes. How they probably happened. Once a plane lost a wing, it would begin spinning wildly toward the ground. If the aircraft was at a high altitude, that translated into two or three minutes of stark terror for those on board. The fortunate ones would pass out from the G-forces which pinned them to their seats. The rest would sit screaming, waiting for the—

I opened my eyes.

Janet Spence was talking again.

"At our last meeting," Janet said, "Margie was pretty upbeat because she'd finally contacted an expert who could prove that the wing box was flawed. Margie said that with his testimony and what she'd gathered, her case would be pretty much irrefutable."

"Douglas McInnes," Simon said.

She gave him a blank look. "Who?"

"Colonel Wildman never mentioned the name of her contact to you?" he said.

"No. But there was a lot of stuff she didn't tell me. She said it would be better if I didn't know."

"And the reason she decided to renew her investigation, what was that exactly?"

"She never said."

"Oh?"

"If you knew Margie, that wasn't unusual. Even in college, she was like that. Always kept everything to herself. She dated Bobby for two months before telling me, and I was her closest friend."

Simon edged toward her, asking, "Do you know if the two men who were following Colonel Wildman ever *identified* themselves as working for the government?"

I knew where he was going. This point had been bugging me, too. Janet shook her head.

"If not," Simon said, "then I'm curious why you think the government might be behind the murders."

"A couple of reasons. During Margie's initial investigation, when she wasn't getting any cooperation from the military, she contacted an FAA investigator she knew. She said he politely listened to her theory, then dismissed it, saying the FAA had already analyzed the wing box and determined it was safe. Once she heard that, she knew the FAA had to be part of the cover-up." She paused, eyeing Simon. "And the day after that meeting was when Margie began receiving threats."

"Hold on," I said. "You're not suggesting the FAA is behind the murders."

"No," she said. "But it's clear they're part of the conspiracy to keep the plane's problems under wraps."

"A conspiracy isn't murder," I said.

"Try this, then," she said. "You know what the authorities did when she reported the threats. Nothing, except then the threats would escalate. That's a big reason why she was so afraid. There was nowhere for her to turn."

There it was, an explanation for Wildman's reluctance to confide in General Mercer. I said, "She contacted military and government law-enforcement agencies?"

"Yes. Regular cops, too. No one did a thing."

"Did she say if she spoke with the Air Force OSI?" I asked.

"No. She just said she'd contacted the military authorities and the FBI, and they ignored her complaints."

I rubbed my face. General Mercer had said someone big was pulling the strings on this. Mercer was right.

Simon asked Janet if anyone from Global Aviation had threatened Colonel Wildman. When she said no, he asked if Wildman ever mentioned General Holland.

Janet shrugged. "Just that he was her boss and could be a pain in the ass."

"So she never said he'd threatened her or tried to coerce her in any way?"

"Not to me. In fact, the last time we spoke, it sounded as if she'd changed her opinion about him."

"What do you mean?"

"We were discussing her case and she brings up his name, saying she'd met with him earlier that day and that he might be willing to help her. Say, you okay?"

I was staring, stunned. But when I looked to Simon, he was sitting quietly. I said to Janet, "You're certain she was talking about General Marcus Holland?"

"My job is to listen, Marty," she said dryly. "You want to tell me why you're so interested in Holland?"

Simon gave me a single head shake.

"Sorry," I said, easing back into my seat.

"Janet," Simon said, "did Colonel Wildman mention if the car of the two men following her had a government license plate?"

"No clue," Janet said. "But I do know she'd copied down the license number and turned it over to the FBI, and nothing happened."

"She mentioned who she spoke with at the FBI?" Simon asked.

"I might have jotted the name in my notes," she said after a moment. "They're in my briefcase, in my car."

"Check. How about the name of her FAA contact?"

"She never told me his name."

Simon gave her a long look. "I'm curious if Colonel Wildman ever mentioned how these two men might have learned she was again looking into the G-626 accident?"

Janet paused, then said no. She seemed unsettled by his gaze.

"She had no idea?" Simon asked. "None at all?"

"No. I know she was trying to be extremely careful, not go through any official channels."

"And these men appeared when . . . roughly three weeks after she began her investigation?"

"About."

"That seems rather . . . quick."

"I guess. I really wouldn't know—"

He cut her off. "Who else knew she was conducting an investigation?"

I was getting annoyed with Simon. He was grilling her like she was a suspect now. Trying to keep her off balance. I knew what he was trying to do, but thought he was overplaying his hand.

Janet swallowed, flustered. "Look, all I know is she confided in me and . . . and that expert I mentioned. Now, maybe there were others . . ."

"Janet . . ." Simon shook his head. "Janet . . ."

"What?"

"The truth. I want the truth."

"I am telling—"

"Isn't it possible that during your research, you mentioned Colonel Wildman's investigation to someone?"

"No. I—" It hit her then what Simon was insinuating. You could see the anger build on her face. Her eyes turned glacial. Her mouth worked, but no sound came out.

Simon said, "Please understand I'm not accusing you—"

And then Janet exploded. "You *fuck*! You think *I* was the leak! You think I tipped someone off to what Margie was doing. You're disgusting, you know that? To think I actually thought I could help— Jesus, you...you *son of a bitch*!" She was so incensed she was shaking.

Simon seemed genuinely stunned by her tirade. "Now, Janet, if you would just calm—"

The crack sounded like a shot when Janet slapped him. Simon recoiled from both pain and surprise. He looked away, embarrassed.

Janet glared at him, her nostrils flaring. She was panting like a runner. She slowly lowered her hand almost in a daze. "You bastard," she croaked.

Simon huddled in his seat. He didn't seem to know what to do.

When Janet looked to me, I saw tears. "I didn't tell anyone. He thinks I did, but I didn't."

"I know."

"I...I was careful. I researched at night, after everyone had gone."

"I believe you."

She nodded, wiped her eyes with a finger, smearing her mascara. Then she calmly gathered her purse, opened her door and climbed out into the night.

We watched her walk away in silence. I kept waiting for Simon to go after her, to try and apologize.

But he just sat there, knees pressed together, fidgeting with his hands.

I glanced at Romero. He jerked his head to the door.

I nodded, clicked the latch, and got out. I shot Simon a glare and closed the door hard. After a couple of steps, I heard the soft whirring of the window motor. I looked back to see Simon gazing up at me. "You think I was too hard on her, I suppose?"

"Big time."

"You believe her, then?"

"For chrissakes, Simon. Why would she lie?"

A tight smile. "Ask her about the Dryke case. You remember it?"

It took me a sec. "Sure. The female lobbyist who was murdered—"

"Ask her, Martin. Let me know how she responds."

"What the hell for?"

But the window was already whirring up.

CHAPTER 24

Janet and I strolled along the sidewalk as the cars along Jefferson Davis raced past. From the Potomac Yards Mall, I guessed it was ten or twelve blocks back to the hotel. Normally, the walk wouldn't be a big deal except for the cold. With the windchill it was close to freezing. Janet's sweater offered little protection, and I could see she was shivering. I took off my jacket.

"I'm okay," she said.

"Take it," I said, draping the jacket over her shoulders. "I grew up in the cold." A white lie, but Virginia did have a winter. I wedged my pistol into my trouser pocket, since I didn't want to alarm any passing motorists.

She smiled her thanks. "Your wife must be a lucky woman."

She'd obviously noticed the wedding band I still wore. I didn't feel like explaining how Nicole had passed away. I glanced back, saw the limo maybe half a block behind, slowly following along the shoulder.

I said, "Maybe we should just get back in the car."

Her jaw muscles flexed. "Not a chance."

We reached an intersection with a flashing DON'T WALK

sign. As we waited, I asked, "So how long did you and Simon date?"

She glanced over in surprise. "He told you about us?"

I shook my head. "You know Simon."

"Yeah," she snapped. "Mr. fucking Privacy."

The light changed. A car rolled by and we crossed.

"We dated for almost a year," Janet said. "We met about three years ago, when I was still doing personality profiles. My editor wanted a story on him, right after he took over the homicide division. I mean, how many rich guys become cops, right? Anyway, Simon and I hit it off and started going out." She smiled to herself. "Actually, I had to ask him out, because I knew he'd never make the first move."

I recalled the article, but hadn't realized she'd written it. I told her I thought it was good.

She shrugged. "Simon didn't make it easy. Wouldn't give me much. I had to dig out his background myself. I was able to find out what he's done since he was eighteen, but before that everything's still pretty much a mystery. You know Simon never talks about his childhood or his parents. Even after dating him, I still don't know anything about his family. I'm not sure he even has one."

"Oh?"

She nodded, stepping onto the next sidewalk. "Romero's the closest thing to family Simon has. In a way, he acts kinda like Simon's father. He's originally from Cuba."

"Romero?"

"Uh-uh. Simon. You been to his house? No? Well, anyway, he's got a picture of this man in a military uniform in his study. Simon told me the guy was an uncle who'd been in the Cuban Army. I asked him about his father and you know what he said?"

I shook my head.

"He didn't have a father. Funny, huh? Not his father was dead, or took off or lives in Jersey. You know, like most people would say."

"How about Simon's money?" I asked. "Where does that come from?"

"All I know is he has a trust fund." She glanced over. "A big one. And he gives a lot of it away each year. Mostly to families. People in need. He sends their kids to college, pays for their housing. Stuff like that."

We strolled past a popular Irish pub. A small group of people were clustered outside, waiting to get in. Most were dressed to the nines, D.C.'s young and beautiful. Someone whistled at Janet, and she flashed him a smile without even thinking.

"That doesn't bother you," I said. "Men always coming on to you?"

She grinned. "Would I dress like this if it did?"

Stupid question. I asked, "So why did Simon become a cop?"

"I'm not sure. I think it's because of Romero. I think he must have been a cop. He's smart, that guy."

I nodded my agreement.

She went on, "I've never understood their relationship exactly. I mean how they ever got together in the first place. And I've asked, believe me. Neither of them will discuss it."

"Mind if I'm blunt?" I said. "Simon wants me to ask you something."

We walked a few steps. She said, "The Dryke case?"

"Yes."

She took a deep breath and pulled the jacket tight around her. I could tell she was wrestling with herself, trying to decide how to respond. I still had no idea why Simon wanted me to ask her about the case. I wondered if it had something to do with the fact that it was one of the few murders Simon had never solved, even though, technically, it hadn't been his case. Simon had been one of maybe a dozen local and federal cops who worked it as part of a task force.

Recalling the details wasn't difficult, because the case had been a headline-grabber locally. There had even been a fair amount of national interest from talking heads like Geraldo Rivera.

Thirty-something Patricia Dryke, a beautiful, high-powered Washington D.C. lobbyist, had been found beaten to death in her upscale apartment. Initially, the cops thought burglary was the motive because Dryke's jewelry collection, valued in the mid–six figures, was missing along with almost a grand in cash. What eventually threw a wrench into this theory was the apartment's extensive security system, which included a full-time security guard who checked everyone in and out, no exceptions. The possibility that an intruder could sneak in seemed unlikely if not impossible. Then there was the brutality of the beating, which suggested uncontrollable rage, as if the killer knew the victim. The papers mentioned a rich boyfriend and an ex-husband as possible suspects, but they were later cleared. Eventually the murder fizzled from the headlines without anyone ever being charged. I'd once asked Simon about the case, but he made it clear that he wouldn't discuss it.

When we reached another red light, Janet finally faced me.

"This is . . . hard for me. Part of the reason is . . . well, I like you, Marty."

The statement caught me off guard. I didn't know what to say. Janet was standing close to me, and I became aware again of how beautiful she was. Suddenly, I felt ashamed. Like what I was thinking . . . feeling . . . was somehow wrong.

"I hope you don't judge me too harshly, Marty."

I shook my head, forcing myself to look away. Finally, thankfully, the feelings faded.

When I gazed back, Janet was staring down the street. Abruptly, she said, "Simon found a witness who could identify the killer. A housekeeper who worked in the apartment building. With her testimony, Simon thought he might have enough to make an arrest. But before he could, the housekeeper recanted her statement. She told him she'd been mistaken and hadn't seen anyone on the day of the murder." She turned to me. "He . . . he blames me for that, her changing her story."

She'd lost me. "I don't understand."

"Simon thinks the killer got to the housekeeper, threatened her." Her voice seemed to crack slightly. "Do you know how the killer found out about her, that she'd seen him?"

I started to shake my head, then remembered. "Sure. It was in the paper. Something about a possible witness—"

And then the answer hit me. "Jesus. Don't tell me you're the one who—" I stopped. There was no point in going on. Never in a million years would Simon have leaked the name of a witness to the media.

But he might have told someone close to him, someone he trusted.

"Now you know," Janet said softly.

Without waiting for the light to change, she crossed the street.

"That's the whole story?" I demanded, catching up with her a few steps later.

"That's it." She wouldn't look at me.

"You actually took something Simon told you in confidence and put it on the front page?"

"For chrissakes, what do you want from me? I made a mistake. I mentioned it to one of the editors to give him a heads-up. He said he wouldn't use it until— Oh, what's the use. I shouldn't have done it. I was wrong. If I could take it back I would. But I can't."

Janet's stride quickened and I had to work to keep up. I took some solace in the fact that she wasn't trying to make excuses.

I asked, "Who did Simon say the housekeeper saw?"

"He never told me. He didn't trust me quite that much."

We went almost a minute saying nothing. I wasn't so much angry at her as disappointed. Simon also bore a lot of the responsibility for what had happened. He should have known better than to reveal confidential police information to a reporter.

Of course, I knew why he did it. Simon had obviously fallen hard for her.

I said, "I have to know. Is what you said tonight all true?"

Silence. Then: "You mean about the Dryke murder?"

"No. Colonel Wildman. The government's role. Was all of that true?"

"Yes."

"And you aren't helping us just to get a story?"

"Of course not."

"You're certain?"

Her jaw tightened. "Knock off the bullshit games, Marty. You're not going to believe me no matter what I say."

"The audiotape might help."

She hesitated, then stopped walking to dig through her bag. A moment later she thrust a small cassette into my hand. "Keep it. It's a copy."

I put the tape in my jacket pocket. "What about your files on Global Aviation, the ones you copied for Wildman?"

"In my office." A pause. "But I've also got a disk copy in my car."

"I'd like that tonight. And your notes."

I expected her to protest. Instead, she said, "Sure. Whatever."

"Now," I said, "do you have anything else we can use?"

"No."

"Is there anything you haven't told us?"

"No."

I kept staring at her.

She sighed. "Marty, give it a rest, huh? You're not good at playing the hardass cop."

She was right, I wasn't really. At least not with women. We began walking again. In the distance, I could make out the Marriott sign on the other side of the road. It still looked a long way away.

"So," she asked, "we still friends or what?"

"Depends," I said. "How well do you know Bobby Baker?"

"In college we all hung out. Bobby, Margie and I, with a few others. Over the years we've stayed in touch." She shrugged.

"And you came to the hotel tonight to talk to him about the murders?"

"Yeah. I wanted to see if Margie might have told him something. They were still pretty close even after the divorce."

"You still planning on questioning him?"

"Damn right."

"Simon won't like it."

"Fuck him."

"It could be dangerous. If someone sees you snooping around—"

"Save the speech, Marty. I'm not exactly stupid. I know what I'm getting into."

"Dammit, this is serious. You could get hurt. Or worse."

"Listen," she said, looking over, "you want to hear me say I'm scared. Fine. I'm scared silly. But I have to do this. So do me a favor and back the hell off."

That was clear enough. "You have a gun?" I asked.

She nodded, patting her purse.

"Know how to use it?"

She shot me a look of annoyance.

I knew Simon would probably be irritated over what I was going to propose. But the way I saw it, if Baker was hiding something, odds were he'd tell someone he knew before the cops. Besides, she was going to see him anyway.

I said, "Janet, I need a favor...."

After I explained, she shook her head angrily. "That's why Margie finally dumped him. The alcohol she could handle, even the the other women. But not the drugs. We really thought he was going to make it this time. *Christ*, how could he be so damned *stupid*?"

"Remember," I said, "anything you get from him comes straight to me. If I read something in the paper—"

A car horn behind us suddenly blared, and we turned to see the limo pulling alongside.

Simon waved anxiously out of the rear window. "Get in, something's come up. We have to get going."

"I'll walk," Janet said flatly. But she gazed at him expectantly, making no move to go. I realized what she was waiting for, but thought she was wasting her time.

"Janet, just get in. You've made your point." Simon sounded exasperated.

"Will you be nice?"

"I'll . . . try."

"Try?"

"Yes. All right. I'll behave. Now, please get in."

Not quite an apology, but close enough to satisfy Janet. She went toward the car, and I followed. As we drove off, I asked Simon what had come up.

"We located Douglas McInnes' hotel." He glanced to Janet as he spoke, making it clear he didn't want to elaborate in front of her.

I gave him a questioning look, trying to determine if McInnes was alive or dead.

But Simon just shrugged and gazed out the window.

CHAPTER 25

During the short ride to the Marriott, I mentioned to Simon that Janet had already turned over the audiotape and was going to give us her research files and notes. He seemed mildly surprised, but refrained from comment.

As we rolled up to the hotel entrance, Romero hopped out to open the door for Janet, an indication that he didn't share Simon's animosity toward her. I found this curious, because I'd never known them to disagree on anything.

As Janet climbed out, I asked Simon if McInnes was dead.

"Don't know. He's registered at the Westin in Rosslyn. I rang his room but didn't get an answer. We're going there now. You on your way back to the Pentagon?"

"Yeah."

"Before you go, I need you to do me a favor."

"What kind of favor?"

"A small one. It won't take long." And then he gave me a little smile.

I sighed. "Baker's car?"

He nodded. "I've arranged everything with Calvin."

Unlike Simon, I didn't like playing fast and loose with

the Fourth Amendment. "We don't know if Baker has left yet. If he comes out and sees me—"

"He's gone. Sergeant Perkins called. Linda and Baker are on their way home." Perkins was obviously one of the cops tailing Baker. I hadn't spotted them when we'd left, but that was the idea.

I tried to think of another excuse. Couldn't. "All right. Calvin has the keys?"

"Yes. And relax, Martin. He's assisted me before and knows what to do." That's how Simon skirted around the legalities of an unwarranted search, by having a third party who wasn't a cop do it.

"If the gun is there, you want me to take it?" This would be illegal without a warrant, but you never knew with Simon.

"I'm not concerned about the gun."

"You're not?" And then it occurred to me what he was looking for. "Shit. A disk. You think Baker's got a copy of Wildman's disk."

"Yes."

"Hell," I said. "That has to be it. That explains why he's so frightened."

"Odds are he wouldn't keep it in his car, but we need to be certain, Martin." Simon shook his head grimly. "Baker's playing a dangerous game. He's a fool."

"Dangerous?" I frowned. "You mean blackmail?"

"Of course. Why else wouldn't he have given us the disk?"

"Hey, guys," Janet called out, "I'm freezing my ass off. You two going to talk all night or what?"

Crawling out of the backseat, it dawned on me why Simon had assigned a team to follow Baker. And it wasn't just to keep him out of trouble. I had a sinking feeling, hoping Simon knew what he was doing. Because he was taking a major risk. If something went wrong . . .

"I have to get my keys from the valet," Janet said. "Say, you okay? You don't look so good."

"Hmm. Oh, I'm fine." And I gave her a smile to prove it.

As Janet drove away, she honked goodbye. I waved back, wedged the notebook she'd given me in my belt, then headed over to the valet stand where Calvin was waiting. I'd spoken to him earlier when he'd returned with Janet's car.

Calvin sprouted a gold-toothed grin when I walked up. "You ready?"

I nodded.

He jerked a thumb. "Meet me out back, by the Dumpsters."

"Huh?"

"Out back," he said again. "Unless you want someone to call the cops about me searching the car."

I went around back.

Simon was right; Calvin had done this kind of thing before.

From the time he'd pulled in between the two rows of Dumpsters and finished the search, he'd taken less than five minutes. And that included looking under the floor mats and popping out the backseat to see if anything had slipped in behind it.

He clicked off his flashlight, closed the trunk and came over to where I was standing a few feet away. "No computer disks. Found the gun jammed under the driver's seat. An automatic, and it's loaded. Here." He handed me a crumpled piece of paper.

Unfolding it, I could just make out a scrawl of numbers in the dim light. "What's this for?"

"What you think? The serial number off the piece. Man, you *sure* you're a cop?" He was grinning as he spoke.

"Anything else?" I asked, ignoring him.

"Nah. Just some books in the trunk. Damn, it's cold."

"What kind of books?"

He shrugged. "All I saw was the top one. Some shit about computers."

"Open up the trunk," I said, already walking over.

There were actually three books in a plastic Waldenbooks bag. Calvin held out his flashlight so I could read the titles. All were instructional manuals on building Web sites.

I shook my head, perplexed. The other stuff Baker had lied about I could understand. But why deny knowing computers? And more specifically, why an interest in Web sites?

"So you done?" Calvin said, checking his watch. "I got to be getting back or Jimmy's going to have my ass."

I nodded, returning the books to the bag.

Calvin winked at me as he shut the trunk lid. "Tell the lieutenant I done good, okay? Tell him next time I want Redskins tickets. Grew up here and never been to a game. And buddy, I'm a *fan*."

"I'll tell him," I said.

As he drove away, I took out Janet's business card. I was still bugged about the books, and Janet was the only person I could think of who might know whether Baker really was into computers.

"Hi, Janet here," her answering machine said in a breathy Mae West imitation. "Sorry I missed your call . . ."

So was I. I left a message at the beep and went over to Amanda's car.

Two minutes later, I was back on Jefferson Davis Highway, driving north. I called Amanda to tell her I was on the way. She answered, sounding agitated.

"I was just about to call you," she said. "I might have blown it, Marty."

"Blown what?"

"The interview with the secretary, Alma Carter. I spoke to her at her desk, which I didn't think was a big deal because I'd seen him leave. But I never thought about his wife. Dammit, I should have checked."

The light came on. "Jesus. Don't tell me..."

"Damn right. Holland's wife was in his office the whole time. When we got up to leave, Alma popped into Holland's office to drop off a note and practically laid an egg when she saw his wife at his desk. Lucille Holland never said a word to me, but I could tell by her face she overheard us. That means she knows we can put her hubby at Wildman's this afternoon. *Fuck.*"

"How can we— Holland *has* a Sable?"

"Not him. But Alma says his wife does. She's got some high-powered job with the Transportation Department. Alma said Holland's been driving it the last few days."

"And the color?"

"Tan."

I stopped at a red light, my body tingling.

"Marty?"

"Still here. What about his alibi?"

"Alma thought he was here, but she can't be certain. Holland told her this afternoon he wasn't to be disturbed, so she didn't. Not even for phone calls. His office has a second entrance to the hallway, so he could have slipped out and she'd never have known."

The light was green, and I stepped on the gas. "I'll be there in five minutes."

➤ I turned on the car radio to find something soothing. I had to think. I passed over two rap tunes and a country number, and settled for a Faith Hill love song. Sitting back, I tried to figure out my next move. Normally, with what I had on Holland now, I'd go in for the kill. Pressure him hard until he talked.

But the guy was an influential general officer, which was

why Amanda was so bothered. She knew Holland could throw up interference, make things difficult. If push came to shove, he could even have General Barlow crank up the heat for us to back off.

And there was a more specific problem.

Even though the Sable at Wildman's matched the description of the one belonging to Holland's wife, we still couldn't *prove* it was the same car. Not without the license number or a witness who had seen Holland in it.

In the end, we had a whole lotta suspicion but little else. Nuts.

I rolled to a stop along the curb by the Pentagon's River entrance, near where the limo had been parked earlier. No Amanda. I left the engine running as I swapped around to the passenger seat. A minute later, I finally saw Amanda emerge from the building, carrying a folder. I started to honk the horn, when I saw Holland and his wife follow her out.

They all came down the walkway together. I shook my head in amazement. Even from this distance, I could made out the friendly smiles on the Hollands' faces.

At that moment, my phone rang.

"I found Douglas McInnes," Simon said.

When I hung up, Amanda and the Hollands were standing at the end of the walkway, still conversing. General Holland handed Amanda something, flashed another smile, then took off with his wife toward the parking area reserved for Pentagon brass. Amanda glanced around, spotted me, and came over.

"Got the bios on Holland and Wildman," she said, tossing the folder in the back as she climbed in.

"Friends of yours," I said dryly.

She gave me a hard look. "Don't even go there, Marty." She handed me a business card. "General Holland wants to meet with us tomorrow. You're supposed to call him in the morning at home, set up a time."

"Oh?"

"To discuss the case. He said it's all a big misunderstanding. He says he can clear everything up. To me it's damned obvious what he's up to. He wants to see what we have on him. Christ, you should have seen him when they came up to me. All smiles. Trying to charm me. *Me.*" She grimaced, disgusted.

Holland and his wife stepped off the sidewalk near where a handful of cars were parked. Without me having to ask, Amanda immediately pulled ahead to keep him in sight.

"He's obviously reacting to what his wife overheard," I said. "Maybe he figures he has no choice but to come clean now."

"No way. Not that guy. He's up to something. By the way, Alma confirmed he's the one who had Wildman's computer removed from her old office."

No surprise there. Holland and his wife were getting into a car now, but I couldn't quite make it out because a couple of vehicles were in the way. Amanda made a quick left for an unobstructed view. I said, "Did you tell Alma whether or not we had the license number of the Sable?"

"Of course not."

"Then," I said, eyeing her, "for all he knows we have it. Connections or not, he's got to be sweating a little."

"C'mon, Marty. You think he'd admit to murder? Get real."

"There's still a chance he didn't do it. Maybe he was just ordered to cover things up."

She looked incredulous. *"He was there."*

"I know, but— They're leaving."

Twenty yards away, a tan Sable was backing out. The brake lights came on and we saw the plate clearly.

It was white.

After I jotted down the number, Amanda said, "He was there and he lied about it. The son of a bitch is in this thing up to his eyeballs." She shot me a look as if daring me to respond.

I just shrugged, watching as the Hollands drove off.

"So where we going now?" she asked.

"D.C. The Excelsior Towers apartments. It's near Embassy Row."

"Why?"

"Simon found Douglas McInnes," I said.

Her head swiveled around. "Alive?"

"Looks like it. Unless dead men go to parties."

CHAPTER 26

During the drive, I brought Amanda up to speed on my conversations with Bobby Baker and Janet Spence. I also told her about Simon's suspicions that Baker might be trying to use a copy of Wildman's disk for blackmail. I avoided mentioning Janet's comment that General Holland had apparently considered assisting Wildman, because I knew Amanda wouldn't believe it. Frankly, I wasn't sure I did either.

"Blackmail who?" Amanda asked, referring to Baker. "Global Aviation? Someone in the government?"

"Take your pick."

We were in northwest D.C. Even though it was almost eleven, the traffic was still heavy, but not quite bumper-to-bumper. Amanda took a right off Massachusetts Avenue toward the posh brownstones near Embassy Row.

"You know," she said, "maybe it's General Holland that Baker's going to blackmail. If it comes out that Holland covered up the G-626 problems, his career would be over."

I massaged the bridge of my nose as I considered this. "Sorry. I just can't buy that Holland would kill Wildman and her children simply to protect his career. Then there's the car. If Holland went to Wildman's house to kill her, why would he park it right out front where it could be identified?"

No argument. I took that as an admission I'd made a point. We turned down a tree-lined street. Ahead we could see the outline of a large apartment building.

Amanda tapped the brakes and flipped on the turn signal. Moments later we saw a granite sign for the Excelsior Towers. She said, "One thing you mentioned earlier confuses me. If Simon thinks Baker is in danger, why doesn't he put him in protective custody?"

"Think about it."

It took maybe a second before she caught on. *"My God,"* she murmured.

I nodded.

She turned to me, her stunned expression visible from the oncoming headlights. "Bait? He's using Baker as bait to draw the killers—"

"Look out!"

Amanda jammed on the brakes, throwing us both against the shoulder harnesses. A split second later, a sports car flew out of the apartment entrance, missing us by inches. I managed to catch the blurred face of the driver as he made a tire-squealing turn and roared off down the road.

Amanda swore viciously, threw up the finger. "You okay, Marty?"

"Yeah, fine." I was still watching the rapidly disappearing taillights. I faced front with a scowl.

"Amen to that," Amanda said, noticing. "Assholes like that shouldn't be behind a wheel."

"You happen to get a look at the driver?"

"I could tell it was a guy driving. Why?"

I shrugged. "I know someone who drives a black Corvette."

"Who?"

"Sergeant McNamara."

"Isn't he off the case?"

I nodded.

"Then why would he be here?"
I couldn't think of a reason.

We cruised up a long, crescent-shaped drive lined with flowers toward a majestic chrome-and-glass building fronted by a large fountain shaped like a waterfall. The expansive parking area was filled with BMWs and Mercedeses, with an occasional Volvo or Lexus tossed in. Amanda pulled into a spot reserved for guests, thirty yards past the glassed-in entrance. Two stretch limos sat across from us, one with the engine running.

"Guess no one here ever heard of buying American," she said, looking around. "What do you figure apartments here go for? Three, four grand a month?"

"At least." I checked out the limos. "Simon's not here yet."

"So whose party are we crashing, anyway?"

"Simon didn't say." I squinted, noticing one of the license plates. "Click on the overhead light," I said, digging out my notepad.

The light came on, and I started flipping pages. I stopped. "Interesting."

"What?"

"Remember I told you I saw Holland arguing with some guy at the Pentagon..."

"Yeah."

"That's his limo. The one with the engine running."

"Imagine that," Amanda said, opening her door.

Striding across the asphalt, we could hear heavy-metal music pulsating from the limo. Through the tinted windows, the vague outline of the driver was visible behind the wheel. I rapped sharply on the side window. A moment later, it slid down, revealing a square-jawed man in his twenties dressed in a dark suit. A diamond stud earring glinted in his left ear. Even though the guy was sitting, you could tell he was heavily muscled.

He frowned in annoyance. "The hell do you want, buddy?"

I held up my badge. "Police. We have a few questions. Could you please step outside?"

"I don't talk to fucking cops."

Amanda shoved her face close to his. "Listen, wise guy, you either talk to us here or at the station. It's up to you." She was bluffing since, without the D.C. police, we had no real authority here.

The man muttered under his breath and got out, leaning arrogantly against the door. He had me by three inches and a good fifty pounds. He puffed up, flexing his muscles, just in case we'd missed them. And as he did, I saw a faint outline in his suit under the armpit. Amanda must have noticed too, because she immediately stepped off to the side, her hand dropping to her waist.

"What's your name?" I asked casually.

"Jake."

"Jake what?"

"Just Jake."

"Did you drive to the Pentagon this evening, Just Jake?"

"I get it. You're a fucking riot, fella."

"I asked you a question."

A shrug. "I drive lots of places."

"Who did you drive there tonight?"

"You listening? Did I *say* I drove there?"

"Hey, shithead," Amanda snapped. "We're conducting a murder investigation."

"Yeah, yeah. My heart fucking bleeds." Jake pretended to pick lint from his suit.

"Fine," I said to him. "You want to be an asshole, no problem. Let's see the permit for the piece you're carrying."

"Sure. I'm legal." Jake dug out his wallet and produced a folded paper.

Amanda and I made a pretense of studying it under her

penlight. "You're in trouble, Jake," she said, shaking her head.

"The hell you mean?"

"It's a forgery," she said. "And *that's* a felony."

"The fuck you mean, forgery? I just got that renewed last month."

I said, "I'm afraid she's right, Jake. You're in big—"

Before I could react, Jake lunged forward to grab the permit. In a flash, Amanda did something to his fingers and he crumpled, screaming. Amanda stood over him, twisting what looked like his thumb and pinkie. "You going to behave, tough guy?"

Jake nodded, gasping, his face etched with pain.

"Will you talk to us?" she asked.

Another nod.

"Get his gun," Amanda said to me.

I reached around and removed it.

Amanda let go and Jake rolled over to a sitting position, grabbing his hand. In spite of the cold, his face was covered with perspiration. "Fuck," he wailed. "I think my thumb's broken. You fucking broke my thumb."

"I saw your car at the Pentagon tonight," I said. "Who was in the back?"

He glowered at me. For an instant, I thought he wasn't going to respond. "Mr. Tatum," he managed sullenly.

"And Tatum is . . ."

"Handles security for Mr. Caldwell."

Amanda and I exchanged glances.

"What did Tatum and General Holland argue about tonight?" I asked.

Jake hesitated. "I don't know. I had the center window up."

"I'll bet," Amanda said.

Jake stared at her with hate.

"Does Caldwell live in this building?" I asked.

"When he's in town."

I glanced to Amanda to see if she had anything.

"So why does a chauffeur carry a gun?" she asked.

"Part of my job. I work security for Mr. Tatum."

Amanda motioned me to hand over Jake's pistol. She emptied the rounds into her pocket, then dropped the gun and the permit beside him on the ground. She gave him a smile. "Our mistake, Jake. The permit's okay after all."

Jake began swearing, his face knotted in rage. He rose menacingly to his feet.

We casually walked away.

CHAPTER 27

As I approached the building entrance, I looked back and saw Jake balancing a cell phone on the hood, trying to punch in a number one-handed.

"He's telling on us," Amanda said.

"Yup."

She glanced to me, her face troubled. "What the hell is going on, Marty? The last place I figure to find McInnes is at a party in Caldwell's apartment."

I shook my head.

We went up the front steps. I stood under a TV camera mounted above the glass doors and pressed the button on the call box. In the black-marbled lobby, I could see a security guard sitting at a circular desk lined with television monitors. He sat up, focusing on a screen.

"Where'd you learn that little trick back there?" I asked Amanda. "The Academy?" The security guard turned, squinting at us. I tossed him a wave.

"Unh-unh," Amanda said. "Growing up, my mother got tired of my brothers always picking on me, so she enrolled me in martial arts classes." She grinned. "After I almost threw my older brother through a wall, they pretty much left me alone."

"I'll bet."

"Oh, one thing I forgot to mention. My guess is Baker has his own Web site."

I frowned.

"Those computer books you found, Marty. A lot of jocks have their own Web sites."

"May I help you?" the call box squawked.

Amanda and I had been sitting in the waiting area across from the guard's station for maybe five minutes when Simon walked in, his face tense. He nodded curtly to us and immediately went over to the guard, who was beaming at him like they were old friends.

As Amanda and I rose, we heard the guard say, "It's good to see you again, Lieutenant."

"You too, Lester," Simon said. "How's your son?"

"Good. Second year at Cornell. I can't tell you how much the wife and I appreciate your help. We could never have afforded to send him."

Simon's face went blank. "What help?"

"C'mon, Lieutenant. The registrar told us it was you." Lester popped Simon lightly on the shoulder.

Simon shifted his weight, his face reddening. He seemed relieved when Amanda and I strolled up. I glanced out the door, expecting to see Romero, but all I saw was a police black-and-white, a uniformed cop standing beside it smoking a cigarette. And beyond him, an empty space where Jake's limo had been.

"Where's Romero?" I asked.

"Running an errand." To the guard, Simon said, "Mr. Caldwell still has the penthouse, Lester?"

Lester nodded. "He's got a big party going tonight. Lots of important people. Political types. Kinda surprises me that Mr. Caldwell is up to it. He's not doing so good, you know. His heart's pretty bad."

Simon nodded as if he understood.

"You want me to announce you, Lieutenant?" Lester said, picking up a phone.

"Don't bother. When did Caldwell arrive in town?"

"Yesterday around two."

Amanda leaned over and whispered in my ear. I shook my head. I had no idea how Simon could know Caldwell.

But before we could ask, Simon walked over to the elevators. He looked anxious again. He impatiently pushed the button, then took out his cell phone. He glanced to us. "You two coming or not?"

➤ The elevator doors opened. As we stepped inside, Simon was saying angrily into the phone, "I don't care about the staffing problem, Harland. I want two men immediately assigned to watch Ms. Spence. That's right. Janet Spence, the reporter. Around the clock. Fine. Patch me in to the chief. Yes, I know what time it is. I'll wait."

As I pushed the button for the penthouse on the twelfth floor, Simon gave me a look of exasperation.

"Good move," Amanda commented as the elevator began to rise.

And it was. With what Janet Spence knew, she was a possible target for the killers. But I suspected that ensuring the safety of a possible witness wasn't Simon's only motivation for assigning Janet protection. To me, it was obvious he still cared for her, even though he'd never admit—

"Chief?" Simon said. "Simon. The *Post* reporter Ms. Janet Spence's house was ransacked tonight. I think it might be linked to the Wildman killings. Ms. Spence was an acquaintance of Colonel Wildman and— All right. I'll fax you a report in the morning. About the men I need for the detail— Thank you. Sorry to wake you, sir." Simon waited. "You get that, Harland? Okay. Tell the officers that Romero should be with Ms. Spence when they arrive. He'll probably remain there overnight. Right. Good night."

"Jesus," Amanda said as he put his phone away.

"Janet okay?" I asked him.

"She's fine," Simon said. "Her apartment was pretty well destroyed. As with Colonel Wildman, the intruders wiped out the memory on her computer and removed all her disks." He grimaced, shaking his head. "I blame myself. I should have seen something like this. But I let my personal feelings cloud my judgment. And that was a *mistake*." He fell silent, staring at the floor.

Looking at him, I could tell he was really shaken. He was thinking about what might have happened to Janet if she'd been home during the break-in.

Amanda watched him with a sympathetic expression. During the drive, I'd told her about Janet's history with Simon.

I gave a little cough. When Simon glanced up, I said, "This ups the ante. It's almost certain the killers will go after Baker now. Maybe tonight. He's the only one left."

Simon nodded.

"Maybe you should just take him in now. Just to be safe. Dammit, Simon, why not?"

Simon was shaking his head emphatically. "*Time,* Martin. We don't have time to wait until Baker decides to talk. We need to solve this case quickly. My guess is we've got a day, two at the most."

"Huh?" Amanda said.

I said dryly, "Isn't that kind of a stretch? How can you—"

"Is it, Martin?" Simon said. "You've seen the signs. You've already experienced the pressure, the interference. That's the first step. And once we begin to get close to the truth, there will be more phone calls. More pressure will be applied." His voice was rising, becoming bitter, almost incensed. "I've been through this before. He thinks just because he has power, the influence, he can do as he pleases. Well, he's mistaken."

The elevator lurched slightly and a chime sounded. The doors began to open.

I stared at Simon, bewildered by his tirade. I heard Amanda ask, "Who the hell are you talking about?"

"Global's CEO, Charles Caldwell," Simon snapped. "The man who may very well have had Colonel Wildman murdered." And then he stepped out angrily into a carpeted hallway.

"Hello, Simon," a man called out.

I blinked, startled. Then I recognized him.

CHAPTER 28

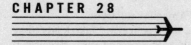

The man stood by a set of mahogany doors in the middle of the hallway, grinning broadly. He gave a little wave. I had the feeling he'd been expecting us.

"That's the guy from the limo at the Pentagon," I murmured, as we continued toward him. "The one who spoke with Holland."

"Long time no see, Simon," the man said as we walked up. He smiled pleasantly at Amanda and me.

"Hello, Tatum," Simon said.

"Hey," Tatum said, pleased. "The big detective remembered me. I feel honored."

Amanda and I shook Tatum's hand as Simon made the introductions. Through the doors, we could hear the faint sounds of violins and the low buzz of voices. Simon said, "Tatum handles security for Mr. Caldwell. He used to be in law enforcement. FBI."

Tatum was a little older than I'd first thought outside the Pentagon. I put him closer to fifty, medium height and build. He was deeply tanned, perfectly groomed, and wore a tailored silk suit that probably cost as much as I made in a month. Add in another couple months' salary for the diamond pinky ring and the gold Rolex.

"Spent twelve years in the Bureau before I finally got smart," Tatum said, focusing on Amanda and me. He smiled easily at us through capped teeth. "I understand you already met Jake."

"You could say that," Amanda said dryly.

Tatum shook his head apologetically. "Jake tends to be excitable. I hope he didn't do anything rash. Because if you have a complaint—"

"It's not a problem," I said. "It was just a minor misunderstanding."

Amanda nodded along.

"What's *this*?" Simon asked, frowning at me.

"I'll explain later," I said.

"So what can I do for you, Simon?" Tatum was smiling again. He seemed to smile a lot. Maybe he liked to show off his teeth.

"We'd like to speak with one of your guests. Mr. Douglas McInnes."

For an instant, surprise flickered across his eyes, but his smile never wavered. "McInnes. No. Doesn't ring a bell."

"He's an employee of Mr. Caldwell's," Simon said. "He works for Global Aviation."

"Hmm, no. I suppose I could check—"

"Please."

"Okay, if you'll just wait here—"

"We'd rather wait inside," Simon said.

Tatum shook his head. "Any other time, it wouldn't be a problem. Tonight, Mr. Caldwell's got a little get-together going. There are important guests. *Influential* guests. And if they realize the police are here—well, I'm sure you understand."

"We'll be discreet."

Tatum sighed unhappily. "No can do, Simon. Unless you got a warrant."

Simon shook his head.

"Sorry."

Simon obediently stepped back. As Tatum turned to

open one of the doors, Simon took out his phone and punched the redial. He spoke rapidly. "Harland, Simon. Get me Judge Lee. I'll need a warrant."

Tatum was halfway through the door. He spun around. "Cut the shit, Simon. You know I can't let you in. Caldwell will have my ass—"

Simon said into the phone, "And I'll need at least two squad cars responding—"

Tatum swore. "*Okay*. You win. You can come in. Just hang the hell up, huh."

"Never mind, Harland," Simon said.

Tatum glowered at Simon. "Mr. Caldwell isn't going to like this."

Simon shrugged, and we followed Tatum into the party.

We stood in the entryway next to an enormous tropical-fish tank built into the wall, peering into the most luxurious apartment I'd ever seen. Directly in front was an ash-white living room that seemed to go on forever, with two sitting areas near the middle and a large buffet table laden with hors d'oeuvres to the left. The decor could only be described as Asian Modern. Oriental pen-and-ink drawings in silver bamboo frames covered the walls, oddly complementing the severe, black leather furnishings and checkerboard flooring. The music was provided by two stunningly attractive women in sheer black evening gowns, who strolled through the apartment playing violins. Over to the right, past a bar that had been set up next to a grand piano, was an enormous plate-glass window that looked out onto a brightly lit patio.

But what really caught my eye was the crowd. Tatum had been right about the guests: they were political heavy-hitters. At least the ones I recognized.

The red-faced fat man hitting on the giggling, twenty-something girl in a short, sequined dress was Congressman Trenton, a prominent member of the House. Richard Matson, the White House Press Secretary, was hanging out by the bar, engrossed in conversation with Senator Mark Slater, a former actor and now a presidential hopeful. Going around the room, I spotted two more senators, a former and current cabinet member, the UN ambassador, and a handful of congressmen. It wasn't quite a who's-who of American politics, but it was close. To me, their presence here was unsettling as hell.

"Damn," Amanda whispered as if she could read my mind. "No wonder Caldwell's been able to cover up the G-626 problems."

I nodded, finally grasping Simon's concern over Caldwell. He was right. The man had power.

"Wait here," Tatum told us. He left, quickly negotiating his way through the crowd toward an elderly, reed-thin man in the sitting area. Tatum spoke into his ear, pointing back to us.

"Caldwell?" Amanda said.

"Yes," Simon said.

Caldwell glared at us from beneath a mane of silver hair. He said something and Tatum helped him to his feet, handing him a cane. They slowly made their way toward a hallway at the back.

Amanda poked me lightly in the ribs. "The patio," she said.

I looked. Two men smoking cigarettes. One I knew.

"Who are they?" Simon asked.

"The bald guy is Hank Clayton, the Undersecretary of Defense for Acquisition," I said quietly. And I wondered if Clayton was the person who'd been pressuring the Air Force chief General Barlow on Holland's behalf. Or maybe it was the Secretary of Defense himself.

A minute went by and we kept standing there, waiting. I gradually began to feel awkward, like a new kid in school who doesn't fit in. Every now and then, someone would glance toward us, then quickly look away with disinterest. The message was clear. We were nobodies, and therefore didn't matter.

A thirtyish woman in a red business suit and a graying man in a tan blazer cruised by, carrying drinks. The man was saying, "Quit worrying, Edna. You can tell Caldwell the hearings are in the bag. I've spoken with Congressman Kelly and he's going to play ball. Grunwald and Steiner have also signed on."

They stopped to look at the fish tank. "What about Marcelli?" Edna said. "He's the problem. He's the one pursuing this—"

"Will you relax, Edna? Marcelli's a fucking freshman. He gets out of line, Trenton will have his nuts for lunch. That's the chairman's *job*."

Edna quietly gazed into the fish tank. "We have to be certain, John. Mr. Caldwell would like a copy of the questions in advance—"

"You kidding? It's a congressional hearing, not a movie script."

"Surely there must be some talking points—"

"It's a *hearing*."

Edna sighed unhappily. "I'm going to trust you on this, John. But I'm holding you personally responsible if anything—"

John blinked. "You threatening me?"

"No, John. I—"

" 'Cause you better not be threatening me, Edna. Your company's the fucking reason we're in this mess."

"Easy, John."

"Screw easy. You should be damn grateful we're covering for you. Damn grateful." He shot her a malevolent glare, then killed his drink in two swallows.

Edna said apologetically, "I'm sorry, John. It's just that so much is riding on this."

"Yeah, yeah. The fucking merger. Well, your boss is going to have to suck it up on that one, because—"

Edna touched his shoulder. "Looks like your boss wants you, John."

John glanced over to Congressman Trenton, who now had his arm around the girl and was waving in their direction. Trenton was swaying and appeared completely wasted. He must have said something funny, because the girl began giggling uncontrollably.

John grimaced. "Looks like lover-boy's found a new girlfriend."

"He's disgusting," Edna said.

John yawned. "Tell me something I don't know. Just remember, he's covering your ass. Call you tomorrow." And he walked away.

Edna stared at the fish tank for a few more moments. I watched her, my heart racing. Another piece of the puzzle had just fallen into place.

Edna suddenly gazed around and caught me looking. "Hello," I said.

She looked flustered. She seemed on the verge of saying something but instead tossed back a tight smile and hurriedly left.

As I watched her go, I heard Amanda say, "You guys thinking what I'm thinking?"

I nodded. "Anyone know what committee Congressman Trenton chairs?"

"The transportation and infrastructure committee," Simon said.

And transportation meant airlines.

"That's it, then," I said. "If we can establish that Wildman knew about an upcoming congressional hearing about the airlines and was going to present evidence..."

"She knew, Marty," Simon said with a trace of sadness. "And in a way, that makes her something of a fool."

"Isn't that a bit harsh?" Amanda said.

"Maybe. But if she'd survived, do you think Congressman Trenton would have allowed her testimony?"

Amanda hesitated, then shook her head. "So why kill her?"

Simon shrugged. "Alive, she would always pose a risk. Killing her insured—"

"Heads up," I interrupted. "Tatum's coming back."

 Tatum led us into a spacious paneled den filled with books. Caldwell was seated behind a desk the size of a pool table and scowling at us. He was shockingly thin, with pasty white skin that hung in loose folds from his gaunt face. He wheezed as if every breath took effort. A large oxygen canister on wheels had been placed beside him. Lester had said Caldwell was not a well man. Lester had been right.

"Get out, Tatum," Caldwell ordered.

Tatum hesitated. "Mr. Caldwell, I'm not sure—"

"I said get *out*!"

Tatum did, drawing the door closed behind him.

Caldwell considered Simon for a moment. "You disappoint me, Simon. I thought we had an understanding."

Simon said nothing.

"Tatum said you want to talk to my company's chief design engineer. Why?"

"We think Mr. McInnes knew the victim of a homicide we're working."

"And the victim's name is..."

Simon looked right at him. "Colonel Margaret Wildman." He paused. "And her two children."

With someone accustomed to operating under pressure like Caldwell, I didn't expect to see a reaction. But I did. You had to look close to catch it, but there it was, a flicker of surprise. And then it was gone, replaced by a look of indifference.

"Why would Douglas know a military officer?" Caldwell asked.

"She was investigating the airworthiness of the G-626," Simon said. "Apparently she was convinced it was... unreliable."

Amanda and I immediately looked at Simon, shocked he'd come right out and said it. Then I realized it really didn't matter. Caldwell would already know this.

Caldwell slowly sat back, tenting his bony fingers. "And you think she contacted McInnes..."

"Yes."

"... to gain detrimental information on the G-626."

Simon nodded.

Caldwell's voice rose angrily. "Preposterous. Absolutely ridiculous. There's nothing wrong with the G-626. Douglas certainly wouldn't have cooperated with this colonel on matters concerning—" He stopped, grimacing. He buckled, grabbing his chest.

Simon hesitated, then stepped forward. "Are you all right?"

Caldwell nodded feebly, waving him back. He reached for the oxygen mask attached to the canister. He placed it over his nose and mouth and took deep breaths. We just stood there, listening to him wheeze. I felt helpless, wondering what we were going to do if he suddenly croaked. I could just see the headlines: Billionaire Dies While Being Questioned by Police.

Then it occurred to me that maybe this was all an act. That Caldwell was just doing this so we would—

Caldwell's eyes opened. He lay slumped against the chair, staring at us. He seemed to be breathing easier. He lowered the mask from his face. "It will pass in a minute."

"We'll question McInnes later at his hotel," Simon said, turning to go.

"No," Caldwell said. "You'll do it now. He'll confirm there's nothing wrong with the G-626."

Simon seemed taken aback. "All right."

"I want you to understand I don't have to do this," Caldwell said, eyeing him.

Simon nodded.

"All it would take is a phone call . . ."

Another nod.

". . . and I could prevent you from talking to McInnes."

Simon was silent, his face a mask. He and Caldwell just stood there, staring at each other. You could feel the tension between them. I was mystified about why Simon was letting Caldwell push him around. Regardless of the man's influence, we were cops doing our job.

"After this," Caldwell finally went on, "I don't want to see you again, Simon. If I do . . ." He left the statement hanging, but the message came in loud and clear. It was a threat. I was outraged by the arrogance.

But Simon just said quietly, "Agreed. But on one condition. We talk to McInnes alone. No interference."

A thin smile. "Of course. I wouldn't have it any other way, Simon." Then he sat up and pressed the intercom on his desk. "Tatum, get McInnes..."

As Caldwell relayed his instructions, I was watching Simon. He suddenly looked worried.

CHAPTER 29

Douglas McInnes' appearance didn't fit the stereotype for an engineer. He was a tall, athletic-looking man in his late fifties, with chiseled features and a mass of unruly blond hair. He seemed surprised when Caldwell and Tatum left the room.

We all sat in the chairs in front of Caldwell's desk.

"So," McInnes said, "what's this all about?" He was perched on the edge of his chair, knees pressed together, back straight. He fidgeted nervously with his hands.

Simon asked, "Do you know Colonel Margaret Wildman?"

McInnes frowned like he was thinking. "Sure. I remember now. She called me a while back, with this crazy idea that the G-626 was unsafe. Wanted my help to prove it. I said I couldn't. You know, because there's nothing wrong with the airplane. Nothing at all." As he spoke, his eyes shuttled constantly between Amanda, Simon and me.

I shook my head. Now I knew why Simon had been worried.

Simon leaned close. "You can tell us the truth. We can protect you."

"I *am* telling you the truth. I only spoke to her that one

time. I told her she was wasting her time, that there was nothing wrong with the plane."

"And your e-mail?" Simon said, nodding to me.

"E-mail?" McInnes said.

"This," I said, placing a copy before him.

McInnes read for maybe three seconds, then glanced up, clearly rattled. "I never saw this before."

"C'mon," Amanda said. "It was sent from your e-mail address."

McInnes licked his lips. "It's a forgery. Or maybe some kind of joke. That's it, someone's playing—"

"She was murdered today," Simon said.

"Huh?"

"Colonel Wildman. She was murdered today along with her two children."

McInnes turned pale. He began to tremble. *"My God."* And then he lost it, covering his head in his hands. "I warned her. I tried. She…she wouldn't listen…just wouldn't listen…she kept pushing…"

"The truth," Simon said sharply. "I want the truth."

McInnes slowly raised his head. He looked miserable. "I can't."

He was pissing me off. "Dammit," I said. "We need your help."

"I *can't*." McInnes jumped to his feet. "You don't understand. I would if I could, but I…" He tried to swallow and coughed.

"I will protect you," Simon said. "I give you my word."

McInnes hesitated, then reached into his jacket to remove something. And when he did, he turned toward Simon so I couldn't see what it was. He stepped forward, handing him the object.

"What about them?" he asked, his voice cracking. "Can you protect them?"

Simon was silent for a few seconds. "I can't guarantee anything—"

He never got to finish, because McInnes pivoted, flung open the door and walked out.

Simon slowly shook his head. I could now see he was holding a photograph. Even though I knew what the image contained, I leaned over for a look.

My stomach knotted. The picture showed two young boys playing on a swing set, taken from a distance.

No one spoke. Somewhere, a clock chimed midnight.

Finally, Amanda said, "Guess you can't blame the guy."

"No." Simon tucked the picture away.

"Now what do we do?" I asked.

There was only silence.

Tatum appeared moments later to walk us out. He seemed upbeat again, almost jovial. At the front door, he said, "Sorry it didn't work out, guys. But hey, no hard feelings. You got any more questions, give me a call." He cheerfully handed us business cards.

"Tatum Security Associates," Amanda said dryly. "Catchy name."

"Yeah. Thought of it myself." He gave Amanda a big smile. "You know, I could always use a good-looking female operative. You should think about it."

Amanda rolled her eyes.

"Hey," Tatum said, defensively. "The pay's damn good. You could do a lot worse."

"Good night, Tatum," Simon said firmly.

As we started down the hallway, Simon looked back. "Oh, Tatum, I forgot to mention something to Mr. Caldwell..."

"Sure..."

"Tell him I know about the merger."

Tatum's eyes widened. "How the hell did you—" His mouth snapped shut. He realized he'd just been suckered.

"I didn't until now," Simon said with a smile.

Tatum's face reddened. He took a couple of steps forward.

But by then we were already going toward the elevator.

"You think that's why Wildman was killed?" I said to

Simon. "Because she was jeopardizing some billion-dollar merger deal?"

"I don't know," Simon said. "The timing is suggestive."

"I still don't see it," Amanda murmured.

I glanced over. "See what?"

"Caldwell looks guilty as hell, right?"

I said, "Sure—"

"Then what's his motive? Money?"

"Of course it's money," I said.

"But that's just what bothers me. Since when does a rich guy with one foot in the grave care about making money he'll never see?"

We reached the elevator. Simon and I stared at her.

"Yeah," she said. "Makes you think."

She pressed the DOWN button.

➤➤➤ "The asshole's still watching us," Amanda said.
       I turned to see Tatum by the apartment door, glowering at us as we waited for the elevator.

"He doesn't seem all that bright," Amanda said. "Makes me wonder how he runs his own security company."

"You're underestimating him," Simon said curtly. "Don't. Tatum's very good at what he does. He's one of the highest-paid private security operatives in the world."

Amanda gave him a dubious look.

"It's true. Tatum's niche, his forte, is his willingness to perform services others won't." He eyed her. "Very *expensive* services."

Amanda blinked at the implication. "You mean *murder*?"

"I don't have any proof, but there have been rumors to that effect. I do know he's been arrested twice on charges of extortion—"

I swore. I'd been looking at Tatum when something clicked. I grabbed Simon by the arm, saying, "Son of a bitch. Janet Spence. Her description of the men following Colonel Wildman. Dammit, you *knew* all along."

"Knew what?" Amanda said.

"I suspected," Simon corrected.

"Suspected, hell," I said, letting him go. "It matches. It has to be him."

"Probably," Simon said.

"Hey, guys," Amanda said, "someone want to tell me what you're talking about?"

The elevator chimed. As we went inside, I found myself confronted by two annoyed blue eyes.

I told her then.

➤ "So Tatum was probably one," Amanda said as we walked out into the lobby. "Who was the second guy?"

"Ask the Shell Answer Man here," I snapped, still ticked off with Simon. "He probably knows."

Simon sighed. "I have my suspicions, but...at this point, it's really just a guess."

I said, "Dammit, Simon—"

"Leaving, Lieutenant?"

We turned to see Lester appearing from a door at the back, carrying a flashlight and a large key ring.

"Excuse me, Martin. I should say goodbye." Simon walked over to Lester, who was smiling at him.

"Man, sometimes he really gets under my skin," Amanda said, watching him go.

I nodded.

"He always act like this? Plays everything close to the vest? What a jerk."

I sighed. "That's just the way he is. He has this aversion to being wrong. So unless he's one hundred percent certain—"

"And what's with his history with Caldwell? They obviously had some kind of run-in before."

"No clue. What?" Amanda had tapped me on the arm and was pointing outside.

"Now, *that's* interesting," she said.

Standing by a silver Lincoln parked a few spaces over from Amanda's Camaro were John and the young girl from upstairs, talking with the cop who'd come with Simon. The girl was disheveled, and even though she wore a fur coat, you could see a strap from her evening gown dangling in front, broken. She kept dabbing at her eyes with a tissue and was clearly upset. And to her left, sitting sideways in the Lincoln's rear seat with the door open, was Trenton, his head resting awkwardly against the front headrest. Moments later, John started gesturing angrily at the cop.

"You know," Amanda said, "we might have just gotten lucky."

"What do you mean?"

"Just thinking maybe we can convince John to tell us about that merger deal."

"Okay . . ."

"Cop cars have cameras, right?"

"Yeah. Both regular and video."

"Even better. Hey, Simon!" She hurried over to him.

CHAPTER 30

Amanda went over to the patrol car while Simon and I joined the ongoing confrontation between the cop and Congressman Trenton's aide, John. "What seems to be the problem, Officer Richards?" Simon asked the cop.

Richards, clearly flustered, said, "Lieutenant, this gentleman—"

"There's no fucking problem here," John snarled, coming forward. He glared at the girl. "Except she's a goddamn liar."

"He tore my dress," the girl said shrilly, pointing at Trenton. "He touched my *breast*."

"She's drunk," John said. "She doesn't know what she's saying."

"*Look.*" The girl held up the broken strap of her gown.

"Is this true, Congressman?" Simon asked, stepping toward Trenton.

Trenton slowly sat up in the backseat of the Lincoln. His hair was mussed and there was a red blotch on his cheek. He squinted like he was trying to focus. Before he could say anything, John stepped around to block Simon's path. "Of course it's not true. She's making this up. Trying to embarrass the congressman."

"Get out of my way," Simon told him. To the girl, he asked, "Did you slap the congressman, miss?"

Her head bobbed. "But I had to. He...he wouldn't let me *go*."

"There," John said. "She's admitting to assault. And I was a witness. I want her arrested for assault." He had stepped back a few paces, but was still in Simon's way.

Simon shot him a look of annoyance. "I told you to—"

"I'm a lawyer," John said. "The congressman doesn't have to say anything. He *won't* say anything. It's clear that this woman is trying to extort—" Suddenly a bright light struck him in the face. He blinked, momentarily blinded. "The hell?" Then his eyes widened in alarm. "Hey, who is she? *What the fuck is she doing here?*"

Amanda had appeared off my shoulder and was focusing a video camera on Congressman Trenton.

John swore, trying to reach for her. Amanda nimbly danced away, all the while throwing out questions like, "Congressman, did you molest this young woman tonight? Did you grab her by the breast? Did you tear her..."

"Stop her!" John threw himself in front of Trenton, trying to close the door. "Goddammit, *stop her!*"

But Amanda ran around to the other door and continued videotaping Trenton through the window. Then she jogged over to the girl and began interviewing her.

John was incredulous. He kept screaming for Simon to do something. Finally, Simon said, "All right, that should be enough, Amanda."

Amanda grinned, clicking off the light.

"Hey, what the hell is this?" John said, suddenly suspicious.

"Let me put the camera away," Amanda called out. She ran over to the patrol car.

John blinked at Simon, uncertainty in his eyes. "Son of a bitch. This was a setup. You fucking set us up."

"Relax," Simon said. "We'll gladly turn over the tape and you can be on your way."

"Huh?"

"We'd just like to ask some questions."

"I told you the congressman won't—"

"Not him. You."

John squinted. "What kind of questions?"

"Easy questions. And we forget what's happened here."
He gave John a reassuring smile.

"Hey," the girl wailed. "What about me? What about my
dress? It's ruined. It cost a thousand dollars. Someone's
got to pay."

"Martin..." Simon drew me aside and handed me a wad
of bills. As I took them over to the girl, I saw Simon leading John away. John was shaking his head, saying, "Not a
chance. No fucking way..." Amanda ran up to them, carrying a videotape.

"Fuck!" Congressman Trenton suddenly slurred. "What
a goddamn night, huh?" He gave me a bleary-eyed look,
belched loudly, then curled up on the backseat.

I sighed, glancing at the cop. He shook his head, grinning.

The girl settled for two thousand dollars, two tickets to a
Kennedy Center gala, and a cab ride.

I thought that was pretty cheap, considering.

The girl left first, followed by John and Congressman Trenton, who was snoring loudly as they
drove off. I watched the taillights disappear, then checked
my watch. Almost twelve-twenty, which meant I wouldn't
get home until around one-thirty. But I still had it easier
than Simon, who had to stop by the morgue to check the
autopsy results, then swing by Wildman's house to see if
everything there was wrapped up.

After Simon called for a patrol car to drive me home, he
walked with us to Amanda's car to pick up Wildman's laptop computer so the lab boys could look it over. I said, "A
merger between Boeing and Global, huh?"

"Yes," Simon said. "Boeing has been trying to acquire
Global for a number of years, but Caldwell resisted. John

explained that it was a power issue on Caldwell's part, that he didn't want to relinquish control of the company his father had started. But now he's being forced to sell by the shareholders."

"So Caldwell doesn't own a controlling interest in Global?" For some reason that surprised me.

"We didn't get into any specifics, but obviously not," Amanda said.

I said, "And the problems with the G-626..."

"Nothing," Amanda said. "John got real anxious when we mentioned the plane. Clammed up and wouldn't give us anything more. Wouldn't even confirm whether there were going to be any hearings. I'll check with LL. They should be able to tell us."

LL stood for the Office of Legislative Liaison, the Pentagon's conduit to Capitol Hill. I said to her, "You know, this sale of Global supports what you said earlier. About Caldwell's motive. I mean, why would the guy care about a company that was being taken away from him?"

We reached Amanda's car. Simon slumped against the side as Amanda reached into the backseat and passed him Wildman's computer. He said, "Caldwell's motive has to be the money, Martin. He would lose millions if it came out that Global was producing unsafe aircraft. And we're not just talking about the merger falling through. Something like this could destroy his entire company."

Amanda started to respond, but shrugged instead. She looked beat. We all did.

But there was one point I had to clear up. I gave Simon a long look. "Tell us about you and Caldwell."

No response.

I said, "Simon..."

He sighed, looking off into the night. "It's a long, complicated story, Martin. We're all tired. Let's discuss this tomorrow."

I'd been down this road before. Tomorrow could be a week or a month or never. "Fine. Then I quit."

Simon looked at me in shock. So did Amanda.

"I'm serious," I said. "If you're not going to trust us enough to confide in us, I don't see any point in continuing." I folded my arms, waiting for him to respond.

But Simon just kept looking at me as if he didn't really understand.

Christ. "See you around." As I turned to leave, I felt his hand on my shoulder.

"I didn't realize you felt so strongly about this," he said.

"I do."

"All right," he said. "But not tonight. Drop by the house in the morning around nine. I'll explain everything then."

I hesitated, glancing to Amanda. She nodded. "Okay," I said.

Simon's expression turned somber. "I want you to know the reason I haven't confided in you has nothing to do with trust. It's something completely different, something... personal."

"Personal how?"

But he just patted me on the back and walked away.

CHAPTER 31

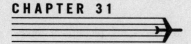

Amanda and I watched as Simon got into the patrol car and drove away. "What the hell was that all about?" she asked.

I shook my head.

"He's one strange dude, that guy." She yawned and massaged her eyes. "So when do you want to interview General Holland?"

"After we meet with Simon. I'll set something up for late morning."

She nodded, opening her car door. She glanced back. "Where do you live, anyway?" When I told her, she said, "I should have mentioned something earlier. That's only fifteen minutes from me. Hop in. I'll give you a ride."

I hesitated. "It's still out of your way. . . ."

"So who needs sleep? Besides, who knows how long until your ride gets here? Now get in before I change my mind."

I smiled my thanks. As I started around to the passenger door, I saw her lift up her jacket to remove a videocassette wedged into her belt.

"Amanda, don't tell me that's . . ."

"The original. I gave Johnny-boy a blank one. Figured Trenton's constituents and his wife might get a kick out of this." She grinned. "Any bets on Congressman Dirtbag's reelection chances now?"

After I called to cancel my pickup—a three-minute hassle because no one seemed to know what I was talking about—Amanda began questioning me about Simon: how long we'd known each other, what I knew about him, the cases we'd worked. I think she was trying to figure out his last comment.

I told her what I knew, and afterward she became quiet, reflective. She asked me if I believed there was such a thing as justice. I knew where she was going. I told her I still believed in the concept of justice, if not the reality.

"Not me," she said. "If you're rich and powerful, laws don't mean a damn thing. Look at O.J., look at Ted Kennedy at Chappaquiddick, look at the JonBenet Ramsey case. The list is endless. In this country, where there's supposed to be justice for all, the ugly truth is that the rich aren't held accountable." She shook her head. "And I got to tell you, Marty, that's depressing as hell."

"So what are you saying? That cops should just give up? Walk away if a wealthy person commits a crime?"

"Of course not. It just . . . Hell, you were there tonight. You saw the people at Caldwell's place. You think we're going to solve this thing? You think we'll be *allowed* to solve this thing?"

I shrugged, staring out into the night. I thought she was overreacting, letting tonight's events jade her. "I don't know. Maybe."

She snorted. "Okay, let's just say we somehow manage to charge Caldwell. You think he'll ever get convicted? Uh-uh. No way. He'll get a team of high-priced attorneys and the next thing you'll know, it'll be the cops on trial. Or maybe they'll go after Wildman, twist everything around so it looks like she was somehow at fault. Or maybe they'll find some poor slob working at Global to blame. Scumbag lawyers."

I didn't even try to respond. Deep down, I knew what she was saying could be true.

"You sound a lot like Simon," I said.

She glanced over. "What do you mean?"

"He thinks our legal system is inherently corrupt, too, like you're saying. That's one of the reasons he often skirts the legalities in his investigations. He figures the ends justify the means."

"I take it you don't."

I shook my head. "We're cops. Our job is to follow the law."

"Even if that means letting a suspect walk?"

I hesitated, then nodded.

Amanda seemed about to reply, but settled back instead. I was glad. This was way too heavy a discussion when you were tired. For the next few miles, we rode without speaking. I blankly watched the light poles flickering by.

As we merged onto the Beltway, Amanda said, "You know why I really wanted to join the OSI?"

I glanced over.

"To make a difference. After what happened to Marcia, I wanted to change the system so guys like Holland would be held accountable. Silly, huh? I suppose that's what really bothers me. The fact that no matter what I do, nothing will change." A pause. "But what the hell, that's life, huh?"

And then she turned to me and I saw her eyes were wet. "I keep seeing the faces of those kids...just lying there..."

"So do I."

"It's not right. Someone's got to pay."

"We'll get Caldwell. You'll see."

A vague smile. "Sure we will, Marty. Sure we will."

Her tone made it clear she didn't believe that. And neither did I. Unlike Amanda, though, I could accept that outcome. That's one of the bitter lessons Nicole's death had taught me.

Life just wasn't fair.

Five minutes later, I was trying to stay awake by going over the contents of Janet Spence's note-book. There were seven entries documenting her conversations with Colonel Wildman. I scanned them to see if there was anything of importance that Janet might have neglected to mention. Nothing jumped out until I read the scrawled name on the second-to-last page.

I angrily clicked off the light and threw the notebook in the backseat.

Noticing Amanda's curious look, I grunted, "Looks like Janet Spence was right about the government being involved."

"Oh?"

"Wildman's FBI contact was Deputy Director Sam Rawlings."

Her face went blank.

"The Bureau's number-two man," I said.

A look of resignation crossed Amanda's face. She stared straight ahead, not bothering to comment. I knew she had to be thinking the same thing I was. We now realized that at a minimum, the FBI had to be part of a cover-up. And at the worst—

My phone rang, interrupting my thoughts.

"Hey, Kemosabe," an annoyingly cheerful voice said. "How you been?"

It was my FAA buddy Rob Sessler, and he sounded drunk.

CHAPTER 32

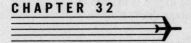

I'm fine, Rob," I said. "Thanks for calling me back."
Amanda was giving me a quizzical look, so I cupped the
phone and told her who it was.

In the background, I heard a woman call out, "Honey,
the dog is whining. You better walk him."

"In a minute, Katie. I'm on the phone."

"Rob..."

"I said in a minute." To me, Rob grunted, "Hell, you'd
think her legs were broken."

"I heard that."

Rob sighed. "Ain't marriage wonderful? So, buddy,
what's so all-fired important it couldn't wait until morning?"

I explained I was investigating the murder of a military
officer.

"So why call me?"

"She's an aircraft investigator. We're pretty certain she
was gathering evidence on an airliner she thought was unsafe."

A pause. "What airliner?" He suddenly sounded sober.

"The G-626."

Silence.

"Rob..."

He lowered his voice as if afraid someone would hear. "Look, Marty, my advice to you is to drop this thing. You understand me? Forget about the G-626."

"Dammit, Rob—"

"I'm telling you this for your own good. I really am. You keep digging into the G-626, you'll get burned."

I couldn't believe what I was hearing. In ROTC, Rob had always been a pain in the ass because he followed the chickenshit military regs like they were the Ten Commandments. A guy that gung-ho was the last person I thought would go along with a cover-up.

I said, "I really need your help, Rob."

"Are you *listening?* I'm telling you I can't, Marty. No one can. This is too big."

The phone hissed in my ear. I forced myself to remain calm. Amanda caught the drift of the conversation and was shaking her head in disgust. I said, "Did I mention Colonel Wildman had two children? They were also murdered tonight. Want to know how?"

"Marty, please..."

"Some bastard cut their throats. They bled to death while their mother watched."

"Don't do this..."

"The girl was nine. The boy was ten.

A long silence. I could hear Rob breathing.

"You son of a bitch," he said softly.

I didn't say a word. I just let him sweat.

"This could cost me big-time," he said.

"I could drop by your office—"

"No. Not there." He was quiet for a moment. "Let's make it the Tidal Basin. One of the benches just east of the Jefferson Memorial..."

"I know them."

"Ten o'clock."

"Thanks, Rob. I'm sorry I have to put you through this."

"So am I." And he hung up.

"He'll help?" Amanda asked.

I nodded.

"I'll be damned."

I just smiled and closed my eyes.

"Marty, we should be getting close."

I struggled to sit up, blinking to get my bearings. We were rolling across a slight rise. I pointed. "That's my house. Turnoff's about a half-mile ahead."

"All the land yours?"

"My father's. Most of it's under lease." She kept glancing over, so I said, "Something on your mind?"

"You think he'd be up to selling a few acres?"

"You serious?"

She nodded, making a face. "My neighbor works nights. He's always complaining about my dogs keeping him up. So I've been looking to get some land where they can bark their heads off. I mean, who sleeps at two in the afternoon..."

But I wasn't listening to Amanda anymore. Instead I was staring at my house through a line of trees. At a bright flickering in my driveway. I felt something churn inside. I tried to fight a growing sense of panic.

Amanda had gone silent. I heard her ask me what was wrong. I had to swallow twice before I could answer. "Car lights."

"So?"

And then she understood. Her head jerked around to look. "Oh, Jesus..."

She punched down on the accelerator while I took out my phone. My finger was shaking so badly I almost misdialed the number.

It seemed to take forever until the phone began to ring.

I saw Amanda take out her gun and thumb off the safety catch.

Finally, a sleepy voice answered.

"Yeah, Chief, I just checked with Lionel. It's him."

I sagged with relief. "Fine. Tell him we'll be there in a couple of minutes and not to get trigger-happy."

A laugh. "Hell, Chief. You know Lionel couldn't hit anything if he tried."

"It's okay," I said to Amanda. "False alarm."

Thirty seconds later, we took the gravel turnoff toward the house. Lionel's compact frame was leaning against the patrol car when we rolled up. He grinned at me as I emerged. I tossed a wave to Amanda as she drove off, then went over to Lionel.

"Everything quiet?" I asked him.

"Sure, Chief. Exceptin' we had to arrest Hank Bruner. We caught him pissing on his ex-wife's rosebushes again." Lionel giggled.

Even I had to smile. "You can knock off patrolling by here tonight, just pick back up in the morning."

"Anybody in particular we looking for?"

"Strangers." And I nodded good night and went into the house.

I put a pork chop in the microwave, then went upstairs to peek in on Emily. I sat on the edge of her bed for a few minutes, watching her sleep. She was lying on her side, and from that angle she looked just like Nicole. I smiled when I noticed the Harry Potter book on the night table. I pulled the covers up to her chin and kissed her forehead lightly, then spent a couple of minutes picking up her clothes from the floor before slipping out.

After I made a pork sandwich, I went down to my study in the basement. As I ate, I scanned the disk on Global Aviation that Janet Spence had given me. I'll say one thing for Janet, she was thorough. Most of the disk consisted of endless pages of detailed financial statements, aircraft production reports, subcontractor listings that numbered in the thousands, organizational wiring diagrams. You name it, it was all there ... someplace.

I started with the company history, reading as I ate.

Global was founded in Dallas, Texas, by an auto mechanic turned barnstormer, Joshua Caldwell, back in 1922. The company scraped by until World War II, when it received contracts to build transports for the military. Shortly after the war ended, Joshua Caldwell died, leaving the company to his two sons, Harold and Charles. Under the brothers, the company successfully transitioned to manufacturing airliners, eventually becoming the number-three passenger aircraft producer in the world behind Boeing and European Airbus. Harold had been the company's CEO until his death in 1998, when his younger brother Charles assumed control. Twice in the last thirty years Global had been on the verge of going under, but it always managed to rebound. The second time had been in 1990, when Global introduced an extremely popular, two-engine long-haul aircraft.

The G-626.

I slowly sat back, setting my sandwich down. Amanda's explanation of the difficulties in manufacturing composites notwithstanding, I'd been troubled as to how an airliner with a major defect could have been built. Now I finally knew.

It all came down to the fact that Global had needed the G-626 to survive.

So corners were cut and the production and testing process accelerated. And somewhere along the way, someone made a mistake, a mistake that should have been caught, and maybe would have been caught if not for the financial pressures.

I shifted to the production figures for the G-626, dated last month.

I felt a chill.

Almost twenty-two hundred in operation.

I clicked to the monthly production numbers. Forty-seven.

Over five hundred and sixty a year.

Maybe they weren't all defective. Maybe it was just a few of the older models. Maybe one out of twenty. Or thirty. Or a hundred. And maybe some of those had already been repaired.

But any way you did the math, the answer was the same.

Too many.

I pushed away from the computer and checked my fax machine. Almost a dozen pages—articles on G-626 crashes that Sergeant Rider had culled from Internet news services. Flipping through the pages, I saw that they were all various accounts of the same three accidents Wildman had on her disk.

I took out a pen and added up the number of deaths in my notepad. Six hundred and forty-two.

I stared at the figure, shaking my head. Even with Caldwell's obvious influence, I kept wondering how the government could allow this.

Possible scenarios went through my mind. I saw a high-level meeting. Intense men in suits arguing around a conference table. Someone writes an enormous dollar figure on the board and underlines it. The worldwide impact of grounding an entire fleet of aircraft. Faces stare, stunned.

And the decision is made.

I was tired. I didn't want to think about this anymore. I queued up my printer to print out the report. As I started to go up to bed, I remembered Amanda's comment about jocks. I clicked on the Internet and typed in a Web site address.

A moment later, Bobby Baker's face grinned out from the screen.

I clicked on the price-list icon. An autographed baseball was thirty bucks, a T-shirt forty-five. But the counter on the main page showed less than a thousand hits, which explained why Bobby was hurting for money.

I closed out the screen angrily. *I don't know nothing about computers,* Baker had said.

The lying son of a bitch.

➤ Twenty minutes later, I lay in the dark, the questions still coming: *What was Caldwell's motive if not money? Why was General Holland at Wildman's house? What was Bobby Baker hiding? Why did the killers murder the children?* And on and on.

Some time later, I felt myself drifting off without a single answer. I rolled over to face the photographs on the bureau. I couldn't see them in the dark, but that didn't matter.

I just wanted to tell my wife Nicole good night.

CHAPTER 33

THURSDAY

I heard birds chirping and groaned, wondering why they would sing in the middle of the night. I wanted them to be quiet, let me sleep. I rolled over, wrapping the pillow around my head. Then someone began calling to me and I knew there weren't any birds.

I cracked open my eyes to find the morning light streaming through the blinds. I felt for the alarm clock and banged on the cutoff button until the chirping stopped. It was seven-thirty, which meant I'd gotten maybe four hours of sleep. I lay there for a moment, waiting for the fog in my head to clear. The bedroom door opened and my daughter Emily tentatively poked her head inside. She was already dressed for school.

"You awake, Daddy?" She spoke loudly so if I wasn't, I would be.

"I think so."

Her face brightened and she came over to the bed. "Mrs. Anuncio wants to know if you want breakfast."

"Tell her just some eggs and toast, honey." I stroked Emily's hair, but she pulled away.

"*Daddy*, I just combed it."

I sighed, thinking how fast she was growing up. I squinted at her. "What's that on your cheeks?"

Her eyes widened in horror. "Nothing. I . . . I gotta go, Daddy." She spun, hurrying toward the door.

"Emily."

She stopped, slowly facing me. She had her guilty look.

"Is that makeup, Emily?"

She kicked the carpet with her toe, avoiding my eyes. "I dunno. Maybe."

"Where did you get it?"

Silence.

"From a friend at school?"

A head shake. More kicking.

"Helen?"

She hesitated, then nodded.

I said, "Does Helen know you're using her makeup?"

Another head shake. "I just . . . just borrowed a little."

"All right," I said. "Go and wash your face before going to school."

She wailed, "Daddy, that's not *fair*. Other girls wear it. Linda and Colleen and Molly—and Molly's younger than me."

"Honey, we've already discussed this. You're too young." Behind Emily, I noticed Helen, watching from the hallway. She had on her flying clothes.

"But, Daddy—"

"No! Now wash your face."

Emily stuck out her chin at me, her eyes misting over. The words tumbled from her mouth. "You're mean, Daddy. If Mommy was here, she would let me. I wish Mommy was here." The tears began. "I . . . I hate you." And she ran from the room.

I stared, stung.

Helen was watching me from the doorway, her face sympathetic. "She didn't mean anything, Marty. She was just talking."

I nodded, not trusting myself to speak. The phone rang. I ignored it.

"Girls her age don't know what they're saying," Helen said. "They don't stop to think."

I forced a smile. "It's okay. Really." But it wasn't okay. I was hurt.

"Look," Helen said. "How about I try and talk to her? Something like this, it might be easier for another woman..."

"All right," I said.

As she started to leave, she glanced back. "You know, Marty, this is just the beginning."

"Beginning?"

She winked. "Just wait until she's a teenager."

I sighed, grimacing at the thought. I heard Mrs. Anuncio calling from downstairs for me to pick up the phone. I checked the caller ID as I reached over.

"Morning, Simon," I said. "You're up early."

"There's been a change of plans, Martin." He sounded tense.

"What kind of change?"

A long pause. "It seems I'm no longer on the case."

I was silent. I wished I was surprised, but I wasn't. As I rolled out of bed into a sitting position, Simon began to explain.

Simon spoke quickly. "Captain Kelly received an advance copy of a story that's going to appear in the *Washington Post* tomorrow. He called me, wanting to know whether it was accurate. After I confirmed that it was, he told me he had no choice but to reassign me until he can decide on the best course of action."

Now I was confused. "Hold it, you're being yanked from the case because of a news article?"

"Yes."

"That's *it*? Just some article?"

"Yes."

"So it's *not* because Caldwell pulled strings to—"

"I'm sure Caldwell is behind the article. In fact, I'm rather surprised it didn't come out earlier."

"Earlier?"

He sounded tired. "It's a complicated story, Martin. It goes back to when I was working on the Dryke case. Last night you probably didn't realize that the Excelsior Arms was the same apartment complex where Patricia Dryke was murdered—the owner changed the name after the killing because of the publicity. Anyway, during the investigation, we learned that Patricia Dryke had been seen going into Caldwell's apartment shortly before her death. A maintenance man also reported hearing sounds of a violent argument—"

"*Caldwell* killed her?" To me that seemed ludicrous, considering the shape he was in.

"No. One thing I know for certain is that he *didn't* kill her."

"Oh?"

"Caldwell was at Global's corporate headquarters in Dallas at the time of the murder. And the witness, a maid who worked across the hall, described two people leaving the apartment. The first was a man, followed by a woman a few minutes later."

"Tatum the guy?"

"No. When Janet told you about the case, did she mention that the witness had been intimidated to remain silent?"

"Yeah..."

"That was part of our problem. The witness had been hesitant about coming forward because, at the time, she was in the country illegally. Once she was threatened, she wouldn't cooperate at all. It took me months to get her to change her mind. She identified Tatum from a photograph as one of the men who had intimidated her. But we couldn't really make a case against him because it was his word against hers."

"So you don't have any idea who the two people in the apartment were?"

"It's likely the man was an executive with Global, since many of them often used the place when Caldwell wasn't in town. I suppose it's still possible that he could have also been a client of the victim, Patricia Dryke."

"Client? You mean she was a lobbyist for Global?"

"Patricia Dryke's firm did some work for Global, but that's not what I'm referring to." He paused. "She was also a call girl, Martin. A very expensive one."

"You're kidding."

"That's also what contributed to the difficulty of the case. She understandably had a number of male visitors. And whoever killed her was smart enough to remove her client list, so we have no idea who most of the men were."

"Hold on a sec," I said, trying to take this all in. "If Patricia Dryke and this guy were getting together for sex, what was the second woman doing—" I stopped. I felt slow. The answer was obvious. "A group thing? The second woman was also a hooker?"

"It's certainly a possibility."

"Couldn't the guard, Lester, help identify—"

"Lester was hired subsequent to the murder. And the guard Patricia Dryke paid off to let the johns in wouldn't talk. We're pretty certain he was bought off by Caldwell to keep his mouth shut."

"Then Caldwell must know who the killer is."

"Of course. The question is, why is he protecting him? When we tried to interview Caldwell, he brought in a team of attorneys to stonewall us. When we persisted, that's when the pressure began. Subtle at first, but it was there. Mostly in the form of phone calls from reporters and politicians demanding to know why we were harassing Caldwell." Simon hesitated, his voice becoming angry. "Eventually the interference escalated to the point where it completely compromised our investigation. We discovered that judges wouldn't approve a search warrant for Caldwell's apartment. Then the DA actually prohibited us from contacting Caldwell. Even the mayor weighed in, essentially ordering us to desist from what he termed a program of unwarranted harassment. It was frustrating. We soon realized that no one wanted the crime solved. So, in the end, it wasn't."

I knew there had to be more to it. No way would Simon walk away from a case, regardless of what a superior said. "And you gave up just like that?"

"I didn't want to. But there didn't seem to be any point...." He was momentarily silent. When he came back, there was an edge to his voice. "No, Martin. That's just an excuse. I *was* influenced by the article. Maybe not consciously, but... At any rate, the fact of the matter is that Caldwell threatened me with its release two years ago and *I backed off.*" He sounded disgusted with himself.

"Christ," I murmured, "just what the hell is in this article, anyway?"

Another pause. "Information about my past."

"For instance..."

"You can read it for yourself," he said quietly. "I've faxed you a copy. I'm meeting in an hour with Captain Kelly to see if we can resolve my status. I'll call you when it's over. By the way, Detective Reardon finally located the neighbor of Wildman's who lived across the street. She's been visiting her daughter in Richmond for the past few days. She mentioned one item of interest. Before she left, she saw Holland's car in front of Wildman's."

"We already know that."

"The neighbor left yesterday, Martin."

"Oh?" I tried to understand the significance but drew a blank. "So what does that mean other than he was there two days in a row?"

"I'm not sure."

I said, "Mr. Frawley mentioned the woman might have had a video camera set up—"

"She only turns it on when she's home. Dr. Marbury also completed the autopsies. Nothing surprising. He determined the cause of death on all three to be the severing of the carotid artery. In addition to Wildman's facial injuries, there were also numerous contusions on her body, including four broken ribs."

"Time of death?"

"Marbury now estimates that Wildman died between

1545 and 1600. Her children up to twenty minutes before."

And the call to the 911 dispatcher came at 1612, confirming that it was probably made by one of the killers. "Okay..."

"One more thing. Captain Kelly told me who he's assigning to take over this case."

I tensed at the disgust in Simon's voice. "Aw, hell, don't tell me it's..."

"Brian McNamara. Be careful with him, Martin. Under no circumstances tell him anything or cooperate with him in any way until I check on something first. Promise me."

"Look, Simon, I know Brian's a jerk, but if I'm supposed to work with him I can't very well—"

"Promise me!"

"Okay, okay. Relax—"

But I was talking to a dial tone. I shook my head, mystified by the extent of Simon's outburst. There had to be more to it than just his dislike of McNamara. If I didn't know better, I'd almost believe he thought McNamara was somehow involved in—

My hand froze as I cradled the receiver. I'd suddenly recalled Janet's description of the second man following Wildman. One particular statement: *He put on a lot of weight.*

It couldn't be. And yet...

"Daddy."

Emily was standing at the door, tears in her eyes. "I'm sorry, Daddy. I didn't mean it."

"I know, baby. I know."

She ran to me, throwing her arms around my neck. As I hugged her, my eyes went to the framed picture of Nicole smiling at us from the bureau.

I'm trying, honey, I thought.

Five minutes later, I was watching out my bedroom window as Mrs. Anuncio drove Emily to the highway to wait for the school bus. By the hangars, Helen and Joe Borazzo, a local handyman she was teaching to work as her spotter, were filling the plane's hopper with pesticide. Spotters helped crop dusters line up the rows, to avoid confusion. The sky was clear and it looked like a perfect day to fly.

I threw on a robe, and on the way to the basement I stopped off in the kitchen for a cup of coffee. The fax was waiting for me in my study as Simon had promised.

As I sat down to read, I was still thinking Simon had to be overreacting, that the story couldn't be that bad.

I was wrong.

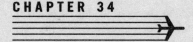

CHAPTER 34

Homicide Investigator's Success Linked to Troubled Past?

The story started off innocuously enough, with a couple of paragraphs rehashing Simon's impressive exploits as a local Arlington cop.

Then came the zingers:

Lieutenant Santos' chosen profession is particularly admirable, considering his lineage. On his official application to the police academy, Santos listed his father as Mario Santos, deceased. In truth, Lieutenant Santos is the son of Arturo Mendez, the Miami industrialist who disappeared in 1972 before he could be arrested for the murders of fourteen young women in the South Florida area. Mendez was thought to have taken refuge in Cuba and there are unconfirmed rumors that he passed away in 1997.

According to famed Harvard forensic psychologist Dr. R. F. Maloney, the fact that Lieutenant Santos, wealthy from his father's fortune, aspired to become not only a policeman but a leading homicide investigator suggests Santos is driven to atone for the crimes of his father.

"Actually, his response is typical of many family members who are compelled to make amends," Dr. Maloney stated in a telephone interview. "In Santos' case, it's also highly likely that his pursuit of killers is his way of proving to himself that he will not fall prey to the demons that afflicted his father."

Dr. Maloney further explained that there had been no documented evidence suggesting that family members of murderers were any more likely to kill than the general population unless they were conditioned at an early age. "However, someone in Santos' position as an influential law-enforcement officer might find it beneficial to seek psychological counseling in order to understand whether he has been influenced in any way by his father," Maloney said. "The concern is not that he will suddenly snap and begin killing, but that he will feel increasingly compelled to solve a case no matter the cost."

I swore, knowing where the story was going now. I was tempted to crumple up the page and fire it at the wall.

Instead I kept reading.

The remaining paragraphs expanded on the theme that Simon's zeal in pursuing investigations could be cause for concern. Citing conveniently unnamed police sources, the article suggested that Simon might not be above fabricating evidence or conducting illegal searches to make an arrest.

"In his nine years as a homicide investigator," the article concluded, "Lieutenant Santos has solved fifty-seven of sixty-one cases, by far the highest success rate in the Arlington Police Department's history. So the question one has to ponder is whether or not Lieutenant Santos' impressive record is due to exceptional police work or whether he has made a habit of skirting the safeguards guaranteed in the Constitution."

I slowly let the paper slip through my fingers to the desk, thinking I finally understood Simon. His foray into the priesthood, his obsessive need for privacy, his becoming a cop—it all made sense now. And while I thought this Dr. Maloney was basically full of shit, the guy was right about one thing. Simon *was* a man haunted by lingering guilt.

I also had to admit that whoever Caldwell had hired to write the article had been one clever son of a bitch. Knowing Simon could probably weather having a father who'd been a homicidal nutcase, the author went after Simon's credibility as a cop, using his own success against him. The fact that there wasn't any proof of wrongdoing didn't matter. That's how smear campaigns worked. Throw out a net of suspicion and doubt and watch the victim drive himself crazy trying to prove a negative.

And Simon's problem was that he could only protest so much, because he *did* occasionally skirt the rules. Like with the search of Bobby Baker's car last night. More than once I had also seen him bully witnesses or suspects. Nothing excessive or illegal, but that didn't matter. Once people began to look into his conduct, just a hint of impropriety would damn him.

It occurred to me that there were only two ways Caldwell could have uncovered the dirt on Simon. The first was from a private investigator and the second was from someone close to Simon. And if you consider the fact that the article was appearing in the *Washington Post*...

I shook my head. Maybe Simon had been right all along. Maybe she was just using us for a story.

I had to know.

My notepad was still on the desk where I'd left it the night before. I slipped out Janet's business card tucked in the flap.

She answered tentatively on the second ring. She sounded relieved when she realized it was me. She started going on about the break-in at her apartment last night.

I cut her off rudely. "Janet, I'm faxing you an article...."

Of course, Janet Spence vehemently denied having any part in the story. She even said she would try to talk to the *Post*'s managing editor to get it pulled. All in all, she came off as sincere and I wanted to believe her. Why, I'm not certain, except that I liked her. In the end, I suppose it really didn't matter. The damage was already done.

I sighed, picking up the phone to make three calls. The first was to my boss, General Mercer. The way I figured it, if Simon was off the case, maybe I was too. As the phone rang, I realized I was making a mistake. One of the first things I'd learned in the military was if you can't stand the answer, don't ask the question.

So I hung up and called General Holland to set up the interview. I'd mentally braced myself for a confrontation, but a woman answered. Holland's wife, Lucille. She seemed downright pleasant, countering my mental picture that Amanda had generated through her disparaging comments. Lucille told me Holland was unavailable but had left a message, asking if I could drop by around eleven-thirty. I said I could.

After I jotted down Holland's Alexandria address, I phoned Amanda. Her sleepy voice told me I'd woken her up. "Man, what a night, Marty. Kept thinking about the case. I finally got to sleep around four."

I gave her the bad news about Simon first.

Twenty minutes later I was dressed, at the kitchen table, wolfing down my eggs and flipping through the *Post* for the account of the Wildman murder. On a stand in the corner I had a TV on, tuned to a local newscast, the sound turned low. I could hear Mrs. Anuncio in the family room, huffing and puffing to her morning aerobics show on

ESPN. She usually did little more than twist around a bit and clap her hands, but she seemed to enjoy herself.

I finally found the story on the murders squirreled away back in the metro section. It dawned on me that not even Caldwell could get the *Post* to bury a triple homicide. Getting a damning article on Simon printed was one thing, but this took real influence. As I read, I couldn't help but wonder just how high up in the government the cover-up went.

The article was a single column only six inches long, giving the essentials about the murders and little else. Two points about it pissed me off. First, the suggestion that robbery was the motive, and second, the omission of the names and ages of the victims, as if the murders of children were somehow irrelevant. Not that I was surprised. The object was to downplay the killings so no one would pay much attention.

The hallway clocked chimed eight A.M. My eyes went to the TV. Considering the press' feeding frenzy last night, the story should have been the lead.

But of course it wasn't. It came on after the first commercial break, just a five-second mention before the weather.

I shook my head, thinking power was an amazing thing to behold.

As I gathered the paper together to toss it in the trash, I noticed an item I'd missed. A small article on the bottom of the second page I'd folded over.

Congressional Hearings Begin Today

The short blurb explained that the House Transportation and Infrastructure Committee was holding hearings on airline safety that same day. Other than the timing, there was little in the article of interest. But that singular point was enough. I sat back, slowly shaking my head at a suspicion that had now become a certainty.

I tossed the paper in the trash, rinsed off the dishes, and then returned to my study to put Janet Spence's report and the cassette tape in my briefcase. As I started to leave, the phone rang. The caller ID read ARLINGTON PD.

I hustled up the steps to tell Mrs. Anuncio to ignore the call. But when I reached the family room, she was waiting with the phone in her hand.

"For you."

"Tell him I'm not here," I said.

She gave me a disparaging look and set the receiver on the end table. "I no lie," she said, and promptly went back to her aerobics.

I sighed, picking up the phone. McNamara was saying, "Marty, you there? Hello..."

What the hell. I hung it up and grabbed my overcoat from the hall closet. Walking to the front door, I saw a dark blue sedan coming down the gravel drive. Almost as an afterthought, I squinted at the license plate.

My mouth went dry.

White.

I stood there, my heart pounding. I forced myself to remain calm, to think. As the car approached, I could make out two men in dark suits sitting in front. Neither matched the description of the men who'd been following Wildman, but that didn't mean much.

Mrs. Anuncio fired off a stream of rapid-fire Spanish as I literally pushed her bulk up the staircase. Outside, car doors slammed. I headed for the sliding glass door at the back, my cell phone to my ear.

As I stepped out into the backyard, the doorbell chimed. I took out my gun and went around toward the front, whispering orders into the phone.

CHAPTER 35

They were standing on the porch. Both were maybe six feet tall, with military-style haircuts. The guy on the left was muscular, mid-thirties, with chiseled features and blow-dried dark hair; his partner was ten years older, heavyset, with thinning blond hair.

I came around low, hugging the bushes along the railing for cover. I heard the bell chime again, followed by the sounds of knocking.

Reaching the front steps, I stood. "Help you, gentlemen?" I asked pleasantly.

They both spun, startled. Then they saw my gun.

"The hell is this," the blond man snarled.

The other man was casually reaching into his jacket.

I shifted the barrel an inch. "I wouldn't," I said.

His jaw went tight, but the hand slowly dropped. "Better put that thing away. We're with the FBI."

"Congratulations," I said dryly. "Now remove your weapons slowly and kick them over."

They both looked incredulous. "Did you hear what I just said?" the dark-haired man said. "We're with the FBI."

"The guns," I said to him. *"Now."*

He hesitated. His partner said, "For chrissakes, just do what he says, Frank."

As they kicked their pistols over, Frank said, "You Chief Collins?"

"Last I checked." I squatted, picked up the guns and tossed them into the yard.

"Smart-ass," the blond man grunted.

"I don't know what your fucking problem is, Collins," Frank said, "but you got us all wrong. We just came out to take you to a meeting."

"What meeting?"

"Mr. Rawlings wants to talk to you."

Rawlings was the FBI's deputy director I'd told Amanda about last night. The one who had met with Wildman. I said, "Next time, tell Rawlings to call first."

"You're way out of line, Collins," the blond man said, his voice thick. "Pulling a gun on a Federal Agent."

"You got a warrant?"

He blinked. "Of course not—"

"Fine. Then you're trespassing. Now have a seat." I waved them to the chairs on the porch.

They didn't move. They just glowered at me.

"Might be a few minutes," I said.

"A few minutes for what?" Frank said suspiciously.

I didn't reply. We stood there, staring at each other like in a scene out of *High Noon*. I could almost see the gears spinning in their heads as they tried to figure out their next move. I kept wondering what the hell I'd do if they decided to rush me.

Thankfully, I heard the faint sounds of sirens.

Frank and the blond agent were sitting cuffed in the back of the first of two patrol cars parked in my drive. While his partner sat quietly, Frank kept busy glowering at me through the glass.

Buddy Medina and Mick Barson, the two young cops who'd responded to my call, hovered around me, their faces worried. In Buddy's hand were the two leather IDs taken from the agents.

"I dunno about this, Chief," he said, tugging on the peach fuzz he called a mustache. "They really are with the FBI."

"I know."

He glanced nervously at Mick. "But Chief, arresting *FBI agents*. Can we even do that?"

I sighed. "Just book them for trespassing, then let them go. I'll handle any flak. And send someone out to drive their car to the station."

Both men nodded reluctantly. Before the cars drove away, Frank began ranting that I was overstepping my authority big-time. That I was in a lot of trouble. And he was probably right.

To me their presence here confirmed what I'd suspected. Now that they'd taken care of Simon, I was next. All I was really accomplishing was buying time. If I was lucky and broke maybe a half-dozen regulations, I figured maybe I could stall getting canned until tonight.

Heading back to the house, I called Amanda to tell her I was running late. She sounded distracted and was surprisingly noncommittal about the visit from the agents. I finally asked what was bugging her.

"I'm a little confused, Marty. I spoke with AFPC a few minutes ago, trying to get a copy of General Holland's personnel file faxed out."

AFPC was the Air Force's Personnel Center down in San Antonio. I said, "And..."

"No file. It's been signed out."

"And that surprises you?"

"It's the *reason* that it was removed that's bugging me. The clerk told me the file was being sent across the street, to the Reserve side of the house."

I was going up the steps. I stopped so fast that I almost tripped. Personnel records were only transferred to the Reserve branch for one reason. When someone separated from the regular service.

"The clerk must have made a mistake," I said.

"No mistake, Marty. I had her check twice. Holland put in his separation papers almost two weeks ago."

"And his last day of duty . . ."

"On the twenty-fifth. Ten days from now."

My bewilderment matched Amanda's. We'd been operating under the assumption that Holland was covering up the problems with the G-626 to save his career. That was the only motive that made sense. But if he was planning to get out of the Air Force all along, then he had no reason to—

"Anyway," Amanda said. "I called Major Sullivan and asked her why she didn't mention to us that Holland was retiring. Know what she said? She didn't know. Funny, huh? That Holland would keep it a secret from his staff."

It was. By definition, general officers had large egos. I'd never known one to skip out quietly and avoid the pomp of a retirement ceremony.

"That's something else we'll have to ask him," I said, throwing open the front door.

I stopped dead. Mrs. Anuncio was blocking my way, her face flushed with anger. She erupted into a stream of Spanish, gesturing toward the TV in the family room, which was now showing an equestrian competition.

"Sounds like you're in trouble, Marty," Amanda said.

She was laughing as she hung up.

CHAPTER 36

Amanda lived about fifteen miles east of me, near the rural town of Buckland, population maybe a thousand if you counted the pets and the people stopping for gas. I was running about five minutes late because I'd stopped to pick up the Backstreet Boys concert tickets I'd promised Emily. The truth was I'd almost forgotten and had to double back about a mile. When I finally pulled up to Amanda's small white-brick house, two large German shepherds ran up to the mesh fence at the back and started barking wildly, announcing my arrival. Moments later, Amanda appeared at the front door, her cell phone to her ear, the same folder from last night tucked under her other arm.

As she climbed into the passenger seat of my late-model Jeep Cherokee, she was saying into the phone, "I know the hearings begin today, sir. I'm trying to find out when Mr. Caldwell is scheduled to testify. That's okay, sir. I'll hold."

I took the folder from her and stuck it in my briefcase. As I drove away, I said, "You talking to Legislative Liaison?"

Her nod confirmed that she was talking with the Pentagon's Legislative Liaison office. Cupping the phone, she said, "You see the article in the paper on the hearing..."

I nodded.

"...anyway, it's supposed to end tomorrow. According to LL, it's a biannual event. Primarily for PR to give the public a warm-and-fuzzy that the government is keeping the skies safe. All the major airline and aviation company CEOs are scheduled to testify—" She held up a finger. "I'm still here, Major Tanner. At 1700 hours today. Yeah. That's it. Thanks, sir."

Slipping her phone into her jacket, she said thoughtfully, "You know, if Colonel Wildman was really intending to present evidence at the hearing—"

"She was."

Amanda nodded. "That means she must have contacted someone in Congress and presented evidence on the G-626. It's the only way she could have hoped to get on the witness list to testify."

I thought it over. "The committee chairman is Trenton. If she contacted him, anything she turned over might as well be on the moon."

"Maybe it wasn't him."

It took me a moment to figure out what she was getting at. "You think she might have contacted Congressman Marcelli?"

She shrugged. "He'd be a logical choice. According to Major Tanner, Congressman Marcelli's making quite a name for himself as a proponent of airline safety. He lost both his parents in a plane crash ten years ago."

"I dunno," I said. "Marcelli's a freshman. I would have thought Wildman would have contacted someone with clout."

"Couldn't hurt to call," she said.

We came to a stop sign. I checked traffic and pulled out onto the highway. Even though I thought it was a waste of time, I said, "All right."

A minute later, she clicked off her phone. The bits and pieces I'd caught told me she hadn't spoken with Marcelli. I said, "So..."

"Marcelli's at some committee meeting. I was talking to his press secretary. Mrs. Thompson. She had no clue who Wildman was until I explained that I was investigating the death of a military-accident investigator with data for the hearing." Amanda shot me a grin. "That's when I caught her interest. She said her boss had canceled a dinner engagement last night to meet with someone who claimed she was an accident investigator, but the woman never showed."

I let out a breath. "At least this confirms the timing of Wildman's killing."

Amanda nodded, gazing outside. "It also explains why they murdered her in the middle of the day. That was risky as hell. Even stupid. But now we know they had no choice. They had to shut her up before she could meet with Congressman Marcelli."

Traffic was picking up. We drove past an enormous new subdivision under construction. In a few years, the suburban sprawl would reach Warrentown.

"Wonder who Wildman told?" Amanda murmured.

When I glanced over, she was reclined back in her seat, looking at me.

"What do you mean?" I said.

"About her upcoming meeting with Congressman Marcelli. Colonel Wildman must have told someone she trusted. That's the only way the killers could have known about it. And so far I can only come up with two suspects."

I thought, and mentioned Bobby Baker.

She suppressed a yawn. "That's one possibility."

"And the second..."

"Janet Spence."

My head snapped around to tell her she was way out of line, that Janet Spence had no motive for compromising Wildman. Hell, they were friends.

But Amanda's eyes were closed now and she was massaging her temples. Then, as if she could read my mind, she added, "You know, Marty, even attractive women can kill."

I decided to let it go.

We rolled up to the Jefferson Memorial about a quarter to ten, early enough to beat most of the tourists and snag a parking space. As I climbed out, my cell phone rang. Amanda shot me a quizzical glance when I clicked off the ringer.

"Analog phone," I explained. "No caller ID. And the way I figure it, if no one actually orders me off the case..." I shrugged.

Moments later, Amanda's phone began ringing. She glanced at the ID box. "Bolling."

"Don't answer it. It's probably General Mercer."

She frowned. "I thought he was supporting us on this."

"He is, but the decision is probably out of his hands now. We talk to him and he might have to order us off the case, even if he doesn't want to."

She hesitated, then turned off her ringer, too. "I hope you know what you're doing, Marty."

I didn't reply, because I wasn't sure I did.

A bus full of school kids pulled in as we wound our way around the back of the memorial, toward the path leading to the Tidal Basin. The air was cool and brisk and the cherry trees were just beginning to bud. Occasionally, a plane from Reagan National would take off over our heads. I spotted my buddy Rob Sessler standing by the third bench down, throwing peanuts to a cluster of squawking ducks.

Even in a suit, Rob still looked like a fighter pilot, a wiry, compact man with intense blue eyes and close-cropped dark hair now going gray. I noticed he didn't have his cane today, which he used sporadically when his leg was troubling him. He glanced our way as a jogger ran by. The look he gave us wasn't exactly welcoming.

He scowled at Amanda as we walked up. "What's she doing here, Marty?"

"Amanda is working with me. There's a problem?" Rob was shaking his head, looking very ticked off.

"Damn right there's a problem," he said. "I talk to you alone or I walk."

I said, "For chrissakes, Rob—"

He poked a finger at me. "And another thing. I want your word this isn't a setup."

"Setup?"

Another poke. "You heard me."

Then I understood. "A *wire*. You actually think I'm wearing a wire?"

Rob was staring at me. "Just give me your word. That's all I'm asking."

I was pissed now. I held open my jacket, glaring at him. "Take a fucking look."

Rob started to reach out, then drew back as if suddenly aware of what he was doing. He forced a smile. "Hey, don't get sore, buddy. You have to understand the position I'm in. If any of this gets back to me—"

"It won't," I snapped.

Sounding apologetic, Rob said to Amanda, "Look, it's nothing personal. . . ."

"No problem," Amanda said amiably. "I'll be in the car, Marty." But as she left, I could tell she was bugged.

Rob continued to toss peanuts to the ducks until Amanda was out of earshot. "Sorry about the scene, huh?"

"Forget it."

"So what do you know about the G-626?"

In response, I handed him the copy of the e-mail from Douglas McInnes.

When he finished reading, he passed it back without comment, then focused out across the water. "I want you to know I wasn't in charge of the certification branch when the G-626 was approved. If I was I'd never have given the okay. I'd have insisted on more tests. You have to believe me, Marty."

I nodded. "So it's the wing box?"

A barely perceptible nod.

"How did such an unsafe airplane ever get built?"

He gave me a cryptic look. "You know you're wasting your time pursuing this."

"Maybe."

"No way you'll be able to prove any of this."

I shrugged.

"You ever tell anyone about this conversation, I'll deny it."

I nodded.

He sighed, emptying the bag of peanuts into the water. Feathers flashed as the ducks erupted into a feeding frenzy. "This is gonna take a while, and my leg's getting tired. Let's have a seat, huh?"

CHAPTER 37

Rob stretched back against the bench, keeping his right leg, the injured one, straight. He spoke in a clipped monotone, like he was giving a military briefing. "Back in 1990, Global was under a lot of pressure to build the G-626. The company was getting their ass kicked by Boeing, McDonnell Douglas and Airbus, and was a gnat's eyelash from bankruptcy. At the time, the G-626 was still in the conceptual phase and no one believed Global would actually be able to build the plane before they went under. But somehow they did, in less than two years. And the experimental composite frame made the plane an instant hit. Compared to similar metal aircraft, the G-626 was almost fifteen percent lighter, translating into a fuel savings of almost eight percent. In the airline business that could mean savings upward of hundreds of millions of dollars annually, depending on fleet size.

"And that's when the lobbying began in earnest to get the G-626 put on the fast track for approval. Global started the ball rolling, knowing they were sitting on a gold mine. Then the airlines started jumping up and down, demanding the plane be certified. And I'm not talking just the U.S. carriers. Practically every airline company in the world got on the bandwagon. Then Congress weighed in, partly in response to the airlines and partly because they knew that if the plane didn't get certified in a hurry, there would be over a hundred thousand very pissed off Global workers looking for jobs. Not to mention all the subcontractors. At one point, Nolan Taylor, the FAA chief at the time, was fielding twenty fucking calls a day from political heavyweights, demanding he expedite the process. Finally, the President called him personally, telling him to quit screwing around and make it happen.

"So it did, Marty. A certification process which should have taken six months to a year—maybe longer because the composite was a new, untried material—was finished in three. And now we've got a flying piece of shit that we keep hoping doesn't fall out of the sky every time it flies."

Rob sighed deeply, shifting awkwardly to face me. "Anyway, that's how this whole mess started. It was no one's fault and it was everyone's fault. But that's the way the system works. It's called a goddamn bureaucracy. End of fucking story."

"All right," I said. "Now tell me about the cover-up."

He shrugged. "What's there to tell? Everyone's got an interest in keeping the lid on this thing. Congress doesn't want the story to get out because they pushed so hard for the airplane to get made. Neither does the FAA. And President Carlson sure doesn't."

The FAA and Congress I understood, but . . . "Why would President Carlson want to keep this quiet? This originated with his predecessor."

Rob flashed a weary smile. "Think, Marty. What was Carlson's job before he won the election?"

I still didn't see the connection. "He was the Oklahoma governor. . . ." And then I dimly remembered something from Janet Spence's report. "Doesn't Global have a plant in Oklahoma?"

"Bingo. Actually there are two, employing over thirty thousand workers."

"So Carlson pushed for the plane...."

"Big-time. His fingerprints are all over this. But that's not the only reason he wants to keep the problem under wraps. The ugly truth is, this plane is too fucking popular to ground. Right now the G-626 is twenty-four percent of the domestic fleet and sixteen percent of the world fleet. It'd create instant chaos if we shut down its operation for the three-plus years it'd take to fix the jets. Not just in the travel industry or the airlines that we'd put out of business. But you're talking commerce, trade—"

"That's no excuse and you know it," I snapped. "You're playing Russian roulette with people's lives."

Rob's face darkened. "Don't give me that holier-than-thou crap. You don't have a clue what you're saying. It's not like the planes are going to fall apart the moment they get in the air."

"C'mon. You said yourself that they're unsafe—"

"Sure. But *only* if certain parameters are exceeded. And we've put out bulletins to the carriers, and as long as the guidelines are followed, the planes should be reasonably safe until they can be fixed. The airlines understand that. That's why they pushed so hard to keep the jets flying."

"Have the repairs already begun?"

"Give us some credit, huh? For the last two years, Global's been working around the clock to fix the problem. But it's a slow process replacing the wing box, because you're completely rebuilding the main structural support. So far about forty percent of the fleet has been repaired. And the new ones coming off the production line don't have the wing box problem."

"What are the parameters?"

"Primarily G-limit restrictions. The numbers vary depending on the plane's gross weight, but roughly anything in excess of four Gs could lead to the wing box cracking. Staying within those limits usually isn't a problem for an airliner. Most can fly for years and never even exceed two Gs."

"Is that right?" I said dryly. "In case you missed it, four

planes have gone down in the past few years. Three civilian and one military."

He tugged on his cheek. "I know. The civilian jets hit severe turbulence that caused the G limits to be exceeded. The military plane broke up when it was flying at a low level. From what I read, the pilot did a high-G evasive turn, causing a wing to separate."

"When did you first learn there was a problem with the G-626 wing box? The military crash?"

He nodded. "It was the first one that went down."

I eyed him for a moment. "Then you must have known about Colonel Wildman. That she had concluded the wing box was defective."

A long pause. He answered carefully, choosing his words. "I didn't know her by name, Marty. I just heard that a military investigator was making noises about the wing box possibly being defective."

"Who ordered her removed from the investigation?"

He shook his head. "We weren't involved in that."

I gazed at him, trying to decide if I believed him. A young couple approached, walking arm-in-arm. They gave us a smile, and I attempted one back. Rob just sat there stone-faced. After they passed by, I asked him, "How many more do you think you'll lose before the rest are fixed?"

Rob shrugged. "How the hell should I know?"

"C'mon, Rob. You guys must have done forecasts. Some kind of risk assessment? How many more do you expect to lose?"

"Originally, we didn't think we'd lose any—" He held up a hand when he saw I was about to respond. "Let me finish, huh?"

I sat back, biting my tongue.

A look of resignation crossed Rob's face. "I wasn't going to get into this. You know anything about composite materials?"

"A little."

"Then you probably know there's no foolproof way to detect internal defects in the lamination process. We had to assume all the wing boxes were compromised. So we came up with the four-G flight restriction that we honestly thought would suffice. And dammit, it should have. One of the main reasons the problem showed up in the military jet first was the constant pounding the wings took from low-level flights. We knew airliners wouldn't be subjected to those kinds of stresses."

It dawned on me what he was implying. "Son of a bitch. You're saying the wing box is even weaker than you'd anticipated."

"Looks like it. From the accident reports on the three airliners, it's pretty clear that we're looking at around a three-, maybe three-and-a-half-G restriction, depending on temperature."

"Temperature?"

"Those accidents occurred during the winter. We think the extreme cold at altitude is further degrading the wing box tensile strength. Making it brittle. But the damndest thing is, we haven't been able to confirm anything in testing." He shook his head. "I'm telling you this is a fucking nightmare, Marty."

"So how many more do you think you'll lose?" I asked quietly.

"Hard to say." He hesitated. "Not more than one or two."

"Jesus—" I caught myself before I said something I would regret.

When Rob spoke, he sounded tired. "Marty, I understand how you feel. Was what we did wrong? Sure. If it was up to me, would I have made a different decision? Absolutely. But it wasn't up to me." He gave me an ironic smile. "One thing you have to remember is that the aviation business is all about accepting a certain level of risk."

A couple of snide comments popped into my head, but I kept them to myself.

Rob shook his head at me. "Marty . . . Marty . . ."

"What?"

"You. Your outrage. The righteous indignation that this could happen."

"You telling me this doesn't bother you?"

A shrug. "It did at first. But after a point you . . . I don't know . . . you just accept things, I guess." His expression turned somber. "You know, this G-626 situation isn't the worst problem we're facing. Not by a long shot. Take the air traffic control system, for instance. You think it's safe?"

I hesitated, uncertain over the point he was trying to make.

"It's a simple question. Do you think the ATC system is safe?"

"Not completely—"

"Exactly. That's my point. There's an element of risk. But we can't shut the entire system down just because we *think* something might happen."

He was talking in circles, trying to confuse the issue. "That's not what we're talking about here. We know the G-626 is dangerous—"

He snorted. "Like the air traffic control system isn't? You know, we spent billions to upgrade our computers in the nineties and we screwed it up royally. It's true. So now we're scrambling, trying to come up with something that will work. In the meantime, we're forced to keep using the old system that was designed for a third of the current traffic. And the congestion problem will only get worse. A lot worse. In the next ten years, the forecasts show air traffic doubling. *Doubling.* And odds are whatever system we do finally implement still won't be able to handle that kind of traffic. Between you and me, it's not a question of *if* we're going to have a midair because an ATC computer fucked up, but *when.* But after a while, you understand that's just the way things are."

I wondered if Rob was making this argument for my benefit or his own. I said, "You're comparing apples and oranges. You're talking generalities and I'm talking specifics. Dammit, we *know* the wing box on the G-626 is defective."

He shrugged. "The logic is still the same. We can't shut the ATC system down for the same reason we can't ground the G-626. Politics notwithstanding, the bottom line is we simply can't afford it. And this is nothing new, Marty. Want to take a guess on when the last time an entire fleet of airliners was grounded?"

I shook my head.

"Never." And he gave me a meaningful look.

"Bullshit," I said.

"Huh?"

I said, "Last year the FAA grounded all the McDonnell Douglas MD-80s because of a stabilizer problem—"

"You're wrong, Marty," he said flatly. "The fleet was never grounded."

"But the FAA announced..."

"*We* issued an airworthiness directive requiring inspections of the stabilizers. Only a handful of aircraft were actually grounded."

"Oh."

"Now, I'm not saying we'd never ground a fleet of airliners. What I am telling you is that decision will always be a last resort. The key consideration will always be the financial impact weighed against the risk to the public."

"So it comes down to money."

"Always has and always will." He shrugged. "That's what I mean about accepting things."

I felt a wave of frustration. "For chrissakes, Rob. That's nothing but a goddamn cop-out and you know it."

Rob's face reddened. "Thanks for the fucking support, buddy." He sat there, tight-lipped, doing a slow burn. He'd always had a short fuse, and I was afraid he'd get up and walk away. And maybe he would have, but at that moment, a jet roared overhead on its departure from Reagan National.

I looked up. "Say, isn't that..."

"Yeah," Rob said. "It's a Global 626."

We watched in silence until the plane disappeared.

CHAPTER 38

A group of schoolchildren went by us on the sidewalk, laughing. Then two mothers rolling baby strollers. I cleared my throat to defuse things. "Look, Rob..."

"Drop it, Marty," he said tersely. "Let's just finish this up, huh?" He wouldn't look at me.

"Fine. How did you cover up the wing box problem in the three civilian crashes? Those all took place overseas out of your jurisdiction."

"We didn't. ICAO handled that."

Made sense. ICAO was the International Civil Aviation Organization. I asked Rob if he knew anything about the upcoming merger between Boeing and Global. He seemed surprised at that, explaining that he was familiar with an old deal that had fallen through a few years ago.

"It's understandable that Boeing is still pushing to acquire Global," he went on, finally looking at me. "Even with their problems, Global's still the leader in composite airframe design. And composites are clearly the wave of the future. Another generation or two, the only metal in an aircraft will be the wiring."

"This earlier merger attempt," I said. "Why did it fail? Caldwell backed out?"

"Actually, I don't think it was him. He never wanted the merger in the first place. I understand he was being pushed by a few key stockholders. At the last minute, Caldwell was apparently able to convince them to nix the deal. Guess they must have changed their minds if the merger's on again."

Checking my watch, I realized I had to get going for the meeting with General Holland. I asked my last question. The most important one.

"Do you think the government could be involved in Colonel Wildman's killing?"

I expected a denial. Instead, Rob surprised me by taking his time. "My first reaction is they wouldn't, but . . ." He finally looked my way, shaking his head. "Hell, I suppose anything is possible."

I slowly rose, gazing down on him. Even though I knew his answer, I had to give it a shot. "I could really use your help."

"You know I can't."

"Can't," I said. "Or won't?"

His head popped up, his face knotting in rage. "You sanctimonious bastard! You got no right! You don't *understand*! You know what I'm risking by just being here. Talking to you—"

Rob was yelling at me now. People were coming down the path. I told him to keep his voice down.

"Fuck you! It's easy for you. You're an outsider. No one can touch you. Me, I busted my ass to get where I am. And you want me to throw that away for what? You actually think you're going to *change* anything? I got a news flash for you, Marty. You haven't got a chance in hell."

A burly man in a Redskins jersey with two small boys at his side called out, "Hey, Mister, watch your mouth. We got kids here."

Rob shot him a dirty look.

The man immediately started to come over when I

said hastily, "Sorry, sir. We'll keep it down."

The man planted his feet wide, staring at Rob. "See that you do."

"Shithead," Rob muttered, as the man led the boys away.

I sighed, focusing on Rob. I kept telling myself that he'd been a good man once and probably still was. That he wasn't to blame so much as a system that had changed him.

"See you around, huh?" I held out my hand.

He hesitated, then shook it. We gazed at each other for a moment. "I do hope you make it, Marty," he said softly.

"Sure." And as I walked away, I wanted to believe him.

Overhead, I watched another gleaming G-626 airliner roar across the sky.

I wasn't sure why I went inside the Jefferson Memorial. Maybe I was hoping to wash away the disillusionment I felt, or maybe I was looking for some sense of understanding that would never come.

Inside the rotunda, the crowd had grown. I hung back by the entrance, gazing up at the granite face of Jefferson. I was surprised by my sense of disappointment. For some reason, the statue seemed smaller than I remembered. I also noticed how the light filtering in made the marble walls seem a dingy gray. I shook my head, remembering a time when I used to feel a sense of reverence being here. That this was a special place.

But as I left, I felt nothing at all.

CHAPTER 39

Amanda was bent forward in the passenger seat of my Cherokee, poring over the documents in a thick folder, while Led Zeppelin's "Black Dog" blared from the radio. She didn't even notice me until I climbed behind the wheel.

"Sorry about Rob back there," I said, turning down the volume.

Amanda closed the folder, which contained Janet Spence's report on Global. "That's okay," she said lightly. "I just figured he's another sexist male who hates women."

I sighed, cranking up the engine. "See anything of interest in the report?"

"Not in Janet's report," she said, tossing the folder into my briefcase, which was lying open on the backseat. She picked up a second folder on her lap. "I did notice something in the bios that's kinda curious."

"What?"

"General Holland and Wildman were stationed together once before."

I frowned. In the Air Force it was common for people's paths to cross during their careers. Especially in a small community like Air Force Safety. Of course Amanda would know that. "You have a point?" I asked.

"Not really. Just thought I'd mention it. You know. That they've known each other for a while."

I suddenly understood. "I get it. You're wondering why Wildman would work for Holland if she knew he was a jerk."

She shrugged. "Something like that." Her cell phone in her jacket rang. She took it out and glanced at the face. "OSI headquarters. We've been getting a lot of calls, so I've been checking my voice mail. You want the good news or bad news first?"

Her phone stopped ringing. I followed a van out of the parking area, then made a left toward the George Mason Bridge. "Doesn't matter."

"Two messages from General Mercer. He wants us to call him. He mentioned he's been catching grief from the FBI over your little stunt."

I shrugged. I'd expected it. "He say if we've been re-moved from the case?"

"Not in so many words, but I'd say it's probably a given. He sounded pretty teed off."

"What's the good news?" I asked.

A cryptic smile. "There isn't any. The other message was from a very pissed-off FBI special agent named Frank Carruthers. Among other things, he threatened to have us picked up if we didn't contact him. Any chance he's one of the guys you had the run-in with this morning?"

I nodded. Truthfully, I was a little surprised by the threat. While I'd expected the FBI to get upset, having us hauled in seemed excessive. I took out my phone, figuring I'd better check my voice mail.

The first message was from General Mercer telling me to call him, then the OSI duty desk, asking me to do the same thing. Next Agent Frank Carruthers' voice came on. Amanda was right. Frank was one very unhappy man.

At the next click, I recognized Brian McNamara's voice: "You cock-sucking son of a bitch—"

I punched in the delete code.

My eyes widened at the last message, which was from an excited Janet Spence, telling me that Bobby Baker had called her, asking her to come over. "You might be wrong about Janet," I said to Amanda after I tucked the phone away.

But after I explained, she said, "Isn't Romero with her?"

I gunned the car, merging onto I-395 southbound toward Springfield. "I think so."

"That's why. He probably had her call."

I gave her a look of annoyance. "What have you got against her, anyway? You can't seriously think she's involved in Wildman's death."

She hesitated. "Probably not. But she's a reporter, Marty. You think she gets a break on maybe the biggest story of the year, she's gonna give it to you? Be serious."

"She's a *gossip* columnist, for chrissakes. Besides, she promised me she would." But even as I made that last statement, I realized I sounded ridiculous. "Look, you weren't there. She wants to find the killers as much as we do."

"Uh-huh." Amanda settled back in her seat, giving me an expectant look. "Anyway, what did your FAA women-hating buddy tell you?"

For the next ten minutes, I filled her in on my conversation with Rob. She shook her head angrily when I finished. "Jeez, this pisses me off. They think they have the *right* to make this kind of decision with people's lives. Makes me wonder what the hell else the government is involved in that we don't know about."

We were in the southwest part of Alexandria now, driving past a high school in an upscale neighborhood of majestic Colonial-style homes on acre lots. "It's troubling."

She went quiet for a moment, her brow furrowed. "No use. Call me naïve, but I can't buy that the government would have been in on the Wildman killing. The cover-up on the G-626 problem, okay. But not the killing."

I still tended to agree, though with more than a lingering doubt. "Who are you calling?"

Amanda was taking out her phone. "My older brother Mark. We still don't know anything about the merger. I think it'd be interesting to find out how much Caldwell would lose if it fell through."

"And Mark is..."

"A Wall Street analyst. Tracks the bond market for Merrill Lynch, but he's pretty well connected throughout the financial community. He should be able to find out what we need."

I made a right at a stop sign near a park, following the road up a hill. Larger homes here, in more eclectic styles. Amanda hung up thirty seconds later. "Not in, but I left a message." She shifted to face me. "So how are we going to handle questioning Holland?"

I shook my head. "*We* aren't. I'll take care of it."

"Dammit, Marty—"

"No. You're too emotional toward him."

"That's damned sexist and you know it."

I blinked. *"Sexist?"*

"Sure. You're implying that because I'm a woman I can't control my feelings to do my job."

Christ. "Being a woman has nothing to do with—"

"Tell me something. Would you accuse a *man* of being too emotional?"

I hesitated.

"That's what I thought." She shot me a look of disgust and gazed out the window.

We rode on in awkward silence.

I sighed, throwing out an olive branch. "Maybe you're right."

She kept staring outside.

"Okay, okay," I said. "We'll question Holland together." When she finally looked my way, I gave her a smile. "Look, I really didn't intend to—"

She waved me off. "Forget it, Marty. I probably overreacted anyway. At the Academy I put up with a lot of the macho me-Tarzan, you-Jane bullshit. After a while it just gets old."

I nodded sympathetically.

"Anyway," she said, "if it makes it any easier for you, I can leave my gun in the car."

"Your gun?"

She flashed a wry smile. "Just in case you're still worried I'm going to shoot the son of a bitch."

"All right," I said. "Put it in the glove compartment. I think that's Holland's home just ahead."

"I was *joking*, Marty."

I wasn't.

We pulled into the circular drive of a sprawling hillside house fronted by white columns and a wrought-iron veranda that ran the length of the second floor. Here inside the Beltway, the place probably went for at least a half-mil easy. A point that struck me as curious, since I knew what a general officer made. We parked behind the tan Sable and a gleaming silver Porsche 911 with vanity tags that said 2STARGEN.

"Little ego there," Amanda muttered dryly as we climbed out.

I nodded, frowning at the Porsche. "Did Sullivan say why the general hasn't been driving his car recently? Maybe that it was in the shop?"

"No. Why?"

"Just curious." Maybe it's a guy thing, but I was thinking if I had a Porsche, I wouldn't go tooling around in my wife's Sable. Not unless I had to.

Walking around a flower garden toward the front steps, I glanced around, saying, "I didn't know Holland had money."

Amanda shrugged. "They're a couple of DINKs with high-paying jobs. Probably up to their asses in mortgages."

By DINKs she meant double income no kids. I nodded. That was probably it.

As we stepped up to the front porch, Amanda said, "You know, when I spoke with Major Sullivan this morning, she mentioned something that struck me kinda funny."

I rang the bell. "And that is ..."

"She said she was giving Holland a briefing this morning at nine."

I gave her a blank look.

"Don't you see, Marty? If Holland already went to the Pentagon, why are we meeting him here at his home instead of his office?"

She had a point. That did seem a little silly.

"I'm telling you, the guy is smart," Amanda said. "He doesn't do anything without a reason. I can't shake the feeling he's up to some—"

"Quiet," I said. "Someone's coming."

CHAPTER 40

A uniformed maid led us into a bright sunroom that over-
looked a shimmering pool with one of those infinity
edges that seemed to flow seamlessly into a forested hillside. General Holland was seated in a rattan chair, back to
us, sipping coffee and staring out the windows. A zipped-
up laptop computer case sat on a glass coffee table in front
of him. I'd expected Holland to be in uniform, but instead
he was dressed casually in a pale yellow polo shirt and
dark slacks. When I cleared my throat, he rose and wel-
comed us with a big grin.

"Right on time," he said, gesturing us to sit. "How about
a soft drink? Maybe some coffee?" He held out a blue mug
with MAJOR GENERAL HOLLAND scripted on the side.

Holland's attentiveness immediately sounded a warning
bell in my head. Outwardly, he seemed genuinely glad to
see us. Until I noticed his eyes. There I caught a flicker of
arrogance that told me he was going through the motions.
Putting on an act.

Amanda and I sat on a floral sofa to Holland's right.
Amanda shook her head at the drink offer. "No thanks, sir,"
I said.

"I'll take a refill in a couple of minutes, Marta," Holland said.

As Marta withdrew, Holland sat down, his handsome face turning serious. "Look, I know we got off on the wrong foot, but I want you to know I was just following orders last night."

The standard military cop-out. "Whose, sir?" I asked.

"The Chief of Staff. General Barlow. But it wasn't coming from him. I'm pretty sure he was getting his orders from someone higher up."

"How much higher?" I asked.

"Sorry. I really can't say."

"The Sec Def?" Amanda asked.

He gave her a vague smile and shook his head.

"The administration," I tried.

The head-shaking abruptly stopped. A tight smile. "Look, I really can't comment."

But it wasn't a denial.

"Marcus! I'm leaving!"

We all looked to the hallway. Striding toward us in a dramatic fashion was Lucille Holland, wearing an impeccably tailored red suit that contrasted with her blond hair. Taking my first good look at her, I immediately detected the coldness Amanda had mentioned. There was an arrogant set to her jaw that was more than a little intimidating. The combination of personal style and her bearing allowed Lucille Holland to project an air of confidence that made it clear she was someone used to getting her way.

In a flash, Holland popped to his feet and met her in the entryway. Amanda and I also rose.

Lucille Holland gave us a surprisingly warm smile before turning her attention to her husband. He started to make introductions, but she cut him off, saying, "I'm really running late, Marcus. I'll need you to call Mort Conrad and tell him we won't be able to make the dinner. Tell him we'll set something up next week. Oh, and make sure you call the gardener about the rosebushes. They really are atrocious. And the cleaners called. I need you to pick up my blue dress before six...."

For the next thirty seconds or so, she ticked off a list of errands. Holland nodded continually, occasionally glancing our way. He seemed embarrassed.

"Walk me out, Mark," she said finally.

"Of course, dear."

Lucille gave Amanda and me another smile as she and Holland disappeared down the hallway.

"Friendly thing, isn't she?" Amanda said dryly.

Actually, I thought she was...kind of.

➤ It was almost five minutes before Holland returned with an apologetic smile. As he sat down, he said, "Now, where were we..."

Amanda said. "You were telling us you were ordered to find Colonel Wildman's file on the G-626—"

"Actually, I was supposed to be looking for two files."

"Oh?" Amanda said.

"Sure. The file on the military crash, and the second file she'd put together to present to Congress."

Amanda's eyes popped wide, mirroring mine. "She *told* you she was going to Congress?"

"Almost two weeks ago," Holland said. "Colonel Wildman wanted my help because I ran the accident board on the G-626. Specifically, she wanted my testimony that I'd been ordered to cover up the wing box problem."

The timing clued me in. "The argument. That's what you two argued about. That's why you relieved her."

Holland nodded, slowly tenting his fingers. "Look, you have to understand I thought she didn't have a chance in hell of getting this out. I was convinced she'd just ruin both our careers if she persisted. But when she told me she had obtained conclusive evidence from a Global engineer that proved the G-626 wing box was defective, I decided to give her a hand."

Amanda rolled her eyes, looking at me. Annoyance flashed across Holland's handsome face.

"Dammit," he said. "It's the truth. Why do you think I reinstated her? Why do you think I decided to resign from the Air Force—" He seemed startled when he saw me nodding. "You were aware of that?"

"Yes, sir," I said.

"Then you know I have no reason to keep this quiet any longer." He stretched back in his chair, appraising me coolly. "You must have checked up on me with AFPC. That must mean you consider me a suspect in Colonel Wildman's death."

I said nothing.

He smiled. "You're goddamn nuts, Collins. I didn't have anything to do with her death."

My jaw tightened. "Sir, your wife's car was seen at Colonel Wildman's—"

"Guilty as charged. I was there, all right. Not only yesterday, but I dropped by the day before...." He paused, glancing at me. I nodded, indicating we knew this. "Anyway, when I left yesterday afternoon, Colonel Wildman was very much alive."

Frankly, I was surprised he was admitting being at the crime scene. I started to mention it when Amanda cleared her throat sharply. The look on her face told me she wanted to handle this. She sensed blood and wanted to go in for the kill. I started to shake her off—

But she was already focused on Holland. Curtly, she asked, "What were you doing at Colonel Wildman's, General?"

He shrugged, taking a swallow from his mug. "I told you I'd decided to cooperate with her investigation. She asked me to come over and review her evidence."

"What time was this?"

"I arrived around two. Maybe a few minutes after. I stayed for approximately forty-five minutes."

"So you left around two-fifty, sir."

"Give or take. I wasn't really looking."

"Could it have been as late as three?"

"Possibly."

"How much later, sir? Five minutes? Ten?" Amanda was trying to pin him down. Get him to admit being at Wildman's closer to the time of the murders.

Holland sighed wearily. "Let's call it three o'clock at the latest."

Watching him, I couldn't believe this was the same guy from last night. I expected him to erupt any moment over the way Amanda was peppering him with questions, trying to trip him up. But Holland seemed remarkably composed.

"Did anyone see Colonel Wildman when you left, General?" Amanda asked.

"When I *left*?" Holland pursed his lips together. "I don't think so."

Amanda sat back, looking slightly smug. "So you can't actually *prove* Wildman was alive, sir."

I tensed, eyes on Holland. Here it comes....

But instead of being angry, Holland responded with a relaxed smile. "I don't think I said that."

Amanda frowned.

"You see," Holland said, "there was someone else in the house. A woman. She didn't actually see me leave, because she was on the phone."

"A woman, huh?" Amanda said dryly. "Any reason you didn't mention her to us last night?"

"I should have mentioned it. It was a mistake. But at the time my only concern was finding the files. I thought if you knew I was there things would become...complicated."

"So who is this woman?" Amanda asked.

Holland glanced down the hallway to the maid who was approaching with a silver coffee decanter. "A friend of Wildman's. The woman was helping her do some research. She's a reporter."

Amanda stared. "Jesus." Her eyes went to me.

Of course, we knew who he was talking about now. I

had to work to keep my voice casual. "Her name, General?"

"Janet Spence. Works for the *Post*. Thanks, Marta."

And then Holland drained his coffee mug and held it out for the maid.

CHAPTER 41

As Marta poured the coffee, I gazed out the windows at the sunlight rippling across the pool. Air hummed softly from a nearby vent. From somewhere outside, I heard the faint sounds of dogs barking.

I felt more foolish than angry. Simon had tried to warn me. So had Amanda. And still I'd believed Janet. Given her the benefit of the doubt. Even now, I still couldn't convince myself she was involved in Wildman's killing.

When I looked back to Holland, he was gingerly sipping his coffee. He set the mug down and grinned at me. "Didn't know Janet Spence was there, huh?"

He was rubbing it in. I shook my head.

"Talk to her," he said. "She'll tell you I was long gone when Colonel Wildman was killed."

I almost mentioned that we'd already questioned her. "We'll check it out," I said.

Amanda leaned forward. In her eyes, I could see her disappointment over Holland's possible alibi. She said, "Maybe I'm missing something, sir, but I still don't understand why you thought Colonel Wildman's files were in her office. Isn't that the evidence you were reviewing at her home?"

Holland shook his head. "We were looking at copies. Colonel Wildman told me the original files were kept in a secure place." He shrugged. "She wouldn't tell me where, so I figured maybe they were in her office."

"These files, General," Amanda said, "if you'd found them, what were you going to do with them?"

The million-dollar question. I edged forward.

Holland's eyes drifted past us to the window. "They'd just killed Colonel Wildman," he said quietly. "What the hell do you think I was going to do?"

I said, "So you were going to turn them over to the chief of staff, General Barlow—"

"Not him," Holland said, coming back to us. "I was told to turn them over to a representative from Global Aviation."

"The man in the limo," I said.

He blinked at me in surprise.

I said, "I happened to see you talking with him, sir."

"I'll bet." Holland made it sound like an accusation.

"His name is Tatum," I said.

Holland gave me a blank look.

"He never told you his name, sir?" I said.

"No. He just said he was from Global."

"Tatum," I said, "handles security for Global's CEO, Mr. Caldwell."

"Figures," Holland said. "He came off as a real hardass. Anyway, once I told this Tatum I couldn't find the files, he got a little crazy. That's when we went at it. He threatened me, told me I had to find the files by today."

"How did he threaten you, exactly?" I asked.

Holland took a deep breath. "The son of bitch mentioned something might happen to my wife."

Amanda looked dubious. But to me, this fit the pattern of threatening family members.

I asked, "What are you going to do now?"

Holland took a swallow of coffee. "What do you mean?"

"If you can't find the files . . ."

He stretched back, uncrossing his legs. "Nothing. The point is irrelevant now."

Amanda and I frowned.

"You see," Holland said, eyeing us, "I went back to the Pentagon last night. Searched everywhere I could think of. Took me over two hours. Finally found the damn thing hidden in an admin safe."

Amanda sucked in a sharp breath.

I felt a little light-headed. "You have the files, sir?"

"Had. I'm afraid I handed them over to that son of a bitch Tatum this morning."

Amanda sagged back in her chair. I shook my head in frustration until I noticed Holland grinning at us.

"Relax," he said, reaching toward the computer case. "I only turned in the files after I made this."

As I looked down, he removed something from the side pocket. He held it up.

It was a computer disk.

 Amanda stared, stunned. "I'll be damned," I said softly.

"Took me half the night scanning everything in," Holland said, passing the disk to Amanda.

She turned it over almost reverently. It was unmarked. "Mind if we take a look at the data, sir?" she asked, looking toward the laptop.

"Still don't trust me, huh?" He didn't sound the least bit disturbed.

Amanda hesitated.

"Sure. Go ahead." Holland waved a hand. "But make it quick. I've got to get going pretty soon." He pushed the laptop case over the table to us.

In less than a minute, Amanda had the laptop up and running. She popped in the disk and clicked the mouse. At least twenty file names appeared on the screen, all with G-626 in the title.

Another click and the screen changed to a cover page with a Global header. The words EYES OF THE CHAIRMAN were stamped across the top in block letters. And below that, G-626 WING BOX ANALYSIS. Amanda scrolled downward, pausing occasionally to read. The report consisted of fifty-plus pages of text and graphs. To me they didn't mean much, but Amanda grew increasingly excited.

She opened a second file: a report citing possible defects in the composite lamination process. She scanned a page, giving a hiss of approval.

She began moving quickly, going down the line of file names, opening and closing each one. Most were reports, but two contained letters from Douglas McInnes to various bigwigs in Global, warning of possible problems with the G-626 wing box. "We got him," Amanda murmured. "Son of a bitch, we got him." She was talking about Caldwell.

A few minutes later she shut down the computer and popped out the disk. She looked a little flushed.

"Okay?" Holland said, rising.

"We appreciate this, sir," I said, as Amanda and I stood.

Holland's demeanor abruptly changed, softening. In a quiet, almost hushed voice, he said, "I am telling the truth when I said I tried to help Colonel Wildman. No matter what you've heard, I liked her a great deal."

I nodded, struck by his tone. Sincerity coupled with genuine emotion. I felt suddenly confused. I wanted to believe him.

But when I looked at Amanda, her face was a mask. Holland gave her a tiny smile. Her expression never changed.

He sighed, stepping back when the maid appeared in the entryway. "Marta will show you out."

"Sir," I said. "We might need your help detailing the problems with the G-626."

"Be glad to help." And he sounded like he meant it.

"Thank you, sir." I turned to go, tucking away my notepad. That's when I saw it. Just a flicker of red across Holland's shirt. At first I thought it might be a small bug or maybe a piece of—

The flicker stood still on his chest. My eyes widened in horror when I realized what it was.

The blur of movement to my right startled me.

"Get down, General!" Amanda screamed.

I lunged toward him, expecting the sound of a gunshot.

CHAPTER 42

Amanda hit Holland first, sending him tumbling over the chair to the floor. I landed next to them, my shin banging painfully on the edge of the table. An instant later I heard glass shattering. Something thumped hard against the wall above my head. Marta began screaming from the doorway. More bullets tore through the window, striking the wall. I rolled over, yelling for Marta to get down. But she just stood there, hands to her face, screaming.

I pushed up and hurled myself toward her. I knocked her to the ground as more glass shattered. The shots were coming every few seconds. Bits of Sheetrock rained down as the bullets peppered the wall. Holland began yelling, "The fucking bastard. The son of a bitch." Then Amanda's voice: "Dammit, General, stay *down*."

Marta was whimpering now, her legs dangling across my face. I looked around wildly, saw we were shielded only by a rattan chair. "Crawl into the house, Marta!" I ordered savagely.

She didn't move. She was frozen with fear.

Dammit. I pushed her hard on the rear. She yelped, then scurried across the floor into the adjoining hallway.

"The shooter's got to be on the hill, Marty," Amanda called out.

"Tell me something I don't know."

"We're sitting ducks," she said. "After the next shot, we're coming your way."

"All right." Rising to my knees, I dove through the doorway as another bullet struck the wall. I landed hard on the pile carpet and scrambled down the hallway. Moments later, Holland followed, still shouting obscenities, Amanda right behind. We all crawled into the kitchen, where Marta was already collapsed on the floor, crying hysterically.

I slumped against the granite-topped island in the middle of the spacious kitchen, breathing hard. A drop of sweat rolled down my brow. I wiped at it with my hand, trying to catch my breath. "Everyone okay?"

General Holland looked at me, wild-eyed and panting. "Fucking bastard," he gasped. "Who do you think he is? FBI? CIA?"

I shook my head.

"Silenced rifle with a laser sight," Holland said. "Shooter's got to be a pro."

Amanda went over to comfort Marta, who was propped up against the refrigerator. "Sounds like the shooting has stopped," she said, glancing over at me.

"Let's give it a few minutes." I took out my cell phone.

"What are you doing?" Holland asked.

"Calling the cops," I said.

"You crazy?"

I frowned. Amanda was looking at us, her arm around a dazed Marta, who was now sniffling softly.

"*Think*, Collins," Holland said. "Whoever the shooter was probably saw me give you the disk. You call the cops, that's the same thing as turning it over to the FBI. Hell, I wouldn't be surprised if they showed up *with* the cops."

"He's got a point, Marty," Amanda said. "We probably should get out of here."

"All right," I said after a moment. "But the police should still be notified—"

"I'll call them after you're gone," Holland said. "The important thing now is the security of the disk."

"You have the information stored on your computer?" I asked.

Holland nodded. "On my desktop upstairs."

"Call General Mercer, sir," I said, speaking quickly. "Tell him what happened here. And have him send a couple men out to pick up your computer and the disk. Do you have a weapon?"

"Sure—"

"Get it and lock yourself and Marta in a room while you wait for the police."

Holland nodded.

"You know, Marty," Amanda said. "They could have somebody waiting outside."

I nodded, already rising. "I'll check." Before leaving, I took a last look at Holland. Just to be sure.

It was there in his eyes.

Fear.

I went to the front door.

 From where I stood, partially shielded from one of the columns on the porch, everything looked quiet.

A red sedan turned into the driveway next door. In the distance, I saw a mail truck working its way toward us. I squinted at a car parked along the curb a few houses down. No one was inside. Three women in sweatsuits walked by briskly. They waved and I waved back.

A minute later, I went back into the house.

Driving away from Holland's house, I kept my eyes glued to the rearview mirror. No one followed. As I settled back, I called Simon to tell him about the shooting.

He sounded irritated when he answered. I could hear a

backdrop of clicking keyboards and ringing phones. "What's wrong with your phone, Martin? I've left two messages."

I started to explain why I wasn't picking up.

"Never mind. We're making progress. I'm at the offices of Larson and Pinard."

That was the name of the high-powered Washington, D.C., PR firm, the one that had hired Bobby Baker. "So you're back on the investigation?"

"In a manner of speaking. I should be leaving here in thirty minutes or so. Can you meet me at Bobby Baker's home in an hour? Romero said Janet has convinced Baker to tell what he knows."

I didn't reply.

"Martin..."

"I'm here, Simon. Look, maybe you were right about Janet after all."

"Oh?"

After I described the events that had taken place at Holland's, there was a long silence. When he finally spoke, I could hear the concern in his voice. "You and Amanda are all right?"

"We're fine."

"The information on the disk, you're certain it's Colonel Wildman's files?"

"Pretty sure. It looked like it."

"So you're convinced General Holland was not involved in her death?"

"I can't see how he was." I hesitated. "About Janet. You still think it's a good idea to have her question Bobby Baker? I mean, if she lied to us about being at Wildman's place..."

"I wouldn't be concerned about that, Martin. Janet called me about an hour ago to tell me she was there yesterday."

"She did?"

"Yes. It's one of the reasons I tried to phone you. So you could verify her account with General Holland."

"So General Holland really was going to help Colonel Wildman?" As I said it, I saw Amanda roll her eyes.

"From what Janet overheard, yes. She also confirmed that she left a few minutes after Holland did."

"You believe her?"

A pause. "Yes. She may be a lot of things, Martin. But she's no murderer."

Hearing him say it made me feel a little better. In the background, I heard a bubbly-voiced woman say, "Lieutenant Santos, Mr. Pinard will see you now."

"Thank you," Simon said. To me he said, "Frankly, I'm puzzled, Martin. We seem to be running out of suspects for Wildman's murder."

"It still could be Caldwell or the government," I said. "Or a combination of the two."

I heard someone knock on a door. The woman announced loudly, "Mr. Pinard, Lieutenant Santos."

Then Simon, speaking very rapidly to me. "That's what disturbs me. I'm not sure either is viable."

I was incredulous. "Not *viable*? Just who the hell do you think shot at us, then?"

"What's he saying?" Amanda asked, noticing my reaction.

In my ear, Simon said, "I have to go, Martin. One question. How many shooters were there?"

"We think one. The shots came from the same location."

"I thought as much. I doubt he's with the government. Ah, Mr. Pinard, thank you for—"

Simon finally remembered to click off his phone.

As I made a left by the park, Amanda said sarcastically, "So Simon doesn't think Caldwell or the government arranged Wildman's killing?"

I shook my head.

"Who does he think did it, then? Bobby Baker? Maybe the bogeyman?"

"He never said."

She made a face. "Simon's mistaken, big-time. Caldwell has to be behind the killings. It's the only thing that makes sense. Unless..." She trailed off, brow knitted. "You buy Holland's story about helping Wildman?"

Her tone made it clear she didn't. "Give it a rest, Amanda. He sounded sincere as hell, and Janet Spence backs up Holland's account. And after what just happened, you can't seriously believe he was lying."

Her look was enough. She still did.

"Besides," I said, "if he was involved in the G-626 cover-up, why would he give us the disk?"

She slowly massaged her brow. "I know it doesn't make sense, Marty. But everything he told us seemed a little too...contrived. To make his actions fit the facts. And you notice, some stuff, he still couldn't explain."

"For instance..."

"Why didn't he tell us about Janet Spence last night?"

"Same reason she didn't tell us. They both probably didn't want to get caught up in Wildman's murder investigation."

"You don't think that's a tiny bit suspicious, huh?"

"Maybe. But I agree with Simon that Janet's probably in the clear. And I don't think there's much doubt now that Holland is too."

Amanda started to say something, but didn't.

"What?" I said.

"Forget it. You'll think I'm crazy."

I smiled at her. "It's the shooting, isn't it?"

Her head snapped around.

I said, "You're wondering how the guy missed us."

"Damn right. The shooter had us dead to rights. And notice how most of the shots hit high on the wall."

I had. "My guess is someone was trying to warn Holland to keep his mouth shut."

"There's another possibility."

We were going by the school again. I put on my blinker to turn at the four-way stop sign. "Which is..."

She eyed me. "So we'd make the conclusion that you

apparently have. That Holland was telling us the truth."

As I braked to a stop behind a plumber's van at the intersection, I turned to argue that the fear I saw in Holland was real. That he hadn't been faking. But just then, I caught movement in the rearview mirror and noticed a dark sedan rolling out behind. It began to close rapidly. I could vaguely make out two men sitting inside. Their faces were obscured by the glare of the—

I swore, recognizing the faces. I spun the steering wheel. "Hang on, Amanda—"

"Back up, Marty! Jesus, it's a trap. *Back up!*"

For an instant I was confused. Then I saw that the van's back door was open. Three men in dark coveralls sprang out, guns pointed. I threw the car into reverse. From behind, we heard a sudden squeal of tires. We turned to see the sedan skidding to a stop scant feet from my rear bumper, boxing us in. The front doors flew open.

I was tempted to go for it anyway, ram their fucking car out of the—

My head spun at a sharp rap on my window. "FBI! Shut off the engine and get out!"

I stared at the man in coveralls pointing a gun at my head.

"The car," the man barked again. "Shut it down! *Now!*"

I nodded dumbly. My hand shook as I killed the ignition. Out of the corner of my eye, I noticed Amanda seeming to fumble awkwardly with her seat belt. I realized what she was trying to do but thought it pointless.

As we got out, the two men from the sedan were walking over. One was young and dark, the other heavy and blond.

I tried to sound nonchalant. "Long time no see, fellas."

"Spread 'em, asshole," Special Agent Frank Carruthers said.

CHAPTER 43

"Okay, you can drop your hands," Carruthers said, as he finished patting us down.

Amanda and I stepped away from the van and faced him. Two of the men in coveralls were already searching my Cherokee, while a third kept a gun on us. Carruthers' blond partner was standing a few yards away, his badge out, motioning the traffic past. "Nothing to see, people," he was saying. "Keep it moving. Nothing to see...."

"Enjoy copping a feel?" Amanda said to Carruthers.

Carruthers was placing our guns on the van's hood, next to our cell phones. His jaw hardened. "Listen, lady—"

"My name's Gardner," Amanda said. "*Captain* Gardner."

Carruthers ran his fingers through his thick hair, looking exasperated. "Look, Gardner, we can either do this the easy way or the hard way. Either you hand me the disk or I take it."

Amanda's face went blank. "What disk?"

"Don't screw with me, Gardner. Barnes here saw you stash it." The big man with the gun nodded. He was the same guy who'd rapped on my window.

"He's lying," Amanda said flatly. "I don't know anything about a disk."

Carruthers threw up his hands. "Fine. Have it your way." He motioned to Barnes. "Cuff her. We'll take her in for a strip-search." He looked right at Amanda as she spoke. Waiting for a reaction. But she gazed back calmly.

Barnes removed a set of cuffs from a pocket and came toward her. I waited for Amanda to say something, but she remained stubbornly silent. While I admired her nerve, she was being foolish now.

"Wait," I told Barnes. "Give it to him, Amanda."

She hesitated, then flashed Frank Carruthers a tight smile. "Hey, you can't blame a girl for trying." She faced the van. I saw her reach down the front of her pants before I looked away.

When she turned, she handed Carruthers the disk.

"Check it out," Carruthers said, passing the disk to Barnes. "Make sure it's legit." As Barnes stepped around to the back of the van, Carruthers shook his head at me. "You know, it didn't have to be like this. You should have cooperated. Would have been easier on you. Easier on everybody."

I almost told him to go to hell. But unlike Amanda, I tried not to antagonize people with guns.

A minute later, Barnes returned. "The disk checks out."

Carruthers nodded, taking out a cell phone. He stepped away to make the call.

"So what do you think they'll do to us?" Amanda murmured to me.

I watched Barnes with the gun. "I wish I knew."

As I leaned against the van to wait, I found myself thinking of my daughter Emily.

A young couple with orange spiked hair drove by, laughing and pointing at Amanda and me. She flipped them off, which brought out a grin from Barnes. The two men finished searching my car and returned, tossing my briefcase into the back of the van.

"He's finished with the call," Amanda said to me.

I nodding, watching Carruthers coming over. He detoured by the hood of the van to pick up our guns, then paused to remove the ammunition clips, which he slipped into his jacket. Then he popped out the batteries from our cell phones.

For the first time, I felt hope. Amanda whispered, "Marty, you think . . ."

"Take off," Carruthers ordered Barnes, handing him our batteries. "I'll wrap things up here."

Barnes pocketed his gun and disappeared into the van. We stepped aside as it drove off. Instead of continuing toward the Beltway, the van pulled a U-turn back into the neighborhood.

"All right, boys and girls," Carruthers said, handing us our weapons and cell phones, "today's your lucky day. You can go."

I tried not to sound surprised. "That's it?"

"That's it. The way I see it, you and me are even. No hard feelings."

No hard feelings? I almost lost it then. It took all my self-control not to take a swing at the son of a bitch. Punch that arrogant smirk off his—

"Oh, I almost forgot," Carruthers said as he turned to leave. "I got a message for you two from a Brigadier General Mercer. Apparently he's been trying to notify you that you're removed from the case." He winked. "Have a nice fucking day, huh?"

Amanda and I climbed into my Cherokee as Carruthers and his partner hurriedly drove off in the direction of the van. Amanda said quietly, "They're going to Holland's."

"I know."

She gave me a sideways glance. "At least we know Simon was right about one thing."

"What's that?"

"The FBI are assholes, but they probably didn't kill Wildman."

"You mean because we're still alive?"

She nodded.

I wasn't sure I agreed. "Lot of witnesses around. Been hard for them to explain us disappearing." I started the engine and put on the blinker, waiting for a car to cross the intersection.

"This is a waste of time, Marty," Amanda said, realizing what I intended.

I drove back to General Holland's to watch the show anyway.

I pulled up to the curb a block from Holland's house. In the circular driveway we could see two dark sedans and the plumber's van parked behind the Porsche. Carruthers and his partner were walking up to the front door, where a woman in a navy-blue pantsuit stood, talking into a cell phone. She stepped aside to let them by. Moments later, Barnes and one of his coveralled buddies emerged, carrying a desktop computer and a cardboard box. They placed the items in the back of the van and returned to the house. They didn't seem in any big hurry.

"Looks like Holland didn't put up much of a fight," Amanda said.

I nodded, thinking the same thing. "Can't really blame him. Probably figured the disk wasn't worth dying for."

Amanda didn't reply. The third man in coveralls came out of the house with what appeared to be Holland's laptop computer. The woman out front began pacing, still on the phone. I wondered if she was talking to Sam Rawlings, the FBI's number-two man, or someone even higher.

"All right," Amanda said grudgingly. "Maybe I was wrong about Holland."

Finally.

"Still," she said, "the timing bothers me."

"Timing?"

She shrugged. "That the FBI just happens to be conveniently waiting to grab the disk."

"No mystery," I said. "The FBI must have the house under surveillance. Shooter probably gave them a heads-up when he saw Holland give us the disk."

She looked dubious. "I thought you said Simon didn't think the shooter was linked to the FBI."

I said nothing. But I was thinking there was no way in hell Simon could know that.

Amanda squinted at the house. "Looks like we've worn out our welcome."

The man with the laptop was staring in our direction, a hand shielding his eyes. He pivoted and hurried back to the house.

I punched the gas and made a U-turn. An oncoming car blared a horn.

As we sped down the hill, Amanda said, "We going to meet Simon at Bobby Baker's now?"

I nodded.

She gave me a long look. "You know, Marty, if we keep digging, they'll probably try and stop us again."

I caught her drift. "There's a Wal-Mart on the way."

"I'll call Mark. Maybe he's got something for us on the merger now. And Marty, one more thing about Holland suggests maybe he did know about the shooter."

I sighed. "And that is ..."

She shrugged. "Might explain why he wanted to meet us at his home."

I had no response.

➤➤➤ This time Amanda's brother, Mark, was in. She was still speaking to him on the Wal-Mart pay phone when I came over with two Diet Cokes and a sack containing two ammo clips and a box of shells. When Amanda hung up, I handed her a can. After a sip, she said, "Mark just returned to his office. He's having a hectic day, so it won't be until tomorrow before he finishes checking out the Global merger. He did confirm what we already knew, that there was a previous merger attempt between

Boeing and Global that fell through. He also told me who Global's largest stockholder is."

"Okay . . ."

"An outfit called MC Enterprises. It owns roughly thirty percent of Global's outstanding stock."

"And Caldwell's share?"

"Twenty-eight percent."

I thought. "Between the two, they have a controlling interest. Since we know Caldwell is against the merger, this MC Enterprises must be one of the entities pushing it. You having your brother look into MC?"

"Yeah. Mark already knew who owned it. MC stands for Marsha Caldwell. She's Caldwell's sister-in-law. She inherited the shares when Caldwell's brother Harold passed away."

I tugged on my chin. "Seems a little surprising she'd go against Caldwell on the merger."

Amanda gave me a knowing look. "Not really. Want to take a guess on Marsha Caldwell's take if the merger goes through?"

I shook my head.

"Up to a half-billion, give or take."

I whistled. "That much?"

"Yeah," Amanda said. "I'd say that puts Marsha Caldwell officially on the suspect list. Could even be one of the other major stockholders who ordered the killings. Mark's going to compile a list to see if we recognize any names. You ready?"

"Give me a minute." Even though we had to get going, I needed to make a couple of calls. I felt a nagging guilt at leaving General Mercer hanging out to dry. Knowing Mercer, he'd probably tried to cover for me until he'd finally been ordered to withdraw me from the case. I wanted to apologize and explain that any repercussions were my responsibility and not Amanda's. That she had simply been doing what I instructed.

Major Barbara Burns, General Mercer's annoyingly efficient executive officer, answered and said Mercer was in a meeting with General Barlow, the Air Force Chief. Not much doubt what and who they were discussing. Barb patched me into Mercer's answering machine and I left a rambling message. Amanda gave me a tiny smile when I hung up.

"That wasn't necessary, Marty," she said softly.

But we both knew it was. Amanda's name was now up in lights before the Air Force brass, tagged as a trouble-maker. Her military career was essentially over unless I could convince them she'd simply been following my orders.

I punched in Simon's number to give him the bad news that we no longer had the disk thanks to the FBI. He was just leaving the meeting. He sounded disappointed but not particularly surprised. "Maybe it doesn't really matter, Martin. There's been a break in the case. It's possible that the disk might not have anything to do with the murders."

"What?"

Amanda cocked an eyebrow at me. I held up a finger, listening to Simon's explanation. Afterward, I cradled the phone, feeling a little dazed.

"What's wrong, Marty?"

I faced Amanda, shaking my head. "Case might be over."

"Huh?"

"Romero," I said. "He just called Simon. It seems Bobby Baker is ready to go on record with Janet claiming responsibility for the murders."

Twenty minutes later, Amanda and I rolled into Baker's North Arlington neighborhood. We said little during the ride. We were both trying to recover from the realization that Baker might actually have committed the killings. As I turned onto Baker's street, I glanced at my notepad for the address.

"My God . . ."

My head popped up to see Amanda focused straight ahead, the blood draining from her face.

Then I noticed the logjam of police cars and ambulances at the far end of the street.

For a moment, I went numb. My mind raced through possibilities. I was thinking it couldn't be.

I heard Amanda say, "Maybe it's a different house."

But we both knew it wasn't.

I came down hard on the gas.

CHAPTER 44

We bounced jarringly over a speed bump as we sped toward the run-down red-brick house. In the driveway, I spotted Janet Spence's BMW sitting behind Bobby Baker's Cadillac. I counted two ambulances and four black-and-whites haphazardly angled along the curb. A half-dozen uniformed officers milled around on the unkempt lawn. Across the street, a muscular cop with a flattop haircut was talking with a gathering crowd. I didn't see Simon.

I squealed to a stop behind the last police car. As Amanda and I jogged toward the front door, two cops interviewing an elderly woman shouted to us. One came over to check out our IDs. He was a large black man with a pleasant face.

Handing back my badge, he said, "Lieutenant Santos said to expect you, Chief Collins."

"Is he inside, Officer Mason?" I asked, reading his name tag.

"On the way." Mason's voice became somber. "Real shame about Mr. Romero. He was a regular guy. Friendly. A lot of us liked him."

Something knotted in my stomach. I almost couldn't say it. "He's dead?"

A head shake. "But it doesn't look good. Took a couple rounds in the chest. Reporter lady's in a little better shape."

"Does Lieutenant Simon know about Romero yet?" I asked.

Mason nodded.

"What about Bobby Baker and his girlfriend?" Amanda asked.

"Don't know. They're not in the house." Mason jerked his head toward the other cop still talking with the elderly woman. "Mrs. Olson lives across the street. She heard the shots, called us. She said she saw the girlfriend leave about an hour ago, so we're figurin' she's probably okay. Baker might be hurt, though. Notice the blood trail?"

He pointed to the front stoop, where another cop was stringing yellow crime-scene tape around a post. Large blood spatters glistened in the sunlight. More drops dotted the concrete walkway, trailing off into the grass.

"Someone's hurt pretty bad," Amanda said, stating the obvious.

"We think Romero got off a round into the shooter before he went down," Mason said. "We're putting the word out to all the area hospitals. It's just a matter of time before the guy turns up."

"Is it looking like Baker was the shooter?" Amanda asked.

Mason shrugged. "We're still trying to get a handle on the situation. Mrs. Olson told us she heard a couple of cars drive off about twenty minutes ago. Said she caught a glimpse of one of the drivers and it didn't look like Baker. Baker's silver pickup is missing, so maybe he took off or wasn't even here."

"Hey, Willy!"

We looked across the street. The muscular cop was standing with a young woman holding a baby. He motioned.

"Excuse me," Mason said, going over.

The patrolman by the entryway had the area almost completely taped off now. Amanda called out to him and he pointed us to the back. As we started to walk around, we saw the garage door begin to open. Moments later two paramedics appeared, rapidly rolling a gurney.

Romero lay on his back, eyes closed, an oxygen mask over his face. His shirt was partially cut away and one of the paramedics was holding a blood-soaked bandage to his bare chest.

As they loaded him into the back of the ambulance, I searched for some movement. Anything. Finally I noticed his chest rising and falling.

"I know he and Simon were close," Amanda said softly.

I was surprised at the emotion I felt. But then I'd always liked Romero. "Very."

As we headed toward the back of the house, I blinked a few times to get the moisture from my eyes.

 We picked our way across the rock-strewn back-yard toward a rickety wooden deck with a rusted-out gas grill, a trash can full of empty beer cans next to it. The sliding door was partly open. As we approached, we heard someone moan.

Then a soothing voice: "Just a few minutes longer, miss. I know it hurts. Hang in there."

Amanda and I put on our latex gloves by the door. Through the glass, we could see into a small living room done up in motel-cheap furnishings. A sturdy female cop was standing just inside, her back to us. Past her, two para-medics hovered over someone on a gurney. One of the medics suddenly stepped back to toss a bloody bandage into a plastic bag.

I recoiled in horror.

"Oh, Jesus," Amanda said. "Her face . . ."

I had to take a moment before following Amanda inside.

 Janet Spence would never be beautiful again.

Her once-perfect jaw was now a mass of mangled flesh. Bits of shattered bone and broken teeth gleamed white against the gore. I kept looking away until the paramedic working on her, a wiry guy with a dagger tattoo on his forearm, began to cover the wound with a heavy bandage.

"Call the hospital, Dennis," Tattoo told his partner. "Tell them ETA eight minutes."

At that moment, Janet's eyes flickered open. They settled on me, widening in surprise. She tried to speak and gurgled.

"Don't try to talk, miss," Tattoo said.

She raised a hand, motioning to me.

Tattoo said, "Now, miss—"

I tapped him on the shoulder. He spun, startled.

"She might be trying to tell us who shot her," I said.

Tattoo hesitated, then nodded. "Make it quick, huh? I got to get her to the ER before she goes into shock."

Janet was making a writing motion. As I handed her a pen, our eyes met. Mingled with the pain, I saw a sadness. I wanted to say something reassuring, tell her that everything would be okay.

But of course everything would never be okay. Not for her. Or Romero.

Amanda and the female cop gathered around as I held out my notepad. "Who shot you?"

Janet slowly began to write.

Amanda swore, even before Janet finished. I stared grimly at the name. Simon had thought he was mixed up in this. As usual, Simon had been right.

"What the—" The cop stared at the name in disbelief. "No *way*. She's mistaken. It can't be him."

"It's him," I said. I started to give Janet a smile, but she was writing again.

For Simon.

I frowned at her.

Then her other hand came up, pressing something into mine. By feel I knew what it was even before I looked.

Her tiny cassette recorder.

Someone touched my shoulder, and I turned.

Simon, his face haggard and sad. "Excuse me, Martin."

I stepped aside as he took Janet's hand.

Simon continued to hold Janet's hand as the paramedics rolled her down the driveway to the second ambulance. Occasionally, he would reach down and tenderly wipe the hair from her eyes. Just before they placed her inside, he kissed her forehead. As the ambulance drove away, he closed his eyes and crossed himself. Then he turned and slowly walked back toward the garage.

Amanda and I were in the kitchen, watching him through a window. "You think he loved her?" Amanda murmured.

I nodded.

Moments later, we saw an unmarked police car with the flashers going double-park next to Simon's green Lincoln that he rarely used. Michael Reardon, the big detective from last night, emerged carrying a thick file. He shouted, jogging up to Simon. Reardon handed him the file and they continued into the garage, heads bent in conversation.

Amanda and I looked expectantly to the door by the refrigerator. It opened and Simon came over to us, carrying the file. Reardon continued into the living room.

Simon and I gazed at each other for a few moments. His face was etched with fatigue as if he hadn't slept in days. "I'm sorry," I finally said.

He nodded grimly.

"Are you going to the hospital?" Amanda asked.

"Later. There's . . . nothing I can do there now. The important thing is to end this before anyone else gets hurt."

I said, "So you've been reinstated— No?"

Simon shook his head. "A decision hasn't been made. The department is waiting to gauge the fallout from the news article. Captain Kelly is allowing me to assist unofficially." He checked his watch. "Forensics will be here soon. So will the press. We need to find someplace quiet to play the tape." He turned to leave the kitchen.

"Wait," I said to him. "Janet identified the shooter."

"I know. It was Brian McNamara."

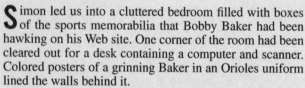

CHAPTER 45

Simon led us into a cluttered bedroom filled with boxes of the sports memorabilia that Bobby Baker had been hawking on his Web site. One corner of the room had been cleared out for a desk containing a computer and scanner. Colored posters of a grinning Baker in an Orioles uniform lined the walls behind it.

"Close the door, Marty," Simon said.

I did, then joined Amanda on a box. Simon camped out behind the desk. I tossed him the cassette recorder.

"So how did you know McNamara was the shooter?" Amanda asked him.

Simon was studying the recorder. "Hmm. Oh, Officer Mason said a young woman reported seeing a black Corvette leaving shortly after the shooting. But I've suspected McNamara's possible involvement in the Wildman murders for some time." He finally pushed a button and the tape began to rewind.

"Because of Janet's description of the men following Colonel Wildman?" I said.

A nod. "That's what initially heightened my suspicions.

I became convinced when I saw the file on Wildman's harassment complaint this morning."

"I take it McNamara was the detective who handled it," I said.

Another nod. He appraised me for a moment. "You suspected him too?" He sounded a little surprised.

"Not until this morning when you told me not to cooperate with him. That means the second man must have been Tatum."

"Yes." Simon sat back, massaging his eyes. "I had an IRS contact check McNamara's tax returns this morning. Over the past five years, he's made almost eight hundred thousand dollars working for Tatum's security firm."

I gave a low whistle.

"The son of a bitch," Amanda said. "That's why McNamara was so pissed when you took over the Wildman investigation. He was looking at a big payday for covering the thing up."

Simon nodded.

"And the Wildman murders," Amanda said. "Tatum and McNamara must have been in on those."

"Probably," Simon said.

I shook my head. In a way, you had to hand it to the bastards. It could have been the perfect crime, with McNamara investigating murders he'd help commit.

"I'm also convinced," Simon went on quietly, "that Tatum was the one who shot at you today at General Holland's."

"I'll bite," I said. "Why?"

He shrugged. "Tatum spent five years as a sniper on the FBI's Emergency Response Team. Frankly, I'm surprised none of you was hit."

I told him our theory, that maybe the shooter had only been trying to frighten Holland so he wouldn't cooperate. Simon pondered this for a few moments, then shrugged. "It's certainly plausible."

The recorder clicked off, finishing the rewind. Simon

stared at it and took a deep breath. As he pushed the PLAY button, his finger trembled slightly.

A soft hiss, then Janet's voice came on.

Simon closed his eyes as if he couldn't stand to listen.

➤   Janet's voice sounded clipped, professional. A reporter's voice: "This is Janet Spence of the *Washington Post*. It is eleven thirty-three A.M. on March sixteenth. I am about to interview former professional baseball player Bobby Baker, concerning the events which led to the tragic deaths of his ex-wife, Colonel Margaret Wildman, and their two children. Are you ready, Bobby?"

"Yes."

"State your full name, please."

"Robert Henry Baker." Baker spoke in a lifeless monotone, as if the weight of the world was on his shoulders.

"Are you being coerced in any way to participate in this interview?"

No response.

Janet again: "Don't shake your head, Bobby. Please just say yes or no."

"No."

"Fine. Let's begin. Who is responsible for Colonel Wildman's murder?"

A pause. "Me."

"Please repeat that statement."

"I'm responsible for the murder of my ex-wife, Margaret Wildman, and my two children."

Silence. The sound of paper rustling. Janet again: "By 'responsible,' are you saying you killed them with your own hand?"

"No. That was someone else."

"I see. Look, maybe it would be easier if you went back to the beginning and described the events that led to the murders?"

"I'll try. Jesus, this is hard." The sound of a match flaring. "I was just trying to make a few bucks. That's all. Just a few bucks. I...never thought anything would happen. Nothing was supposed to happen. It began when I started working at this club a couple years back. The Pentagon Club over in Crystal City. A lot of rich people. Influential people. One day this guy I'd seen around the club, Benny Tatum, comes up to me and hands me a thousand bucks. I ask what's the catch. Benny says there's no catch. He says he's just a fan and figured he'd help me out. Next week the same thing. Another thousand. For a month that's how it goes. Then one night Benny invites me to a party. Tells me the host is a guy who's big-time connected and might be willing to get me a cushy job.

"So I go. The place is plush. Decked-out penthouse with a view of the city. Broads and booze everywhere. Big silver bowls of coke and weed. Right then, I knew I should have left. I was trying to kick the drugs. But everyone's so friendly. Treat me like I'm still somebody. You know... asking for autographs, taking pictures. Especially the guy who owned the place. His name was Rick. Young, good-looking guy. We hit it off. Rick says maybe he can line something up for me that pays six figures. Promises to call me later that week. That's all I remember, because the party really got wild after that. The women started taking off their clothes and the next thing you know, people are humping on the floor. Crazy shit. Reminded me of when I played ball. When these women would be all over us.

"Anyway, the son of a bitch Rick never called like he promised. After a couple of weeks, I realized he was just bullshitting me. You know. Just some rich guy getting laughs showing me off to his friends. It happens.

"Then out of the fucking blue Benny and Rick show up at the club last month. Rick apologizes, gives me some song and dance about being sent out of the country. He tells me the offer is still on the table. He swears he can get me a nice-paying job. I play it cool 'cause I think he's screwing with me again. Anyway, he invites me to another party at his place. I figure what the hell. I got nothing to lose.

"Only this time, when I get there, there's no party. Just me and Rick and Benny Tatum and some woman I remembered seeing at the party. And a briefcase full of money sitting on the dining table. Rick says it's a hundred grand. Then he hands me a drink and pushes the briefcase across the table. 'Take it,' he says. 'It's for you.'

"I don't move. I just sit there, because I know he wants something. He has to want something.

"And I was right. Rick finally gets around to telling me he works for Global Aviation. Rick says he needs a favor. He tells me my ex-wife Margaret is causing his company problems. Making waves about one of their airplanes. The G-626. He wants me to convince her to stop. Says if I do, I get half a million and a great job. Says if she wants, Margaret gets half a mil too.

"I knew it was wrong. I knew I shouldn't do it. Margaret had told me about the plane, how dangerous it was. All that.

"But I'm sitting there, staring at the money. So much money. And the woman says for me to think about my kids, think about what I could do for them with the money. So I say yes and walk out with the briefcase.

"The next day, I went to see Margaret and tried to get her to agree to the deal. She never let me finish. Just threw me out of the house. I don't know what I was thinking. I should have known she wouldn't go for it. Not her. When Rick calls me later, I tell him to forget it, there's no way Margaret's going to change her mind. Rick gets pissed, tells me if I can't get her to back off, then I've got to get her evidence, her proof. I tell him I can't. I tell him he can come over and pick up the money. Then I hang up on him.

"About an hour later, my doorbell rings. I'm expecting Rick or Benny, but instead it's a cop. He says he needs to ask me some questions. He goes on about how he's been hearing that I'm dealing drugs. I tell him he's crazy. Then easy as you please, the cop pulls a bag of crack out of his jacket. A big bag. I'm talking fifty vials. I'm sweating now. I know he's setting me up. The cop doesn't say anything.

He just smiles and makes a call on his cell phone, then hands it to me.

"It's Rick. He's calm. Kinda friendly. He asks me if I understand the situation, and I say I do. What else could I say? It would be my third fucking bust. With a conviction for dealing, I was looking at ten years easy. Maybe more.

"For the next couple weeks I tried to get the stuff from Margaret's office, but she always seemed to be at home. There was never a good time. Finally the cop pays me another visit. Tells me I have to have everything to Rick by yesterday. Wednesday. The fifteenth.

"From my kids, I found out Margaret was going to a meeting in the morning. I knew this was my last chance. I'd only been in the house for maybe ten, fifteen minutes when Margaret suddenly comes back. She catches me in her office and we have a fight. I break down and tell her the whole story, how I'm looking at prison time, all of it. She starts crying. She says she's scared too, but she can't give me her evidence because . . . because she just can't. It's too important. She comes up with this idea that I should take the kids and leave town until everything blows over.

"So that's just what I was going to do. Leave town.

"After I left Margaret's, I call Rick to try to stall him. Ask for another day. I was trying to buy time for Margaret, so she could do what she had to do. Just one more day. That's all she needed. Then everything would have been out of her hands.

"But that didn't happen. She didn't have a day. My kids didn't have a day. And it was my fault. My goddamn fault."

Baker fell silent. The tape ran for a few moments.

Janet: "I'm not sure I understand. How exactly are you responsible for the murders, Bobby?"

Baker, his voice rising with emotion: "Because I happened to mention to Rick about her meeting that night. That's why he was so anxious to get the information. He knew Margaret was going to turn over everything to this congressman. That's why he had her killed. Don't you *see*? He had to—"

He broke off. We could hear him crying.

"Congressman?" Janet asked. "What congressman?"

Before Baker could reply, we heard a doorbell. Then urgent knocking.

Romero's voice: "I'll see who it is." Moments later, he said, "It's Sergeant McNamara. I'll get rid of him."

A pause.

"Hello, Romero."

Romero again: "What the hell are you doing—"

Then Baker's voice: "That's *him*! That's the cop who—"

A single coughing sound. Someone groaned. We heard Janet shout, "Don't. Please..." More coughing noises. Janet started screaming. Another cough and her screaming stopped.

An instant later, we heard a single loud gunshot followed by a grunt of pain. Then McNamara: "You *son of a bitch*!" Another coughing noise and the sound of something heavy falling. A man was groaning and swearing. It sounded like McNamara. Faint, staggering footsteps and a door slammed shut.

Silence.

The taped hissed.

Finally, someone began to moan. Then Baker's anguished voice: "I'm sorry, Janet. Christ, I'm so sorry."

Rapid footsteps, fading. Another door slammed closed.

The moans grew louder, almost guttural, as if Janet was trying to call to someone.

Simon couldn't take any more and turned off the tape.

CHAPTER 46

In all the years I'd known Simon, he'd always been able to control his emotions. He never let himself get too high or too low. But hearing the tape had really shaken him. For a couple of minutes afterward, he just sat quietly, taking deep breaths, dabbing his forehead with a silk handkerchief.

"You going to be okay?" I finally said.

A barely perceptible nod. He carefully refolded the handkerchief and tucked it into the top pocket of his jacket.

"So what's our next move?" Amanda asked him. "The tape pretty much settles the question of Tatum's guilt as well as this guy Rick's. Plus Caldwell's, since they were obviously acting on his orders."

"How do you know that?" he said mildly.

My eyebrows went up. Like in our phone conversation this morning, Simon seemed reluctant to link Caldwell to the murders. "Get real, Simon. You know Tatum wouldn't take a crap without an okay from Caldwell. And the penthouse Baker described. Fifty bucks says it was Caldwell's."

Simon shrugged. "Even so, that still doesn't prove Caldwell was behind the killings. Remember, he rarely used his apartment more than a few times a year."

Amanda and I looked at him in disbelief. "Why the change?" I asked him. "Last night you were practically ready to throw the cuffs on Caldwell and haul him to jail."

He took a moment to gauge his response. "I was letting my bias against him cloud my objectivity, Martin. I wanted him to be guilty, so I assumed he was. It's similar to Amanda's attitude toward General Holland." He paused to give her a tight smile. "Your comment last night made me realize I was making a mistake."

"*My* comment?" she said.

He nodded. "You asked why a wealthy man with one foot in the grave would care about making more money. I finally accepted that he probably wouldn't. At least not to the point of committing murder."

I wasn't buying this. Not now. Not after the tape. I said, "It has to be Caldwell— What's this?"

Simon handed me a folded sheet he'd removed from his jacket. As I opened it, Amanda leaned over my shoulder to see.

A copy of the front page of a 1040 tax form. Two lines were highlighted in yellow. The first was the name block: Benjamin L. Tatum. And farther down, the block for Tatum's employer.

That's where Amanda and I were looking now when she gave a little gasp. I did a slow head shake.

We'd expected to see either Caldwell's name or that of Global Aviation.

Instead the line read: MC Enterprises.

My eyes went to the GROSS INCOME block. Almost a million dollars.

"Okay?" Simon said.

I nodded, passing back the paper. To Amanda, I said, "Looks like you were right to check out MC."

"You're *familiar* with MC Enterprises?" Simon said to us.

Amanda quickly explained how we'd learned of the

company. That it was the majority stockholder in Global and was run by Caldwell's sister-in-law.

"Frankly, I haven't learned much more than that yet," Simon said. "But this is a troubling development. I've uncovered two additional references to the company this morning. I spoke with Archie Peters at the Pentagon Club. He confirmed that MC Enterprises holds a corporate membership that wasn't on the individual listing he gave us."

Amanda said, "That's how Tatum got into the club to contact Baker?"

Simon nodded. "And probably Rick."

"Anyone named Rick or Richard on MC's membership?" I asked him.

"Archie's pulling the account," Simon said. "I told him I'd swing by to pick it up."

Amanda said, "You mentioned two references...."

"Yes. It seems MC Enterprises is also a major client of Larson and Pinard."

It took me a few moments to grasp the significance. Amanda beat me to it, saying, "You're telling us Bobby Baker got his PR job—"

"Precisely," Simon said. "MC Enterprises got him hired. *Not* Global."

"Pinard," Amanda said. "Did he say who runs MC?"

"On paper, Marsha Caldwell is the CEO," Simon replied. "But she's in her late sixties and lives in Europe. She has little to do with the day-to-day operations; she leaves that to a board of advisors. Pinard said she's officially going to step down later this week."

I felt my pulse quicken. "And her successor?"

"Pinard didn't know," Simon replied. "He says it's being kept very hush-hush. An announcement is expected anytime."

My head was spinning, trying to make the pieces fit. I said, "Let me see if I've got everything straight. You're working on the assumption that Tatum and Rick worked for MC Enterprises and ordered Wildman killed so she wouldn't jeopardize the merger..."

"Yes."

"...and that Caldwell didn't know anything about it. Played no role."

Simon hesitated. "I think Caldwell is probably aware of what's taking place. My question is whether he had anything to do with ordering the actual murders. I'm inclined to think not for the reasons I've mentioned."

"I dunno, Simon. That seems like a helluva stretch to me."

Simon slowly tented his fingers, watching me. "It's more than just blind supposition, Martin. Think back to last night."

"Last night?"

"In Caldwell's study. Remember his reaction when I told him about the murders of Wildman and her children?"

I frowned, trying to recall.

"Sure," Amanda said. "He seemed surprised."

"Ah," Simon said, as if she had said something important.

But Amanda still seemed confused. She said, "Couldn't Caldwell have been putting on an act for our benefit?"

"That's what I thought at first," Simon said. "If you'll recall, he quickly caught himself. To me that point is suggestive. He was trying *not* to show he'd been surprised by the news. So I concluded he was."

"But the news article on you," I said. "That shows he's trying to cover up the murders by having you removed from the case."

Simon sighed, massaging the bridge of his nose. "I know, Martin. I don't think there's any mystery about why he's protecting the murderers. He's probably concerned that their arrest could somehow implicate him. At the very least, it would lead to the G-626 problems becoming public."

I kept looking at him. I knew there had to be more behind his sudden change of attitude toward Caldwell. And Simon knew I knew. I waited for him to explain further, but he sat there quietly.

Through the door we heard a growing murmur of voices. Simon shifted in his chair, avoiding my eyes. He carefully folded Tatum's 1040 and slipped it into his jacket. Amanda started to say something, but caught my head shake. Simon glanced at his watch, then the desk and back to his watch. Stalling.

"Enough," I finally said. "Tell us the rest of it."

A resigned shrug. "All right, Martin. I want you to understand it's only a theory. But the timing and the location make me think there's a connection."

And as he spoke, he casually reached down and flipped over the thick folder on the desk, the one Detective Reardon had given him.

"Huh?" Amanda said. "You serious?"

We were looking at the case file for Patricia Dryke's two-year-old murder.

CHAPTER 47

Simon remained silent, watching us. Amanda continued to gaze dubiously at Patricia Dryke's murder file. I said, "I don't understand how this—"

At that moment, the answer hit me. I sat there looking at Simon, but I didn't really see him anymore. Instead I was focused on Baker's voice from the tape, playing in my head.

The women began taking their clothes off...

People were humping on the floor...

Reminded me of when I played ball. When those women would be all over us...

And then Simon's own words: *The timing and location are suggestive.*

"Son of a bitch," I murmured.

Simon seemed to smile. Amanda still looked puzzled. I spoke rapidly, trying to keep up with my thoughts. "Patricia Dryke was a hooker. She lived in Caldwell's building. Hell, she must have been at the party with Baker."

"Yes," Simon said.

"My God," Amanda said.

I was on a roll. I kept on talking, shifting through the

possibilities. "Patricia Dryke must have *heard* something, *seen* something at the party. Maybe figured out what was going on. Maybe she—" I paused. "Blackmail?"

"Possibly," Simon said. "Patricia Dryke was a girl with very expensive tastes. Perhaps she got greedy. Or maybe she simply knew too much. Not that it matters why she was murdered; she was."

We became quiet, taking all this in.

I decided to mention something else about Baker's interview that had struck me. I said to Simon, "From Baker's account, it seemed as if Rick was making most of the decisions. Could be he was the person Tatum has been working for all along."

Simon nodded. "At the very least, he's a key player. What we need to do now is identify him."

"How do we do that?" Amanda asked.

Just then the bedroom door opened and Detective Michael Reardon stuck his head in. He held out a phone to Simon.

"Lieutenant," he said quietly. "You've got a call from the hospital."

Simon stepped outside to take the call. Amanda and I sat in an uneasy silence, watching the walls. I took a moment to mouth a prayer. From the front yard, we heard a car drive up followed by the sound of voices. I went over to the window and saw the forensics team piling out of a van and a Suburban.

Turning, I saw Amanda sitting at the desk, powering up the computer. I understood why. Even though Baker never got around to mentioning it on the tape, she was considering the possibility that he had gotten hold of one of Wildman's disks and installed the information on the computer. I went over and began to search the desk drawers. Not so much because I really thought I'd find anything; I just wanted to keep busy.

More books on computers. The three I'd seen in his car

on Web site building, plus a couple of manuals on word processing and spreadsheets. Another drawer contained what had to be at least a hundred disks, some labeled, most not. I started flipping through them.

"Martin."

Simon was standing in the doorway. His face said it all. He swallowed hard a couple times, looking lost. "I . . . I need to go to the hospital."

"I'll drive you," I said.

Amanda gave me a questioning look, asking if she should come. I shook my head. At a time like this, Simon would be more comfortable with a close friend. By default, that responsibility now fell to me.

I gave her my car keys since we would take Simon's car, then picked up Patricia Dryke's case file and followed Simon out.

The Arlington County General Hospital morgue was located in a corner of the basement, near the loading docks that the hearses used to pick up the bodies. The young female attendant led us across a spotless tiled floor to a bank of metal refrigeration doors. She opened one, rolled out a body covered by a sheet, then quietly withdrew.

Simon stepped forward and slowly uncovered the face.

Romero looked as if he were asleep. The indentations from the oxygen mask were still visible around his nose and mouth. Simon stared at him for almost a full minute. "Do you know how long I've known Romero, Martin?"

"No."

Simon began speaking softly, in a faraway voice. Remembering. "Since I was twelve. After my father's disappearance, my mother lived in fear that he would return and try to harm us. He was angry with her, because she'd cooperated with the authorities. So she hired Romero. Over the years, he became more than my protector. He . . . was my closest friend, the one person I could always count on. My mother had trouble coping. The guilt, my father's crimes. It was too much. She began to drink heavily and..." He closed his eyes for a moment. "Anyway, a boy needs someone to provide guidance. Romero..." His voice quivered. "Romero taught me so many things...so many lessons. Without him I'm not sure I..."

Simon couldn't finish. He reached out and gently stroked Romero's cheek.

Seeing his grief, I was having trouble reining in my emotions. It reminded me of my own devastation when Nicole had died.

Abruptly, Simon withdrew his hand and began talking again. "There was a time in my life when I was very confused. I was young. Twenty-one. I wanted to do something with my life that...that mattered. For almost three years, I searched. I tried teaching...the church. But nothing felt right." Simon turned to me. "You knew Romero was a police officer?"

I nodded.

"Anyway, it was his idea that I become a cop. I resisted at first, but..." Simon managed a faint smile, returning to Romero. "He was perceptive that way. He always knew what I wanted before I did."

"He was a good man," I said.

Simon didn't reply. I could tell he was close to losing it. Removing rosary beads from his jacket, he bent his head over Romero and began to pray.

Somehow, Simon got through it. When he ended the prayer, he gave Romero's face a last caress and drew the sheet over his face.

"I loved him, Martin."

"I know."

We left to check on Janet Spence.

Leaving the morgue, we walked down a long hallway past the elevators toward the emergency room. Simon said, "Hate diminishes you. I'm trying hard not to give in, but it's difficult. I want more than to solve this case now. I want those responsible to suffer."

"But how? Baker's interview tape is little more than hearsay. The rest of the pieces are only theory and supposition. We still have no proof that will stand up in court. We haven't even identified Rick."

"I don't see that as much of a problem," he said with feeling. "I fully expect to learn his identity within the next few hours."

"You mean once Baker is located?"

"I was thinking more of McNamara. He's injured. He'll have to seek medical help soon."

"He still might not talk," I said.

Simon shrugged. "He was seen by at least two witnesses leaving Baker's. My guess is he'll try to cut a deal. And even if he doesn't cooperate, it's not the end of the world. We still have options."

"Caldwell?"

"That's one possibility." We'd reached the double doors to the ER. Simon opened one and we could hear a woman screaming.

CHAPTER 48

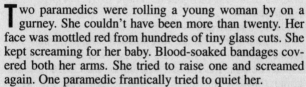

Two paramedics were rolling a young woman by on a gurney. She couldn't have been more than twenty. Her face was mottled red from hundreds of tiny glass cuts. She kept screaming for her baby. Blood-soaked bandages covered both her arms. She tried to raise one and screamed again. One paramedic frantically tried to quiet her.

"But my baby! Where's my baby?"

The gurney disappeared down the corridor. The woman's cries faded into silence.

We walked up to the admissions window, where a heavyset nurse was talking into a phone. "Dammit, Rita, I don't know where Dr. Anderson is. He's not answering the page or his beeper. Fine. I said fine. I'll try. But the son of a bitch better be there."

She banged down the phone, then noticed Simon. She smiled wryly. "Well, well. Lieutenant Santos. What brings you to the war zone?"

Simon attempted to smile back. "Hello, Ann. I was wondering if you knew the status of . . ." He frowned in annoyance when his cell phone rang. He answered it, listened, then wordlessly passed it to me.

"Simon . . . Simon . . ." It was Amanda.

"It's me," I said, stepping away. "Simon's busy. What's up?"

She spoke quickly. "A couple things. Linda Green, Baker's girlfriend, showed a few minutes after you left. She was out grocery shopping. She doesn't know where Baker might have gone, but she's worried he could be suicidal. She said he was particularly distraught last night. She even caught him putting a gun to his head. He tried to convince her he was just playing around—"

I felt a chill. "Baker take one of his guns when he left?"

"Reardon thinks so. We found the one in his Caddy, but the one he kept in the house is missing."

Christ. I ran a hand over my face.

Amanda went on, "Now, don't get your hopes up, but I think it's also possible Baker did obtain one of Wildman's disks. Linda said he spent the entire night working on his computer."

"Have you checked—"

"The hard drive. Yeah. Just finished. Initially, I had trouble because a lot of his stuff was password-protected. But Linda knew the passwords. Nothing on the G-626. I'm still going through his disks. I have to tell you I'm kinda stumped, Marty."

"About what?"

"Baker. If he had a copy of the disk, making additional copies would have taken minutes. What was he doing the rest of the time? He sure as hell wasn't playing video games."

Simon had finished talking with the nurse and walked over. I said to Amanda, "Maybe Baker was reading the information instead of—"

"Hang on a sec, Marty. Something's going on." In the background, I heard a jumble of anxious voices. Amanda called out, "Where are they?" A garbled response, then a man, angrily: "I can't fucking *believe* this. What the hell are *they* doing here?"

Even before Amanda came back to the phone, I knew what had happened.

"Three guesses who just fucking showed up waving a federal warrant," she said sarcastically.

➤ I passed Simon back his phone, explaining what had just occurred. He didn't seem overly concerned at the appearance of the FBI, or at Amanda's comment that Baker could be suicidal. We left the ER, retracing our steps down the hallway.

He glanced over. "You look discouraged, Martin."

"I am."

"Don't. It's a waste of time."

"It's hard not to be. Every time we get close, the FBI cuts us off at the knees."

"This time their interference is little more than an annoyance. If Baker had a disk, he certainly wouldn't have left it behind."

I knew what he was saying was probably true. "So how do we find Baker?"

A head shake. "We don't, I'm afraid. He's desperate and frightened. There's simply no way to predict his next move."

I felt a trace of exasperation. "So we do nothing. Just hope some cop spots him before he eats his gun."

"For now. Unless you can think of something better."

He knew I couldn't.

We reached the elevators. Simon pushed the UP button.

I said, "Janet's upstairs?"

He nodded. "In surgery."

➤ Thirty minutes later, I drained the last of my coffee, looking at Simon, who was seated next to me. We were hiding out in a private waiting room near the back stairs because the main waiting area was packed with Janet's press colleagues, a number of whom had tried to question us. At the moment, Simon's eyes were closed, his chin sunk to his chest. He'd been this way for almost ten minutes, ever since he'd had me recount in detail my confrontation with Holland in Wildman's office, the shooting at Holland's home, and my conversation with Rob Sessler on the G-626's problems. Before settling back, Simon also asked me to describe Holland's and Sessler's appearance. And I had a nagging suspicion why.

I sighed, firing the paper cup into a nearby trash can. I'd seen Simon go on like this for hours, trying to resolve the facts of a case in his mind. He termed it getting quiet, listening to the voice inside his head. I called it a waste of time.

I picked up an issue of *Newsweek* from the table, flipped a few pages, and tossed it aside. I felt increasingly restless. The way I saw it, Baker was the key now. Even though we had little chance of finding him, I wanted to try. Anything was better than just sitting—

Simon's eyes opened. He sat up. "You have the photograph from Wildman's office, Martin?"

I nodded, telling him I'd planned to drop it off at Wildman's house later.

"Let me see it."

I handed over the framed picture of Wildman and her kids at Disney World. Simon looked at it for a few moments, then said, "And General Holland expressed an interest in this?"

"Not so much an interest really. He just mentioned that it was missing."

"But the comment struck you as odd. Why?"

I thought back. "Nothing I can put my finger on. But the guard said the picture was under Holland's hat. I began thinking, what if that wasn't by accident? Maybe Holland wanted the picture for some reason."

"He didn't ask you for it?"

I shook my head.

Simon flipped the photograph over and started sliding out the cardboard backing.

"I already checked," I said. "There's nothing in it."

Simon nodded, slipping the photo into his jacket. "I'll

return it. Wildman's parents are flying out in the morning."

I folded my arms, looking at him. "So when are you going to tell me?"

He frowned. "Tell you what?"

"That Baker's description of Rick fits General Holland to a T."

He hesitated. "That still doesn't prove they're one and the same."

"C'mon, Simon. Holland's the one person who's been in on this thing from the beginning. He knew the victim, had a motive for the killing—"

"That's what bothers me, Martin. What exactly is his motive? Saving his career?"

"Look, I didn't buy that either at first. But someone could be paying him. Probably is. You should see his house. The man lives well. Besides, how many other young, good-looking guys have we come across in this case?"

"I can think of another."

"Oh?"

He thought for a moment, then shook his head. "But he's really not worth mentioning. He's rather an unlikely suspect."

Simon's phone rang. He spoke for maybe a minute, then cupped it, waiting. From his grim expression, I could tell the news was bad.

I said, "Baker's dead?"

"McNamara. Reardon said he's been found in his car in the parking lot of an abandoned restaurant in South Arlington. He'd been wounded in the stomach. Someone finished him off with two shots to the head."

"Tatum?"

A nod. Simon sounded angry. "Or one of his men. Tatum couldn't have allowed McNamara to talk."

I understood why Simon was upset. As much as he despised McNamara for killing Romero, he realized his best opportunity to break open the case was gone.

"What are you waiting for now?" I asked him.

"Reardon is getting Amanda for me."

"FBI still at Baker's?"

"Just left. They had a federal warrant authorizing them to take possession of Baker's computer and disks. Do me a favor, Martin. Ask the nurse if we can use their fax machine."

"Sure." As I stepped out into the hallway, a possibility occurred to me. There was someone else who fit the description of Rick. Someone unlikely. The big driver of Caldwell's limo.

Then I wondered how Simon could know what Jake looked like, since Simon hadn't been there during the confrontation.

Not that it mattered whom Simon had been alluding to. This time his intuition was wrong. Holland had to be Rick. It was the only thing that made sense. The fear that Holland displayed after the shooting could have been an act. And the disk he gave us was, as Amanda suggested, an attempt to throw off suspicion.

And yet . . .

I sighed, recalling the one hole in this theory that I couldn't resolve. The one that had bugged me from the beginning.

The damn car, and why a killer would park it out front.

As I went to the nurses' station, I felt the beginnings of a headache. I reminded myself to ask for some aspirin.

Over the next fifteen minutes things progressed rapidly. In that time, Simon called Archie Peters at the Pentagon Club with the nurse station's fax number, then chatted with the guard Lester from the Excelsior Arms apartments. When I returned with Archie's fax, Simon was talking to someone about obtaining photographs from the Virginia Department of Motor Vehicles. Three names he mentioned were Tatum, Holland and Caldwell.

Simon's sudden energy wasn't surprising. McNamara was gone now, and the odds of Baker turning up alive were iffy. Realistically, we were down to our last option, which was what he was working on now.

Simon ended his call and gave me an expectant look.

I passed him the fax with the last names and initials of the seven people on the MC Enterprises corporate membership list.

"Tatum's on it," I said. "And so is Marsha Caldwell, MC Enterprises' CEO. But there's no Holland and no one with a first name beginning with R. That probably doesn't mean much. No way Rick is the guy's real name."

Simon carefully scanned the sheet. He put it away, saying, "Rick could have been a guest of Tatum's. Did you ask how much longer Janet will be in surgery?"

"Another couple of hours."

He rose. "Amanda will meet us at Caldwell's apartment."

"Odds are he won't talk. Probably just sic his lawyers on us."

Simon shrugged, carefully adjusting his bow tie and smoothing his suit.

I said, "We should check out Marsha Caldwell. It could very well be she's the one pulling the strings on this."

"Perhaps. But Pinard described her as not financially astute. Besides, she's been in Europe for over a year."

"What about the other members on the list? One of them could be Rick."

He started for the door and stopped. "I rather doubt that, Martin."

I held back a smile. "Because you've finally decided Rick is General Holland."

A grudging nod. "He's the most likely candidate. Still, I can't completely rule out the other individual—"

We were interrupted by a sharp rap on the door. A scholarly-looking man with a beard poked his head in. He said cheerfully, "Ah, there you are, Lieutenant Santos. I'm

Randy Speers with the *Washington Post*. I was wondering if you could answer some—"

Simon rudely pushed past him and into the hall.

Randy Speers and a half-dozen other press types followed us all the way to the parking lot, yapping out questions and taking pictures. They kept darting in front of us, and we had to constantly step around them. A number of the questions were about Simon's father, which told us that Simon's story had already made the rounds of the *Post* staff. It seemed to take forever until we finally got into the car and drove away.

"Bastards," I said.

Simon said nothing. His face was a mask.

"Don't let them get to you," I said. "They were way out of line. You're not responsible for your father's actions."

Again no response.

I took the hint and concentrated on driving. We rode in silence for the next fifteen minutes. The whole time Simon kept staring grimly outside. I wanted to tell him something reassuring but knew it would be pointless. Romero's death and now this—what do you tell someone whose world was suddenly falling apart around him?

Finally, I cleared my throat, saying, "It's Holland's car, isn't it?"

Simon faced me, frowning.

"Because it was in front of Wildman's," I said. "That's why you're not convinced Holland's guilty."

He hesitated. "Actually I'm more troubled by Janet's comments concerning Holland's discussion with Colonel Wildman. How he kept urging Wildman to leave—"

"What?"

Simon blinked at me. "Didn't I tell you?"

I gave him a look of annoyance. He knew damn well he didn't. "Are you saying Holland was trying to get Wildman to leave her home?"

"Yes."

"Right before the murder?"

A nod. "But not only then. According to Janet, Holland had been concerned for Wildman's safety for some time. He'd been wanting her to go into hiding until she turned over her evidence."

"Jesus." I felt completely off balance now. As I turned up the winding drive to Caldwell's apartment complex, I said, "Maybe Holland was just feeding Wildman a line, trying to gain her confidence."

"And if he wasn't, Martin?"

I didn't even try to answer.

CHAPTER 49

I thought you said Lester's expecting us," I said.

Simon and I were peering through the sliding glass door at Lester's empty guard post in the lobby of the Excelsior Arms.

Simon didn't reply. He rang the call-box buzzer again while I rapped on the glass.

"Lester might be making a security check," I said.

Simon nodded, taking out his cell phone. He punched in a number and we heard the faint sounds of ringing from within. He hung up, looking at me. I shrugged.

A white Volvo rolled past us, pulling into one of the covered spaces reserved for residents. A young woman in a beige pantsuit emerged, carrying a briefcase.

"Martin..."

When I glanced over, Simon had stepped back and was staring down the line of parked cars.

"What?" I asked.

But Simon had begun to walk rapidly toward the cars.

I tried to follow his eyes. Simon seemed interested in an area just past where the woman had pulled—

I swore.

Maybe three spaces down from her Volvo, I saw the end of a vehicle poking out; a battered silver pickup.

Simon suddenly pivoted, anxiously waving his ID at the woman. He jogged toward her. "Miss, we're police officers. We need your ..."

As he explained, I took out my pistol and chambered a round.

Simon hurried over to me, barking orders into his cell phone. The woman ran back to her car. Simon hung up, jamming the phone into his jacket. "Dispatch says it will be three minutes."

I asked, "You want to wait or go now?"

He hesitated.

"It could all be over in three minutes," I said.

He responded by taking out his gun. He slipped the woman's entry card into the keyless lock.

The doors slid open. Simon left the card in the slot and we went inside.

A quick look confirmed that the lobby was empty. We found Lester facedown behind the guard station. A dark red welt glistened on the back of his head. Simon checked his pulse. "He's alive."

To me this point was telling. Bobby Baker wasn't on a homicidal rampage so much as a mission of vengeance.

I checked Lester's belt for his keys. Gone.

We spun at the *ding* from an elevator. A man in a jogging outfit stepped out. His eyes popped wide when he saw our guns.

"Police," Simon said curtly. "There's an armed man in the building. When the patrolmen arrive, I want you to tell them that Lieutenant Santos has already gone up to Mr. Caldwell's apartment. Twelve-E. Can you remember that?"

The man nodded dumbly. He practically ran out the front door.

We stepped inside the elevator and I pushed the button for the twelfth floor.

"We need to take Baker alive," I said.

"If we can."

 The elevator doors opened.

I went out first, keeping low, Simon on my heels. The hallway was empty. Silent.

We kept to the wall as we made our way to Caldwell's apartment. As we approached, we saw the door slightly ajar. We listened.

Nothing.

Simon looked at me. I nodded.

He slowly pushed open the door with a foot. We saw a large man in a dark suit sprawled faceup in the entryway. Jake, the chauffeur. A fist-sized contusion covered his forehead, and his nose was shattered and bleeding.

I studied him. "He's breathing," I said.

Simon was already stepping over Jake into the empty living room. Just past the bubbling aquarium, he froze and gestured my attention to the dining area on the left. On the table were three dinner plates, each with a partially eaten sandwich. One chair was lying on its side.

And next to it, I saw another man crumpled in a fetal position. His chest was a mat of blood, and he stared at us with unseeing eyes.

"Tatum," Simon murmured.

I nodded, felt a breeze. I motioned Simon to the terrace. The drapes over the sliding doors were billowing open. An instant later, we were startled by a thumping sound followed by a muffled cry.

I spun, ears straining, finger tight on the trigger.

Simon mouthed, *hallway*. He went first, and I followed. The thumping and crying grew louder.

A woman, I realized.

 We stopped at a small bedroom at the far end of the hallway. I pushed the door open and we entered a room filled with medical equipment, including green oxygen canisters and what appeared to be heart-monitoring equipment. The thumping was coming from a closet door to our right. Someone had wedged a chair under the knob.

At a nod from Simon, I kicked the chair away. The door flew open and a young woman in a nurse's uniform burst out.

"Jesus! This man. He just burst in—" The words died in her throat. Terrified eyes locked on our guns.

"We're police," I said, lowering mine and taking out my badge.

"Thank God." She began shaking with relief, the words tumbling from her mouth. "This . . . this crazy man burst in and shot Mr. Tatum—"

"We know," Simon said. "Do you know where he went?"

"No. He just threw me in here."

"How many people are in the apartment?"

"Four. Mr. Caldwell. Me. And—"

That was enough. Simon cut her off. "Stay here and lock the door."

We went back into the hall.

The silence told us what we would find, but we still took our time working our way to the terrace. Simon covered me as I pulled back the drapes.

They were both just sitting there.

Baker and Caldwell sat across from each other at a wrought-iron table shielded by a large umbrella. In front of Caldwell was a half-full cup of coffee and a partially eaten salad. Both men were slumped forward, and from a glance you might have thought they were dozing.

Except that most of the top of Baker's head was blown away.

It was all too much. For a moment I couldn't speak.

Then I exploded. "The stupid bastard! How could he do this! Dammit, we needed him! We needed Caldwell. *Fuck!*"

"It might not really matter, Martin."

"The hell it doesn't matter!" I shot back. "The only witnesses against Holland are now fucking dead!"

Simon shrugged, stowing his gun. "You're forgetting. We still have a witness left."

"The chauffeur?" I said, jerking my head to the door. "Fat lotta good he'll do. We going to try and sweet-talk the son of a bitch into confessing?" I was sarcastic because I knew Simon was blowing smoke. Even if Jake was involved in the killings or knew who was, we had nothing on him to make him talk. We'd hit another wall that we couldn't get around.

Simon shot me a look of annoyance and stepped onto the terrace.

I followed, shaking my head.

Simon checked Caldwell's pulse but didn't bother with Baker. Instead he patted Baker down, checking his pockets. He straightened, holding another metal pipe and a glass vial with a white powder that was probably cocaine.

But no computer disk.

Moments later, a voice called out, "Simon, Martin. You all right? Everything okay? I got some officers with me."

Amanda with the cavalry.

"Everything's fine," I hollered back.

Which, of course, was a damn lie.

CHAPTER 50

Amanda and I stared down at the two bodies on the terrace while Simon spoke to a couple of the uniformed D.C. cops. Jake was still sprawled out by the entryway, unconscious, awaiting the paramedics. We could hear a female officer in the living room trying to comfort the nurse, who was hugging herself, saying over and over, "I thought he was going to kill me. Jesus, I thought he was going to kill me." A cool breeze touched my face. In the distance, we heard the sound of sirens.

Baker hadn't been dead long. Blood still oozed from his grisly head wound, matting what was left of his hair and running fingers down the side of his face. His gun lay a few feet away on the terrace floor, which glistened with bits of pulverized bone and brain tissue. My anger toward Baker had ebbed, and I couldn't help but contemplate the tragedy of his life. How he'd screwed everything up. Even this final, cocaine-fortified act of vengeance, which he probably saw as heroic, would ultimately allow the person most responsible to—

"No marks on Caldwell," Amanda said, breaking in on my thoughts. "You think maybe it was his heart?"

"Probably," I said. "If not, Baker would have killed him."

She drew in a deep breath, scrutinizing me. "Baker got Tatum and Caldwell. And with McNamara dead, that only leaves General Holland."

"You figured he's Rick from Baker's description?"

She nodded.

That made it two against one. I didn't feel like setting her off by getting into Simon's reservations over Holland's guilt. I also didn't mention the fact that, with Baker dead, Holland would walk. Then, of course, there was still the underlying matter of the G-626, which we were no closer to proving was unsafe.

Amanda's eyes dropped to Baker. "Wonder why he offed himself before going after Holland?"

I shrugged. "Maybe he figured Caldwell was responsible for the murders. Once he was dead, Baker might have thought his job was finished."

"Wouldn't Caldwell have told Baker about Holland?"

"Not if Caldwell died before he could talk." I frowned. I was looking at Baker's left hand, the one opposite the gun. It was cupped into a fist. Taking out my gloves, I carefully stepped over, avoiding the blood.

"See something?" Amanda asked.

I snapped my gloves on and crouched. "I'm not sure... hang on." I pried open the fingers and removed a small piece of paper. "Baker's business card," I said, rising. "He's written Simon's name—"

That was as far as I got. I began to tremble.

"What's wrong, Marty?" Amanda asked.

But I kept staring at the card, at the line scrawled at the bottom.

Lt. Simon Santos, please look.

And just above, Baker had drawn an arrow to his Web site address.

"Marty, what the hell is it?"

I didn't answer her. I kept standing there, thinking of the books in Baker's car. And Amanda's comment earlier:

Baker spent last night working on his computer.

I grinned. No wonder Baker didn't have a disk on him. He didn't need one.

Amanda suddenly snatched the card from my hand. When I focused on her, she was studying it. Her eyes widened. "Jesus. You think—"

"Yeah."

Three minutes later, Simon and I watched as Amanda typed Baker's Web site address into the computer in Caldwell's office. At first Amanda couldn't find the right link. Then she slowly ran the cursor up and down the main page. I realized she was searching for an invisible link hidden in the background. In the far right corner above Baker's picture, Margaret Wildman's name magically appeared.

I tensed when Amanda clicked on it, but the information on the G-626 was there.

Amanda scrolled through the pages, shaking her head in amazement. "That son of a bitch. He hid it where no one would ever think to look."

"That's enough, Amanda," Simon said. "Here's what I want you to do now."

Amanda and I left while Simon stayed to debrief the D.C. homicide detectives. Since neither of us had our laptop, he'd given us a wad of bills to buy one. We spent a little over two grand on a model Amanda said could scream. It was almost two-fifteen before I buzzed the door to the Pentagon Club. Marla, the spectacular brunette from the night before, let us in with a dazzling smile and even more dazzling cleavage. She told us Simon was already waiting upstairs in the Roosevelt Room.

As we passed through the crowded lobby and up the stairs, Amanda did a lot of head turning but never said a word. I asked what she thought about the place.

"You don't want to know, Marty."

"Try me."

She sighed. "I think the concept is disgusting and promotes an extremely sexist attitude toward women. I think any male who frequents a place like this is simply an immature adolescent who is probably hiding feelings of sexual inadequacy. I also think—"

"You're right," I interrupted. "I don't want to know."

Simon didn't answer my knock. From within, we heard muffled voices. When we walked into the Roosevelt Room, Simon was relaxing on the leather sofa, a glass of wine in his hand. His eyes were glued to the big-screen TV in the corner, which was showing a congressional hearing. A white-haired man I didn't recognize was testifying into a microphone about how much safer airline travel had become. The view changed to a panel of somber-faced congressmen gazing down upon him. Congressman Trenton sat in the committee chairman's seat, looking remarkably clear-eyed considering his drunken escapade the night before.

I gave a little cough to get Simon's attention, then deposited my briefcase on a chair by the door.

He glanced over disapprovingly. Patricia Dryke's murder file and a thick manila envelope sat on the glass coffee table before him, next to a bottle of wine. On the couch were the TV remote, another file, a stack of small pictures—probably the driver's-license photos he'd requested, since Holland's grinning face was on top—and the framed photograph from Wildman's office. "You're late, Martin."

"Traffic was pretty bad." I noticed a lunch buffet laid out on the conference table. Finger sandwiches and a tureen of what was probably soup. I realized I was hungry.

Amanda squinted at the TV as she set the laptop on the conference table. "Which one is Congressman Marcelli?"

Simon killed the sound with the remote and sat up. "The blond gentleman seated at the far right."

I looked. Marcelli was maybe thirty-five, with an angular, intelligent face. I noticed that he was the only one taking notes. The screen switched back to the man who was testifying.

I asked Simon if he'd spoken with Congressman Marcelli yet. Simon's plan was to essentially follow through on what Wildman had originally intended. Once Amanda downloaded the G-626 information from Baker's Web site, we would turn the disk over to Marcelli for use in the hearing. Then sit back and watch the show.

Simon nodded, saying, "Marcelli will see me around four." He looked over at Amanda, who was connecting the laptop to a phone jack built into the table. "Will that give you enough time?"

"Plenty. How many copies you want of the disk?"

"Three. One for Marcelli. One for us. And one for Archie to lock in his office safe downstairs."

I nodded my approval. Simon wasn't taking chances. "Who's going to testify in Caldwell's place?" I asked. The killings were all over the radio now, with Baker already tagged as the murderer.

Simon shrugged. "Take a look at the television, Martin."

I did, struck by something in Simon's tone. On the screen, the white-haired man was still talking. "So?"

"The gallery," Simon prompted.

I saw him then. He was sitting off to the right in the front row, wearing a gray suit.

"Shit," I said. "General Holland."

"This clinches it," Amanda said from the table. "This proves the son of a bitch is tied to Global."

Simon nodded slowly. "He's obviously connected somehow. But frankly, that's what confuses me."

Amanda frowned. "Confuses you?"

He faced her. "Yes. Because I know for a fact that Holland had nothing to do with Wildman's murder."

Amanda stared, incredulous. I said, "For chrissakes, Simon. How did you suddenly decide that? Just because Holland wasn't at the scene doesn't mean—"

I clammed up because Simon wasn't listening. He was bent forward, staring intently at the TV. My eyes returned to the gallery. I saw a woman in a red suit sitting down beside Holland.

Simon suddenly turned to me. "Who is she?" he demanded.

I was caught off guard. Amanda answered, "Holland's wife, Lucille. Why?"

But Simon was again focused on the screen. He looked increasingly agitated. "Of course. *Of course.*" He snatched up the thick file on Patricia Dryke's murder and pawed through it. He stopped, then began to read.

Amanda gave me a quizzical look. I shook my head. I had no clue why Simon was so worked up.

Moments later, Simon glanced up, his face grim. "I now know, Martin."

"Know what?"

But he was rising to his feet, yanking his cell phone from his jacket. When he did, something shiny fell to the carpet. As he thumbed in a number, Simon stooped to pick the object up and stuck it into his pants pocket. Moments later, he began to speak in rapid Spanish.

Amanda went over to the couch, picked up Patricia Dryke's file, which was lying open, and took it to the conference table. I joined her. The pages contained a portion of an English translation from Simon's interview with Mrs. Guerrero, the maid from the Excelsior Arms.

"She's the one who saw the killers?" Amanda asked.

"Yeah. You notice what Simon dropped?"

"It looked like a magnifying glass."

"That's what I thought."

We began to read.

⟶ In the interview, Mrs. Guerrero spoke of seeing two people leave Caldwell's apartment. A man first, then a woman a few minutes later. Mrs. Guerrero's description of the man was vague because she'd only glimpsed him from behind. Medium build with short dark hair and sunglasses. He could have been anybody.

But not the woman.

Mrs. Guerrero described her in detail because they'd ridden down in the elevator together. In that short time, Mrs. Guerrero had also formed an impression of the woman. Besides describing her as rude, she'd called her something else.

Puta, a word my housekeeper Mrs. Anuncio often used when she got angry. It was usually used to describe a woman who was a bitch, though the word actually meant whore.

And maybe that's why Simon had thought the woman might have been a high-class hooker like Patricia Dryke. But of course she wasn't. Not by a long shot.

"I'll be damned," Amanda murmured. "She's describing Lucille Holland."

CHAPTER 51

After Simon completed his first call, he made a second. This one lasted almost ten minutes. Much of the discussion centered around Lucille Holland. Amanda continued to download Baker's Web site while I tried to think things through. To understand.

From the bits and pieces I overheard from Simon's conversation, a fuzzy picture began to form.

I reread the account of Patricia Dryke's murder to be certain. She'd been stabbed seventeen times, mostly in the face. I could only stand to look at a couple of the crime-scene photos before it got to be too much. Patricia Dryke had been butchered. Her eyes had been gouged out, her flesh hacked to the bone. Like Colonel Wildman's brutal beating, Dryke's killing suggested an inexplicable rage, as if the killer had hated the victim.

I flipped back to Mrs. Guerrero's interview, to the line where she'd described the woman's hair as wet. Almost soaking.

As I sat back, the remaining pieces slowly started falling into place:

Amanda's suspicions that Lucille Holland had terrorized her friend.

The 911 call reporting Wildman's murder, made not by a man but by a woman.

Holland's selection to cover up the military's G-626 crash.

The money the Hollands seemed to have.

And their presence at the hearing, confirming their connection to Global.

The picture finally crystallized. The how and the why. Not everything, but enough.

When Amanda finished downloading the file, I told her what I now knew. She'd already figured a lot of it. On a few points, we disagreed. Like me, she still didn't understand the extent of General Holland's role, and whether he'd actually been involved in the murders.

I had just started eating a sandwich when Simon finally ended his conversation. He came over, carrying his wineglass. His face was flushed and I knew it wasn't from the alcohol. He told us he'd spoken with Pinard, who'd told him that Global had made the announcement for the company's new CEO.

Of course, we knew who it had to be. Amanda said the name anyway. "Lucille Holland."

When Simon nodded, I said, "That explains why she's at the hearing. She's going to testify in place of Caldwell."

"Yes."

"In support of the merger?"

"Correct. It seems Congress is going to vote on whether to approve it. Amanda, how much longer until you're ready?"

"Couple minutes. Just need to copy the info to the disks."

Simon paced as Amanda swapped disks. I understood his anxiety. He was impatient to deliver the disk to Marcelli and ensure the public destruction of Lucille Holland.

I wanted that, too. But right now, I almost wanted something else even more.

I said, "So you've figured everything out, Simon?"

"I think so, yes." He was still pacing.

"Both murders?"

"Yes."

I slid out the chair next to me. I put an edge in my voice as I spoke. "Then tell us, dammit."

Simon stopped pacing. He looked at me in surprise. "Why, of course, Martin."

As he took the seat, I shook my head. Sometimes, with Simon, you had to be firm.

Simon described his recent phone calls. Once he'd realized that Holland's wife matched the description of the woman leaving Caldwell's apartment, he'd called the witness, Mrs. Guerrero, at her employer's home, and had her tune in to C-Span, which was televising the hearings. Mrs. Guerrero verified that Lucille Holland was the same woman she had seen coming from Caldwell's apartment. As expected, she didn't recognize General Holland because she'd never seen his face that day.

Next, Simon phoned Pinard to determine whether Lucille Holland had a connection to Global, as her presence in Caldwell's apartment suggested. Pinard immediately recognized Lucille Holland's name for two reasons: she was Marsha Caldwell's niece, and she held a seat on the board of MC Enterprises. Pinard considered Lucille Holland's appointment to head Global only mildly surprising. He bluntly called her an ambitious bitch who'd been sucking up to her aunt for years.

Simon then switched topics to the murders, starting with Patricia Dryke's. As he explained his theory that Lucille Holland had been the killer, Amanda interrupted him, pointing out that two people were seen leaving Caldwell's apartment.

"And the guy had to be Holland," she said.

"No doubt," Simon said.

She eyed him. "So Holland could have been involved in the murder. Probably was."

"You're mistaken, Amanda," Simon said. "The evidence clearly indicates that Lucille Holland alone did the killing."

"You mean because Lucille's hair was wet?"

"That's one factor. The stabbing was extremely violent. As the killer, Lucille Holland would have been virtually covered in blood. She would have needed to wash before leaving."

"Maybe Holland washed up, too," Amanda said. "You just don't know that because your witness never got a good look at him."

Simon thought, then shook his head. "You're not taking into account Caldwell's reaction, which essentially confirms that Lucille Holland was the killer."

Amanda frowned. So did I. "Caldwell?" I said.

"You'll recall, Martin," Simon said, "that Caldwell used a great deal of his political capital to protect the killer. For two years I have asked myself why he would do such a thing. Now I know. In reality, he was protecting—"

"His niece," Amanda said grudgingly. "Okay, maybe you have a point."

"Actually, they're not related. Lucille is Marsha Caldwell's niece, not Charles Caldwell's. Caldwell's concern wasn't for Lucille but his company. Her crime provided him a way to retain control."

Amanda's face went blank.

I wasn't following this either. Then it dawned on me where he had to be going. I said, "Sure. The first merger attempt two years ago. No wonder it fell through. Caldwell must have found out about Lucille's role in the murder. Probably used that knowledge as leverage against her aunt so she would vote against the merger."

Simon nodded approvingly.

"Hold on," Amanda said. "If what you guys are saying is true, why would MC Enterprises now be supporting the merger?"

I hadn't thought things out that far. I looked at Simon.

He said, "I can only venture a guess. But I suspect Lucille Holland didn't believe Caldwell could afford to go to the authorities now. His attempts to curtail the investigation are well known, which opens him up to a charge of murder after the fact. Plus his ill health is almost certainly a consideration in her decision. She probably concluded that Caldwell had more pressing concerns than trying to hold on to his company."

With a knowing glance to me, Amanda said, "I understand that the motive for Dryke's murder never was blackmail." This was Simon's earlier theory, that Patricia Dryke had found out about the cover-up and was blackmailing Global.

Simon shrugged. "I doubt it. If Lucille Holland had wanted Dryke silenced, she would have had Tatum handle it quietly. No. This murder was completely unplanned. A spontaneous act."

Amanda returned to me, acceptance in her eyes. "Looks like you were right after all."

I nodded.

To Simon, she said, "General Holland has a big-time reputation as a womanizer. Marty thinks Lucille Holland might have caught her husband humping Patricia Dryke. Went crazy."

"I agree."

"So it was a crime of passion."

"Yes."

"Simple as that."

"Simple as that."

Amanda tapped a finger to her tooth for a moment. "The way I see it, Holland's still not in the clear. I mean, he was there. He could have stopped the killing, right?"

"I would have thought so," Simon said.

"And afterward, he never went to the cops."

"No."

She frowned, chewing her lower lip. "Maybe I'm missing something, but I'm still not clear how the maid's statement links Lucille Holland to the murder."

"Did you follow the case?" Simon asked mildly.

"Some," Amanda said. "I wasn't a junkie, if that's what you're asking."

Simon filled her in on much of what I'd read in the report: how a maintenance worker had seen Patricia Dryke enter Caldwell's apartment around three-fifteen P.M. on the day of the murder, less than ten minutes before the ME said she died. He explained how that point, coupled with the lack of blood evidence at Patricia Dryke's apartment, essentially confirmed that Dryke had really been killed at Caldwell's and subsequently moved.

"Let me get this straight," Amanda said. "Dryke was killed around three-twenty-five and Mrs. Guerrero saw the Hollands leave the apartment at . . ."

"Less than fifteen minutes later," Simon said. "At approximately three-forty for General Holland; his wife a few minutes later."

"Okay," Amanda said, "so you've got the Hollands at the crime scene near the time of death. It's still not exactly open and shut."

"Patricia Dryke didn't die quietly," Simon said. "We found skin samples under her fingernails. DNA tests should prove her assailant was Lucille Holland."

"Hell," Amanda said, sitting forward. "So we've got her."

Simon hesitated, looking uneasy. "Maybe."

Amanda furrowed her brow in thought. Then came a slow nod of understanding. "Because of the government?"

"I'm afraid so. They have no choice but to interfere with any legal proceedings against Lucille Holland. They simply can't afford for her to reveal the government's complacency in the G-626 cover-up."

"That's why you want to get the information to Marcelli," I said. "Once the cat's out of the bag, the government's motivation to protect Lucille will be reduced."

"Even that might not be enough," Simon said wearily. "In the wake of the G-626 scandal, the government will engage in extensive damage control. The last thing they'll want is the word to get out that they had covered up for a murderer."

Amanda's jaw hardened. "You mean the bitch could walk?"

"It's a possibility."

No one spoke for a moment. The laptop, which had been chirping softly, went quiet. Amanda wordlessly passed Simon two of the disks, then popped out the third and pocketed it. She began to shut down the laptop.

I checked my watch. We still had a few minutes. I was about to ask Simon about the Wildman murders when his phone rang.

Simon answered it and spoke in Spanish again. He seemed to be arguing. Finally he rolled his eyes and held out the phone to me. "You talk to her, Martin. Mrs. Guerrero is frightened. She's not sure if she wants to testify now."

I frowned, taking it. "Me? Why? I don't speak Spanish."

Then I heard Mrs. Guerrero say my name, and I almost dropped the phone.

➤ Mrs. Guerrero wasn't crying, but she was close. In her broken English, she told me she was frightened not for herself but for my family. In case the bad men came again. It took me almost a minute to get over my shock and another five to convince her it was okay to help.

I hung up, glaring at Simon. "You should have told me."

He smiled apologetically. "She made me promise, Martin. She thought you wouldn't hire her if you knew the truth."

"Whoa," Amanda said. "What is *this*?"

"Dammit, Simon," I said. "I had a right to know."

Simon shrugged. "You needed someone to help. She needed a place to stay."

"But her references—"

"I arranged those."

I tried to stay angry at him but couldn't keep it up. I said, "Well, just don't do anything like this again." Even to me, the statement sounded lame.

Amanda gazed at me in growing incredulity. "Jesus, Marty. Don't tell me Mrs. Guerrero is—"

"Yeah," I snapped. "She's my housekeeper."

Amanda burst out laughing.

My face reddened as I sat there feeling stupid. There was nothing I could say.

Simon gave a sudden grunt of surprise. When I glanced over, he was kicking back his chair and rising from the table. "Pack up. We have to go. Now."

I frowned, checking my watch. "What's the hurry?"

But Simon was already striding to the couch. Almost frantically he began to gather up the items and throw them into a folder. As he did, he kept looking back at the TV.

Then I heard Amanda say, "*Shit.* She's early. She wasn't supposed to testify until five."

I looked at the screen. A beaming Lucille Holland was taking the witness stand.

CHAPTER 52

I t was still almost ten minutes before we rolled out of the Marriott parking lot, because we'd swung by Archie's office to drop off a disk. I drove, Amanda camped next to me in the passenger seat. Simon sat in back. Even with traffic, the trip to the Rayburn Building near the Capitol would take less than thirty minutes.

Simon made two quick phone calls. First to the Capitol Police to give them a heads-up that we were on the way. I thought this meant we were going to arrest Lucille Holland, but Simon was vague about our intentions, saying we were only going to interview Congressman Marcelli. When he hung up, I said, "We should just get the damn thing over with. Arrest her after the hearing."

"We will."

"Then aren't we going to need the assistance of the Capitol police—" I broke off. I got it now. "You don't want to risk tipping our hand."

"Not yet."

His second call was to the hospital to check on Janet Spence. She was out of surgery and resting. When Simon passed us the news, he had that same lost look from the morgue. As if he still couldn't accept what had occurred.

He slowly slid back in the seat, closing his eyes.

I kept looking at him in the rearview mirror. Waiting. Finally, I said, "I've got a couple questions about Wildman's case—"

"Give me a moment, Martin."

A moment became minutes. Simon didn't move. He was obviously hurting, and I decided not to bother him.

Crossing the Memorial Bridge into D.C., Simon abruptly began to talk. He kept his eyes closed and his voice low. We had to strain to hear.

"Colonel Wildman's murder," he said, "came down to money. A great deal of money. According to Pinard, Lucille Holland stood to gain almost forty million from the Global/Boeing merger. Once Lucille learned of Wildman's renewed investigation into the G-626...probably through her husband...she sent Tatum and McNamara to intimidate Wildman. To scare her into backing off. It had worked before, and Lucille was undoubtedly confident that it would work again. But of course it didn't. This time Colonel Wildman refused to be intimidated. Lucille probably began to panic. When she learned that Wildman was going to present her evidence to Congressman Marcelli at the very hearing where the merger would be voted on, she decided to have her killed. My guess is that Tatum or McNamara handled the actual murders. But it's clear Lucille was also present. I believe she's the one who administered Wildman's beating."

Simon fell silent. His eyes flickered open and he sat up. From his jacket, he removed the photograph of Wildman and her children. He stared at it, doing a slow head shake.

I watched him in the mirror. I knew he hadn't given us all of it yet. "You didn't detail Holland's role in all this."

Simon lowered the picture. "He was obviously part of the cover-up."

"But not the murders?" Amanda said.

"No."

"So Holland was Rick," she said.

Simon shrugged. "Probably."

Probably hell, I thought. I said, "And the 911 call..."

"Lucille Holland made that to establish her alibi. Not General Holland's."

"Then," I said, "she must not have known her husband had gone there."

"I think not. I imagine she was quite enraged when she realized he had driven her car."

I said, "So Holland really must have been trying to help Colonel Wildman. Protect her."

"No question."

"Back up," Amanda said to him. "Why are you so convinced that Lucille Holland beat Wildman?"

"Because," Simon said with sudden feeling, "that was the reason she went to Wildman's. Why she took the risk of being there. She wanted to participate in Wildman's destruction. She wanted to exact her revenge."

"Revenge?" I said. "I thought you said Lucille Holland did this for money."

"Money was her primary motive, Martin. But there was also a second, more personal one."

Amanda said, "Which was..."

He gave her a vague smile. "One question. Do you know if General Holland and Colonel Wildman were ever stationed together?"

I glanced at Amanda. She had brought this point up earlier after looking over their bios.

"Yeah," she said. "They were based at the Air Force Safety Center in Albuquerque."

"When?"

She thought. "About ten, eleven years ago."

"Perfect," Simon said softly. To me, he said, "Martin, what did I tell you was the key to the case? Do you remember? It was last night...."

We came to a red light. I slowed to a stop. "Sure. At Wildman's house. You didn't understand why the children were killed."

No response, so I turned around. Simon had another

oddly vague smile. He held out Colonel Wildman's photograph.

"What's this for?" Amanda asked, taking it.

"The second motive."

And then he passed her something else, which glinted in the sunlight. I knew at once what it was.

The magnifying glass.

Amanda and I held the picture between us in the front seat. Wildman and her two children, smiling with Mickey Mouse. From behind, Simon said, "Look at the faces in the crowd. The person standing on the left edge. Tan slacks and blue pullover.

Amanda placed the magnifying glass where Simon directed.

A man. Slightly blurred. Amanda shifted the glass. The image sharpened until—

We saw the face clearly.

Amanda gasped. My mouth went dry. I stared until I was certain, then turned to Simon.

"Now," Simon said. "Look at the daughter."

So we did. When you were looking for it, the resemblance was there.

"That sick murdering bitch," Amanda snarled.

A car horn blared. The light was green.

I drove through the intersection in a daze.

CHAPTER 53

The House Transportation and Infrastructure Committee met in the immense Rayburn House Office Building on the northwest corner of South Capitol and C Street. We worked our way around the H-shaped structure to the underground parking garage, where a matronly female Capitol cop was waiting. After checking our IDs, she had us park in a red-coned slot, then escorted us past security through a labyrinth of hallways, talking and pointing like a tour guide. At a stairwell, she directed Amanda and me to the committee room before escorting Simon upstairs to Congressman Marcelli's office.

We slipped into the committee room around a quarter till four. We spent a few minutes hanging back by the door with a couple of press types. On TV the room had looked huge, but it really wasn't much bigger than a large court-room. The only real difference was that instead of one judge, there were more than forty, gazing down from a double-tiered polished-mahogany dais. The gallery to our left was maybe half full, with a number of open seats toward the back. I spotted three TV cameras placed throughout the room, two with C-Span logos and one from a local affiliate. Like the people in the room, the cameras were focused on a lone woman in a red power suit sitting at the witness table.

Lucille Holland was reading from a prepared statement about why the merger between Global and Boeing should be approved. As I listened, I looked for Congressman Marcelli, but his seat was empty, probably because of the meeting with Simon. I gave the remaining legislators a once-over. Most were slumped back, clearly bored—unlike Chairman Trenton, who was gazing down at Lucille Holland with what could only be described as beaming approval.

For a moment, I saw red. I kept thinking of his aide's comments in Caldwell's apartment last night, about the hearings being in the bag. I wondered if this was the way these things were always handled. If hearings were just a show for a decision already made.

Amanda nudged me, indicating General Holland, still sitting quietly in the same seat we'd seen him in earlier. The supportive husband.

"You want a seat?" a tentative voice asked.

We turned to see a woman with a press pass smiling at us from the last row of the gallery. She was an attractive redhead in her early forties. She drew in her legs, indicating the line of open seats next to her.

I smiled my thanks and Amanda and I edged past her. We took the seats at the far end to avoid advertising our presence.

Lucille Holland went on for another ten minutes before the questioning on the merger began. Each congressman had seven minutes for questions. Most used less than five, and instead of querying Lucille Holland, they usually just made a statement in support of the merger. The G-626 was never mentioned. I shook my head. No doubt about it. The fix was in.

"He's coming back," Amanda said.

I nodded, watching Congressman Marcelli slip in through the door behind the dais. He started for his seat, stopped and looked toward Trenton, who had pushed back his chair. Trenton stood and went over to Marcelli. They spoke for maybe thirty seconds. Trenton seemed to do most of the talking. Marcelli just nodded back a couple of times. He looked a little unsettled, almost flustered.

As both men went to their seats, Amanda said, "Ten bucks Trenton's telling Marcelli to behave."

"No bet."

Moments later, we noticed Simon by the main door. I waved him over. As he sat next to Amanda, she asked, "How'd the meeting go?"

Simon hesitated. "I'm not quite sure."

I said, "What do you mean?"

"Congressman Marcelli seemed less than enthused. Anyway, we'll know in a moment. Looks like Marcelli is about to take his turn."

We all focused on the young congressman, who was bending his mike in toward his face. He kept looking over at Trenton. Finally he cleared his throat and focused on Lucille Holland, who was staring back expectantly.

Over the mike, Marcelli's high-pitched voice sounded tinny. But the words came out loud and clear.

"I have no questions, Mr. Chairman."

Trenton smiled broadly. So did Lucille Holland. So did another half-dozen congressmen.

"Why, that miserable son of a—" Amanda caught herself, realizing where she was. She shook her head in disgust.

I didn't say anything. I just sagged back in my chair, more deflated than angry.

"Trenton," Amanda spat. "He must have gotten to Marcelli."

"Perhaps it wasn't him," Simon said quietly.

I gave him a look of annoyance. "C'mon, Simon. Who else could—"

I stopped. Simon was pointing to the door behind the dais, where a knot of staffers were standing. To their left, I spotted a familiar face staring at us.

It was Special Agent Frank Carruthers.

Carruthers suddenly smiled and held up something. He was at least fifty feet away and it was hard to tell what it was at first.

Finally I realized it was a computer disk.

My eyes immediately went to the main door. Carruthers' blond partner was there. And I knew there had to be others I couldn't pick out.

"We've been set up," Amanda said.

As the hearing continued, we watched the two FBI men and they watched us. No one spoke of the tension, but we all felt it. They seemed to be daring us to make a move.

"Now what?" Amanda said. "They know we have the G-626 info. No way they'll let us just walk out of here."

"No . . ." I said, looking to Simon. He was sitting quietly. He didn't seem worried at all. Abruptly, he nodded.

"Okay," he said.

"What's okay?" I asked.

"We are. We can get out of this."

Amanda snorted. "How? The entire building is probably surrounded. They'll pick us up as soon as we try to leave."

"I doubt there are any more agents. Carruthers wouldn't dare risk it."

"Why not?" I asked.

But Simon was already leaning close, outlining a plan.

When he finished, I shook my head. While his plan ensured the release of the G-626 data, I still wasn't sure how it helped us get away.

Simon looked to Amanda. "Go ahead."

She hesitated. "You know I'll probably have to hurt him."

Simon nodded.

Amanda seemed to smile. She rose and went over to where General Holland was sitting. She spoke to him for a moment, then pivoted and headed toward the exit.

After she walked out, the blond agent hung back, as if uncertain what to do. After a couple of false starts, he finally left.

I checked my watch. Three minutes later, Holland rose and discreetly made his way to the door. As he passed us, he didn't even glance our way.

A minute later, Simon and I followed him out.

At the door, I paused, looking for Carruthers.

He was gone.

We stepped into the hallway. Holland wasn't in sight. Neither was Amanda or the second FBI man. Simon and I walked quickly in the direction we'd first come. Simon took out his phone and called Archie Peters. After he hung up, we made another left and a right.

The small conference room was where Simon had remembered it, a little past a women's washroom with an OUT OF ORDER sign. The door contained a rectangular glass cutout. As we approached, we looked inside.

He was standing there, waiting, back to the door.

When we entered, General Holland faced us. The change in his appearance since the morning was shocking. His skin seemed to hang on his face, and there were dark shadows under his eyes. He blinked often and his upper lip twitched.

"I understand this is about . . . about my relationship with Colonel Wildman," he said.

"Yes, General," I said.

Then Simon stepped forward and handed him Wildman's photograph.

"Specifically, your daughter," he said.

There was a long silence.

General Holland stood there, staring into the picture. When he finally looked up, his eyes were moist. He spoke barely above a whisper. "She . . . she never knew I was her father. I wish now that I'd..." He swallowed hard. "I loved her. You have to believe that."

"We do," Simon said.

"I never wanted anything to happen to her. I tried to talk Margie out of going forward with the investigation. Told her it was too dangerous."

Simon and I nodded sympathetically.

"But Margie wouldn't listen. She just... wouldn't listen." He stood there trembling.

"Will you talk to us now?" Simon said.

A nod.

"Tell us everything?" Simon said.

Another nod.

"Fine. Let's begin."

As he filled us in, General Holland spoke haltingly, pausing often to gather himself. He told us about the brief affair with Wildman eleven years ago, how she became pregnant, and her decision to have the child.

"To avoid a scandal, we had no choice but to keep the paternity quiet. Our careers would be over. But it was more than that. I was... worried about Lucille's reaction. She would never have understood. Over the years, I tried to help Margie out financially. But it was difficult. Lucille... Lucille was always suspicious of me. Watched me. And it was my fault really. I...I wasn't ready for marriage. Women always seemed attracted to me. And sometimes... sometimes I couldn't resist. I wish I could have, but..." He trailed off, staring at his shoes.

"Tell us about the Dryke murder," Simon said.

Holland looked stunned. "You... you know about that?"

"Yes."

Holland took a deep breath and sat on the edge of the conference table. "I...I really had nothing to do with it. It ...just happened. I'd gone to the apartment to pick up some papers Caldwell had left. Stock transfers for Lucille arranged by her aunt. Lucille was supposed to meet me, but she'd called, said she probably wouldn't make it. The doorbell rang. It was Patricia Dryke. We'd met at a few parties. I knew she was a little wild. Anyway, one thing led to another. We had a few drinks. And then... Hell, I never saw what happened next. Next thing I knew, Patricia was next to me screaming. And there's all this blood. A lot of blood. And I see Lucille standing over her. With this knife... I don't know what happened after that. All I remember is seeing Patricia lying there. And the blood. And Lucille screaming at me. Afterward, I wanted to go to the cops. But Lucille said she'd tell everyone I'd done the killing. Said it would be my word against hers. With her money and her lawyers, I didn't have a chance. From then on, she always held that over my head. To make me do what she wanted."

"Like covering up the G-626 problem," I said.

A nod. "But it wasn't just Lucille. Everyone wanted that problem hushed up. The military, the government, congress, the airlines. Everybody. I was given a direct order to keep it quiet. Hell, in my mind, I was being a good soldier. Doing what I was supposed to do."

"But Colonel Wildman wouldn't go along."

He shook his head.

"So your wife had her killed."

"I don't actually know that—"

"Don't quibble," Simon said. He tapped his chest. "In here, you know."

Holland hesitated, looking miserable. He slowly nodded.

"Your wife's car," I said. "Why did you drive it to Wildman's?"

He gave me a long look. "You won't believe me."

"Try me," I said.

"I... I thought maybe it would help protect her. I knew Lucille had people watching Margie. I thought, you know, if they saw Lucille's car there maybe... maybe they wouldn't try anything."

Simon said, "Your wife knew you were trying to assist Colonel Wildman."

"Yeah. I...I finally told her about my daughter. I wanted Lucille to know I wouldn't allow anyone to harm Margie or the kids. That's...that's what the goddamn shooting at my place was about. A warning. To make sure I knew who was in charge." He laughed harshly. "The *bitch*."

I said, "And the disk you gave us..."

"Lucille's idea. To throw you off."

Simon asked, "Were you Rick?"

Holland didn't answer him. He was again staring at the photograph, lost in thought. He said, "You know it's my fault. I should never have told Lucille about her. The affair was bad enough. But the fact that I had a child. I should have known...how crazy that would make her. Lucille can't have children and...*dammit*, I should have realized. But when you're desperate, you don't think. You just..." He closed his eyes for a few moments before looking at us. "You know you're wasting your time. You saw the hearing. They'll never let you touch her. They can't."

We didn't reply. "Were you Rick, General?" Simon asked again.

Holland looked puzzled.

I said, "You didn't help set up Bobby Baker? Get him to pressure his wife?"

"No. That was Lucille and that bastard Tatum. And Tatum's ex-partner at the FBI."

Simon nodded like he understood. At that moment, I made the connection. But before I could say anything, I heard the sound of a door clicking closed behind us.

"You talk too damn much, Marcus," a voice said.

CHAPTER 54

Agent Frank Carruthers stood there holding a gun. He looked completely calm. He slowly shook his head, staring at Holland. "I told Lucille you would be a problem. Told her we should have taken care of you."

"Go to hell, Frank," Holland said. He tried to sound tough, but the fear in his eyes gave him away.

Carruthers shrugged. He nodded to Simon. "Hello, Simon. Been a while."

Simon didn't say anything. He just gazed back coldly.

Carruthers' eyes flickered to me. "Collins and his sidekick, I wasn't worried about. But you, Simon. I knew you'd eventually figure things out. You got another disk on you?"

Simon nodded, reaching into his pocket. After he handed it over, Carruthers said, "I take it I'm too late. You've probably got a backup plan to release the information."

"Of course," Simon said.

"What the hell. Can't win 'em all." He waved the barrel fractionally. "Your guns."

We took them out.

"Kick them over. Collins first. Then you, Simon."

We did as he asked.

Carruthers picked the guns up, then stuck his and Simon's into his belt. "Time for a little improvisation." He paused, tossing Simon a smile. "The way I see it, Holland took Collins' gun, shot him and you. Lucky for me, I heard the gunfire. I came in and had to shoot Holland. How's that sound?"

No one spoke. Carruthers seemed disappointed. The barrel came around to me.

"Nothing personal, Collins."

I tensed, my mind racing. I told myself to rush him. That it was my only chance to—

The flat crack of a gunshot startled me. I expected pain but instead saw Carruthers pitch forward, blood spurting from his neck. The gun clattered to the floor.

For a moment, I was confused. Then I saw the jagged hole in the glass inlay on the door. A moment later, the door flew open. Amanda stood there, panting, holding out her gun. "Fuck. I saw him. I was next door. I wasn't sure when I should—"

I didn't hear any more because I was suddenly knocked down from behind. I looked up in time to see Holland bulling Amanda out of the way as he ran out the door. Then I heard Amanda shout, "Shit! He's got a gun!" She took off after Holland. Simon hesitated long enough to check that I was okay, then bolted out.

By now I was pushing myself to my feet. Carruthers lay in a growing pool of blood, gurgling softly. He took a final ragged breath and went quiet. He'd dropped my pistol but it was gone, so I wrenched Simon's from his belt. I sprinted into the hallway just as Simon disappeared around a corner.

I tore after him. After a few steps, I realized where Holland must be going and why. For an instant, I was tempted to say screw it. That we should just let him go.

But instead I picked up the pace.

I was maybe thirty feet behind Simon as we approached

the committee room. He flung open the door and went in. As I entered, I heard the sound of a gunshot.

Too late.

The committee room erupted into pandemonium. People started screaming and shouting. I had to fight my way through a crowd pouring toward the exit. Pushing through, I saw Lucille Holland slumped forward on the witness table, the back of her head blown away. Holland stood over her and calmly fired again. Her head kicked off the table. Bloody chunks flew from her scalp, striking the dais. Panicked congressmen and staffers clawed each other, trying to escape out the rear door.

I saw Amanda walking toward Holland, weapon pointed, yelling for him to drop the gun. He slowly turned to her. He looked dazed.

Simon appeared behind Amanda. He shouted something and she stopped. He continued past her, extending his hand to Holland. I could tell Simon was talking to him, but the noise made it impossible to make out the words. Holland seemed to be listening. He slowly lowered his gun and gave Simon a faint smile.

Then it happened.

In a single, sudden movement, Holland put the gun to his temple. He still had the smile as he pulled the trigger. Blood spurted and he toppled. More people screamed. A woman cowering to my right fainted. No one stopped to help her; they just stepped over her. I managed to grab the woman's arm and drag her off to the side.

I went over to Amanda. She was shaking, her pistol still pointed at Holland. "I've got it," I said gently.

She blinked, letting go.

Simon was standing over Holland, shaking his head pityingly. He bent down and pried something loose from his hand. I knew what it was even before I saw it.

The photograph, its frame broken.

Simon rose, looked at the picture, then knelt down again

and slipped it into Holland's jacket. He took out his rosary beads and dipped his head.

Behind us a voice shouted, "Hands up. Get your hands fucking up. Now!"

We looked back at the two very nervous-looking Capitol cops with their guns pointed at us.

We raised our hands.

On the television, CNN again replayed the shooting.

We saw Holland come up behind his wife. We saw him aim the gun and fire. We saw her head explode in a mist of red. We saw Holland calmly shoot again. We saw Simon walk up to him. We saw Holland suddenly turn the gun on himself. We heard the screams and saw the gore.

Over and over.

I couldn't take watching any more. I got up from my chair and turned off the television.

It was almost seven-twenty P.M., and Amanda and I were alone in the small anteroom outside the basement office of Lieutenant Tom Sanders, the Capitol police shift commander. Once all the turmoil upstairs had finally subsided, a very irate Sanders had us brought here for questioning. Simon had insisted on going first. His session wasn't going well. Occasionally, we could hear Sanders and Simon shouting at each other through the closed office door.

As I sat back down, I glanced to Amanda sprawled out in an easy chair. "You okay?"

A tight smile. "I'm fine."

Which was a lie. Since our arrival here, she'd barely spoken. She spent most of the time staring vacantly at the wall.

I said softly, "You had no choice. You had to kill Carruthers."

"It's not that," she murmured.

"Oh?"

She gave me a long look. "I could have stopped him."

"Holland?"

"Yeah. I had a clear shot. I could have winged him easy. But . . . I couldn't make myself pull the trigger."

"Because you wanted Lucille Holland dead."

A pause. Then a nod.

"Forget it. It's over."

She kept staring at me. "What would you have done?"

I hesitated. This was the question I'd wrestled with earlier. Amanda wanted me to tell her that being the judge and jury in this case was okay. That the ends justified the means. But when you really thought about it, it wasn't okay. It was never okay. "I can't say. I wasn't there."

"Dammit, Marty—"

I was saved from a response when the office door flew open. Lieutenant Tom Sanders stormed out, shot us a withering glare, and continued through a second door into the hallway.

I frowned at Simon, who casually trailed behind, digging into a paper sack.

"What's with Sanders?" I asked him.

Simon handed me my pistol, then gave Amanda hers. "Sanders is upset because he has to let us go."

Amanda and I looked at him in surprise.

Simon balled up the sack and tossed it in a trash can. "The investigation is out of his hands. I just spoke with Deputy Director Rawlings from the FBI. Once I explained that he would not be able to prevent the release of the G-626 data, we reached a mutually beneficial understanding."

I caught the drift. "Starting with Carruthers?"

Simon nodded. "Officially, he will have died in the line of duty." He looked to Amanda. "The FBI's final report will also conclude that you could not have fired on Holland without endangering bystanders."

"Bullshit," she muttered.

"Look at me," he told her sharply.

She did.

"When you are asked by the press, you will say you had no clear shot. You could not have prevented General Holland from killing his wife. Do you understand?"

She grimaced but reluctantly nodded.

Turning to me, he said, "And you, Martin, will file no report with the OSI."

I saw this coming. "You cleared this with General Mercer."

"Director Rawlings spoke with General Barlow. The Air Force is in the process of releasing a statement explaining that General Holland was overworked and under extreme pressure. That he and his wife had marital problems and he just snapped."

I said with a trace of sarcasm, "And the FBI's role in the G-626 cover-up . . ."

Simon smiled blandly without answering. Still, his message came in loud and clear. Now that those responsible for the murders were dead, he saw no point in pursuing other facets of the investigation. Not necessarily because he didn't want to. But Simon was pragmatic enough to know that anything else would be unprovable. A waste of time.

And the depressing thing was, I knew he was right.

As Amanda and I stood, he said, "One more thing, Amanda. Director Rawlings is concerned about the whereabouts of Agent Masters."

"Masters?"

She blinked. "*Shit*. I forgot . . ."

> We approached the women's restroom with the OUT OF ORDER sign. Ahead we could see a paramedic rolling a gurney into the conference room where Carruthers had been killed. Two men with blue FBI blazers and walkie-talkies milled around outside. I said, "They don't waste much time, do they?"

Simon shook his head.

I asked, "So did Masters also work for Lucille Holland?"

"It's doubtful. According to Director Rawlings, Masters and Carruthers have only been a team for the past few weeks."

"And you believe that?" I said.

A weary sigh. "Let it go, Martin."

We stopped at the restroom door. The FBI men watched us but made no move to come over. Simon asked Amanda, "How did you get Masters inside?"

"Didn't. He followed me."

She pushed inside. The room was dark. She clicked on the light.

At first I thought the bathroom was empty and Masters had escaped. Then I saw bare feet poking down below the end stall. Amanda went over to it, saying, "It's locked from the inside."

She dropped down and crawled under the opening below. Moments later, the stall door opened.

The sight that greeted us was startling.

Agent Masters sat naked on the commode, staring up at us with pleading eyes. There was a large bruise on his forehead and a balled-up sock had been wedged in his mouth. His feet were cinched together with a belt and he was secured to the commode by his hands, which were tied behind his back around the plumbing with strips of what looked like a shirt.

I winced, noticing the end of a tie knotted around Masters' penis. I said, "That's a little extreme."

"Figured if he struggled, he might attract attention." Amanda pointed to a loop on the other end of the tie, then indicated the hook on the door. She gave a little smile.

Simon looked at her in horror.

"Jesus," I said. "If someone had opened the door—"

"Hey," Amanda said defensively. "I locked it first. So, you want me to untie him or what?"

"No," Simon said. "Better let the FBI handle it."

We went next door to tell them.

CHAPTER 55

As we drove away from the Rayburn Building it began to rain. A crowd of press were camped around a barricade by the entrance. Because of the dark, they didn't realize who we were until it was too late. I burned rubber as they ran toward the car. To make sure we weren't followed, I drove around the city for a few minutes. I noticed how the rain made the streets look shiny and clean. But of course they weren't clean. Not if you looked close.

I rubbed my eyes. I was tired and I wanted to go home. I didn't want to think about this case anymore, or how close I'd come to dying. I just wanted to see my daughter. Hold her close and tell her I loved her.

But we still had one thing left to do. The most important thing.

So Simon called Archie Peters at the Pentagon Club, who said the reporter from the *Post* was waiting in his office. When Simon first told me he wanted the *Post* to break the story, I was surprised. Then I figured out his rationale. I did think it ironic when Simon passed on the name of the reporter who would handle the story: Randy Speers, the guy who'd harassed us at the hospital.

We arrived at the club around eight-thirty. Simon went to Archie's office to talk to Speers while Amanda and I headed for the bar. The usual clusters of serious-faced power brokers sat around drinking and plotting. A few heads turned to stare at us, but most didn't even look up. I usually drank beer, but this time I ordered a double Bourbon for myself and wine for Simon. Amanda had a vodka and tonic.

Amanda and I were halfway through our drinks when a nearby table suddenly burst into laughter. I glanced over, and recognized two of the faces. The silver-haired man was a ranking senator who had a rep as the pork-barrel king. The guy slapping him on the back was a flamboyant billionaire known for his ruthless business deals. And on it goes, I thought.

Amanda snorted in disgust. "This is so wrong, Marty."

I nodded.

She went on, "This is the kind of crap that led to the G-626 problem in the first place. Elected officials are supposed to protect the public trust, not play fast and loose with one special-interest group after another. Hell, in some respects, guys like Trenton are almost as bad as Lucille Holland. By covering up the plane's problems, they were ultimately responsible for the deaths of hundreds. Bastards." She angrily sucked down a swallow from her drink.

"Wait until the data on the disk becomes public," I said. "The outcry will take a number of them down. You don't think so?"

Amanda was gloomily shaking her head. "Not a chance, Marty. Thanks to Bobby Baker, they got the perfect patsy to lay the blame on."

"Caldwell?"

"Sure. With him dead, the politicians can claim they were never told of the plane's problems. Who's going to say anything different?"

I said nothing. But I knew she was correct in her assessment. The responsibility would be deflected to Global. From the President on down, politicians would publicly express shock and outrage while privately circling the wagons. No one in the government or the military would be held accountable. I'd been naïve to expect anything more. I asked Amanda if she'd sent off the videotape of Congressman Trenton yet.

"Tomorrow."

"That's something, at least."

"Not enough."

I eyed her. "The important thing is that the planes will be grounded until they're fixed."

"I know, but . . ." She stared dejectedly at her glass, then sighed, looking up. "You're right. I'm losing my focus. Hell, it's not like we can do anything about it anyway."

"No."

"When you think about it, we did okay, considering."

I nodded.

"And we're still alive."

"Yes we are."

We drank to that.

Simon showed up a few minutes later. He told us the *Washington Post* would run the G-626 story on the front page tomorrow. The paper would also launch a major investigation of its own.

"And they'll drop the article on you?" I said. Because I knew that was the reason Simon had given the *Post* the story.

Simon sipped his wine. "No. It's still running. In fact, I insisted on it."

Amanda and I stared at him.

He smiled faintly at our reaction. "No, I haven't lost my mind. The story would come out eventually. Too many people are aware of it. I thought it best to get it over with now."

"It could mean the end of your career as a cop," I said.

"I rather doubt it. There will be a fuss, then people will forget. They usually do. And if not . . ." He shrugged.

No one spoke. The senator and the billionaire were laughing again, playing slap-and-tickle with a giggling waitress. Amanda made a face but kept quiet. I could feel the bourbon now. There was still one item about the case I didn't understand. I asked Simon about it.

"I've known Carruthers," he explained, "since the task force on Patricia Dryke's murder. He was the FBI's representative. At first I thought it was just coincidence that he happened to be assigned to that case and was now in charge of the government's G-626 cover-up. When I realized that he matched the description of Rick, I still couldn't convince myself that there was anything to it. Part of the problem was that I liked Carruthers. He'd impressed me when we'd worked together. It wasn't until I saw him at the hearing that I made the connection."

"You mean that he was Rick," I said.

Simon nodded.

"How?" Amanda asked. "Because he had the disk?"

"Partly," he said. "The disk suggested that Carruthers had somehow found out about my meeting with Marcelli. That point puzzled me. I knew Congressman Marcelli wouldn't have told him."

"How do you know that?" Amanda asked.

"Because," Simon said, "on the phone Marcelli was eager for the data. Very eager. He had every intention of presenting the information at the hearing. But in the time between the phone call and our meeting, his mood changed to one of reluctance. I suspected then that someone had gotten to him."

"And you think that person was Carruthers?"

A head shake. "Chairman Trenton probably pressured Marcelli after being told of the meeting by Carruthers. Again, that was the troublesome point: How could Carruthers have known about our meeting in the first place? The obvious answer was that he had arranged some kind of surveillance on Marcelli. Perhaps bugged his office or tapped his phones. But the question was, why he would do such a thing? What made him think we might contact Marcelli? And then I realized it wasn't us Carruthers had been concerned about when he initiated the surveillance, but Colonel Wildman."

Amanda still looked puzzled. I didn't get it either. "So what if it was Wildman?" I said.

Simon gave me a long look. "Who knew Wildman was going to turn over the evidence to Marcelli?"

I tried to remember. Amanda said, "Bobby Baker."

"Correct," Simon said. "Wildman was careful about her intentions. She wouldn't even tell Janet Spence. Only Baker knew. Now think back to Baker's interview. Who did he—"

"Shit," Amanda murmured.

Simon nodded.

"Rick," she said. "Baker told Rick."

It was a little after nine when we got up to leave. Simon wanted to drop by the hospital to check on Janet before visiting hours ended at ten. He'd mentioned he might spend the night there. He said Janet didn't have any family in the area and would need someone. He also told us he'd spoken to one of Janet's doctors, who'd confirmed what we already knew, that she was going to require extensive plastic surgery. The doctor had given Simon the name of a prominent facial-reconstruction specialist out of L.A. Simon was going to contact the guy tomorrow, see if he'd be willing to take Janet's case.

The rain was down to a misting drizzle. Amanda and I walked Simon to his car. I told him to call me if he needed anything. Or if he just wanted to talk. The next few weeks were going to be tough on him emotionally as he tried to adjust to the loss of Romero. I wanted to be there for him the way he'd been there for me when Nicole passed away.

Simon didn't say anything about my offer. Instead, he turned to Amanda and told her that she'd done well and that he hoped to work with her again. And he wasn't just giving her lip service; he sounded like he meant it.

Amanda responded with a wry smile, "Let's not make it too soon, huh? I'm not sure my career can handle it."

"I won't. Take care, Amanda."

"You, too, Simon."

Afterward, we all stood around in an awkward silence. Taking the hint that Simon wanted to talk to me alone, Amanda said, "Take your time, Marty," and went over to my car.

Simon gazed at me for a few moments. I saw the sadness in his eyes now. "Thank you, Martin."

Something caught in my throat. "Anytime."

We stood in silence. The tiny droplets felt cool on my skin. Simon gazed up into the night sky, lost in his thoughts for a few moments. Softly, he said, "I miss Romero."

"I know."

"When . . . when does the pain go away?"

I wasn't sure how to respond. I knew he wasn't looking for a feel-good line, so I decided to tell him how it was for me. "It never really does."

Simon continued to stare up at the sky for what seemed a long time. Finally, he returned to me and held out his hand. We shook, and I told him again to call me.

"I will, Martin."

As I watched him drive away, I decided that this time he probably would.

Maybe it was the alcohol or the realization that the case was indeed over. Whatever the reason, Amanda and I hardly spoke during the drive to her house. When I rolled to a stop out front, I told her I would call General Mercer in the morning, see if I could get him to go to bat for her with the Air Force brass.

"Don't bother, Marty. I'm thinking about transferring from the OSI."

"Oh?"

She shrugged. "You and I both know I was wrong about

the shooting. Regardless of my personal feelings, I had a duty to stop Holland. I didn't."

"Don't be too hard on yourself. It was a tough call."

She opened the car door and got out. She paused, looking at me. "Wouldn't have been for you," she said softly.

Without waiting for my response, she closed the door and slowly walked to her house.

CHAPTER 56

I finally arrived at my house a little after eleven. The porch light was on and I smiled, approaching the front door. Taped to it was a hand-drawn map to RFK stadium. Across the top, in big letters, Emily had written, "BACKSTREET BOYS." And below: "Don't forget, Dad."

I carefully removed the map and stared at it. "I won't, honey," I murmured.

The moment I entered the house, the living-room light came on. Mrs. Guerrero, which is how I tried to think of her now, was standing in the foyer in her pink robe. She immediately came over and surprised me with a hug. She told me again how sorry she was that she hadn't told me the truth. She said if I wanted her to leave it would be okay. She would understand.

I led her to the sofa, explaining that there was no need to leave now because the bad people would never bother her again. I also told her Emily and I needed her and would be very sad if she left. At that she began to cry. I kept reassuring her, and after a while she finally stopped crying, wiped her eyes with her sleeve, and asked if I was hungry. She seemed disappointed when I told her I wasn't. She mentioned that there had been a lot of phone calls for me. She said "newspaper," which told me most were probably from reporters. She left the names in my study. Then we just sat for a while. After I gave her another hug, she finally headed off to bed.

I went upstairs to check on Emily. She was curled up on her side with a tiny smile. I thought how much I loved her and how much Colonel Wildman must have loved her children. As I gently pulled the covers up around her chin, I wondered what kind of people could hurt someone so young. But they had, and brutally. In my heart, I knew Amanda had done the right thing. Lucille Holland had deserved to die. But I also felt conflicted by the knowledge that we were cops. Our job was to play by the rules. By that standard, Amanda had no right to make the decision she did.

At that moment, standing in the semidarkness and looking down on my daughter, I remembered all the other victims. The children and families who had died in terror when their planes crashed. It still bothered me that no one would be held accountable for their deaths. But that was the problem with bureaucracies. Responsibility was diffused. You can never find anyone to blame. It's never anyone's fault.

Maybe Simon was right after all. Maybe the system wouldn't change because the public doesn't care and never would. But as I slipped out from Emily's room, I found myself hoping that Simon had misjudged the American people.

For the sake of all the children like my daughter.

So much to do tomorrow. Between putting in some face time at work so I'd at least keep my job and taking Emily and her friends to the concert, I wanted to drop by the hospital to visit Janet Spence. I also had to call General Mercer, and my father, to see if he might sell Amanda a few acres—she'd mentioned her interest again during the ride home.

Even though I should have been getting to bed, I knew I was still too wired to sleep. Besides, I still had something to do. A final obligation. But first I went to my study to check my messages.

There were more than a dozen Post-it notes on my desk. Most of the names were misspelled. I didn't see the name of anyone I knew.

As I started to leave, I noticed a small packet lying in the plastic box where Mrs. Guerrero left the mail. I frowned, picking it up. No postage markings. Just my name printed on the—

I stiffened. I slowly ran my hand over the packet.

And then I knew.

For an instant I was tempted to throw the packet in the trash. But I had to be certain.

So I peeled back the flap. Inside was a yellow Kodak envelope. My hands shook as I removed the dozen or so photographs.

I was looking at a picture of my daughter Emily, standing along the highway by my house. She wore the same clothes I'd seen her in this morning. I went to the next picture. Emily with Mrs. Guerrero. I started flipping faster. Two more photos of Emily and Mrs. Guerrero. Then Emily getting on the school bus. Another of her walking into her school.

I couldn't look at any more. Something twisted inside me and I sagged back in my chair. It took me a couple of minutes before I could return the pictures to the envelope and go upstairs.

I used newspaper to get the fire in the fireplace going. Then I tossed the pictures in one by one. As I watched them burn, I called Amanda. I wanted her to know.

"You did the right thing," I told her.

After my call to Amanda, I put on a coat, grabbed a couple of beers from the fridge, and went out onto the porch to fulfill my final obligation. I sat there for a few minutes, slowly rocking in the quiet and the dark, and then I heard the front door open.

"I thought I heard you come in," a voice said. "Saw the shooting on the TV. You okay?"

I gazed up at the face of my stepdaughter, Helen. She was wearing the flannel nightgown Nicole and I had given her two Christmases ago. "I'm fine."

She frowned. "What are you doing out here? It's freezing."

I hesitated. "You might think it's a little silly."

"Try me."

I shrugged, staring into the night. "When I'd finish a case, your mother always made me tell her about it. We'd usually sit outside with a couple of drinks and I'd go over everything."

Helen didn't say anything. I saw her step into the house and reemerge moments later, zipping up a down jacket over her nightgown. She sat across from me, and I saw tears in her eyes.

"Tell me, Marty," she said softly.

So that's just what I did.

The COMMANDER

PATRICK A. DAVIS

author of THE COLONEL

PUTNAM